THE LIGHT BRIGADE

KAMERON HURLEY

ANGRY
ROBOT

ANGRY ROBOT
An imprint of Watkins Media Ltd

Unit 11, Shepperton House
89 Shepperton Road
London N1 3DF
UK

angryrobotbooks.com
twitter.com/angryrobotbooks

First printed in the UK by Angry Robot, 2019

Cover by Eve Ventrue
Set in Adobe Garamond Pro

ISBN 978 0 85766 823 3
Ebook ISBN 978 0 85766 824 0

Printed and bound in the United Kingdom by TJ International Ltd.

9 8 7 6 5 4 3 2 1

For Hannah.
This is all her fault. . . .

Don't just fight the darkness. Bring the light.

They dragged the insurgent out of the ruins of Saint Petersburg. Ash danced in the sky. The insurgent had the bruised knuckles of a fighter, and broke a soldier's nose: crunch and splatter of blood and snot. When they finally got the insurgent to the ground, they heard a terrible howl: not one of fear, but of triumph.

"You poor ageless grunts," the insurgent said, showing teeth: one rotten incisor, a chipped canine. "I've been waiting for you."

1.

They said the war would turn us into light.

I wanted to be counted among the heroes who gave us this better world. That's what I told the recruiter. That's what I told my first squad leader. It's what I told every CO, and there were . . . a couple. And that's what I'd tell myself, when I was alone in the dark, cut off from my platoon, the sky full of blistering red fire, too hot to send an evac unit, and a new kid was squealing and dying on the field.

But it's not true.

I signed up because of what they did to São Paulo. I signed up because of the Blink. All my heroes stayed on the path of light, no matter how dark it got. Even bleeding-heart socialist drones who play paladin can take an oath of vengeance to justify violence. I did.

The enemy had eaten my family and the life I once knew; a past I now remember in jerky stutter-stops, like an old satellite image interrupted by a hurricane. I wanted to be the light: the savior, the hero, sure.

But more than that, I wanted the enemy obliterated.

How many other corporate soldiers signed up for money, or voting rights, or to clear a debt, or to afford good housing, or to qualify for a job in one of the big towers?

I believed my reasons were nobler.

When I signed up after São Paulo, me and my friends were shocked that the recruiting center wasn't packed. Where were all the patriots? Didn't they know what the aliens had done? I thought all those people who didn't sign up were cowards. While you were all upgrading your immersives and masturbating to some new game, we were fighting the real threat. We were the good guys.

You were cowardly little shits.

I didn't think about what would happen after I signed up. Or who I would need to become. I thought the world was simple: good guys and bad guys, citizens and ghouls, corporate patriots and socialist slaves.

You were with us or against us.

Pick your side.

I was at a party not long after the Blink, drinking a jet-fuel tasting concoction out of a pulpy compostable bag, when a kid from my basic education class wandered over. I'd signed up with the Tene-Silvia Corporate Corps with six friends, four of whom shipped out immediately. Me and the other two, Rubem Mujas and Andria Patel, managed to make the party. Rubem had gone inside, probably to pass out, leaving me and Andria on the lawn to answer everybody's questions. Andria was in high spirits. She didn't drink alcohol; her good cheer was all coltish excitement over our new career.

"You get a signing bonus?" a snaggletoothed kid asked. "They give you citizenship on the spot?"

"No."

Andria laughed outright. Pushed back the heavy cascade of her black curls. Freckles smeared the apples of her cheeks. I remember thinking she was thin, back then, leggy and athletic, but I hadn't seen what true starvation did to a person, not until later.

"You have any other family but the ones they blitzed?" asked another girl. I knew her from basic physics class, one sponsored by Teslova Energy.

"No," I said.

"Be kind," Andria said. "The war has taken a lot from all of us. I look forward to bashing in alien heads."

"I heard they'll teach you eighty ways to kill a man," the snaggle-toothed kid said, "when you get to Mendoza."

"I don't want to kill men," I said. "I want to kill aliens."

"I heard they were human once," the girl from physics said.

"Bullshit," the other kid said. "No human would do what they did to São Paulo."

"I guess I'll find out."

"They'll take away your name," said a tall guy coming over from under the balloon of the main party tent. "I bet that's the biggest advantage for a ghoul like you."

I grimaced. Franklin Kowalski outweighed me by over twenty-five kilos and was almost two meters tall; I had to kink my head up to meet his look. He had beaten me out for first-string quarterback two years before. All the streams preferred faces like his, the coach said, and the corp could only justify an American football team if they kept their viewership up. I could play second string. I told the coach to fuck herself and played two years of rugby instead, until the Blink. I didn't like people telling me what I could do.

Ironic, then, signing up for the goddamn military.

"I hear they eat the rich in the corporate corps, Frankie," I said. "I'm sure you'll be delicious. Why wait to sign up?"

"Already did." He hooked his big thumbs in his pockets and gave a wry little smile, the one I knew preceded the word-vomit of some shitty-ass thing he'd just thought up.

Andria rolled her eyes. "I'm going to check on Rube. He's probably vomiting into a messenger bag." She reached for my sleeve, but I stepped away from her.

That was Andria—always looking after me. And me? Always self-destructive.

"You know you'll have to fight the aliens," I said, before Frankie could get a word out, "not just fuck them."

The snaggletoothed kid snickered. Andria made a moue and got very still. The girl from physics got all big-eyed and turned abruptly and marched back to the party tent. She was probably the smartest of us all.

"Didn't they call your dad Mad Dietz?" Frankie said. "The one Teni had reeducated four times? I heard they sold him off to Evecom for stock options."

"Go fuck yourself, Frankie."

He leaned over me, faster than I expected—I was a couple drinks in—and mashed his tongue against my cheek, leaving a long tail of gin-soaked saliva. I recoiled, so startled I froze. I'd think about that moment a lot, later. I'd wonder what I should have done immediately, instead of freezing like a dumb kid. In some other time line things went differently. I would have broken his nose, kicked out his kneecap—all in an instant. It's what a soldier would have done, what I would have done, later. But I didn't know anything about proper fighting—just the grappling we did on the field. I hadn't been conditioned for violence. I still had to be provoked. If I'd acted differently, I wouldn't be me. We wouldn't be here.

He ducked away, laughing. "You keep dreaming about that, you little fucking grunt."

Andria cut in, "Hey, leave it—"

I leaped at Frankie in a full tackle. The smile fled. He went over.

Yells from the crowd. Some cheers. Smell of grass and dirt and the chemical tang of fertilizer. Frankie slobbering, spitting at me. I shoved my elbow over his throat.

"Yield," I demanded.

"Fuck you," he said, and punched my temple.

A flash of bright light. Darkness juddering across my vision. I swung, but he was already up on his hands and knees. I tackled him again and bit down hard on his left ear.

He screamed and clawed my face. A hunk of his ear came away. I tasted coppery salt. Spit the chewy bit of flesh.

Somebody grabbed me then, many hands pulling me away and dragging Frankie up. The world spun. The thump-thump of the music inside beat in time to the throbbing in my head. My face was wet. He'd busted my nose. The wet was blood. I bared my teeth. I spit up my blood and his. I raised a fist at the sky, blotting out the distorted specter of the moon. A great chunk of the moon was missing, had been for nearly a year. It still took some getting used to, that silhouette with the blinkering satellite of debris spinning around its equator. It had rained hellfire for weeks afterward, each shattered piece hurtling toward Earth like a nuclear warhead.

"You keep your eye up there," I yelled at him. "That's where I'll come from when I kick your ass."

"They only took you because you're a ghoul," Frankie hissed. "You'll be dead your first drop."

The BLM—Business Loss Management squad—showed up, fit men and women wearing Kevlar and riot glasses, Tasers already out. They swarmed us from the mouth of the tent. Andria ran, probably to grab Rubem. I didn't blame her.

"Shame," said the woman who zip-tied my hands. She turned the recording feature on her riot glasses off. I winced. The glasses were meant to reassure us that the agents weren't using personal retinal displays to record encounters with us. Personal retinal displays were worn as external lenses in the eyes; they were almost impossible to detect unless actively streaming data across the eye. I'd been a ghoul long enough to know that a BLM agent turning off her external device was often prelude to a good beating—or outright death.

She leaned over me and whispered, "Shame to get worked up with your whole future ahead, huh? You want to be a soldier?" BLM's all had face recognition built into their riot interfaces and a direct line to our files. She no doubt knew all the intimate details of my last relationship and where I took a shit this morning.

I kept quiet. Never talk to the BLM unless they invoke the Corporate Disclosure clause in your residency contract. My mom had drilled that into my head after we became residents of Tene-Silvia. She and my father had worked their asses off to get us all attached to a corp, but it came with a whole new set of rules. Those rules were probably why I wasn't getting beaten up or murdered like I would have if this shit had gone down before then.

"We need good kids up there," the BLM agent said. "You've gotta figure out what side you're on. Don't waste your life here, kid. The fight's on Mars." She turned her recorder back on.

I wanted to be the hero who would have known exactly what to do when Frankie pulled his bullshit that night. The sort of kid who had a family to go back to, after that party, instead of a dorm for unaccompanied minors. The sort of kid who was driven by more than some dumb gory oath of vengeance. I didn't care if signing up killed me because I didn't understand what dying was, then.

Be a hero, I thought. *Get revenge.* End of story.

But that's not really living.

I had no idea why living mattered at all, after the Blink.

Not until the end.

2.

About the war . . .

There are many fronts in this war. Humans are spread out as far as the asteroid belt. We were on the moon, too, before the enemy hit it so badly that we cleared out.

Our corp, Tene-Silvia, had a lot of interests on the moon: mining operations, research labs, and citizens engaged in top secret work. Some of the bigger corps, like Masukisan, ShinHana, and Evecom had interests there too, but most of the Big Six had moved core competencies to Mars by the time a chunk of the moon got blown out. Mars was the next frontier, for the corps. They didn't care that there were already separatists from Earth up there building cities and calling themselves Martians. The corps all put some flags in the ground and tried to muscle their way in using friendly words like "science" and "research" and "building community relationships."

So how do we get around, on so many fronts?

That's the trick, isn't it?

How do you get out further than Mars? Humans aren't

designed to leave Earth. We're bound to it—blood, guts, and bone.

The biggest hurdle to traveling outside Earth is the distances. They're massive. I still look at the sky some nights and think about the universe—the sheer enormity of it. It makes my head hurt. The Big Six built on concepts like quantum entanglement and particle physics to figure out how to build an instantaneous communication technology that could span those distances. But moving people?

Well, mass is harder.

I guess if you know anything about the limits on the speed of light, it makes sense what they came up with to solve the mass problem.

The fastest way to travel from one front to the next is to turn us into light.

Think about it. How long does light take to get to Mars? About twelve and a half light-minutes. The asteroid belt? About twenty to forty light-minutes, depending on its orbital position.

Like most world-changing discoveries—like penicillin or the cure for cancer—the switch to busting us down into light happened by accident. The Seed Wars ended, and the Big Seven became the Big Six after the Great Corporate War. In the aftermath, people tried to pull away from the Big Six and start their own communes and radical republics. It was a scary and dangerous time. That's what's on all the immersives. Desperate times call for desperate plans of action. How do you preserve a way of life that's unraveling on all sides, descending into lawless anarchy? Everyone likes to pretend they'd be high and mighty about it, but how would *you* govern five billion people?

They turned us into light.

My mother said she remembered the first time she saw somebody corporealize in front of her. Hearing voices, she walked into the shared kitchen on her work floor. Two women in the gray garb of military police stood around the food printer, waving away a worker who had come up for coffee. A burned lemony scent filled the air. Sagging out from the center of the food printer was the torso of a young man.

"His face was so peaceful," my mom said, telling me the story years later. "That's what stayed with me."

She had immediately gone back to her console. "I knew what happened to people who saw things the military didn't want them to," she said. "That coworker of mine they were waving away disappeared that day. Never saw her again. The official line was there had been a military training accident."

A decade passed before they formally announced the new tech. Until then, all the piloting was done manually. My father spent the next war working as a freight laborer on shuttles that ferried the dead from Mars to recycling plants on the moon. That's where he learned to pilot. He and my mother served Teni during early conflicts between Mars and the moon. Their service is what got us residency.

There's a lot to say about the world leading up to the Blink. What I knew for sure was that something happened on Mars between the actual Martians who had left Earth decades before and the increasing corporate interests trying to bully their way onto the planet.

Whatever happened, coms on Mars went dark.

Most corps pulled out their researchers and scientists from Mars, leaving the civilians. What happened to the civilians from the corps, they wouldn't say.

Tene-Silvia gave us the corporate line about how the Martians were crazy socialists bombing their research stations, but Evecom had a different story about how Martians were dragging corps civilians into cults; and the other four corps shared equally strange stories. It happens sometimes; they can't all agree on reality. Listening to the Big Six—when you're allowed to get media outside your corp at all—is like listening to a bunch of nattering old people at a dinner party trying to remember some esoteric event from when they were kids. Everybody has a different memory. When they get frustrated, they start talking real loud, like that will make their memory more true.

What I knew for sure was that nobody had talked to anybody on Mars for almost ten years. And Mars hadn't talked to us. I didn't know what kind of tech they had, or what leverage, to keep the Earth corps out when they went dark. It was like Mars didn't exist anymore. Everybody left on Mars became unknowable. Someone else. Alien.

A decade after they went dark, a splinter group of Martians opened communications with us. They said they yearned to help out Earth, and were chafing under their own socialist government. They said they could mend our most contaminated land with new tech, if only we let them come on down and colonize those blasted hellscapes from the Seed Wars. . . .

A few corps allowed it. And the Martian colonists made the north grow food again, better and more than ever before.

And then . . .

One thing the Big Six all agreed on was that the Blink was unprovoked.

Two million people were in São Paulo one day.

The next . . .

Blinked.

Was the Martian government mad because we accepted the colonists? Or had they just been biding their time until we got complacent, so they could destroy us once and for all? Maybe they had never gotten over the corps trying to take over Mars. Maybe they had been planning to get back at us all along.

Mars had always been ahead of us when it came to tech. You wouldn't hear the corps say it, but we whispered about it. How else could they have broken away? How else had they Blinked two million people out of existence?

The Martians who had settled here were rounded up and interrogated. But nobody seemed to know anything. Some revolted. They were still being tolerated when I signed up. For how long? That was the big question.

That's the war I knew. The events as I understood them. That's how I decided which side of the war to be on. And I was. On the right side, I mean.

Nobody ever thinks they chose the wrong side.

We all think we're made of light.

3.

It's tough to understand a thing just by hearing about it or looking at it. It's like having sex or getting into a fight. You don't get it until you do it.

That's what the Corporate Corps is like.

They inject you with a lot of stuff during that first week of mandatory training. They don't even wait to see if you wash out, because even if you wash out, they still need you for support duty; dangerous drudge work they don't want civilians doing. I had residency. I could have worked in a chemical plant or soldering military hardware until my teeth fell out and the corp approved me for a humane send-off cocktail of Pavulon and potassium chloride.

But I didn't.

You don't "opt out" of this war anymore, not like you could in the early days. If I wasn't in the corps, I'd be supporting the war some other way. I've been hungry; I didn't like it much. Having residency with a corp isn't citizenship, but it's better than being a contractor, or worse—a jobless ghost, a ghoul. Being a ghoul means being hungry. Living in other people's waste. Praying a cough won't turn into pneumonia. Being a ghoul is knowing what gangrene smells like. It's dying from a scraped knee that gets infected. It's shitting in a ditch. It's eating roadkill.

I'd rather be a hero.

When you go through processing the first thing they do is strip you down and punch in your VT—vitals tracker. They inject that between your shoulder blades so they can get a bead on you at any time. That position also makes it tough for you to get it out on your own.

"Afraid I'll run away?" I asked the tech, thinking I was pretty funny.

"It's to ensure swift medical evac," she said, "if necessary. And to ensure we can monitor your physical and emotional state."

"Emotional?"

"We can't take away your emotions," she said. "Not yet."

"Gotcha," I said. There was something in her face that, even now, I'm not sure I understood. "What's this other stuff?"

"Don't worry about that," she said, and jabbed me with another preloaded syringe of milky goo.

She kept bringing out more of those syringes, working her way through a tray of them. I'd already been inoculated against everything, I thought, because the corp knows sick people aren't productive people. Yet they gave me at least a dozen more shots *after* I saw her, moving me from room to room. New faces, new gloves, new needles. Nobody said what was in the vials and I didn't ask again. It felt . . . rude. I'd turned my body over to them and signed all the forms I didn't read. I figured it was my fault for not understanding what they were doing.

We got outfitted with our heads-up displays next. The name makes it sound like a clunky piece of tech, but you just slide lenses into your eyes, like the retinal displays civilians have. The lenses give you access to coms, schematics, anything that the CO wants to beam out to you. You can even blink over to see your vitals. All the info runs at the bottom left of your left eye. You look down to bring it up and lift your gaze to clear it.

I wasn't impressed when we first got it. I had worn retinal displays before to run immersives and take classes. They pegged me as slow when I first came to school at six years old, after we got residency. I'd never been to school before. I spent a lot of time with immersives to catch up.

I had never accessed the knu before I became a resident either. The knu was a complex system of quantum-entangled data nodes that stored and transmitted information for all the corps. The knu had tiered access to information, and not all the knu nodes from different corps could even talk to one another. As a resident, I had pretty low-level knu access. As a soldier, that was restricted even further. We were completely cut off from the outside world during mandatory training. Every time I tried to reach for the knu icon, I'd get a "restricted" warning and kicked out.

The corps kept the coms pretty light those first few days. The messages rolling across the bottom of our vision, blinking at you to acknowledge them, were reminders about PT, wake-up times, lights-out, stuff like that. You could almost forget they were using them to record everything you saw and did, too.

I heard rumors that they were inoculating us against diseases the enemy had brought with them. The diseases are what Mars had used to gain leverage over the Big Six. What better way to declare a prolonged lockdown than some engineered plague? Others said they were punching us full of drugs that were supposed to make us faster, smarter, tougher. Everybody wants to be tougher, right?

That's what Muñoz thought.

I met Muñoz after processing and orientation. Everyone had the same regulation haircuts in the Corporate Corps. What was left of hers was black as midnight, same as her thick black brows. She was all knees and elbows, so underweight I wasn't sure how she'd made the cut. They put her on double rations to fill her out. One corner of her mouth quirked up when she talked, so you always got the impression she was either amused or disgusted with you.

All one hundred and thirty-seven in our class shared the same bunkhouse, stacked three high. Muñoz tried to take the top bunk of our rack. I dragged her out of it and got fifty push-ups from the drill instructor for it. Muñoz wasn't fazed.

"Your push-ups suck," she said, handing me a piece of gum, after. It wasn't from the ration kit, which meant she'd smuggled it in. No small feat.

I took it. "The hell you know?"

"I can do a hundred."

"Bullshit."

"Didn't you do any training before coming here? Hope you're smart enough to keep up, or really fast. Gotta admit, you don't look fast."

"Easy to be fast when you're so goddamn small."

"Played American football."

"Flag football?"

"Fuck you."

"Kicker?"

She rolled her eyes. "You a receiver? A quarterback? You have an attitude like a goddamn quarterback."

"Rugby. What, you on debate team? Corporate messaging? You here because you want a multiple marriage license?"

"Better luck with that as a ghoul. You don't need a license. You look like somebody who'd know that. I'm here to go into corp intelligence."

"Oxymoron."

"Big word, jock."

"Lots of syllables."

"I'm Muñoz."

"Dietz." We bumped elbows.

Muñoz and I sat together in the cafeteria after our first PT. That's when she gave me her theory on what the medical orientation maze was about.

"They're making us into superheroes," she said.

We were eating ground protein concentrate on mashed tubers, maybe sweet potatoes, all piled on toast.

"Grandpa called this shit on a shingle," Muñoz said, stabbing into the chunky, dripping mess and letting it slide off her biodegradable spoon. "Said they ate it out on the belt, because it was the only thing the printers could shit out with any accuracy. Still true, I guess."

"Thought heroes ate better," I said.

"Maybe it gets better."

It did not get better.

We all got sick the next day.

The drill instructors—the DIs—made us do PT anyway. When you're running, shitting, and vomiting, it puts you in touch with the fact that you're just a bag of guts.

"We're all shit," Muñoz said during that first PT. She stumbled along the track during and puked up her breakfast. "Shit that's gonna move at the speed of light."

I slapped her on the back, yelled, "Only if you can keep up!" and hauled ass past her. The drill instructor barked some expletive, but I didn't hear it. I thought I was in good shape, before. Could run eleven kilometers without stopping. But the meds ruined us that week. In two cases, it killed. A wiry kid called Faros and a young woman, Acosta—both on their second attempt at getting through training—died, choking on their own vomit, dehydrated, raving at ghosts. Me, I wanted to crawl out of my own skin. Got hooked up to a saline drip. It was like having stomach flu, a twisting monster in my gut, trying to claw its way out.

"It's gonna eat me, Dietz," Muñoz said that night, heaving over the side of the bed.

Our third bunkmate, Rache, swore at her, and threw a blanket over the mess. He rolled over and went back to sleep.

I stumbled to the head; barely made it before a stream of shit left my body. It was so intense it felt like I'd busted something in my ass.

I wasn't the only one in there. The sounds of misery rose like a chorus of zombies denied dinner.

"Average person only shits about a pound a day," said the kid on the can next to me, his dark, round face slathered in sweat. He was bent forward; moisture collected at the end of his broad nose and dripped to the floor, a mixture of sweat and snot. He was a stout guy, about a meter seventy-five tall, and soft around the middle.

"Heroes don't shit," I said.

"What's that make us, then?"

"Soldiers." I laughed until I felt the bile rise in my throat again.

"I'm going to shit my way through this whole fucking war."

"We can dream."

He snorted, moaned. Another explosive burst of wet gas moved through his body. "I'm Jones," he said.

"Dietz."

"Can't wait to be a soldier."

"All starts here," I said, and vomited all over my feet.

4.

How will you react, when you're physically broken?

Can you use a compass to find your way?

Do you have the skills to scavenge when you're a starving soldier dropped into enemy territory? Will fear paralyze you?

These are the questions they need answered in mandatory training. If you can't learn, you wash out. You are stripped of citizenship if you have it, residency if you've earned it. You become less than what you were when you came in, and they still own you. They use you somewhere else.

Let me tell you how they break you.

You are shit. Everything you do is shit. From the minute you step off the transport at the training base in Mendoza, you aren't doing anything right. You don't walk right. Look right. Talk right. You are a bag of human excrement. No one likes you, let alone loves you. In great shape? It's not enough. Smart? That's worse. Nothing is ever good enough for the Corporate Corps. They want blind obedience.

After a week of that, you're hungry for anything. Hungry

for a "That's right," or a "Good job." You want love, acceptance. Humans want connection. I thought that was bullshit until mandatory training. I didn't believe we were all bags of meat propelled by emotion, but I was wrong. The DIs know. They know exactly what we are, and how to play us.

That's how they teach you to kill.

You might be surprised, but it turns out most people don't want to kill anybody. We aren't born murderers.

You want to gouge out the eyes of a stranger? You tried it? How did that go? Hardly anybody does that shit. If they do, it's in a fit of rage or madness. But cold, calculated killing? Only one percent of people are psychopaths. The rest of us have to learn.

I'd been in fights, before mandatory training. With guys like Frankie, mostly, and a few women who were the same. But fighting isn't about killing. It's about posturing. Submission. What good is it to kill the guy who screws you over when instead you can beat him to the ground, force him to yield, and show everybody else what happens when people fuck with you? One submission can save you a lot of shit later. Rugby, hard living before residency, my basic education, they all taught me that kind of fighting.

Mandatory training taught me to kill. They taught me to *want* to kill.

They made me want to kill more than I wanted air, more than I craved food, more than the desire to fuck. You yearn to kill because it's the only thing that gets your DI to love you. When you withhold all praise, people will do anything to get it. They'll eat each other, if they need to.

Do you know how they train fighting dogs?

The dogs are raised alone and captive from when they're small. They attach them to chains, close to other dogs, but far enough away that the dogs can't reach one another. They add weights to the chains, to increase the upper body strength of the dogs. The dogs are beaten, prodded, antagonized, starved.

They get trained by using "bait animals." Could be rabbits, sure, but mostly it's other dogs. You chain up the bait dog and let your starved, beaten, antagonized dog get riled up with it in the enclosure.

When you think the dog is ready—when it's nine or ten months old—you let it loose. You let it kill the bait dog.

When it kills the bait dog . . . you praise it. You feed it. You reward it. You tell it, "Good job." The first time it's ever known any human kindness in its life is when it kills one of its own kind.

We are not so different, me and that dog.

I wish I had known that back then.

I wish I'd known a lot of things.

"Why you join?" I asked Jones in the mess hall, two weeks in, while Muñoz gagged over her food.

"My family's all citizens," he said. "We all joined, going way back to the Seed Wars. Everything's different than what they went through, though, before Mars went dark. You?"

"I had my reasons," I said. "But my family, they—"

"Ghouls," Muñoz said, waggling her fingers next to her face. "All ghouls."

"Fuck you, Muñoz," I said.

"You a citizen?" Jones asked her. It was a rude question, but that was Jones.

"Just got legit," she said. "Both my dads had citizenship, but when mom came in, she didn't. She just got it, though, right before I turned eighteen."

"That's a lucky fucking break," I said. "You can't pretend that isn't lucky."

She shrugged. "I'd already signed up for Corporate Corps. I would have made citizen on my own."

"In, like, twenty years," I reminded her.

She glared at me.

"It's good," Jones offered. "I mean, we all start somewhere."

"I'm not a ghoul," I said. "I'm a resident."

"And your mama earned that when you were a kid, right?" Muñoz taunted. "Don't tell me yours is fair either. *You* didn't work for it."

"I'm working for citizen," I said. "I'm not going to die of fucking cancer, or get ground down by some chronic bullshit like my mom."

"My great-granddad was a resident," Jones stated proudly. "Drove a bus until he fell over. Died in the seat. Earned his way. You'll make citizen. If not you, maybe your kids."

"Nobody can expect handouts," I said, because that's what my dad always said.

"Right, right," Jones said. "No free lunch."

The drill instructor appeared. Mealtime over. I forked in a couple more bites. I never ate fast enough.

Everything we did those first few weeks got us beaten or yelled at. The way we stood. The way we talked (or didn't). The way we said "sir" (or didn't). The way we ran. How we did push-ups. How we took a shower. They teach you how to walk. How to eat. How to dress. Make your bed. They bust down all those basic things you thought you knew. Hygiene! Who doesn't know how to wash themselves?

But there the DIs and handlers were in the head, barking orders while we showered. There was a sign on the wall for people who forgot:

LINE UP.

MARCH TO SHOWERHEAD.

WET YOUR HEAD.

SOAP YOUR HEAD AND FACE.

RINSE.

SOAP YOUR LEFT ARM.

RINSE.

SOAP YOUR RIGHT ARM.

And et cetera. If you thought you knew how to wash your own genitals, the Corporate Corps was there to say you're wrong. The military knew better. It knew better about everything.

We relearned how to dress. How to shit (Knees up! Squat, don't sit). How to clean our boots. How to talk (Sir! before you speak, and Sir! when you're done). You adapt quickly or you wash out. You lose everything.

You need to remember that a lot of us had no real choice once we got into this. They tell you you've got all this freedom. Freedom to work. Freedom to leave the corp. And that's true. You could not work. And get kicked out of the corp. You could leave the corp and live in some squatter labor camp like me and my parents did, hoping you don't die of the flu. But that's hardly a real choice, is it? That's how they fool you. It's like playing one of those immersive games where you get a choice of three doors, but all the doors lead to the same final boss. There was never any choice at all.

I'm competitive. That worked well the first couple weeks when we were mostly performing on our own. Every morning but Sunday we ran five kilometers and did two hours of PT. I came in top three every time, but there was no praise for that. No praise for performing the expected.

They saved the praise for the killing.

We met our weapons in week two.

Our pulse rifles only weighed half a kilo. One shot breaks apart biomass with such explosive power that there isn't much left to clean up. It's like having a personal laser-guided grenade launcher, without the shrapnel. All that's left when you make a direct hit is a fine red mist.

We slept with those rifles. Took them apart and put them together so many times that by the end of that week, we could do it blindfolded. I was a good shot, but Muñoz was better. That didn't seem to give her as much satisfaction as I thought it would.

"Not exactly high on the list of skills you need for intelligence," she said. "I mean, you're a case in point."

We had four hours of personal time on Sunday mornings. Most people caught up on corp news, slept, and—finally, in week two—watched and recorded personal messages. Getting access to those messages made pretty much everyone giddy, except for folks like me, who weren't expecting any.

There wasn't much privacy in our unit; wasn't privacy anywhere in the corps. We viewed our messages in open booths outside the cafeteria. The line the first day was too long after breakfast, so I went later, toward the end of our Sunday free time. I had six messages waiting from Vi Ruiz, my ex-girlfriend. I deleted those without watching them. They were just ghosts; I'd gotten a lot of them before. I learned to just trash them. The others were from Andria and Rubem, the two friends who'd been at that last party with me before I joined up. It already felt like a lifetime ago. They had ended up in another class a week before me, in Mendoza.

Our heads-up displays ordinarily would have been able to manage messages for us, link us in directly with who we needed to talk to. But they didn't want us getting anything raw from the outside. Every message that got through to us was filtered, censored, and filtered again—then we had to watch them out in the open.

I activated Andria's message. Her face bloomed on the screen, so detailed I could count the specks of turf that smeared her chin, and the individual burst vessels under her bruised left eye. Her sallow complexion was mottled and peeling from too much sun. Despite knowing her hair would be cropped I found it shocking to see her massive black curls shorn away, revealing a delicate, sloping forehead and pate covered in black fuzz. Behind her, Rubem signed something at me, but it was obscured by a passing recruit.

"Dietz!" Andria crowed. "You're in week two, right? Knowing you, you don't even check messages until week three, ha! Oh shit, there's so much I wish I could tell you, but I bet they censor it. Me and Rube are great, fine. Don't wash out! We need to deploy together. The three of us. Somebody's gotta do the grunt work, right? Shit!" She held up her left arm. Her left hand was missing at the wrist. In its place was a semiorganic replacement. You could tell the ones that were fake, because the skin was still too shiny, and the color never matched. She made a fist, surprisingly fast. "Live fire exercise," she said. "You should—" the video cut out, a black background, and REDACTED over the top of it. I waited. The video cut back in. Andria, looking over her shoulder, yelling at Rubem. "Yes, two minutes!" Turned back to me. "We're going to win, Dietz." She held up both hands, pointer fingers raised. "Over and out!" The video cut.

There were a couple more like that, mostly pep talks from Andria. She knew me too well. Maybe felt sorry for me. I hoped not.

"Anything good from home?" Jones wanted to know at lunch in the cafeteria the next day. I wasn't sure if he was asking me or Muñoz.

"When do we get black-out drunk?" Muñoz moaned. "That's what I'm waiting for. How many more weeks until that?"

"Bad news?" Jones asked.

"Nothing," Muñoz said. "Same shit. What about you, Dietz? You got friends?"

"Yeah, Muñoz, I have friends."

"I mean, you being so charming and all," she said.

"It's all those big words. Has folks falling all over themselves for me."

Jones said, "You ever read Jorge Amado? Or Machado de

Assis?"

"I don't think Dietz reads."

"I heard of Amado," I grunted. "Not the other one. Aren't they censored?"

"Not for citizens," Jones said. "Machado de Assis once said, or wrote, rather: '*Everyone knows how to love in his own way; the way, it does not matter; the essential thing is to know how to love.*'"

"What's that have to do with anything?" I said.

"I saw you delete a bunch of messages," Jones said. "From a girl." He raised his eyebrows.

No goddamn privacy.

Muñoz perked up. "You have a girlfriend, Dietz?"

"Not anymore."

"Does *she* know that?" Muñoz grinned.

I wasn't going to talk about Vi here. "You got one of those quotes for every occasion?" I said to Jones.

Jones poked at his protein cake and chewed slowly, rolling his eyes upward. Then, "*I like eyes that smile, gestures that apologize, touches that can talk, and silences that declare themselves.*'"

"Those quotes work on all the girls?" I said.

"Jealous?"

"If it works, yeah."

"I have several someones back home," Jones sighed. "So yeah, it works. But shit, it was easier to sign up than deal with all that drama."

"Quote some dead guy and get laid?" Muñoz said. "You must come from a real small town."

"Why didn't you become a poet, Jones?" I said.

"You think Teni supports poets? C'mon, Dietz, your ghoul is showing."

"I was being sarcastic."

"There are some writing jobs that come with good perks, that's true. I'd love to be a corporate journalist. Maybe after the war."

"Don't they tell you what to write?"

"Nah, you just have to get stories approved by the Corporate Communications Office before you publish. You have a lot of freedom in how you write something, as long as you're writing about approved subjects."

"If you're a citizen," I pointed out.

"Only citizens can become journalists," Jones asserted.

"Why?" I said.

Jones shrugged. "Just the way it is."

"You benefit from the citizenship model," Muñoz said. "Citizen journalists have more to lose if the corporate message isn't consistent. I mean, if Dietz here bashed Teni publicly, they couldn't take much away."

"Fuck you," I said.

"I think that's very pessimistic," Jones said. "Citizens are just better equipped to talk smartly about these subjects. We have been, you know, educated."

Muñoz laughed so hard it sounded like a squeal. "You old citizen families. You're all the same. Like talking to a propaganda poster."

"What?" Jones said.

"Andria wasn't allowed to tell us what's next," I offered, because I didn't like where the conversation was going. I didn't like to talk about politics.

"What does that have to do with anything?" Muñoz said.

"It was censored," I said. "What she was trying to tell us happened this week."

"Great," Muñoz said, stabbing her food and glaring at Jones. "That's always a good sign."

There was good reason for the censorship. The corps has its

reasons. It protects itself.

Next up was the torture modules.

We got in formation on a Tuesday morning; it was hot, muggy, and a fine drizzle coated everything.

"The enemy is going to do a lot of terrible shit to you," the drill instructor said. "It's our job to prepare you for that. That's why we're going to do the terrible shit to you first."

Muñoz rolled her eyes.

I didn't. I fixed my gaze on the DI. I wanted to get some idea of what was coming.

I'm not going to tell you about the torture modules. Not yet. I'm going to say it was three days of shit. I'm going to say: Immersive experiences are pretty fucking immersive. I'm going to say: They should have sent us all to a shrink, after.

But they didn't.

Not yet.

We kept going.

We kept going.

Because that's what war is.

You keep going until it's over.

Or you're dead.

5.

It has come to my attention that this is the week we teach you not to starve," the drill instructor said. "I suppose that's necessary, considering we're going to throw your soft asses out into the woods next week to sink or get eaten by jaguars and parasites."

We were in formation, day one of week three. I had never been so tired in my life. Muñoz stood next to me, swaying on her feet. What the DI hadn't said about virtual torture camp was that reliving horror after horror meant you weren't going to get a lot of sleep. After that had come the nightmares. I still thought I saw shit out of the corner of my eye: kids with busted heads, men holding up bloody machetes. I still smelled the coppery stink of blood. I snorted to try to clear it.

"We have a hike today, children!" the DI said. "At the end of this hike, you will know what pain is. You will understand real exhaustion. Most importantly, you will be able to feed your goddamn selves instead of trying to eat each other."

A few recruits tittered, from the back. I figured they were among the few who had outwitted the torture modules. It was possible to beat the modules, I'd heard, but maybe only three or four in any class managed it, and they were always promoted to intelligence. Muñoz hadn't been one of them. She was still pissed about it.

The DIs marched us nineteen kilometers into the jungle. We followed a worn path at first, but then it was hard hiking for all one hundred and twenty of us left in the class. We had a fifteen-minute break around noon for water, pissing, and some protein bars, then we were marching again.

Jones started to lag behind me and Muñoz. He had the long gaze of somebody who wasn't really there. I splashed his face with water.

"Move your ass, Dietz!" the DI yelled from up front. "Muñoz! You're wasting your breath back there with Jones. You get behind, you won't catch up. Move!" The DI was in a jeep that paced us on the road below. Why the fuck we didn't get to hike on the road was beyond me. There was a second jeep at the back to harass the stragglers.

We moved.

It was after dark when we got to rest again. The DI and the handlers parked ahead of us in a clearing. Eight folding tables stood at the center, and around the periphery of those: a bunch of wooden boxes.

I, honest, thought the boxes were full of munitions, grenades. Thought they were going to run us out and see who survived a live fire exercise. Who knew, with them?

They gave us water. Then the show started. We stood around the tables, expectant as lambs to the slaughter.

"All right, children," the DI said. He climbed up on one of the tables and fixed his fists on his hips. "You all hungry? You're working for dinner tonight!"

The handlers kicked over the boxes.

Two dozen fat white rabbits tumbled out. The rabbits hopped

away from the boxes. Nibbled at the ground cover. Hopped some more.

"Simple task, children," the DI said. "You and a partner catch your dinner. Kill it. Skin it. Eat it. Before something else in that jungle does. Handlers here will help you along, should you so desire. Move!"

I snapped up a rabbit, the first to manage it. I stared into its flat black eyes. Muñoz and Jones came over, no doubt ready to have me do the dirty work. It was probably the first time they'd ever stared their own dinner in the face.

"What's wrong, Dietz?" the DI said. "You squeamish?"

"Sir. No, sir," I said.

"Get going! Or you wanna starve? That more familiar to you?"

I stared at the rabbit kicking in my hands. All around me, other kids who had never done so much as squash a spider were trying to figure out how to off a rabbit. Injured rabbits wiggled away and hopped into the forest, pursued by exhausted recruits.

"Sir, I know how to kill a rabbit, sir," I said. "Just not sure it's necessary."

He leaned over me. "Kill and eat that rabbit, Dietz. That's a fucking order. More necessary now?"

I met his look. You aren't supposed to do that. I have a problem with authority, though. I hate it when people tell me what to do. I want to push back at them, hound them, evade them, punch them, push them, defy them.

I pulled the utility knife from my belt, still looking at the DI, and gouged the rabbit in the jugular. Blood squirted into the DI's face. A more humane way would have been to break the rabbit's neck using a branch, but there were no sticks lying nearby. The blood made a better point.

"Goddamned!" the DI said, wiping away the spray.

I broke the rabbit's neck then, pulling sharply. It'd been

terrorized enough. Oath of vengeance or not, I wasn't a monster. Not yet.

"Drop and give me fifty, Dietz!" the DI yelled.

"Fuck you!" I said.

He hit me. Hard.

I flailed, lost my balance.

"There's one of you in every class," the DI said, looming over me, "some ghoul-spawn trying to prove their mama wasn't garbage. I have news for you, Dietz. You'll always be garbage."

I lay with my face pressed to the ground, wondering if I really wanted to come up and get another hit. He wasn't some Frankie, flailing around trying to look tough. He knew how to kill me. He knew how to hurt me without leaving a mark. He'd done it before.

"Sir," I said.

"What was that?" He pressed my head deeper into the mud.

"Sir. Yes, sir!"

"Up," he said.

I crawled up from the mud. The others were dutifully hacking and skinning their rabbits, badly. One skinny pair of recruits already had a carcass cooking. The smell reminded my exhausted body I was ravenous. Hunger roared back, a sharp, gnawing pain that bent me double. Jones and Muñoz had my dead rabbit in hand, still puzzling over it.

"Haul your ass to camp," the DI said to me. "Stand at attention at the flagpole until I relieve you."

Camp was nineteen kilometers back the other direction. I was exhausted and dehydrated. I had a good idea of how bad that could be. I stood with my mouth open, leaving that unsaid.

"Haul ass, Dietz! You think I'm a fucking parrot? Not going to repeat myself."

I stumbled past him, still disoriented from the blow to the head. Muñoz caught my eye, but quickly looked away. I staggered, trying to find the way back. The DI kicked me in the ass. I pinwheeled, just caught myself, and pushed on toward the path we had marched in on. My legs burned, two hunks of dead meat at the end of my body.

Nineteen kilometers. Shit.

I huffed down the track.

I had done the hump. I had earned the meal. Earned the rest. Earned the sleep. What was I doing, going back? What were my choices? Turn around and get drowned in mud? My vision swam.

The only way out is through.

Fear and panic fueled me the first thirty paces. Then I zoned out. Oh shit, oh shit, nineteen kilometers. The whole way here flashed in front of me. The vomiting, the squatting in ditches, and the shakes, fuck, the shakes, the endless slog.

I stumbled along, chest already burning. I'm stronger than this, I thought. I can endure more than this. He wants to psych me out. Wants me to squeal. Wants me to turn back and get down on my knees and beg for water, beg to eat. He wants me to wash out, wants me to clean his latrines until I goddamn wash out and cry for my dead mom and my dead dreams of citizenship.

This was his real-life torture module.

Don't think about your body. Don't think about the distance. Don't think about water, glorious clear puddles of it, cold and clear as spring rain. Don't think about how your body's burning up your fat, searing it away until it's gone and then starting in on the muscle.

Don't think.

Hunger burns, then goes away. Burns. You think it will kill you, but it doesn't. It fades, like exhaustion. I know this already, because I grew up with hunger. Woke up hungry. Went to bed hungry.

I remember scavenging on the beach of a sludgy river called the Tajo Luz, me and my cousins. My brother was too young, still slung across my mother's back. She walked ahead of us, scraping at the beach with a homemade rake, uncovering bits of discarded junk.

Farther up the beach, where the sand turned to scrub, a flash of movement caught my eye. I climbed the shallow dunes. Nestled at the top was a twisted mat of plastic ties, broken twigs, aluminum shavings, and synthetic fibers. A baby pigeon rested there, half in and half out of the nest. One wing lay outstretched, flapping uselessly. I took the poor little creature into my hands.

"It's all right," I murmured. I ran my finger over its quivering head. Its heart fluttered against my palm.

I slid down the dune and ran to catch up with my mother. I was barefoot, but the rough ruins of the beach hardly bothered me anymore. My feet were dirty, calloused things, hunks of sturdy meat.

"Mama!" I called. She turned, her dark hair blowing back over her shoulder. The sun rose behind her, thick and runny as fresh egg yolk.

"Mama," I said, holding up the injured bird. "It's hurt. Can we help it?"

"Let's get that home," she said, and she smoothed the hair from my face. It reminded me of how I had stroked the bird's tiny head.

I beamed at her.

We took the baby bird home along with six mollusks, some copper wire, and a meter-long metal hunk that bore the faded gray circles of the NorRus logo.

I slept that night next to the baby bird. In the morning, my mother boiled off the bird's feathers and cooked it whole. I'd like to tell you I had no stomach for it. But if you think for a minute I didn't want to shove that weary bird down my gullet despite having sung it to sleep the night before, then you have never been hungry.

My mother ate the bird herself, to ensure she made enough milk for my brother. I sat across from her on the floor and watched her consume the entire fledgling in three crunchy bites.

I didn't cry until she left to greet my father, just home from an expedition to the dumps of medical waste outside the nearby military training academy. Until Teni needed more pilots for the war with Mars, years later, we were nobodies. Ghouls. Just like everyone else there.

I clutched my knees to my chest and cried because I was so hungry. I cried because I wanted the pain to end.

I tripped over my own feet, the memory hot in my mind, and went into the mud. The fall was a relief. I lay there, chest heaving, snorting the earthy scent of the loam, rotten leaves slimy between my fingers.

The first time Tene-Silvia corporate security came for my father was seven years after we got residency; seven years after he started running shuttles between Mars and the moon. Teni made real housing available to us, and baseline rations. But my mother was already dying by then, riddled with some chronic disease only citizens could afford to cure. Only citizens get access to advanced care, and we were a long way from that. I was in my early teens, both proud of and embarrassed by my parents. My brother stayed home to care for my mother; he was a little slower than me and hadn't tested into basic education. Only citizens could get help at home; as residents, we had to figure shit out on our own.

My father listened to a lot of illegal broadcasts. Watched video and took hits from immersives that weren't approved by the corp. I didn't understand, back then, why he did it.

When corporate security kicked down our door, I was sitting at the kitchen table complaining about eating plain toast. I remember that specifically, because it seems so stupid now, but as a teen, it was important that we be just like everybody else, and everybody else got butter on their toast. Why didn't we?

My father grabbed me by the shoulders. "Do as they say," he urged.

"On the ground, on the ground!" they yelled.

My father pulled me down with him.

"What about Tomás?" I hissed.

"My son!" my father said. "My son is in the bedroom, there, with my wife. Please don't hurt him. He's a simple boy."

"Stay down!" Two of the security techs trained their guns on my father and I while the other four pounded into the back room.

The security personnel wore black: black masks, black helmets, black boots.

My brother wailed from the bedroom. I heard my mother's thin, wispy voice.

"We've done nothing wrong!" I howled.

"Shut up!" said the beefy tech holding the gun at my back.

They dragged my brother into the room with us. Pushed him to the floor. He screamed and thrashed. He was only ten years old, but he was big. One of the techs bashed him in the face with the butt of her gun. His nose burst. Blood splattered.

My father reached for him. The woman smashed her gun to the back of my father's head. He went down. Two more techs restrained my brother. My brother sobbed and sobbed, spitting blood and snot and his two front teeth.

I lay there shaking.

A woman wearing a long white coat entered through our broken doorway. Two soldiers accompanied her, proper soldiers, not security. Her boots were red. She clasped her willowy arms behind her back. She stood very straight and was so lean she put me in mind of some great crane, head slightly cocked, inquisitive. She paused just inside the door, surveying the bloody floor, our humble flat.

"There's a mother here, is there not?" she said.

"She's sick, Sergeant," one of the techs said. "In the back. Hooked up."

"Well, unhook her."

"I left Martiana back there," he offered.

"Is that what I asked you?"

The tech yelled, "Martiana, the sergeant wants you to bring the woman out!"

"Please," my father said, "please leave her. She is very sick. She is in pain."

"You are Captain Dietz?" the tall woman asked. She wore white gloves. She ran her gloved finger over our mantle, the one that framed our media screen.

"I am," he said.

My father's title referred to his career piloting shuttles, and wasn't a military rank. The way the interrogator said "captain" was almost mocking. I hated her in that moment more than I had ever hated anyone.

"Martiana!" the security tech said, again.

The woman in white held up her hand. "A moment on that. Dietz is a German name, is that right, Captain?"

"What does that have to do with . . . I don't know."

She continued running her fingers along the mantle. "Germany. Germania. The Germanic region. Old Europe. Now Evecom territory. After one of the early capitalist wars, a number of Germans came here, to what was then Argentina. You know it? That area is split now into twelve zones. Most of those immigrants ended up in what's now New Buenos Aires. That's quite far from here, isn't it?"

"I don't know it," my father said. "My family is from São Paulo."

"Ah, of course. The labor camp. I always wonder how ghouls manage to escape that camp."

"I was useful," my father said.

"Clearly. To whom were you useful, though? The highest bidder? Did Teni outbid Evecom? Masukisan? Did Mars ever approach you?"

"Please. My family's done nothing wrong."

"About twelve thousand of those German immigrants were former Nazis," she said. "Do you know what a Nazi is, Captain?"

"I've heard the term."

"You know the slur, perhaps. But not the history. They were highly organized. Single-minded. High as balls, too, which helped. They had some of the world's best-educated chemists and engineers. They made good use of them. Every factory worker, soldier, shopkeeper, and childbearer was hopped up on a low-dose methamphetamine called Pervitin. Depression, fatigue, PTSD, post-partum depression—they prescribed it for everything. A wonder drug. But they were myopic, ultimately. Extended use causes delusion and psychosis. They got too greedy too quickly. The way you have become greedy."

"I have given everything to Teni—"

"Let us know where to find the contraband," she said, "and we won't ransack the flat. We won't disturb your wife. We can still be civilized here, captain."

Her fingers paused just below the right side of the mantle. I heard a soft click.

"Ah," she said. The media screen woke; a clear vista bloomed across its surface. A crumpled mountain in the distance, just visible over a swaying field of lupines. "Interesting viewing," she said, "for a secured channel. Did you know we were coming, Captain? Is that why you changed where this transmission was coming from?"

"My office," my father said. "I can take you there. Please, just leave them alone."

She turned off the screen. "Captain Dietz is taking us on a tour of his office."

When they brought my father back two months later he was . . . different. I know they must have tortured him, but there were no visible marks. Yet he had grown old in those two months. When he looked at me, it was as if he saw through me. He would sit on the back balcony and watch the ships passing in the harbor; he liked it best when it rained.

One day, I came home from school and he was still out on the balcony, soaking wet.

I took him by the arm and said, "Come inside."

He put his hand over mine and met my look. "You accept reality. This reality. That will keep you safe for now, my little mouse. But promise me that when you come of age you'll ask questions. Promise me you'll strive for some other future than the one we gave you."

"Okay," I said, without knowing what he was asking. Not really.

I still wasn't sure, lying in the ditch. But the memory reminded me of how far we'd come. My family was all dead, now. All gone. They had wanted to get me here so I was in a position to get citizenship with some big corp. What kind of child would I be if I gave up now?

"Get up, Dietz," I said. "Get up."

I pulled myself up; achieved it by pretending I was operating someone else's body. I ignored the insistent pain that told me I was ruining myself, doing permanent damage. What did it matter if the body didn't belong to me?

I belonged to Tene-Silvia.

Up, Dietz.

I was up. One foot in front of the other.

The Corporate Corps wants to break you, I know that. They want to break you down and rebuild you. They want to carve away all the softness, all the gooey bits, the fatty deposits that keep you warm and safe. They want to break you down to the bones, see glistening, gleaming muscle and pulpy viscera.

As I labored on that black road, shivering, hallucinating, I had a moment of terrible fear. When they broke me apart, what were they going to find inside?

6.

Dawn came over me like a hangover. I sensed the sky lightening for a long time; so long I figured I was hallucinating it. The hooting and hollering of the rising birds and other crawling, pouncing things convinced me I had made it to see another day. I found a stone along the path and put it under my tongue, like my mother had taught me. When I was younger, we were always hungry and thirsty; sucking on a stone makes the mouth produce saliva and eases the need for water. But as an adult, I knew it was just a trick. I tried to concentrate on something besides my discomfort. The sky, the birds, the trail. I had no idea where I was.

I stumbled around a bend in the path and saw the trailhead marker. I came up short. Leaned against a tree. Below me, the cleared parade grounds around our barracks went on and on. The flag at the center of camp already flew high. I wanted to throw myself on the ground and hope gravity did the rest.

But seeing the barracks gave me a fresh burst of energy. I moved my dead legs. I kept shuffling until my fingers touched the base of the flagpole. I wanted to go to the cafeteria and beg for water, for food, a shower, and sleep, sleep, sleep, but the DI's face kept flashing in front of me, his mealy, doughy little mouth. His fist. His certainty that I would quit. That I was shit. That my family was shit.

The barracks were quiet. I figured my class hadn't gotten in from the night's exercise yet. No doubt they all ate fresh rabbit and got hours of sleep before marching in. I pressed my back to the flagpole and stood there as the sun came up, high and hot, burning the mist away.

You can do a lot more than you think you can. That's what mandatory training is about. Seeing how far they can push you. How far you can push yourself. I'd marched, stumbled, and jogged almost the length of a marathon in twenty-four hours. But I wasn't going to fall yet. Not yet. Not until I saw the DI. Not until I spit in his face.

I must have blanked out. The sound of my class's marching cadence brought me back. One vehicle led, with another taking up the rear, just like they'd come in.

As the lead vehicle parked outside the parade grounds, I straightened my weary body and stood at attention.

The DI got out of the vehicle with one of our handlers. They marched up to me. The DI's expression was unreadable.

"Get out of my face, Dietz," he said. "You're dismissed."

"Sir. Yes, sir." I took one step away from the flagpole, intending to march back to the barracks. My legs gave out.

I fell hard, snapping my chin on the tarmac.

The DI called for a medic. The DI squatted next to me. "You want to lead a squad, Dietz? We don't value narcissistic heroes here. Know what a narcissist is? It's some idiot kid drunk on his own shit. Heroes get themselves killed. They get their squads killed. You aren't shit without your team. You're hardly shit with them."

The medics showed up with a stretcher and hauled me to the

infirmary. I got hooked up to a line and treated for dehydration and general exhaustion.

I learned later that my group was also punished for my transgression. They lost two hours of sleep and had to hump back to the barracks early. When I returned from the infirmary the next day, not even Muñoz wanted to talk to me.

We kept going.

No rest for the Corporate Corps.

"What do you know about the enemy?" said Sergeant Older from the head of the classroom the next afternoon. She was a steely woman, all hard angles. She must have been fifty or so, though it was hard to tell, with half her face scarred by acid or some explosion (I never asked. Nobody else did either). She wore a shit-brick of military honors on her jacket. Her left arm was an organic-machine hybrid, and she walked with a hitch in her step. I wondered if she was supposed to serve as a warning or a promise.

We had at least three hours of classes every day. I've never been one to volunteer first, but she called on me.

"What do you know, Dietz?"

"Sir, they're aliens, sir," I said.

Four or five people guffawed.

"Well, that's a good start. You learn that in a book?"

Martinez said, "Sir, they turned on us after we gave them land up in Canuck. Started shooting babies in their beds . . . sir."

I hadn't seen propaganda billboards outside Tene-Silvia. I didn't know you just say the same shit about whatever new enemy you've got. All I knew was what I was told. Every enemy shoots babies in their beds. It's kind of amazing.

"They are indeed aliens," Sergeant Older said. "How did this conflict begin?"

"Sir," Martinez chimed in again, "they hate our freedoms, sir."

"Why?"

Silence. One woman in the back was asleep. She snored so loudly the sergeant rapped her on the forehead and sent her out to do a lap.

"Is this boring you?" Sergeant Older asked. "Knowing your enemy is the best way to defeat them."

"Sir," Jones said, "I think military strategy is a better way to defeat them than that . . . sir."

"And what will you base your strategy on, Jones?"

"Experience," he said. "Sir."

"Experience of what?" she said. "Being a citizen?"

Jones's complexion was dark, and it deepened even further.

"We are fighting an enemy who bit our extended hand," she said, "like a rabid animal. Such an enemy is unpredictable."

"Aren't all of them?" Muñoz said.

"No," Sergeant Older said. "Who are we fighting? We gave these alien people half the northern hemisphere to rehabilitate, because it was such a wreck after the Seed Wars, and the climate shifted. Nobody cared who settled it, not even CanKrushkev. It was their territory. Nothing would grow there until the aliens came. They had technology that they developed when they split from us on Earth and made their communist colonies on Mars."

"Sir," Jones said. "What tech was it, though? That reseeded Canuck?"

"That's not important, Jones," the sergeant said. "Let's stay on target. We cut ourselves off from them when they left, so it was a real surprise when some of them asked to come back. I guess they thought they were saving us, but we don't need saving. The tech, whatever it was, got rid of all the radiation and restored the soil, probably the same way it did on Mars after the Water Riots. And stuff grew. We trusted them, but they betrayed us. I don't just need to tell you. You can experience it."

Sergeant Older pulled up a series of augmented experiences

and immersives for us to engage in firsthand, so we could feel like we were there, seeing all the horror our parents did when these aliens turned on us. It wasn't pretty. It never is. They know what to show you. They know how we work. They know how to turn people into aliens. Kids into monsters.

After that was marksmanship. We lined up for bayoneting practice, skewering dummies made of real flesh and skin grown in a lab.

The DI yelled, "Hit that slab like you mean it! This is the enemy! Give me your fighting face, you scuttling little roaches. This is the enemy that blew up the goddamn moon! They Blinked two million of our own! Gore them! Gore them!"

All our targets looked like people. All our targets were meant to be Martians.

People ask what aliens are like. I can't say I'd seen an alien outside of a corp news bulletin back then. The images they gave to us were of lanky, sneering men and women bundled in colorful clothes and carrying outlandish, oversized firearms painted with the number of their kills. They were just people. Like us.

This is who you kill. This is how you kill. You kill without thinking. You kill. You kill. You kill.

I remember the first time the DI praised me. Remember it starkly, even now. Me and Muñoz at the firing range, me at the sniper rifle, her stretched out just behind me, acting as spotter. Using her direction, I adjusted for wind, corrected the angle.

The target staring back at me through my scope was a lean, wrinkled woman. She wore dark glasses and a red headband. The flesh wasn't real in this extended range exercise, but she looked as real as they could make her. She even moved; the hands coming up and down, the eyelids fluttering.

I took the shot.

The shot hit her just above the left eye. I pulled away from the scope, and there was the DI above us, checking my shot with his heads-up.

"That's a good shot, Dietz," he said. "Muñoz."

I huffed in a breath. I felt such a profound sense of relief that it's almost embarrassing to talk about now. I wanted to please him, no matter how much I hated him. And the only way to please him was to kill without hesitation.

This is how they break you.

7.

The next week they sent us with our guns on a mock recon: a team exercise. It was capture the flag, basically, with real stakes. They called the course "land navigation," and it seemed like a dumb idea, since we all had GPS devices integrated with our trackers and heads-up displays.

"The winning team skips PT tomorrow," the drill instructor said. "Winning team gets two extra hours of sleep. Gets an extra hour checking messages from home. How does that sound, children?"

Four weeks into mandatory training . . . skipping PT and sleeping sounded absolutely treasonous.

"My colleagues will *not* be shooting live rounds during this exercise," the DI said. "But your coms will be disabled throughout. We will be monitoring your trackers but will not intervene unless absolutely necessary. Your teams get to navigate to the rally point. You will retrieve the payload and hump it back here to this flag. You have three days."

I got paired with Jones, a slack-jawed kid named Hadid, who

everyone called Jawbone, and a tall, meaty woman, Vargas, who our group called Grandma because she was a good five years older than the rest of us. She didn't think the nickname was funny. I never used it to her face.

We got our pulse rifles, a water slug, a folded paper map, and a compass.

"Who the fuck uses a paper map?" Grandma muttered.

The DI rounded on her. "You think we're fucking with you, Vargas? You think Teni is wasting your fucking time? Dumping money into some negative ROI exercise? You may find yourselves cut off, your gear fried by an EMP. You know what that is, children? It's like somebody frying the shit out of the little smart boxes that gear out your apartment blocks and civ houses. It'll fry your interface, your tracker, all that expensive shit the corp wires into your head. You will be *blind,* children. And when you are blind, what do you learn?"

"Sir," Jones said, "you learn Braille, sir."

"That's fucking right, Jones. Give this kiss-ass a gold fucking star. Your map and your compass are your goddamn tools when the shit hits the fan. Just because Teni can add two and two for you doesn't mean we take math out of the corp core."

Grandma rolled her eyes.

"I saw that, Vargas," the DI said. "How about we make Jones squad leader for your little tea party? Dietz and Hadid don't have a goddamn brain cell between them, and any more laps for you, Vargas, and you'll be able to outrun a goddamn ghoul with dysentery. Making you listen to Jones is punishment enough."

They flew us into the jungle and kicked us out of the transport like shipping containers. I hit the ground hard. Lost my breath. Hell of a way to start another exercise.

I got my blindfold off. I didn't see any other teams nearby. I wondered how far apart they dropped us. Jones had the map. Me, Jawbone, and Grandma crowded around him. We wore military slicks, organic sheaths that regulated temperature and kept off the worst of the bugs. We called them condoms, which was as good a name as any. Nice to have some protection, but uncomfortable as hell. It was the middle of December, hot and muggy, and the mosquitos rose from the bushes in waves. The insects worked their way around the fine seams between our skin and the slicks, hungry.

Jones folded the map over. It was a topographic map, which must have looked like some mystical scrying tool to a citizen like him.

"Hope you paid attention in that class on terrain," Jawbone said. "I was asleep for half of it."

Jones swung the compass right, then left.

I sighed. "Give me the compass."

"You slept through every nav class, Dietz," Grandma said. "Don't shit us. I can navigate."

"I didn't grow up with access to a GPS. What do you think ghouls use?"

"What, no ghoul has an interface?" Jones said.

"Tech belongs to corps," I said. I took the map from him and followed the lines of the terrain. "There's some bootleg stuff, but not as much as you'd think. Got a direction for me, Vargas?"

"North is this way, up that ridge."

My mother had taught me how to read a map when I was five. Most navigation we did while scavenging along the edges of corp territory was by dead reckoning. But a few times a year, my mother and I would head deeper into the jungle in search of treasures from the pre-corps world that others left untouched. The map she used was old—her grandmother's, she said—made of some silky material that repelled water. You could shove the thing into your pocket like a handkerchief and pull it out again, crisp and unwrinkled, like new. Hold it in the sun for a while, and the contour lines and elevation markings even glowed in the dark. I loved that map. I wondered what happened to it after my mother died.

This map wasn't nearly as nice; plain paper, laminated, but clearly not going to glow after dark. We were in the shade of some big trees. The map was already tough to read. I oriented the map so the top faced the same way as the compass needle. I examined the ridge ahead of us.

"That's a spur," I said, pointing at the feature. "Slopes down there on three sides, up on the one facing us. Can you locate any water?"

Grandma pocketed the compass and forged off south a bit, following the slope. She paused at the edge of a little gully and picked a few violets. She tucked them into the place where her bayonet clipped to the end of her rifle.

"You're a weird one," Jawbone said.

"Enjoy yourself, kid," Grandma said. "It's not going to get much better."

Jones and Jawbone fanned out with her, one heading southeast, the other southwest.

"Oh, hey!" Grandma yelled. "Stream down here."

"Found it," I said, locating us on the map. "If we head over that stream for forty meters, we should reach a field. It's marked here. Keep heading south. Vargas? Jones? You want to verify?"

Grandma took a cursorily look at the map and nodded. "I'm good with it. Big elevation change after that."

"Faster to go this way," I said. "You're in good shape, right? Jawbone?"

"We have three days of this," Grandma said. "Let's pace ourselves."

"Don't you want to win?" I said.

"I'd like to survive."

"Hardly anybody dies during these," Jawbone said.

Jones said, "How do you know that?"

"I looked it up on the knu before I enlisted," Jawbone said. "Mostly, you get into trouble with water. We make sure we have water, we're fine."

"You know they censor that shit on the knu," Grandma said, "even for citizens."

"Could we talk and move?" I headed off south in the direction of the field.

The others followed, still bantering. If nothing else, I'd be glad for the altitude change because all the huffing and puffing meant they wouldn't talk so much.

"Censorship is highly overrated," Jones said. "It's all done by AI. It looks for keywords. Don't use the keywords, and your stream won't get tagged for review."

"They randomize it, though," Jawbone said. "Like when they check for terrorists at the roadblocks."

"Not as random as you think," Jones said. "They say that to keep you on your toes. But one of my moms works in Corporate Security. She says they only access your streams if you do something bad, or you're suspected of something."

"Literally anyone could be suspected of anything at any time," Grandma said. "Some guy in security doesn't like you, you're fucked."

"You going to report us to your mom, Jones?" Jawbone snickered.

We made it over the stream, which wasn't much wider than I was tall, and headed across the field. The position was exposed, but we weren't expecting live fire. As we made our way across, I realized the DI hadn't said anything about messing with other teams. Would that invalidate your victory? Were other teams already talking about how they were going to trip up the others?

I kept my mouth shut, but my eyes open. Every few kilometers we repositioned ourselves using the map. The terrain was tough. The heat and bugs were intense, despite our slicks and good boots. I pulled up the hood of my slick to get some relief and conserve water.

We hiked all day, argued three times about position, and finally agreed to stop for a meal and an hour of sleep. The jungle had cooled enough that Jawbone insisted on snapping our pop-up heater on. It sat at the center of our little circle, pumping out heat but no light. We kept our headlamps on and divvied up dinner; flat MREs that you could fancy up by adding water, if you wanted, or choke down as-is. Either way, they weren't great, which was why Jawbone called them Meals Rejected by the Enemy. I was pretty sure he'd looked that up on the knu too. It sounded too clever to be original.

"These bugs are awful," Jones said. "Bet there aren't any bugs on Mars. Why aren't we training in a desert?"

"Put up your hood," I said. "It helps."

"I'm not putting up my goddamn hood," Jones said. "Makes me feel like a giant dick."

"That's different than any other time?" I said.

"Jealous, Dietz?"

Grandma said, "We don't all need to be a big dick like you, Jones."

Jones got up and headed away from the heat source. His headlamp swung with him, illuminating the big, wet trees and massive vines snaking through the understory. The whole place was crawling with bugs; his headlamp gave us a good view of the leaping, fluttering, stinging mess of them. I don't generally mind bugs. I grew up with a goddamn pet cockroach, because it was one of the few things my mom wouldn't try to kill and eat. But even this was a little much for me.

"Where you going?" I asked.

"Going to take a shit," Jones said.

"You've been pissing in your suit all day," I said. "What's the difference?"

"The difference is, I want to take a shit like a goddamn human being."

Jones forged into the buzzing jungle, crashing and swearing as he went.

"The reward is sounding less great," Jawbone said. "We don't sleep for three days so we can win sleeping in for two hours?"

"Prove you can read a map and not die," Grandma said. "You'll pass."

"How do you know?" Jawbone said. "How many times you done this?"

"This is my second time," Grandma said.

"Thought you were just old," I said.

"I'm twenty-five, you little shit. Signed up right after basic education. Made it five weeks in. Had some issues. Had to wash out."

"Why?" I said. "You bust open your head? Piss on somebody like Jones?"

Grandma hugged her knees to her chest. We heard Jones's noisy flatulence some ways distant. Him and his ass problems.

"Feeling better?" Jawbone yelled.

"Fuck you!" Jones, muffled.

"Nothing like that. I couldn't make the first drop," Grandma said.

"What, when they deploy you?" I said. "They turn you into light?"

"Yeah. The drop. They tried to break me apart. It didn't take."

"What's that mean?" I said.

"You haven't done it yet," she said. "Hard to explain until you do it."

"It didn't kill you," I said. "You look like you have all your limbs and shit."

"I didn't break apart. Not once. Couldn't lose a limb. Never was able to move them. Everybody else, well"—she pointed at the sky—"they got beamed up like superstars. And I stayed grounded. Just stood there. Boots in the dirt. Staring at the sky. Guess I'm too full of shit to bust up into light."

"I didn't know that happened," I said. "We're all made of like, atoms and stuff. I mean, how could it not work? We're all made the same."

"I'm not a fucking scientist," Grandma said. "All that shit they shoot us up with? It changes us, like . . . your body, how it comes together. And they reformulated it the last couple years. They retested me and said it would work this time. I guess a lot of people don't get it. Like, if you want to change the rules to bust people down and put them back together, you need to change human beings. You know? We're all a bunch of guinea pigs. It's why the corps love war. Gives them a rationale for putting investments into genetics."

Jones swore; we heard him bumbling around in the bush again.

"The fuck is that?" he yelled.

"You okay?" I said.

"Stepped in shit."

"Your shit?"

"No, goddamn. Some other shit. Fuck."

"It's the jungle," I said. "It's full of shit."

Jones stomped back into the circle of heat, kicking at the undergrowth. "Fuck these Martian socialists," he said, "and their fucking war."

"What's the difference between a communist and a socialist?" Jawbone said.

We waited, thinking there was a punch line.

"You serious?" Jones said.

"Sure. I mean, I know they're bad, but people use the names the same."

"They both want you to labor for somebody else," I said.

"They want to bleed you out and feed you to lazy people."

"Think about it like this," Jones said. "We're here starving and sweating for the corp and shitting in the goddamn woods."

"You didn't have to shit in the woods," I said.

Jones said, "And for every fifty push-ups you do, they go out there and feed some lazy ghoul who sits around pushing out babies and doing nothing, sucking off your labor."

"My family were ghouls," I said. "We weren't lazy."

"Well, sure," Jones said. "You worked hard and got residency. Not all ghouls are lazy. Just, you know."

"Most of them?" I said.

"They wouldn't be ghouls, otherwise."

"What exactly did *you* do," I asked, "to earn all your voting rights and health benefits before you signed up?"

"Fuck you," Jones said. "We earned everything."

"Didn't your great-grandparents earn it?" Jawbone said. "I mean, Dietz has a point."

"I don't have to pick through trash," Jones said, "because my family did better than Dietz's. So what? Good genetics. Right side of the Seed Wars. Life isn't fair."

Grandma snorted. "But you're trying to say it's fair. That if everybody works hard, they get the same treatment you did. My dad was a resident, my mom a citizen. My dad always had to work harder. He didn't have access to a lot of things she did. Neither did I. I have to earn citizen on my own."

"It doesn't work that way," Jones said. "Why are you ganging up on me?"

"I was just asking," Jawbone said. "I'm here to make citizen, too. And yeah, I sure deserve it more than a ghoul who isn't here."

"I'm fine throwing ghouls at the war," Jones said. "My mom—"

"I'm tired of hearing about your fucking moms," I said.

We all had our headlamps off now, so I couldn't see his

expression.

"We aren't going to win this, Dietz," Jones said. "Why don't you fucking relax?"

"The war, or the exercise?" I said. "Why are you really here, Jones? You get into trouble with the corp? Your moms kick you out of the house? Get your feelings hurt on the football field?"

"What would you know?" he said. "I'm tired of your arrogant bullshit. You aren't anyone special."

"Both of you shut up," Grandma said. "You're making me tired." She rustled around in the undergrowth. Her sleeping mat squeaked against her slick.

I leaned against the tree behind me, which I knew wasn't the best idea. A big branch or a snake could come down on me, and then it was lights-out, no matter how great my training. Anger kept me awake despite my exhaustion. I wanted a shower and a real shit. I understood why Jones had hiked out into the bush to take a crap. You started to feel like a robot, all wrapped up in this suit, hauling around a big gun.

I didn't mean to nod off. I wanted to stay angry. I was thinking a lot of angry shit to keep myself up. I sure as hell wanted to get out from under the tree, but my body betrayed me. This superhero human-suit we were supposed to have . . . If we were all so great now, why did we get tired? Why did we get thirsty? The only reason they used us instead of robots is because we were cheaper. They'd send us in before they sent in some drone army. I'd learn later that Martians were still more skittish about killing people than drones, too.

Go figure.

I came awake to Grandma shaking me. It was still dark, but the sounds around us had changed. Some animal whoop-whooped in the darkness.

"Another squad just passed us," Grandma said. "Jones went ahead to lay a trap for them."

"A . . . trap?" I said. "They'll hear him coming. He's as graceful as a goddamn bear."

"He turned on his suit's dampener."

"Why? Shit."

"You said you wanted to win."

"Where's the map?"

"He took it."

"You got the compass?"

"He took that too. I fell asleep. Jawbone filled me in."

"Goddammit, Jawbone," I said.

"You wanted to win!" Jawbone said.

I tried to picture the map. "There's a ridge south of us. That's what we were going to have to hump up next. Going around would take us five more kilometers. We'd have lost a lot of time."

"I'm tired, Dietz," Jawbone said. "Let's wait until he comes back."

"We aren't here to fight one another. We're not the enemy."

"You're going out in the dark?" Jawbone said.

"You think being a soldier was going to be a party?" I said. I sounded like the DI.

We packed our gear and headed in the direction Jawbone had seen the other squad go. They had turned on their headlamps and they were a good quarter kilometer ahead, working their way up the ridge.

"Which team?" I asked.

"Muñoz is leading," Grandma said.

Of course. I yelled, "Muñoz!" No answer. No change in the movement of the lights. "Muñoz! Watch out for Jones up there!"

"Why you give him up?" Grandma asked.

"Because we're not here to eat one another. I want to win fair."

"War isn't fair, Dietz," Grandma noted.

"It's an exercise."

I went toward the headlamps. Jawbone and Grandma followed. If Muñoz was leading us the wrong way, fine. But I figured Jones was going to be waiting to see those lights. Muñoz's squad didn't slow down. I'd ask why they kept the headlamps on, but like I said—it was an exercise. It wasn't some covert operation.

The jungle around us was heavy and wet. Dark, so dark. When you grow up just outside some big city, like I did, you don't appreciate the dark. You don't get a real grasp on it. Darkness is what happens when you close your eyes. It's something you choose, not something thrust upon you. But out here, the darkness was absolute. Our headlamps seared through it; lightning during a storm.

I slid into the gully, not waiting for the others. The team ahead picked up their pace. They couldn't have had any time to sleep. I wondered what was keeping them upright; Muñoz, probably, poking them all with a sharp stick.

"Goddammit!" somebody yelled from the squad. Their lights swung wildly. Sound of broken branches, snapping leaves.

The ground under me went soft. Mud slurped around my boots. I grabbed hold of a thick vine. It broke in my hand. It was rigid enough to hook another one. I pulled myself out using it. Further on, the mud thinned to water. I sank waist deep. I shuddered, thinking about parasites and snapping, biting fish and snakes. My rifle wasn't going to be much use against them. I hoped the slick ate leeches.

Raised voices. Jones, arguing. Muñoz's shout.

"Jones!" I yelled. I got to the other side of the swampy mess and crawled up the bank. I ran as fast as I could, slapping away massive leaves and snarled branches.

I heard Grandma and Jawbone behind me. I tripped. Snapped my knee on a sharp rock. I bit back a howl. I leaned against a tree as pain shimmied up my leg. Grandma went past me.

"You okay?" she said.

"Yeah, go. Don't let him be shit."

She went ahead.

I limped after her. I got close enough to see Muñoz and her team; their faces were filthy and exhausted. They had their rifles out. Jones stood in front of them, waving his rifle like a goddamn idiot.

"Hey!" I said. "Put the guns away!"

Grandma strode between the two parties, palms out. "Everybody's tired. Let's—"

A gun went off.

The sound came from Muñoz's team; that's what I remember. I swore and stumbled back. Jawbone bumped into me, swore, and fumbled for his own rifle.

"Don't shoot!" I said. "Don't—"

Everything went dark. They'd turned their lamps off. I couldn't see a damn thing except what was directly in front of me.

"Shoot!" Jones yelled.

Two more shots, both from Muñoz's side. I heard them crashing through the undergrowth. Jones cried out. "I'm hit! I'm hit! Shit!"

"Hold fire!" Muñoz ordered. "Who's firing? Dietz, did you fire, you fuck?"

"I'm on the goddamn ground, Muñoz! Control your fucking squad."

"We're out. We're out," she called.

"Jones is hit!" I said.

"Call for evac. He probably shot himself!" And then her squad was moving away again, crashing through the bush.

I crawled over to Jones. A broken tree branch jutted from his left thigh. He was covered in shredded leaves, splinters, and blood.

"What's all this?" I said. "Is this your—" I brought up my

head. The light from my headlamp crawled across a meaty, twisted wreck just behind Jones. I recognized Grandma's hands, short, stubby fingers tipped in callouses.

I went to Grandma's body. Her chest was blown open. A yawning wet mouth of viscera gaped back at me. The branches of the tree behind the body glistened with blood and bits of tattered flesh. The blistered tree trunk was exposed, as if mashed by a tremendous fist. Her rifle lay a few centimeters from her outstretched hands. The wilted violets she had affixed to her bayonet were scattered across the fleshy red smear where her head should have been.

I stood over the rumpled wreck of Grandma's body and had an irrational urge to try to put all the pieces of her back together.

Jawbone behind me, "What do we do?"

"They'll . . . send evac."

"You sure?" Jawbone said. "Shit. Wouldn't we hear them already? They're recording, right? They'd know, from her tracker. And what we saw. They'll see that Muñoz—"

"I didn't see who shot. You did?"

"I . . . I mean, they'll review it."

"Dietz! Jawbone! My . . . leg. Do you have—"

"Yeah," I said. It felt good to have something to do. I ripped open my med kit. Yanked out the branch from Jones's leg. Jones screamed. Blood bubbled. I shoved coagulating gel into the wound. It made contact with the blood and expanded, filling the wound, stemming the flow.

Jones palmed the pills I gave him. I shot him up with a vial labeled "For pain," just to be sure. We had had basic CPR and medical training by then, but my mind was having a hard time recalling much of it.

Jawbone squatted across from me, rifle still out. "We can leave him and go ahead," Jawbone said. "You stay here and I'll hit the objective, then hump back and meet you."

"We'd still have to hump him back, after," I said. "It's a team exercise. And Vargas is . . . she's dead. Jones isn't good."

"I'm right here," Jones said. "And nobody's humping me. Leave me. I won't get eaten by ants."

"Vargas will be," I said.

"They'll send a team," Jones said, but his voice trembled. "For her and maybe for me too. Complete the mission."

"I wanted to win," I said, and it sounded stupid, then, while Jones squirmed and the bugs began to crawl all over Grandma's ruined corpse. I could almost hear her tell me, "Life isn't fair, kid."

"No, it isn't," I said aloud. Then, to Jones, "Hey, I'll stay with you. Jawbone, you nab the objective; get it logged on the GPS. We'll carry him back, the two of us. It won't take long, all of us together."

"We're going to lose a lot of sleep," Jawbone said, "and we aren't going to win. Why don't we just wait?"

"Is that what we'd say out on Mars? That we'd just wait?"

"This isn't Mars, Dietz."

"Not yet. Do it."

"I'm not going alone. They shot at us."

"Jawbone, shit!"

"Go," Jones said. "I'm not a threat to them anymore. Why waste the firepower? I can shoot. My fingers are just fine."

"All right," I said. I couldn't look at Grandma's body again.

Me and Jawbone got Jones hopped up on some more painkillers. I left him Grandma's water slug and rations.

"We aren't far from the objective," I said. "Give us a few hours."

"Sure," Jones said, and he gave me one of his cocky smiles, but he was sweating badly, and that smile didn't reach his terrified eyes.

"Let's go," Jawbone said. "What's the map say? We can't be

far."

I unfolded the map. It trembled in my hands. *Is there a wind?* I thought, but it was my own shaking fingers.

"We're maybe . . . another eleven or twelve k's."

Jawbone grabbed at my elbow. "C'mon."

The DI. I saw his face again: angry, maybe, but disappointed, mostly, like my father's. I wanted to win. Jawbone wanted to win. We had one man down. Another dead.

We weren't going to win. We had already lost.

"Jawbone, we need to take Jones back."

"They will send—"

"And if he dies?"

"We have to complete the objective."

"This is the objective. The team."

Jones protested, but I'd made up my mind. As we dragged Jones between us, one painful foot in front of the other, drops of his blood made a shiny little trail behind us.

We marched, slogged, dragged, moaned, kicked, screamed, and yeah, we even stopped to cry a couple times. The jungle cover masked the sun, made sunrise come later and sunset earlier. If we just sat down, would they come for us? I imagined the DI again. His spitting, hissing contortions as he told us how worthless we were, how unfit. And me, always me: I was stupid, not two brain cells to rub together. Why did we bother coming back at all, he'd say, when we had so clearly fucked the dog?

Dusk came early to the jungle. I smelled our rally point before I saw it. The mouthwatering scent of roasting protein, real meat, even, and spicy bean mash. My stomach cramped so violently with hunger I thought I'd fall over.

We came around a bend in the trail, its width well-worn now. There was the rest of the class, sitting under the darkening sky at long tables, talking and laughing like kids at some end-of-year dance social. The flag waved above them, emblazoned with a stylized red eagle gripping a bouquet of arrows tipped in stars, flying on a blue background.

"Medic!" I yelled.

A few people looked up. Two handlers came over from the edges of the rally point and met us on the field. The flash of their heads-up displays sparked in their left eyes as they scanned us.

"Medic's on the way," one said. "Put him down. Dietz, Hadid, report to your DI."

"What about Vargas?" I said. "There was live fire. She got hit. She's . . . she died out there."

"We know," the other one said. "The body's been retrieved."

"You knew about Jones but didn't come out?" Jawbone said. "The fuck?"

"Report to your DI, recruit."

I grabbed Jawbone's arm and led him away to the temporary barracks.

The DI was in his office, just off the rec room. He had his face turned away from us. Held a big cup of tea in his meaty left hand.

"Dietz and Hadid reporting, sir," I said.

We saluted. I wasn't sure how I was still standing. The little rush of adrenaline on seeing the DI's face must have kept me mobile.

"Jones alive?"

"Sir," I said, "yes, sir. We got him back. Sir."

"You two fuck-ups were the only squad to lose a unit, you know that?"

I decided that was rhetorical, but Jawbone said, "Sir, no sir. We're sorry, sir."

"Sorry?" the DI said. "You know how many idiots I've lost on what should be a pretty basic fucking exercise?"

"No, sir," Jawbone said.

"Sixteen," he said. "Sixteen in the five goddamn years I've

been trying to teach kids like you not to shoot off their own dicks."

"Pretty tough for *all* of us to shoot off our own dicks, sir. Considering."

"Shut up, Dietz," the DI said. "Don't argue semantics with me. You're the one who got Vargas's goddamn face blown off."

"Sir, I don't know where the shot came from. You can check our rifles. We never fired. It was some other team."

"And you didn't return fire?"

"Sir, no," I said. "They were our people, sir. If we started shooting, there would just be more shooting. You'd have two or three more bodies."

"What if they'd been your enemy, Dietz?"

"They weren't. Sir. There was nothing in the mission brief that said we could or should shoot one another."

"Nothing saying you couldn't, either."

"Sir, I believe you are arguing semantics now, sir."

"Goddamn right I am. Hadid, you shoot anything?"

"No, sir."

"Did you want to?"

"I . . . sir, yes, I did."

"Why didn't you?"

"Dietz said not to."

"And Dietz was your squad leader?"

"Sir, no, that was Jones, sir."

"And what did Jones tell you to do?"

"Sir . . . uh . . . he said to shoot."

"And you disobeyed your squad leader?"

"Sir . . . I, shit, I'm sorry, sir. It was . . ."

"Sorry is for your mom. Do I look like your fucking mom, Hadid?"

"No, sir."

"Get the fuck out of here, Hadid. Dietz, you stay."

A shiver moved up my spine. What was he going to do to me *now*?

When Hadid was gone, the DI fixed me with his undivided attention. "You look like shit, Dietz."

"Sir, I feel like shit."

"You sleep any?"

"Sir, maybe an hour. Sir."

"We record everything that happens out there."

"Sir. Yes, sir."

"You kids are all a bunch of walking, talking, recording devices, you know. I've seen more kids wank off and awkwardly fuck each other than you can imagine. I don't know how they find the fucking energy."

I had no idea what to say to that, but luckily—or not—he kept on.

"I don't like kids like you, Dietz. You know that. Kids like you come out here with something to prove. They put their squads in danger. They risk their lives before the goddamn corp can get any use out of them. But some kids, they get the others to follow them. You can call it dumb luck, or charisma, or some inbred talent. I don't think you have much of that but the first. So I can do one of two things. I can pair you up with somebody you will actually fucking listen to or I can kick you the fuck out as some fuck-up who will never follow orders."

It wasn't a question. I waited. My legs felt like two cold pillars of dead stone. My eyelids kept sinking closed.

"You listening to me, Dietz?"

"Sir. Yes, sir!"

"Get a shower. You've got blood all over you. Dismissed."

I got as far as pulling off my slick and bunching it up at the end of my bed. I couldn't make it to my bunk, so I crawled into Muñoz's—she was still out with the others.

She woke me up some time later and offered a hard roll

slathered in butter and cheese. I gulped it down gratefully before anyone caught us with food in the barracks.

"You stink," Muñoz said. "Take a shower."

Being physically ground down is like being drunk. Sometimes you can only process what you're doing in hazy bursts. It's like your lizard brain takes over, the same part of you that regulates breathing and digestion. I went through the motions on instinctual memory. MARCH TO SHOWERHEAD. WET YOUR HEAD. SOAP YOUR HEAD AND FACE. RINSE. SOAP YOUR LEFT ARM. . . .

I woke in the middle of the night to someone moaning. Everyone had racked up in the temporary barracks. In the morning, we were getting lifted out, back to Mendoza.

I rolled over. "Shut up!" I said.

"It's Jones," Muñoz whispered. "He's been doing that for an hour."

"Didn't they give him painkillers?"

"I think he's having nightmares."

"Somebody should wake him up."

"Too tired to move."

We both lay there in the dark, surrounded by more than a hundred other snorting, snoring, whispering, shifting, sleeping bags of human blood and bone and flesh. As I closed my eyes, I saw Grandma's burst chest again, a tortured animal, something from some awful, over-the-top immersive about parasites or aliens or wars in other corps.

"Know what gets me, Muñoz?"

"What?"

"Grandma washed out cause she couldn't break down into light. They fixed her, though, some new treatment, she said. She was going to deploy to Mars like the rest of us, beamed up in a bolt of light. They can fix all that. They can make us into goddamn sunbeams, but they can't keep us from dying."

"Not yet."

I listened to Jones moaning. "I'm not sure," I said, "if that's good or bad."

"I didn't shoot her," Muñoz said.

"You know who did?"

"No."

"You bullshitting?"

"Doesn't matter which one. It was my squad, and I didn't control them. They'll throw me out."

"They won't."

"I'm not making intelligence. They made that totally fucking clear. Now I'm not going to be anybody."

She left the rest unsaid, but I heard it in the silence. *"Now I'm nobody, just like you."*

I guess that brings us to week five. The week you wanted to hear about. Because in week five?

We jumped.

Interview #1
SUBJECT #187799
DATE: 21|05|309
TIME: 0900
ROOM: 97

I: Interview beginning at oh-nine-hundred with Subject one-eight-seven-seven-nine-nine. This is an audio-only recording. Please note that all recordings with this subject have been classified audio-only. Subject, you will be asked a series of questions to which we require your honest answers, to the best of your recollection. Do you understand?

S: What do you think?

I: I'll need an affirmative.

S: You'll need a body bag.

I: For the record, I take the subject's response to indicate that they understand my line of inquiry. When did you arrive in Saint Petersburg?

S: What?

I: Your arrival in Saint Petersburg. When was it?

S: (LAUGHTER) There is no satisfying answer to that. You have no idea what you're asking.

I: Be unsatisfying. At what time did you arrive in Saint Petersburg?

S: Too early for dinner.

I: What specific time period did you arrive in Saint Petersburg?

S: Before dinner.

I: Who sent you to Saint Petersburg?

S: What?

I: Who was your commanding officer?

S: For what?

I: There was no outside agent?

S: That's a good question

(SILENCE: 08 seconds)

I: Do you need to go back to your cell?

S: No, I can shit here. Sorry, talk here. Talk here, shit here. Either, or.

I: What were you doing in Saint Petersburg?

S: Following orders.

I: From who?

S: I told you.

I: You've said nothing.

S: You aren't listening. But that isn't what you're here to do, is it?

I: What am I here to do?

S: You know what the trick is to an interrogation, Sergeant?

I: You are quite certain I'm a sergeant? Do I look so young?

S: No, I know who you are. And I know that's likely no longer your rank, but it pleases me to piss you off. We've met before, though I suspect you don't know that yet. I can't imagine you still have access to a complete DNA database to test me against, do you? If I'm Martian, the odds that I'd be in there are slim, aren't they? It pleases me, though. I could give you name, rank, and serial number, but that will get me straight to the next room, won't it? And we all know confessions gained under torture are circumspect at best. I'd say anything, just to make the pain stop.

I'd tell you your mother sent me to Saint Petersburg to murder your commanding officer with a bowl full of cherries, if that's what you wanted to hear. The trick is to not offer up anything. You answer the question and only the question. Don't start building up a story you can't substantiate. The standard interrogation technique for TenisanaCom is PEACE: Preparation and Planning, Engage and Explain, Account, Closure and Evaluate. I have to assume you've done your preparation and planning. Now you're engaging and asking me to explain and account for my actions so you can figure out how I achieved it. I know we're starting here because you haven't just jumped into enhanced interrogation techniques. . . . Those techniques are reserved for the very worst interrogators, the ones who will not only fail to get what they truly desire from a POW, but who will create a lifelong enemy whose goal on leaving this prison-if, indeed, they ever leave-will be to share their story and teach an entirely new generation of young people to hate the organization that captured and tortured them. It's one of the most fascinating and heartbreaking cycles of violence, on par with parents who abuse their children. Did you know that the abuse of children by corporate bosses has been shown to create more loyal adult employees? They are told they could simply leave their home corp and become a ghoul, or sell themselves off to some other corp. They are told they have choices. If we choose to stay with a corp, we have to justify our reasons. We become complicit in our own oppression. This was referred to as Stockholm Syndrome—

I: I'm not asking you about Norway.

S: Stockholm, Sweden. You know, that's interesting, an interesting slip. Was it a slip, or were you testing me? I've often wondered what it must be like here, living through the final days of the war. I bet it's overwhelming to see so many dead and dying, to see your whole way of life destroyed. Sweden is where Stockholm used to be. Most of it's still there. You know why it's not all under water like so many old capitalist strongholds? Much of the North is still rising. It was glaciated so long that the land beneath those glaciers was compressed for hundreds of thousands of years. Imagine the earth there is like a piece of bread that's been squashed. Then the pressure eases when the ice melts. Every year the land rises about a centimeter. Since the last ice age, there's one stretch of Swedish coastline that's risen over three hundred meters. There are ancient settlements that used to sit up against the sea. Now they're stranded far inland. An entire geography completely transformed in a relatively short amount of time. . . . Much like what happened in the Pacific as the oceans rose a century ago. The unrest that caused . . . well, that got us the Seed Wars and the Corporate Wars and the Big Six. There's a fascinating course of study on the rise of fascist states that posits that they become more popular the more people fear death. And really, most corporate states are fascist, though they would have you believe they're oligarchies, ruled by tables full of rich old people with humanity's best interests at heart. The more fearful and out of control we feel, the more we look to some big man on a horse or a tank or a beam of light to save us. The survival of truly egalitarian societies requires—if not an absence of fear—then a harnessing of it. Consider—

I: Why were you in Saint Petersburg?

(SILENCE 17 seconds)

S: Why don't you tell me, Sergeant?

I: Let us establish the facts. You planted an incendiary device at the Taleon Imperial Hotel in Saint Petersburg. We know it was you because you stood on a vehicle outside of the hotel as your device went off and called for the TenisanaCom CEO by name. If he had not been in residence at the hotel, you and I certainly wouldn't be having this conversation. You'd have been shot on the spot. But he was. And that leads me to believe you got some intelligence from someone on my team. There's no one else who knew he was staying there. I'd think you _meant_ to get caught, but you ran from my security forces and we had to root you out of an abandoned cellar. Why announce yourself and then run? Who sent you there?

S: I almost called for you, instead, but I figured you were less important. Say his name, though, and you'll come after, like his little dog. I enjoyed yelling "Papa Martin!" which is such a textbook "Hey, let's try to have the supreme leader sound benevolent" name that I laughed when I first heard it. Was his nickname your idea?

I: On the outskirts of the city, we found an abandoned Martian shuttle with your DNA and fingerprints all over it. What are we to make of that?

S: I don't know. You're the one in intelligence.

I: So you are Martian? The Martians sent you to Saint Petersburg to intimidate our CEO? Or plant some other contagion? We suspect you're the one who set the artillery on fire outside the city as well. You know that fire spread? Innocent people lost their homes. We don't have the resources to put out such a blaze at this point in the war. Wanton destruction. A dramatic act of arson. By order of Mars?

S: Oh, now, I didn't say that, did I, Sergeant?

(SILENCE: 05 seconds)

I: Your incendiary device had a name scrawled on it. Three letters. "Hal." What was that supposed to mean?

S: Just a little joke. You remember jokes, Sergeant? I always expected you to be better at this. Maybe all those years on Mars taught me something besides geography and history. Did you know there isn't any banned media on Mars? Of course, they only allowed me books and audio recordings, no immersives. Books, imagine that! Paper, even. How decadent. You can get a lot of reading done, sitting in a ten by twelve cell.

I: You were a prisoner? Why? Deserter? Is that why you left? You were escaping to Saint Petersburg? Why choose that city, and why intimidate our CEO? When <u>exactly</u> did you arrive in Saint Petersburg?

S: Exactly when I was supposed to.

I: End Interview.

(END RECORDING #1)

8.

'd been anticipating my first de-corporealizing drop from the very beginning. Or maybe the end.

It happened our fifth week of mandatory training. After hearing from Grandma about how she wasn't able to get deployed, I admit I was surprised they waited so long to get the drop over with. Wouldn't they want to know early if we could handle it?

That first drop, the training drop . . . they brought us all out to some field and made us stand an arm's length apart. Told us to be still and find a point to concentrate on and begin a meditation. We got a list of the rules, and there were a lot. Some examples:

1. Don't move once the drop sequencing starts.
2. Don't take off your helmet.
3. Don't use the coms until you have fully corporealized at your final location.

4. Respond to medical team requests immediately on returning to the base drop point.

They even had a sequence you had to run through, giving your name and rank, showing both your hands, reading a flashing number they projected on an LED-film display on the field, all sorts of tricks the medics used to make sure you came back right.

I remember all that instruction. I remember getting in formation, and starting to shake, worrying I wasn't going to come back right no matter how well I stuck to the rules. . . .

And then . . .

Heat and noise, my own breath loud in my ears, the sound of my beating heart.

It was just a test drop, but they landed us into some shit. I remember gasping for air that wasn't there, because my lungs hadn't come together yet. Two recruits started coalescing over the same spot; they were saved at the last minute by some tech, no doubt, who redirected one of them and put her somewhere else before they had fully merged. That near miss scared me badly. I was down on my knees for a long time. Then . . . a missing chunk of my memory. Just more heat and noise. I heard after that they were shooting live rounds over our heads and setting off artillery. Maybe it was good I couldn't recall much of it.

We all had to do forty-eight hours of quarantine so they could make sure we were mentally and physically fit afterward. They drew a lot of blood. Ran us through cognitive exercises. Physical fitness tests. One kid didn't make it—she came back wrong when we dropped back to base, her head jutting out of the center of her torso. Another recruit couldn't pass the cognitive or physical tests, after. He got discharged. Latrines all the way down, no doubt.

I may not remember much about that drop, but at least I'd survived it intact.

We graduated in week six. One hundred and nineteen of the one hundred and thirty-seven who first signed up made it out the other side. We had the day of graduation to get black-out drunk, just like Muñoz wanted.

Then we got our assignments.

The orders came in, and they scattered us. I got posted to some infrastructure unit in La Paz, doing what looked a lot to me like desk duty. Muñoz and Jones got posted to Isla Riesco, in an active, front-facing platoon that was getting immediately sent to the Martian front.

When I challenged my post, the posting officer said, "Your numbers came back bad after your drop."

"What's that mean?"

"It means the logistics geeks said you can't handle drops."

"They didn't say anything during training."

"You scored fine. It's just something that happens. Not everybody is cut out for getting burst apart, you get me?"

"I'm fitter than damn near anybody here."

"I don't make the rules. I enforce them. Just keep requesting a transfer. We're . . . taking some losses. There may be a place that opens up despite your rating. It's not the worst rating I've seen."

"Can I see the file?"

"You're asking for classified corp intel. Sorry."

Maybe it's good I didn't remember much about that training drop, but I'd have liked to have a better idea about why I'd been disqualified.

I spent my first six months as an enlisted soldier rebuilding infrastructure taken out by the Martians. I traveled all over Tene-Silvia, and even did a couple joint operations with Evecom and ShinHana. Muñoz and Jones kept in touch, when they could. A lot of their drops were classified, and they were stuck in quarantine often. It wasn't just the lack of combat that bothered me—I'd trained for combat, not ditch digging; it was the loneliness. I got on all right with my platoon, but knowing Jones and Muñoz were at the front and I wasn't the one covering their asses started to get to me. I sent in a new transfer request every six weeks, right after command denied the last one.

"I didn't come out here to do data entry," I told Muñoz once when we both had access to time with the com. Her noisy platoon hooted and hollered in the background. I got the impression they'd come back from some great victory.

"You've got a fast line to citizenship, though," Muñoz said. "And a real career. Being front line is bullshit. They treat you like meat."

"I still think your other numbers were good. You aced every class."

"Doesn't fucking matter," she said, and sighed. I saw a familiar face behind her.

"Is that Jawbone?" I said.

He waved. "Hey, Dietz!"

"Shit, you have Jawbone *and* Jones?"

"Lucky me," Muñoz said. "They're the only ones stupid enough to get rolled into my platoon. He just got transferred yesterday. When *you* coming?"

"I'll get there."

I followed my other friends during that time—Andria and Rubem sent the most messages, mostly Andria. Andria got promoted on her first drop, and brought back a fistful of Martian soil. She tossed it into a water bottle and drank it while making a recording for me.

"Tasty!" she announced in front of her gawking platoon, but the look on her face gave it away. I imagined she got sick right after.

I tried to find the others who had signed up ahead of me

that day at the recruiting office. I knew Garcia and Orville had dropped out. And I lost track of Marseille and Timon. If they were alive, they were difficult to find. I suppose I could have requested to transfer to Andria's platoon instead of Muñoz's, but it wasn't the same. There's something that happens to you when you've been through the most grueling ordeal of your life with somebody. It's like you're closer than blood, after. Closer than family. There's nothing else like it.

The war would have gone a lot differently if I hadn't pursued a place at the front line. I know that. But when my persistence finally paid off, all I thought about was myself. The war I would experience. The war I wanted to fight next to people I trusted. Even if, like Jones, sometimes they were assholes.

After six months of transfer requests, I finally got approved to join Muñoz's platoon. I felt like I'd won some kind of life lottery. But it didn't turn out the way I hoped, for me or for Muñoz.

Life never does.

When I got to Isla Riesco, the CO assigned me to Muñoz's team. Muñoz was squad leader for one of the three fire teams under our CO. Jones and Jawbone were both on her team, along with a lanky woman called Squib who had a loud, brassy voice and Xs tattooed on her knuckles.

"You request me?" I asked Muñoz as I threw my stuff into my rack. Squib sat next to Muñoz on the bed across from mine, polishing her boots. Jones and Jawbone were out checking messages.

"Bad drop," Muñoz said. "They gave us six fresh recruits to make up for people we lost. None of them have seen combat. At least I knew you were a pretty good shot." Her eyes were already different; she had that faraway look that people get when they're reliving the past. "That's probably why they finally agreed to the transfer. All my idea."

Squib said, "More fodder for the grinder."

"I came to fight."

"I give this one two drops," Squib said.

"What's that?" I said.

"She means two drops before you're killed," Muñoz said. "We've dropped seven times already."

"Twenty-eight, for me," Squib said.

"Why aren't you squad leader then?" I said.

Squib showed her teeth. Her left incisor was missing. "I'm not so good with people."

"And we've lost a lot of good people," Muñoz said. "You remember Moskowitz? From mandatory? Dead first drop. Corporealized right inside a goddamn atmo plant on Mars. Can you believe that?"

"Sorry," I said.

"Not your fault. You ready for this? I mean, you could be repairing some bridges."

"Rather be here. Don't get sad about me blowing up, Muñoz."

"Never," she said, and there was the grin I remembered. "You hungry?"

Muñoz introduced me to some others in the platoon. Prakash was a lean young woman with a quick laugh and easy smile; like Muñoz, she was little. A bigger guy, Herrera, was a specialist on another squad.

"And Tanaka is that handsome prick over there," Muñoz said, pointing him out in the cafeteria. He sat with who I figured was his squad. I didn't usually agree with Muñoz and her taste in men, but thought I might be convinced this time. Tanaka was tall and lean and had a kind face that I didn't expect to see on a soldier leading a fire team. A rough beard covered his face, and he had grown out his sandy hair.

"He get flak for the hair?" I said.

"Naw," Muñoz said. "He lost a bet."

The CO of our platoon was Second Lieutenant Valenzuela, but we just called her the CO. She was one of those squat, wide linebacker types who I imagined could bench press the lot of us one-handed. For all her swagger, she wasn't much taller than Muñoz. She had one of those ageless faces all the higher-ranking soldiers had; she could have been thirty or fifty—neither would have surprised me.

"Today some of you will see the enemy for the first time on the field," the CO said during our first mission briefing. I tried not to get cocky about it. I figured I'd go into everything like it was a training exercise. I wasn't going to get busted apart and see only darkness. Not this time. I wasn't going to go nuts or shit myself.

"You will probably shit yourself," the CO said. "That's fine. Your slick will eat it up. This is a Mars recon mission. You are acting as backup to the main mission. That means you don't shoot shit unless I tell you to shoot it. Before you start hyperventilating, yes, you can breathe air on Mars. But the reason I've had you in the tanks is because it's like breathing air on top of goddamn Everest. Keep your oxygen line clear, and use it. Don't be a goddamn hero. Gravity will fuck with you there. You've all had the training. I suggest you use it. Don't go shooting one another's heads off. Too many goddamn rookies in this bunch."

Jones was out with a minor injury: a broken leg from crashing down the stairs drunk while celebrating my arrival and imminent first combat drop. Our med unit was good enough that he'd only be off his feet for a few days. Most bone breaks in training had healed cleanly in the same time frame.

"Go kill a Martian for me," he said from his bunk. He was settled in with some immersives and a long list of rehabilitation exercises. I had never seen him look so anxious about what was going to amount to three days of light duty.

The CO swapped in a seasoned soldier, Specialist Abascal,

from another unit and integrated her into our squad. Abascal had almost three years of service. I figured she was about Grandma's age, maybe midtwenties. Though they looked nothing alike, Abascal's presence on the team reminded me of the firefight that night during mandatory training. I watched the back of her head as we got in formation; she had tattooed two dueling snakes onto her shaved skull.

"You look long enough, they'll bite," Abascal said, without turning.

"It's good work," I said.

"I've got more."

"Really?"

"Ask me, after."

Shit, I thought. She was going to be trouble.

They crammed us into a drop ship. For a while I thought maybe we were going to go in that way, even knowing better. I sweated bad in my suit.

"Why they shuttling us?" I asked Muñoz. "Defeats the purpose, doesn't it?"

Muñoz grimaced. "It's in case something goes wrong. They fuck up the sequencing, it's like a nuclear bomb goes off."

"Red mist."

"Nah," Squib said, rubbing at some invisible blemish on her rifle, "ain't enough of you left even for that."

The drop ship vomited us at the launch point.

We ran off the ship and into the middle of a rocky beach. The ride hadn't been long, so we couldn't have gone far, but the sky was brighter, and the air was different. Cleaner, maybe. Cold arctic air, like something straight from an oxygen bar. I wondered if we were down at one of the bases in Antarctica. I knew three of the corps had territory down there. Last I heard, that was where Andria and Rubem were deployed.

They got us into formation. The CO held up her arm and

gave the signal that we were about to break apart.

My stomach seized. I forced myself to focus on a bare-knuckled tree on the horizon, tried to center myself like they taught us. Think about nothing. My stomach churned. The air burned. I was aware that the weapon in my arms was made to murder people.

The sky above us exploded.

When you drop, you burst apart like . . . Well, first your whole body shakes. Then every muscle gets taut and contracts, like you're experiencing a full-body muscle spasm centered in your core. The CO says it's like a contraction when you're having a kid, and if that's true, if just one is like that, then I don't know how everybody who has a kid isn't dead already, because that's bullshit.

Then you vibrate, you really vibrate, because every atom in your body is being ripped apart. It's breaking you up like in those old sci-fi shows, but it's not quick, it's not painless, and you're aware of every minute of it. You don't have a body anymore, you're locked in.

You're a beam of light.

9.

When we started to come back together, I expected to suck bad air, to leap with easy confidence, to see the ruddy mountains of Mars. But before our feet had even corporealized, we drew enemy fire. We burned up a dozen of the enemy right there even as we were getting our bearings. Our goddamn coms weren't even online yet.

I lay flat on the ground, unsure where the live fire was coming from. Churned brown dirt left rutted trails in thick, chewy crab grass. I peered at the sky, which looked awful blue to me, for Mars. When I confirmed all my body parts had come through all right, I tried to ping Muñoz over our squad channel. I couldn't locate her call sign.

My squad mates' call signs and positions popped in on my display. I had a moment of vertigo. Jones was tagged as squad leader. That threw me immediately. Jones was supposed to be back at base, cozying up with his immersives.

As more came online, the situation didn't get any clearer. Prakash's name came up; I saw her just ahead and to the left, her slim form obscured by early morning fog that snaked along the ground. Yes, that was definitely Prakash and not Jawbone.

Abascal and Squib were missing too. In their place were two people I didn't know; a tall women tagged as Omalas and a heavy man called Marino. My mind went back to all the people Muñoz had introduced me to back at base. I had no memories of these.

"Where are we?" I said into the squad channel.

"Holding pattern," Jones said. "They fucked something up. Stand by for evac."

"What?"

Flashing lights. A smear of red across my vision, as if the world itself tore open. I burst apart.

Shit.

We came down in the middle of a banana field and immediately traded fire. I shot blindly this time. Our rifles seared through banana trees, sprayed the fine remains in great clouds of residue. It's confusing when you come down in the middle of something already going on. Sometimes the energy weapons go right through you because there's not enough of you stuck together yet. But sometimes you've come together just enough, and they hit you, and either you're meat enough for it to kill you, or all your atoms break apart, and you're nothing. You ghost out.

I've seen a lot of people ghost out.

I came together and started firing. I saw the DI's face as I fired.

I hit an alien girl—some civilian at the banana farm. She was just a kid. I heard her and her mother screaming on the other side of the irrigation ditch. Their whole family, screaming, because I'd hit her and her legs were gone.

"Hold fire! Hold fire!" the CO over our platoon channel.

I lay on the ground and pressed my face across the butt of my rifle.

"Dietz?" Jones, over the squad channel.

Goddammit, he wasn't supposed to be here. The logistics people had fucked this up.

"Where is everybody?"

"Don't shit your pants again, Dietz," Jones said. "Prakash?"

"Alive and ready to burn up Martian ass!" she said.

"Omalas?"

"Here."

"Marino . . . Marino, ping me you shit-fucker."

"Yeah, yeah. Cleanup mission," Marino said. He sounded like some career soldier with everything to prove. "They get it right this time?"

We rallied around Jones, who was still listed as squad leader. I stumbled over burst banana trees; smears of overripe fruit ground into the loam. The other units were moving too, checking losses. I didn't see the CO, but her rally point pinged my GPS.

"There weren't supposed to be civilians here," Jones said. He gazed at the farmer family and the screaming girl, about a hundred paces up the dirt track.

"I don't get it," I said. "Where's Muñoz?"

The whole team turned to me. They wore fire helmets that covered their faces, and I was almost glad for it. I could imagine the faces behind the stances.

"You need to spend more time with your psych, Dietz," Jones said coolly.

My coms came online. I looked down and to the left, and the encrypted mission schematic came up.

I reviewed the mission brief. My stomach dropped. I tasted bile. The mission had updated. It wasn't a Mars recon mission.

I wanted to confirm this with the squad, to ask if I was nuts, but Jones's quip about the shrink gave me pause. Had I missed something? Something obvious? My heads-up display said our mission was to hunt for subversives in one of the civilian towns the Martians had set up in southern North America—CanKrushkev territory. The brief was clear. Was it my memory that was fucked up?

"This is bullshit," Marino said. "Wiping baby alien asses."

"Rally point's up," Jones said. "Head to the CO's position."

I clamped my mouth shut and did as I was told. I remembered the DI telling me to follow orders. Remembered what happened when I didn't. *Relax, Dietz,* I told myself. It will make sense. Something went wrong, that's all.

We rallied with the rest of the platoon at the center of the civilian town; it wasn't more than a main street, really. I tried to ping Muñoz again, thinking she was with the wider platoon, but she wasn't. Jawbone, Squib, and Abascal were missing, too. There were new names in this place: Markesh, Leichtner, Sandoval, Landon. I had no idea who they were, and—hidden behind their opaque helmets—I couldn't even scrutinize their faces to determine if it was a technical glitch giving me the wrong names on my heads-up.

Two more platoons wearing CanKrushkev fatigues worked their way up from the other side of the street, kicking down doors as they went. Our platoon had two prisoners: tall, thin Martian settlers with dark hair. They wore jeans and T-shirts. One of the shirts said *I love my CEO.* Nice joke, kid. Someone had taken away the protective lenses they used to shield their eyes from the sun, which was more intense here than Mars. The lenses also served as connected displays like ours. Removing those glasses blinded them in more ways than one.

"Where the fuck have you been, Jones?" the CO said.

"Just got a little turned around, sir."

"Turned around? You've got a fucking GPS. There some malfunction I should know about?"

"No sir," he said. "Just, you know—we've got Bad Luck Dietz with us."

"Sir," I said, "a civilian was hit, back that way."

"Christ, Dietz," she said. "We'll send a medic when this area's clear."

The platoons from CanKrushkev met us outside the town hall. They had six more insurgents with them, all zip-tied, their lenses stripped from their skinny faces. They were young kids, younger than us, pock-marked and in need of dental work. Martian settlers on Earth weren't considered residents, citizens, or even ghouls. They paid a tithe to the corp, and their access to basic care and humanitarian rights was largely self-governed.

Our CO went over to confer with the COs from the other platoons while we regarded one another over the heads of our respective prisoners.

"Jones," I said.

"Shut up," he said. "Don't say anything."

"Just tell me where Muñoz is. Did the mission change halfway through the jump? That's fine, but I don't have anything in the brief about it."

"Shut up, Dietz. Just . . . let's try to get through this mission without anyone dying. We can talk all you want at base. Don't freak everyone out with this stuff when we're on mission."

I had no idea what he was talking about, but he was squad leader. I bit back my retort. I'd save all this for base like he said, but then I wanted answers. The entire point of mandatory training is to get you to stop asking questions.

When the COs got word the area was clear, I went back with Prakash and our medic to help the alien I'd shot, but it didn't matter. She wasn't going to walk unless somebody regrew her legs, and only citizens have those benefits. Shit, these people couldn't even get their teeth straightened.

I had only fired once. But one is all it takes.

I stood over her while she screamed, and kept trying to remember all the horrible immersive they had shown us in training, about how Martians starved their own people and took away their free will. They're aliens. They're the enemy.

Right?

Prakash walked back with me and the medic. "You seem weird, Dietz," she said. "I mean, weirder than usual. It bother you, about the alien?"

"No." That lie tasted bad. It wasn't a lie a paladin would tell.

Prakash rubbed at her left arm. Shook it out.

"You injured?" I asked.

"Naw. Something from the drop. Just hurts. Feels funny. No big deal."

"You tell the medic?" The medic walked ahead of us. We spoke on a two-way channel.

"Don't worry about it," she said. "Didn't affect the fight. Area's clear."

We navigated back to where our platoon waited for extraction. The prisoners had been turned over to the CanKrushkev forces. I went over the names of the platoon on my display again. Same glitch. Same new names. Still no Muñoz.

"Prep for evac," the CO said over the platoon channel.

We lined up; kept about a foot between the soldier on either side of us. Secured our weapons. Jones was on my left, Omalas on my right. Prakash was just in front of me, still scratching at her arm.

"Be still, Prakash," Jones said on our squad channel.

This was one of the most vulnerable times for our platoon, right up there with when we first corporealized in the field. A platoon from CanKrushkev stood on the next rise, supposedly to guard our backs, but I wouldn't put it past another corp to smoke us where we stood if they thought they could get away with it.

"Something's fucked with my arm," Prakash said.

Jones said, "We'll deal with it at base. Hold for extraction."

Our bodies began to vibrate.

I locked my jaw, though I knew I wasn't supposed to. You're

supposed to meditate, but I've always been shit at meditating. I fixed my gaze on the back of Prakash's head, trying to use that as a concentration point.

"Fuck, fuck!" Prakash said. Her whole form juddered, stutter-stop, like a broken image on a projection. She was there, then gone, then there again.

The rest of us vibrated.

"Hold!" the CO said. "Hold for extraction. Stay calm."

The pain came. The massive contraction.

Prakash winked out. Came back. Her left arm was twisted around behind her. It now snaked through her torso, jutting out the front of her chest. Her fingers spasmed. The sound she made over the squad channel was inhuman. A moist gurgling heave. Her mouth twisted impossibly, like wet clay thrown on a slab.

We broke apart.

I could still hear the alien girl screaming.

10.

We corporealized.

The screaming was mine. I was on all fours, shrieking my guts out at the broken grass beneath me.

"Dietz? Dietz?" Jones's voice.

Someone grabbed my helmet, pulled it clear. It was Jones, knees in the dirt beside me, a look of fear and concern on his face. I'd never seen him look so scared for anybody but himself. "You okay? You come back okay? Show me your digits, Dietz."

I held up both hands. Jones pulled me into a massive hug. I fell into him, still shaking hard.

"That Dietz?" The CO said, and pulled Jones away and flashed a pen light in my eyes. "Name, rank," she said.

"Dietz. Private."

"And where have you been, Private Dietz?"

"I . . . I don't know."

"We did fine," Jones said. "You were great. All of us came back whole."

"Prakash?" I said.

"Aw, you miss me?" Prakash said, pushing up her visor. She stood behind the CO, giving me a little half smile. "It because I saved your ass on Mars?"

"What?" I said.

"Pretty sure it was Dietz who saved *your* ass," Jones said.

"That's enough chatter, Jones," the CO said. The scroll of her heads-up display winked in her left eye. "Logistics wants to see Dietz. Dietz, you hear me? Intelligence and logistics will want to see you. They're sending people down now. Stay clear."

Jones moved away. Prakash pulled off her helmet. Two medics were checking the status of the platoon. A vehicle came down from base, carrying two science officers and a corporal. Those ones, I figured, were for me.

"Private Dietz, can you tell us what happened on Mars?" The woman across from me was all lines and angles, that ageless face the officers all had, bushy brows that met like caterpillars over her eyes. I found myself watching her brows as she spoke. She had introduced herself as Lieutenant Ortega.

"I don't remember," I said. "Sorry. My numbers are bad for drops. Don't you have recordings?" What I wanted to tell her was that I'd never been to Mars. But saying that out loud wasn't looking like a good idea. I was still processing the girl I shot in a banana field and here they were chattering about Mars when I'd never seen it.

"We need to know what you remember."

The cramped room was painted a soft, calming blue. I knew there must be more people watching, but couldn't figure out which walls they were behind. It was all flat, blank surfaces.

"I remember . . . bursting apart. Coming back together."

"You came back screaming."

"Shouldn't my recording—"

"Private Dietz." She tapped the metal table between us. I tensed, but she did not give away where the other watchers were. Her gaze stayed on the table. I figured she must be conferring with her superiors, hiding her heads-up flicker from me.

"Here's what we can tell you. I do have recordings of your performance on that last drop, the Mars combat mission. You performed well. Better than well. It's why I can almost excuse the shit that happened the first time."

"The first time?"

"Don't play dumb, Dietz. People died."

I eased back in my chair. Hard metal.

"What gets me, Dietz, is that every time your medical records come back, your cellular structure has degraded faster than anticipated. This is one reason you weren't authorized for the first line of drops. I'm willing to—grudgingly—believe that maybe you don't have recall after some drops. This is the second time we've had this issue. At least this was . . . better than the first. My recommendation, at any other point in the war, would be to ground you. But we need all the good soldiers we can get. So if you're redeployed, well . . . Maybe something will come back to you. If it does. Tell us."

"*If* I'm redeployed?" I said, because that seemed to be the safest question.

The light of her heads-up display went out. "You still need to clear your psych evaluation. C'mon, Dietz. This isn't your first rodeo."

They sent me to the psych evaluation. I guess they sent the rest of my squad too, though clearly our memories of what had happened on the last drop differed dramatically. Everyone gets a basic psych evaluation before they recruit you, but this felt different. Me and the rest of the platoon were housed in the decon barracks for our forty-eight hours of decompression and quarantine after they returned us to base. There were no clocks in there. No live broadcasts. No access to the outside at all, just stuff to read and listen to, immersives, games, and plenty of workout equipment. I spent the first day after we came back running on the treadmill and doing shooting simulations. I had no way to ask about Muñoz or Jawbone or Squib or Abascal on any outside communication system, and I feared asking anyone in the platoon. I kept my mouth shut and listened. Another good tip from my mom. People are always looking for reasons to imprison or kill ghouls. Stay quiet. Keep your head down. Be polite. They may still kill you anyway, but maybe they'll kill the other guy first.

I got called in to see the psych on day two.

"How was it?" I asked Jones when he came back from his time with the shrink.

"Just stick to the mission brief," Jones said. "You especially."

The brief was the only thing I'd been able to study with any detail since I got back. While there was no access to our performance, or our platoon's recordings, I could always see the brief for whatever our last mission was. It hadn't been a Mars recon mission, or an insurgent roundup in the southern half of North America. We had been on a straight-up Mars combat mission to retake a base under heavy artillery fire. I had absolutely no memory of that. I really wished I had. It sounded great.

One of our handlers beckoned to me from the hallway. "Dietz!"

The handler escorted me to a windowless room painted the pale blue of a robin's egg. A great shrub took up one corner. LED film lined the ceiling, displaying the image of sunlight trickling through cherry tree branches exploding with blossoms. The branches moved softly, as if tickled by the wind. I enjoyed the view; it was soothing, as it was no doubt meant to be. A lot of the rec spaces had them, and so did our barracks in quarantine. They gave you the illusion of being outside. I figured we were stowed away underground somewhere, and somebody had put in the imagery for morale. A beige couch and matching chair sat facing each other over a low wooden table that was probably synthetic. I'd watched enough immersives about soldiers and shrinks to figure the couch was for me. I sat up straight, hands between my knees. Stick to the brief, Jones had said.

The door opened. I stood, reflexively.

A small woman, shiny black hair pulled into a bun, fixed me with a warm smile. Like our CO, she was older than thirty, not older than fifty. I wondered if they gave shrinks the same drugs they gave us, the shots that were supposed to make us stronger and fitter for longer. She wore civilian clothes; loose beige trousers and a white blouse. Flat black shoes. Would the drugs make us live forever? Would the drugs make us nuts the way they had made those Nazis nuts?

"Private Dietz?" The scroll of her heads-up display flared briefly in her left eye; no doubt she was accessing my file.

"Sir . . . yes . . . uh. Ma'am?"

"Doctor is fine. I'm Dr. Elaine Chen. We haven't met?"

"Uh, no? I mean, isn't that in the file?"

"We're testing your recall."

"Well, no, then. We haven't met."

"I see." Her gaze flicked to the left, flagging that part. I hadn't met her before, had I? The shrink I saw during orientation was a short dark man called Mufoz. I remembered that clearly because his family was originally from Evecom, and we talked about what it was like to sign a contract with a new corp.

"You want to know about the mission?"

"Just your recollection." She sat neatly in the chair across from me. Her movements were so precise and elegant I thought she must be a dancer. I wondered what would compel someone who had the talent of a dancer to become a psychologist. Maybe it paid better. It was like Jones trying to get corp support to be a poet.

"I don't remember much. Intelligence already went over that. Can you see their report?"

"Do your best. The first real heavy combat drop can be stressful, physically and emotionally."

"There were banana trees," I blurted. It just came out. "I was distracted. It was just an alien girl."

"I'm sorry?"

"I shot a girl. An alien girl."

Her eyelids flickered.

"I see. Was this your first kill? Tell me about that."

"Uh, yeah." That seemed like a rude question, like asking if you'd ever had sex. But I related the full story, just like I remembered it—or, the part about killing the alien, anyway. I didn't say where.

The doctor sat with her hands in her lap, but that heads-up display of hers continued to blink in her eye, probably recording me. I thought about what it must be like for somebody viewing her recording of me and my recording of her at the same time. Like placing two mirrors in front of each other.

"Could you tell what time of day it was?"

"No. My coms didn't come online, and . . . I guess, just . . . that's all I remember. That part. I wasn't there long enough for it to register."

"But you know you were on Mars?"

"Sure. I . . . No, I don't think I was on Mars. Do they grow bananas on Mars?" Shit, I was fucking this up. My mom would be tearing her hair out and telling me to shut up.

"Let's stick to what you recall. You were still aware of your mission objective at that time?"

"Yes? I mean, for the mission we were briefed on before we dropped. But on the ground . . . we just . . . fought. I remember some fighting."

"And what time was that?"

"I don't know. They only give us mission time on our displays. Not real time."

"Did you tell your team about your confusion?"

"No."

"You didn't talk about it?"

"I just wanted us all to come back alive, all of us, sir . . . Doctor."

"How did you feel during the battle?"

"Fine."

"It's common to have moments of confusion. Memory loss. Deep emotional feeling. It's a normal part of being a soldier, and the drop process can . . . amplify some of those effects."

"Okay."

"One last question, Private Dietz."

"Sure."

"Confirm your age for me, please."

"My age?"

"Yes."

"I . . . have no idea. How long has it been?"

Something shifted in her posture. "I see," she said. "Could you tell me what happened to your prior squad?"

"Don't you have those records? Shouldn't you tell me?"

She regarded me like an especially interesting insect. "I see," she said. "I suggest you take this opportunity to quiet your mind and get some rest. Have you been practicing your meditation?"

"My head moves too fast for that."

"Try the guided programs included with your entertainment applications. You still have twenty-four hours of quarantine before you rejoin your company. I want to caution you, however. You may find that some soldiers are experiencing this war differently from you. That's normal. There's a great physical and psychological toll with each successive drop. You may find yourself confused, angry, even violent. If you feel that way, I want you to go to your commanding officer and request a psychological evaluation. Do you understand me?"

"Sure."

"This is very important. Not only for your own personal safety, but for the safety of your squad and your platoon. You wouldn't want them to come to harm."

Hearing her talk about my mental state as a danger when we were fighting an enemy that shot at us was laughable. But I didn't roll my eyes. I didn't talk back. I was still fairly fresh out of mandatory training and feeling my way around. Having everyone think I was nuts wasn't going to help my position here.

"I understand, Doctor."

"Good," she said. "Good." She stood and held out her hand. "I will see you again, Private Dietz."

"If I don't die before then."

Her smile was thin. "I'm sure we'll be able to clear up these issues with your drop resonance. Oftentimes, it's simply a matter of making a technical adjustment."

"Sure."

She let me go. I went into the common room and sat next to Jones. We watched the monitors as Omalas and Prakash sparred in some immersive tournament. Both were hooked into virtual performance harnesses for safety, lunging and grunting. Omalas was a tall, beefy woman, well over two meters tall, with shoulders like a linebacker. Her voice was deceptively soft, though. Even her movements in the harness were purposeful, almost graceful.

"All good?" Jones asked. He didn't look at me. Omalas landed a hard punch to Prakash's face. Her avatar on the screen tumbled back, spit blood.

"All good," I said. I thumped him on the shoulder, then went to the head and vomited my guts out.

11.

When we got out of quarantine and released to our regular barracks, everything looked . . . different. I guess I should have expected that. Someone had made marks on my bunk frame, thin lines in sets of five. I counted. Ninety-three lines.

"Who's been in my bunk?" I asked.

"Nobody," Jones said. He threw his stuff into the locker at the head of our bunk, tossed his jacket onto the upper bunk. Muñoz's bunk.

In the platoon barracks we were only stacked two high instead of three. Even so, Muñoz had made sure I got a bottom bunk. She'd told me she outranked me now, and it was an order. Funny, at the time. Now, I stared at the slats of her old bunk above me and traced the lines. You could only see them if you were lying down like I was. I guess everything we did was recorded, but I couldn't imagine anybody bothering to cycle through recordings of when we slept.

Ninety-three marks. For what? Kills? I shuddered.

They cycled us into the next drop slot eleven days after we

got out of quarantine. I was getting along better with the platoon by then, reorienting myself. Mostly, I pulled it off by keeping my mouth shut. The CO called me into her office and had me shut the door.

"You know what they're calling you?" she said.

"Bad luck," I said.

"Huh? No. You performed well on that Mars drop. All things considered."

I was getting tired of people telling me about this Mars drop where I did really well. If I was so great, why couldn't I remember it?

"Thank you, sir," I said, because that's what a normal person would say.

"Your shrink gave you clearance to go on the next drop," she said.

I didn't have an answer for that.

"What, you quiet for once?" she said. "You're always hot about getting back into the grinder."

"I signed up to fight, sir."

"I want you to know that your file says I recommended you get taken out of rotation. I recommended it last time too. But those shits and their shit ideas outrank mine, and yeah, I hope some tech is going over this recording right now and quotes that back up to them, those little pig-fuckers. There are some soldiers who don't do well on drops. Get sick, go nuts. You're showing classic signs of that, but I can't make that call."

I waited.

"Why do I have to spell out every goddamn thing with you, Dietz? I want you to be honest with them. Tell them what the fuck is going on. I know you're nuts. I've seen nutty soldiers go through here, and every single fucking one of them gets themselves killed. They shoot themselves up, light themselves on fire, go on some Martian killing spree, and run through a minefield wearing underwear on their heads. I don't buy this bullshit about not remembering. I've heard that before. I heard it about your first fuckup drop. I don't believe it. Come clean, get discharged, go spend the war cleaning out goddamn latrines."

"That's not what I signed up for, sir."

"And I didn't sign up to babysit nutters. They have other kinds of institutions for that."

"I'm not crazy," I said, only half believing it myself. She was confirming what I had feared all along. If the truth came out about where I'd been, what I'd really seen, they'd take me out of the platoon. "I performed well on Mars," I said. "You all told me so. I can do it again."

"Don't tell me I didn't try, is all I'm saying." She grimaced. "Go get in formation for the next drop."

The transport took us to the drop field. We still hadn't been briefed, but I could see the flickering of the CO's heads-up display. Her helmet wasn't on yet. I figured she was still getting her brief.

We got in formation. I lined up between Jones and Omalas. Prakash and Marino stood in front of us. The CO's voice came over the platoon channel, "Got a smash and grab for you today, children. We will be deploying to a Martian settlement in CanKrushkev, old Canuck territory and assisting Kev's forces in rounding up some insurgents."

I chewed that over. That mission sounded . . . awfully familiar.

She said, "I don't want to hear a word of jaw vomit over this one. The Martians here are legal, even if most of them are trouble. This isn't my call, but shit rolls downhill. We will drop. We will secure the area with our CanKrushkev friends. When the area is secure, we will round up our targets."

"Babysitting fucking Martians," Marino muttered.

I stared at Prakash's strong back. The image of her with her arm torqued through the middle of her torso flashed before me.

No, I thought. No, we're not doing this now. We're not doing this again, are we?

Oh shit.

We burst apart.

12.

You aren't supposed to see anything when you break apart. I know that. Knew it then, too. But when the light took me this time, I found myself aware of a great landmass beneath me surrounded by a roaring black ocean.

We came together over a jagged, dusty peninsula thrust into a churning sea. A curled ridge of mountains wound across the back of the peninsula like a dragon circling its own tail. The ruins of some city gave off a thick pall of smoke. But as we came down the smoke resolved itself into a dense blanket of clouds kissing the mountaintops, bleeding over its edges into the broken warren of the city below. The age of the place struck me even before I fully corporealized. Ancient layers of rock, worn by wind and sea from time immemorial, lay exposed along the coastline.

The violent sea welcomed us. That black, black sea. Harbor seals. Giant sharks. As we came together again, grabbing for our rifles and our genitals and praying to whatever deity we worshipped that our heads would be on the right way, we found ourselves facing a most peculiar flock of disinterested penguins.

I let out my breath. Watched my left arm materialize as the penguins cocked their fat heads at me. I was ankle deep in water. I scrambled out of the sea, terrified that my molecules would merge with it, or I'd sink into the sand before I'd finished coming together, and recorporealize inside a sand bank.

I ran onto shore and pushed the safety off my rifle and got down on one knee, waiting for coms to come back online. Up ahead I saw a larger gaggle of waddling penguins. I'd only seen penguins in immersives, and once at a zoo my mom took me to when we had residency. Zoos depressed me, though, all those animals locked up with nothing to do and nowhere to go. I still remember the grim look on my mother's face when she stared at a sad-faced orangutan sitting in its own piss.

Around me, four other soldiers flexed and shuffled; the littlest one moved up the coast.

"Prakash?" I said over the squad channel. Maybe we weren't doing this again. I'd gone somewhere else instead. "Wait for Jones."

The figure stopped. Turned. "Who? You come through all right?"

The voice was completely unfamiliar. I tried to access the names on my heads-up, but it wasn't online yet.

"I'm . . . all right?" I said.

The figure pushed up her visor. A small, fine-featured blond woman. I had never seen her before in my life—not in the platoon or the company. I was absolutely certain.

"Who are you?" I asked. It just slipped out. Shit.

"I am the goddamn team leader," she drawled. "Are all your brain cells still there? I'm Akesson. Shit, Tanaka said this might happen." She pointed at the others on the beach. A curly haired man with his helmet off, vomiting into the sand. "That's Toranzos." A tall, dark woman with a face like a shovel, staring down at me like I was a broken thing. "Chikere." And last, a woman about my height, with bruises under her dark eyes. "That's Sharpe. Got it? Jog your memory?" It occurred to me that they all looked hungry and exhausted and very, very dirty.

"Sure," I answered, which was a terrible lie. I must not have sounded convincing even to her, because she rolled her eyes. She wore a loose tactical jacket over her armor. She patted at the pockets, came out with a slug of water, and threw it at me. "Take a breather," she said.

I drank the water gratefully. A strand of her light hair stuck to her forehead.

Exhausted people without regulation haircuts. Even their gear looked worn.

"Akesson," said Chikere, gesturing up the dunes. "You have some gum?"

Akesson dug around in her jacket and tossed it to Chikere. "Girl can never have too many pockets," Akesson said, and winked at me. "Hey, Toranzos, you all right?" She bent over him, offering him a slug of water.

He rinsed out his mouth, nodded his big square head. "Thanks. Let's get this party started."

Akesson scanned the beach. "Coms up for anyone yet?"

"I don't see fuck-all," Chikere said.

"Heads up, team," Akesson barked. "I want an official count. Check your digits. Chikere?"

"All here," she replied, chomping gum.

"Toranzos?"

He struggled to his feet, patting at his chest, his crotch. "All accounted for."

"Sharpe?"

She flexed her fists. "Fine," she said. "Considering."

I raised my rifle. Coms flickered back online. The mission flag tapped at the corner of my vision. I looked left and down. The mission brief scrolled up. Where the hell were we supposed to be and what the hell were we supposed to be doing? Was I really messed up or was it logistics? Had they sent me out with the wrong team? No, *they* knew who *I* was. I was the one in the dark.

"Verify your mission logs, people," Akesson said. "Norberg wants us to ensure the island is clear before we head into the main structure. Remember that this is sensitive shit we're dealing with. I want all your heads on straight."

I scanned the general area. It came up completely clean. No signs of any other platoon trackers.

"Akesson," I pleaded, "Something bad is going to happen. Maybe we should wait."

Akesson smirked. "The worst has already happened. We're just cleaning up. It's all right. Just follow my lead, Dietz. This is as safe a place as any right now, but we have to verify it's clear. Chikere?"

"Yeah," Chikere said, popping her gum. "My GPS is up. Looks like this island's about two kilometers long, a kilometer wide, total. Lot of it's underwater. I suggest we go east, clear the coast and the docks first, then head up the ass end of the main drag where the buildings are."

"Why not the buildings first?" I asked.

Akesson peered at me. "Because we need to clear the island, Dietz. How about you shut up and follow orders."

I nodded. One call to the CO about how nuts I was and I'd get pulled out and sent back to building bridges. I wasn't leaving until I found out what the fuck was going on, and what had happened to Muñoz.

"Great," Sharpe snorted. "Think anywhere's open? Let's find ourselves a drink and a fuck."

"I don't think there's anywhere here to buy beer," Chikere said, deadpan.

Toranzos said, "We could eat penguin."

"I'm not eating penguin," Sharpe snarled. "That shit's disturbing."

"You think penguin tastes like chicken?" Toranzos said. "Or fish?"

"Who the fuck said anything about eating?" Sharpe said. "You were just horking up your rations two minutes ago."

"Why am I having flashbacks to my babysitting days?" Akesson muttered. "Get your rifles up."

We hiked east, following a dusty road along the shore. Scrub brush, sand: there were rundown buildings in the distance, but no signs of fresh human habitation. No tracks. No smoke. No radio transmissions. No knu nodes.

We passed a lighthouse huddled against the rocky coast. Abandoned structures peeked out from the waves, most of them ground to ruin by rising sea levels and powerful storms.

"Lots of penguins," Toranzos said. "Should we clear the penguins?"

"Leave the fucking penguins alone," Sharpe said.

Chikere snorted.

"Clear the buildings," Akesson snapped. "I haven't seen any water craft docked but that doesn't mean anything. Could be insurgents camped out. Stay alert."

Akesson led us up the remains of a street. The buildings had fallen into themselves a long time ago. Others had signs of more recent activity: charred roofs, patched doors, the telltale wavering scar of a pulse blast. Most of it had been colonized by penguins.

"Nobody home," said Sharpe.

"Hey, Akesson," Toranzos said, "you get eaten by penguins, I get your bunk?"

"I get eaten by penguins and you gotta lead these shitheads," Akesson said. "So watch my six. Clear this one!"

She and Toranzos took point at the door of the next building, some old schoolhouse, maybe, mostly intact.

We cleared two more structures and Akesson called a water break. The air was hot and dry; felt like you could set a tree on fire just by gritting your teeth. We took cover in a building with a roof that was half collapsed.

Akesson offered me a protein bar. I shook my head. I was thirsty, but not hungry. Took a lot to get me hungry, I found out, after a drop.

"So how you know Tanaka?" Akesson said. "How long he been your platoon leader?

I blinked. "I . . . don't know." Sometimes the truth worked.

"Just funny," Akesson mused, "figuring out why it is some of us are still alive here at the end."

"The end of what?" I asked.

"The end of everything," Akesson said.

"I really wish they sold beer," Sharpe whined. "You think Norberg's intelligence people have beer?"

"Pretty sure the beer's all gone," Chikere said. "I don't think there's any mama here tending a shebeen."

"As long as anybody's alive," Sharpe said, "someone will be making beer."

I fixed my gaze out the window at the biggest building in the complex.

"Used to be a prison," Akesson remarked, when she saw where I was looking. "Shipped all their prisoners out here for centuries. Was a museum for a while, showing how great ShinHana is to citizens, now. Comparatively."

"The fuck are we?" I said. "It's like the goddamn ends of the Earth."

"Southern Africa," Chikere said. "My grandmother grew up in the desert, just north of here. Nairobi, maybe? What territory is that in? It's changed hands so many times, I don't know." As she gazed out over the ocean, I saw something wistful in her eyes. It was the look of somebody ready to throw away a gun and walk.

She caught my look. Showed her teeth. "Water's full of sharks. We'd never make it. Plus, you know, the trackers. They can pick us up from anywhere. Bitch, huh?"

I checked my display and confirmed. The local map gave me the positions of our team. I zoomed out to get a view of the rest of the platoon, maybe even a division, thirteen kilometers inland. But as I swept the map, I couldn't pick up any pings.

They had really sent us out here by ourselves.

"All right, enough chatter," Akesson said. "Let's clear the main compound and go meet Norberg. See what intelligence wants us here for. They always call the grunts when there's some danger they don't want to put their soft, precious asses in front of."

"All hail intelligence ass," Sharpe said.

"Best name for intelligence I've heard all year," Chikere quipped.

"Shut it," Akesson said.

All chatter ceased. I wondered how long she had led this team, and how I'd ended up on it. We moved.

Akesson led. Chikere and I flanked the door to the old museum; the glass was gone, most of the floor and ceiling charred. Sharpe took point and went in rifle first. Chikere and I came in after, scanning as we went. Toranzos took the rear. Our displays registered heat as a fine red mist, and carbon monoxide as blue. Radiation would register a soft green. Aside from what our team was putting off, I didn't see anything.

We swept through the ruins of the museum, past the sordid, violent remains of some bygone era. For all the bullet holes and broken glass, I only saw one body curled up under a fallen display, and that one was long dead, dry and desiccated in the heat.

Akesson waved us forward.

Sharpe took point again. We cleared all three rooms in the next crumbled structure. Signs of recent activity, here: two

Masukisan-branded tents, a pack of rations hanging from the rafters away from bugs and lizards, a cold portable cook stove.

Akesson pointed at a basement door. Even with the door closed, I could hear the rise and fall of voices trembling up from the cellar. The scuff of boots. A woman, laughing.

Akesson pushed past me and leaned in to the door frame. The stairs were too steep to see much at the bottom but a dirt floor. "Lieutenant Akesson here," she announced. "We have orders from the chief executive of war."

The woman, laughing.

"Something's fucked up," Sharpe said.

"Dietz, Sharpe, take point," Akesson ordered. "The area could be compromised. May not be our people down there. You understand?"

I nodded. Sharpe grunted.

Sharpe went down first.

I followed, with Chikere coming up behind me, and Akesson and Toranzos hanging back to cover us.

What do I remember?

The rotten smell of sulfur. Sharpe blocked most of my view, but I was aware of the bodies of a squad lying on the concrete floor ahead. Blood and dust. And the sound . . . that woman, laughing. At the bottom of the stairs, I caught a waft of voided bowls, the coppery stink of fresh blood. It crept into my nostrils, cloying and sticky. I still smell blood, in the warm months. The light came from a single LED bulb hanging from a coiled power cord nailed to the wall. Two doors. One open, the other closed.

And there, through the open door—

I will tell you what I didn't tell my shrink. I told my shrink that the last thing I remember is the light from the door, but it's not true. I remember seeing straight through it. I looked through that doorway, and it was clear the basement was just a front for some larger enterprise. I saw a long metal hallway. A series of stainless steel numbered doors. The holding cells there were far more sophisticated than this facade would lead anyone to believe. A gun turret mounted to the ceiling swiveled toward us.

Sharpe said, "Shit."

The sounds of the rest of the squad coming after us.

I remember putting my arms out, spreading my body wide, hoping to shield the others for what was coming.

A fiery pulse blew apart the gun turret. The pulse had come from the metal hallway. I heard the *slap-slap* of bare feet on the floor. A tattered figure came at us, barefoot, filthy, dressed in a torn gray jumpsuit. Whoever it was had a standard low-yield gun, and shot Sharpe. Sharpe's return shot went wide. I had a choice—shoot back or continue trying to shield Akesson and the others. I was blocking their descent into the room.

I chose my team.

The figure fired at me. I wheeled backward, thrown with tremendous force. Voices. Darkness.

That's my last memory from that drop.

13.

arkness.

It's more comforting than you think, to be alone in the dark.

I came to flat on my back in a room with two flared canlights flickering overhead. A dozen people hovered over me. Didn't they have places to be? It was like being at the center of a swarm of angry bees.

A doughy-faced man, balding, gave me a tight smile and said, "Do you know where you are?"

"Doctor's office?" Seemed like as good a guess as any.

"You experienced an emergency evac. You may be disoriented."

Darkness, again. I came to in an elevator, or maybe a tram. I lay on a gurney. Three women were trying to move me to another one.

"Still covered in blood," somebody said. "None of it's the private's." Then I was out again.

And . . . awake.

A man knelt on one knee next to me, like he was going to propose. He had a thick needle in his hand. Blood poured down my right arm. "I'm sorry, I'm sorry," he said, digging into my flesh.

The pain snared up my arm. A jagged flash of it, then a persistent gnawing. It must have been what woke me.

I wanted to comfort him. He looked so terrified, so out of his element. Some people are good at putting in a line, at sticking a vein just right. My brother had been good at it, when he cared for my mother during her long illness. But this man wasn't. My blood pooled on the floor.

I lifted my gaze, sensing movement at the door. A young woman stood on the threshold, her mouth a moue of concern, face knotted in grief. She wore a short, flowy skirt and a yellow cardigan. I knew her and didn't know her, because while my brain insisted she was familiar, reason told me it was impossible that she was here. I wanted to say her name but feared the man on the floor would hear me. I was already on intelligence's radar.

A fresh jab of pain. I cried out.

"Sorry! Sorry!" the guy said. Blood kept pumping out. I wondered how much blood could come out of my arm before I passed blissfully back into the darkness.

The girl in the doorway came to me then. My heart caught in my throat. I thought I might choke.

"Vi?" I said, even though it was impossible.

"You look like shit," she said. She had never been one to mince words. Her eyes were wet. She grabbed my good hand and squeezed it. Her hands were soft, just like I remembered, the nails cut short and lacquered with plain polish. She smelled the same, like baby powder and herbal shampoo. I wanted to kiss her just to prove she was real. Why had I let her go? "What are you doing here, Vi? You . . . shouldn't be . . ."

"They won't tell me what happened."

"They can't."

"Can you?"

"I don't . . . know. War is . . . I should be in quarantine . . ." My mind spun. I felt a little nauseous. Found it hard to focus. It was impossible she was here. "We can't be together," I said.

"Why? Because I'm older? Because of your parents?"

"I'm not going back there."

"I am," she said. "There's work to do there, and I'm qualified to do it. What are you so afraid of?"

I knew what conversation we were having. A conversation we'd had before. Our last. I took her hand in mine, squeezed. I knew she wasn't real, knew this had to be a hallucination, because the words were falling out of me just as they had then, every poisonous, stupid thing I'd said.

"You saw what happened to the moon," I said. "You think you can stop that with negotiating? You think words are going to help? You're deluded. It's time to fight. I'm going to fight."

"Fight what. Another corporate war?"

"You've never been a ghoul. You don't have anything to fight for."

The look on her face killed me then, and it wrecked me now. She pulled her hand from mine. Her eyes filled. "You need to grow up," she said, poking at the age difference for the first time, trying to wound me as I'd wounded her. "When you grow up, you come find me. Or wallow in your own guilt here, fine. It's up to you."

In my memory, this is when I had gone, but she was still here. So I said, "I needed to do this myself."

"We were a team. We were going to—"

"Not like my team."

"What?"

"This team," I said, and now the past and present became muddled. "They are my team. They have my back. You couldn't understand what we've been through. What we're going through."

"I had your back. You never had mine."

"I didn't want to lose you. But I fucked that up, didn't I?"

Pain shot up my arm. I rounded on the little man. "Sorry, sorry!" he said. "I'll try the other arm."

I turned back to Vi. She was gone.

I blinked furiously. Stared at the doorway. No one. Just me and the morose doctor.

"Where did Vi go? Did you see?"

"Soldiers see a lot of things, after. Emergency evacuations are especially traumatic."

"That was . . . a memory, but not. Like she was here."

"What is the mind, but an interpreter of stimuli? I'm sorry, but it can misfire after drops like this."

"You need to know about the island. Who sent us to that island?"

"You were deployed to Mars. But you are safe now. There will be a debriefing. You'll feel better soon."

He stuck the line in, one clean jab, and then they were pumping me full of drugs, and I drifted off.

14.

was in quarantine for seventy-two hours. A woman from corporate intelligence came in once I was able to eat solid food.

"Where's my CO?" I said. "Lieutenant V?" *Please let me have the same CO,* I thought.

"We need a report, first, Private Dietz," the woman said. "I'm First Sergeant Jasso. We need your report of the operation."

"Where's Lieutenant Ortega?"

"I don't have any record of you speaking to an Ortega."

Of course not.

"Private Dietz, you were deployed for a Mars recon mission," she said. "Very simple, your first real drop. Something seems to have happened to you."

"No shit. Logistics is fucked up. Where's my squad?"

"You tell us, Private Dietz. Our last communication from your squad was a distress call from specialist Muñoz."

Mars recon. The first drop. Muñoz missing now, here. *All right,* I thought. I was getting a handle on how this was going— or thought I was. I needed to give them the names of the right squad. The Mars recon squad, right? "So my squad . . . Muñoz, Jawbone . . . er, Hadid, Abascal and . . . uh, Squib . . . Specialist Hussain—they went missing? During this mission? The Mars recon mission?"

Jasso's eyes narrowed. "You tell me."

"Listen, I don't know. I'm trying to figure this out too. You have recordings, don't you?"

"We have some limited recordings from others in your platoon. When they arrived on Mars, your fire team was caught in a Martian ambush and we lost all communications with you."

"Shit."

"Indeed."

"I don't remember any of that. You can test me."

"Oh, we are. I have someone on the intelligence team monitoring you right now."

"Then you know I'm telling the truth."

"On dropping to Mars, we have a record from your platoon. You and your team got cut off by a group of Martian insurgents. They deployed smoke, an EMP, and . . . something else. Your trackers were disabled. So were coms. When the noise and confusion cleared, you and your team were missing. If you were captured by the enemy, Private Dietz, any information you have to share with us would be very useful in this conflict."

What she left unsaid, of course, was, "And we want to know if you're a spy now."

This was the first fuckup, I realized. The first fuckup everyone kept talking about on the banana drop. Bad Luck Dietz. Shit, no wonder. I'd come back. My squad hadn't.

"I don't know what happened," I said. "My memory is . . . bad. Penguins. It wasn't even like we were on Mars." I had to give them something, I thought, but as soon as I did I knew it was a mistake. Never, ever, give them anything. The more complex your story the more you have to remember.

She leaned in to me. "What else, Private?"

"I don't know. Maybe it will come back."

"If it does, we expect to hear from you. We're on the same side, Private."

"Yes, sir."

"Your medical report came back clear." I saw the flicker in her eye. "No augments. No additional trackers. There's some unaccounted for anomalies related to your cellular tissue; it indicates that this drop did some damage at the cellular level, an amount we haven't seen in soldiers who are this early in their drop cycle. That's a concern. If you are cleared to drop, you will be receiving additional medical screening before and after each mission."

"How did you find me? On Mars?"

She stood. The flickering in her eye darkened. "We didn't find you on Mars. We found you in Cape Town. ShinHana territory. A child found you. You had no tracker. It was completely missing, unaccounted for. You were still bleeding from its removal. I'm deeply concerned you seem to have no memory of *that* either."

"I thought there weren't any people on the Cape?"

"I realize your geography may be lacking but the Cape is a perfectly functioning little town. The desalinization plants have kept them in clean water since ShinHana repaired the old ones. ShinHana has numerous launch facilities there. It's no New Buenos Aires, but it's coming along again."

I sat with that. "What about the island, off the coast? Robben Island?"

"It's a museum, Dietz. A record of all the horrors unchecked capitalism can lead to, and a celebration of ShinHana's progressive work policies. You can look it up on the knu if it fascinates you. I just had a bottle of wine from Cape Town last week. Lovely red. You know they couldn't produce wine there for a hundred years, after the climate debacle?"

"I'm just wondering why I was there."

"So are we. What was the significance to Mars, to drop you at the Cape after an interrogation, memory wiped, with no discernable alterations or tracking devices on your person? Until you tell us what you know, it's a great mystery."

I didn't rise to her bait, and changed the subject. "I heard them say . . . the doctors, that I was covered in blood when I came in. Whose blood?"

"That's an interesting detail as well," Jasso said. "None of that blood was yours. It was blood we could not trace, which means it had to be Martian, or from someone who hasn't been recorded by the corps. So you see, despite your protestations, it's clear you *were* on Mars. Whether you escaped or were beaten near a Martian prisoner . . . we don't know. Your tracker is missing. We have no recordings."

I was very quiet.

"I know drops can be confusing. When you're physically fit, I'm going to recommend a psych evaluation."

"Yes, sir."

"And Private Dietz? Let's not do this again. Stick to the mission brief." She left me alone in the interrogation room.

I stared into my palms. Opened and closed my fingers, watching the play of light across the seams and callouses. Stick to the mission brief. But securing that island had been our mission brief once we actually came down on that island.

I closed my fists. Caught a whiff of baby powder and herbal shampoo. What was happening to me?

Interview #2
SUBJECT #187799
DATE: 24|05|309
TIME: 0500
ROOM: 98

I: Interview beginning at . . . see the notes for time, with subject one-eight-seven-seven-nine-nine. Tell me about what you know of the Sick.

S: The what?

I: The unleashing of the chemical agent that murdered four billion people in ShinHana and NorRus. We learned it began in CanKrushkev territory. The people there have been completely undone. All civilians. Little children. Helpless. Innocent. Was it your idea?

S: Have you moved on from Saint Petersburg so soon? Are you already trying to implicate me in the murder of billions instead? I suppose that would be a more neat and tidy story. Tell all the media that you've got some important Martian terrorist in here instead of a greasy homeless grunt throwing around Molotov cocktails.

I: Did you have some time to contemplate your actions in Saint Petersburg?

S: I did, of course. But really, lights on all the time? I thought you'd go for the darkness, let me drown in it. That's what I would have done. Paint the whole thing stygian black. The darkness is far more frightening than the light.

I: I'm told you kept yourself busy while

cooling in the cell.

S: I have a lot of experience with waiting. We're all trained in it. Weren't you?

I: What are you referring to?

S: The torture modules. What did they call them at Evecom? There can't be that many names. Black box? tVu? Kid I knew once called it the agony box. The Bene Gesserit. He was a funny kid, quoted a lot of Herbert. You know Frank Herbert? The litany against fear? I always found the litany more helpful then any meditation.

I: Tell me about your experience with the black box.

S: Tell me about yours.

(SILENCE: 05 seconds)

I: I spent sixty days in the black box. But that was before your time, before you were born. It was a different animal, then. More of us went mad.

S: Sixty full days, Sergeant? Real time or virtual?

I: There was no virtual time then. It was all real time. Sixty full days in the box.

S: I must convey my respect, then. That can do hell on one's mental health. You must have been rehabilitated. I'm surprised they kept you in that long. I suppose it's necessary, for intelligence work.

I: In my day, they kept you in until you cracked it. We're not as soft as later generations. I still hold the record for beating the virtual mods.

S: Ah, I see. Yes, in the virtual box you know the torture will end at some point. Easier when you know it's constructed. Easier to fight a constructed thing, especially if you've been taught how to survive real torture. No matter how real it all feels, you know that you will wake up from that nightmare and be whole again. You may have terrors, the shakes, after, sure. You might have to go through aversion therapy so you can function again in the real world. But you come out alive and intact. That's how you can endure it. You know it ends. There's a huge mental release in knowing there is an end to pain. A human being with hope can continue on far longer than one without. Did you know those who are mildly depressed see the world more accurately? Yet they don't live as long as optimists. Aren't as successful. It turns out that being able to perceive actual reality has very little long-term benefit. It's those who believe in something larger than themselves who thrive. We all seem to need a little bit of delusion to function in the world. That belief can be about anything, too. Could be a god, a corporation, a social calling or ideal, like our various militaries. A sense of belonging. Could be national pride. Or the desire to make the world a better place. Or see the world burn. Personal or political. But . . . something bigger. Something greater.

I: I understand how to beat the torture modules. But what about you? How are you enduring this? You think we won't start to take you apart piece by piece, in real time? Perhaps those hands won't be mine—I like to keep even my gloves clean—but others will if I can't get results. You know that, don't you? We won't put you in the box. We'll do it live.

S: Live! Yes! Stream it! That would be exciting.

I: To who?

S: Whom? Yes, that's an interesting question. How many are left, after the Sick was unleashed? I have a good idea, a far better idea than you may believe. You've done an admirable job destroying yourselves. How can I endure this? I know I'm not in a box. There are ways to tell, even with the more advanced modules. This is real enough. So that's a very good question. I should be full of despair. Maybe I can endure this because I have a good idea of how it all turns out. Maybe I can endure this because I know we've done this before.

(SILENCE: 07 Seconds)

I: Did you know how the Sick would turn out?

S: Did you? I wonder about that myself, about who knew about the Sick, and when. Did you already know you would blame it on Mars? Morale was low by that point in the war. The Big Six had become the Big Four. But I'm thinking the Sick may have really been Mars after all, even if the fingerprint of the contagion was clearly Evecom's. The contagion was released after we came up with the final solution to the problem with Martians on Earth. Did you ever consider that maybe you did it to yourselves? That if you had pulled back, not administered the final solution . . . perhaps you could have saved what will certainly amount to five billion lives?

I: I'm most interested in why you were in Saint Petersburg.

S: Oh good, you did come back to Saint Petersburg! Wonderful. It's curious to me, however, why you are so insistent on having me tell you, when you already have a good idea. I'm sure you've run all my metrics. You know who I am. If you didn't have an idea, I wouldn't be here. What is it you think that knowledge will get you? You think you can change what happens, if you know what I know? Let me tell you something. Everything that's going to happen has already happened. You just haven't experienced it yet. We are, all of us, caught within a massive loop of time, bouncing around in the spaces between things.

(SILENCE: 12 Seconds)

I: You don't believe in free will.

S: People believe what they want to believe. You aren't here because you want your horizons shattered. You want your worldview reinforced. Maybe that's really why you're asking—you're hoping to get some other answer from me than the one you have. But that's not what I've got for you, no matter how long you leave me alone in there, in the light.

I: What <u>do</u> you have for me? Because we can go around in circles for months.

S: No, we can't.

I: No? It's rare we're in agreement.

S: No. I haven't asked how long you've kept me awake to stew. I don't need to know, because it couldn't be more than a few days. You're on a timetable, Sergeant. The old world is over, has been for a while. You and I are living out the end of it.

I: What did you want to accomplish in Saint Petersburg?

S: The endgame.

I: End? We're just getting started.

S: Maybe you are. But I'm finishing a very long game, Sergeant.

I: Tell me how your game ends.

S: The same way it started.

I: If you think we're on an accelerated timeline, then you know our next interview won't be so cordial. I suggest you be more cooperative. Neither of us wants to be here. Neither of us wants to drag this out. In this, I am not your enemy.

S: (LAUGHTER) You presume a lot, Sergeant.

I: And you still have nothing to tell me about why you were in Saint Petersburg? Who sent you? What were you really planning?

S: You're still asking the wrong questions.

I: What should I be asking?

S: Ask me when I'll be getting out of here. I know exactly when that will be.

I: When you're dead?

S: No. After I kill you. Finally.

I: End interview.

(END RECORDING #2)

15.

rivate Dietz." Dr. Chen smiled and held out her hand. "Refresh my memory. Have we met?"

"Uh, yeah." I was still in quarantine. She was the first person I'd seen in at least four days who wasn't a medical grunt or security tech. Even the rec room was empty; all of it just for me. I wondered how many facilities there were like this, spread out around Teni.

"And when was that?"

I paused, sensing a trap. "The last time." Shit. This was supposed to be my first psych evaluation, wasn't it?

"And what did we discuss? Please, have a seat, and tell me where we left off." Was she humoring me?

"Isn't that in my file?"

"I'd like to see how your recall is." She sat across from me. She appeared unchanged, which felt weird because I felt so . . . different. Like years had passed since I last saw her. In my head, it had. Time was all screwed up.

"We met already," I said, trying to feel her out. "And we

talked about . . . why I'm bad luck. Listen, it doesn't matter. Let's . . ." *Stick to the mission brief,* I thought.

I told Dr. Chen everything I told Jasso, which wasn't much. I did tell her what Jasso said, about how they found me. The hospital. But I didn't tell her about Vi. There are lots of crazy things that the military will put up with, but I didn't think seeing people or jumping around to somewhere you weren't supposed to be were among them. Even I knew what it meant when you started hallucinating things that weren't there. Bad enough I was supposed to drop in . . . Who knows where I was supposed to drop? But I'd turned up in Southern Africa. And how was that my fault? I didn't control the drops, the corps did. This was their fuckup.

"How are you feeling?" Dr. Chen said. "Since the event?"

"My entire squad is missing, probably dead. How do you think I'm feeling?"

"I'm here to listen, not make judgments."

"Well, everyone is going to make judgments. I guess they have a right to. I would. Maybe it's just that something went wrong, something with . . . the light thing."

"The deployment?"

"Yeah, like, the process. I mean, I hear it's not perfect. I feel like they're trying to pin this on me, and I didn't do anything but follow orders."

"What have you heard about the deployment?"

"Well, sometimes people come back with their bodies put back wrong. Sometimes they get confused. It was in our prep class."

"I see. Does that worry you?"

"I . . . guess? I don't want to let another squad down."

"You think you let this one down?"

"I'm here. They aren't. So, yeah."

"If you truly have no recollection of what happened, surely

you can't blame yourself for those events."

"I should have saved them."

"How?"

"I don't know. But it's what I should have done. Wouldn't you?"

"Difficult things happen during wartime. Do you feel you had control over what happened to your squad?"

"I like to have control over things, yeah. Muñoz was squad leader, but I had her back. That's my job. I stick with my team. I try to make sure they don't get shot. I don't know what happened to them, but I can't imagine it's anything good."

"You see yourself as a protector?"

"I want to help people."

"There are other professions where you can do that. You could have gone into medicine, or—"

"I'm not a citizen. All those options? I don't have those options."

"Why did you choose the military?"

"I wanted to be on the right side. A fucking paladin." It just slipped out. I backtracked. "Sorry, that's stupid."

"A paladin . . . A knight?"

"Sort of. A holy knight. Like . . . you not only fight people, you can protect them too."

"I see. It's important that we tell ourselves stories, Private Dietz. There's a theory that consciousness itself begins with story. Stories are how we make sense of the world. All of us have an internal story that we have told ourselves from the time we were very young. We constantly revise this story as we get older, honing and sharpening it to a fine point. Sometimes, when we encounter something in our lives, or do something that does not match up with that story, we may experience a great sense of dissonance. It can feel as if you've lost a piece of yourself. It can feel like an attack on who you are, when the real world doesn't match your story. What happens if one of these knights fails to save someone?"

I wanted to say, they swear an oath of vengeance and join the Corporate Corps, obviously. But I didn't. I knew what I needed to say. I'd already told her too much. "They just keep going. They do better next time."

"Do you feel you can do that?"

"I'm sorry I said that."

"Don't be sorry. It helps us understand each other. Do you feel that you can go forward? What does the idea of being part of another squad feel like for you?"

"It'll be hard, but it's . . . It's what I'm here for. So, it feels fine. I guess."

"You consider this a calling? What is a personal calling, to you?"

"It's . . . just that. It's a thing you should be doing. No matter what."

We went on like that until the doctor said, "I see our time is up."

"Is that it? When do I drop again? Will they put me on a desk? Building latrines? I'm a good soldier. I can be on another squad. Maybe they'll find the others." I didn't think about all the blood they'd found on me. Whose blood? I didn't buy that it was all Martian. I chewed my lip. Did I dare ask? Would they even tell me?

"That's not up to me. It was lovely to see you again, Private Dietz. Wait here and a handler will see you out."

She left me. Didn't look back. Here she was, this shrink who had my future in her hands, a future she figured out based on a lot of rambling from me about paladins and feelings. Shit, if this got back to the platoon I'd never hear the end of it. If I ever got back to serving with my platoon. Or any platoon.

Whatever she said, it couldn't have been all bad, because

they released me from solitary quarantine a few hours later and shuttled me out to join my platoon.

I should have known what would happen, but I gnawed on it for a long time. If they didn't let me drop again, how could I become Bad Luck Dietz? I had to fuck up more to get there. But then, how did I know that every time I dropped, I wasn't coming back into some other place, some other . . . time? Some other . . . me? I had no idea. My head hurt. I could be anywhere in . . . time?

I went back to my rack. Jones was already there. At first I figured, sure, of course, this was his rack too. But it wasn't. Not yet. He sat on mine. They hadn't moved him yet. The top was Muñoz's. They still hoped she would turn up. But I already knew the future. Didn't I? I opened the trunk at the end of our rack, and her shit was still there. Something caught in my throat. I had to take a minute to keep from losing it.

"What happened?" Jones said.

"I've told a million people. I don't know, Jones." And then, because I wanted to confirm it, "You were injured. You couldn't go on the mission because you were injured, right?"

"What did that jump do to you, Dietz?"

"Yes or no?"

"Yes. I was here fucking around in an FPS while you got my squad killed. Are Muñoz and Jawbone dead?"

"I don't know. I didn't see her die. Or the others. I don't know."

"How does only one member of a squad come back?"

"I don't know."

"Nobody else lost a single soldier, except you."

"So, you weren't there?"

"No, are you listening? You went. I wasn't there. You need me to repeat myself again? You are losing it."

"It was something with the tech. They did it wrong."

Jones peered at me. "Bullshit," he said, and left.

I was permitted to do PT drills with the platoon, and cohabit with them as usual, but even compared to my last drop back to base, they were cold toward me. Soldiers are superstitious. Jones wore the same pair of socks for every drop—despite the fact that all our socks looked the same. He marked them with little safety pins, said they were his "lucky" socks. I was still too new to combat to trust in anything, not even myself, but I knew I'd become bad luck. Nobody wanted me on their squad. I didn't blame them.

We got a fresh group of recruits in. I felt my stomach heave as their names were called.

"We're welcoming four fresh meatheads," the CO said. "Private Landon, Private Markesh, Specialist Leichtner, and Specialist Sandoval."

I closed my eyes after the names were read. Maybe I was hopping through different time lines, different futures, different . . . or maybe Mars was just fucking with me. Maybe, this whole time, I was still stuck on Mars in some looped immersive. I had a sudden, jarring memory of the torture modules, and lost my breath. What if none of this was real—nothing had been real since we first lined up for that Mars recon mission?

I had failed at the torture modules back in mandatory training, failed to acknowledge its unreality and break the construct. There are some things you can't kill your way out of, and the torture immersives were one of those things.

I took a deep breath as we were dismissed. The new recruits were left to mingle with us.

Private Landon was a tall, lanky guy, pale and dark haired, with perfect teeth. "You Dietz?" he said. "You the one who lost a squad on Mars?"

"Yeah. I'm Bad Luck Dietz."

"Bad Luck Dietz, huh? That's funny."

He reminded me of my brother, too handsome for his own good, bighearted, constantly trying to be a better human. There was no malice in how he spoke, just honest interest. People die. Like my mom. They get disappeared, like my father. They get Blinked, like my brother and cousins in São Paulo. No use getting attached.

"Why you looking at me like that?" he said.

"You remind me of my brother."

"Good. I'm not into you either. Where's your brother?"

"He was in São Paulo."

"Sorry."

"Wasn't you who did it," I said.

"Got anybody else?"

"Naw, just you shits. Ate my aunts, cousins, uncles, everyone."

"Parents?"

"You this chatty with everyone?"

"Habit. I worked in sales."

"Selling what?"

"Governments."

"Huh?"

"I mean, the corps sell these ideas to one another. I was one of those people."

"The hell you here, then? Sounds like a cozy job. Boring, but cozy."

"My wife's family died on the moon," he said. "That's what we think, anyway. This is my wife." He fumbled in his pocket for something. I took the laminated card in my hand. It had been folded many times.

"I had it printed out," he said, "so I could see them when coms are still out on drops. Reminds me what I'm fighting for." His own little good-luck charm. It was funny how we still clung to these physical things. They were harder to erase.

His wife looked like a pleasant enough sort of person, a

soft, round young woman with thick black hair and a tawny complexion. Big smile. Dimples. Not the sort of person I expected him to be with. She held a fat baby in her arms, a look of such pride on her face, like that fat baby was a gold medal from the corporate games.

When was the last time I looked at a picture of my family? My mother? Father? The dead were dead to me, and even the living, well . . . I knew they would die too. Muñoz gone, Jawbone . . . all gone. I had done Vi a favor by breaking up with her. That's what I had thought at the time. Fate was funny that way.

I peered at Landon's affable face. He reminded me of an especially friendly golden retriever. He would die, too. And if this war went on a long time, maybe his family would die. Maybe all of us. I handed back the picture.

"Good to have," I said. "A reason."

He tucked the photo away. "Jones says you've read Amado and Machado de Assis. Have you ever read Vega or Martínez Herreros? They were banned in, like, four corps."

The call for dinner came. Thirty minutes to chow down before they took it away from us.

"Some other time," I said.

"I'll send you some files!" I didn't bother telling him reading wasn't exactly my favorite pastime. He was nice enough, and I knew I needed allies right now. But after you lose people—you don't want more people.

I still figured I could fix this. New people like Landon didn't know any better; but he would soon. The way the rest of the platoon treated me would get better once we dropped again, I figured. I'd fight. I'd have their backs. They'd have mine. It had to get better, right? Because I'd jumped ahead further than this, and they were all right. Or, better than this.

But when we were called up for the next drop, the CO said, "You're grounded for this one, Dietz."

"But I did the eval."

"They asked we ground you for this drop. Sorry. They'll keep you busy in coms training. You need to work toward that specialist promotion, right? Good op for that."

"Yes, sir." I didn't like the look on her face. I didn't like that she understood, that she felt sorry for me. Had she ever lost a team? Of course she had. She lost mine, same as me. Shit. I was a fuckup. But I remembered how, after my second fuckup, she was going to recommend that they ground me, and got overruled. Had she been the one to ground me this first time? Or was it intel? And if it was intel, why did they agree to reinstate me in the . . . future? But not . . . now? Or . . . shit, this version? If this was a Martian torture module, it was terrible.

I spent my time during their drop running through training on the torture modules. I didn't go through the modules themselves, but the guided training, which was less intense.

In the immersive, I hung chained at the center of the room. My training guide stood nearby, hands behind her back, coaching me through it. Your guide can be whoever you want it to be, but I chose the generic avatar, one based on Admiral Sokai, the trim, dark woman who had led Tene-Silvia to its first victory during the last Corporate War. Something in her stance reminded me of Muñoz, and I found that vaguely comforting.

"You aren't trapped," the avatar told me. Three suited soldiers came in behind her, passing through her like she wasn't there, and I guess she wasn't. None of us were. "This is the lie they tell you. That you are trapped. That you have no control."

I concentrated on my breathing. I was bad at meditation, but it was pretty much the best tactic here.

"You are waiting for them," she said.

"To do what? Kill me?"

"You are waiting for them to believe they have broken you."

"What if they really do break me?"

"Then we start over."

"Shit."

"Focus." The guards brought out their shock sticks. They began to beat me. I registered pain, but it was dulled, like watching pain happening to a body that had once been mine. I had turned down the settings on purpose. The worst wasn't going to happen to me here, not until I could figure out how to control it.

"Take control," the avatar said.

"Of what?"

A stick came down on my face. My nose burst. Blood sprayed. In the world of the construct, the blood seemed to float in the air like dust before dropping, flat and wet, to the floor and disappearing.

"Your enemy is not these soldiers," she said. "Your enemy is your own mind. Your mind is also your only means of liberation. Take control."

"How?" The *thwap-thwap* of the shock sticks against me, the lightning flare of pain that was meant to register a broken rib. "There's nothing to control!"

The avatar moved to my side as I writhed. She regarded me coolly, black eyes so deep I felt lost in them. "You must rip yourself open. Break yourself apart. That's the only way to leave this world."

"End construct!"

I came back to myself. I sat in one of the padded immersive chairs, safely strapped in, room dim. All around me were a dozen other rigs, most empty. My platoon was gone, living real life. I was here, still trying to figure out how to hack real life through a fake one.

When the platoon came back, I was having my heads-up display recalibrated; just regular maintenance. Jones came into the med tech room and hopped onto the bed beside me.

"Go well?" I said.

"Sure."

"What you in for?"

"Caught something in my display." His left eye drooped; a smear of tears wet his left cheek, with no sign of stopping.

The med tech examined him and popped out his display lenses. "I'll get your right one cleaned and issue you a new left," the med tech said, and walked out.

For the first time since outside the immediate aftermath of a drop, I sat with another human being without anything I did or said being recorded. Jones figured that out before me. He rounded on me as soon as the tech was out of sight.

"What really happened?" Jones said. "Did you kill them? Did you fuck it up?"

"Don't lecture me about fucking up, Jones. Compare our records on fucking up." I saw the bloom of Grandma's burst torso again, the glistening innards. Wondered if I'd have to spell it out for him.

"Just tell me."

"I don't know what happened. But"—I glanced at where the tech had gone—"I don't remember going to Mars, Jones, not ever. Me and some other team I didn't know—we were in the fucking Cape. But . . . dead. It was dead there, nobody alive, except: Masukisan uniforms? In ShinHana territory. That was weird, too. I don't know. There was a blast, a burst . . . Everything went dark. I swear to you."

"Maybe it was fake. Some immersive the Mars people put you in when you were captured."

"It felt real."

"No shit. It's supposed to feel real. The torture modules all felt pretty real in training, too."

"What if I'm still stuck in one?"

"What, now?" Jones laughed. "That would make sense, I

guess. Who'd be left in your ultimate torture scenario? Muñoz down, Jawbone down—and you're stuck with me. What next, they dig up some old girlfriend?"

Something must have shown in my face because Jones said, "What?"

"After the drop, in the hospital. I saw . . . somebody I used to be with. Not somebody I wanted to see. Then she was just . . . gone. Have you ever had this shit happen, Jones? Am I going nuts for real?"

I thought Jones would look at me like the psych did, like intelligence, like I was crazy, but he just nodded slowly. "Yeah, I mean, no—I don't think it's what you think it is." He lowered his voice even further. "You're not the only one to go through this shit. Muñoz did, before you. She had one real bad drop; she told the CO, and the CO told her she was imagining things, just overexcited, but I know code when I see it. The CO didn't want the conversation to get tagged for review by intel."

"If the CO knows this happens, why does she want me to quit?"

"Maybe because she doesn't want whatever happened to Muñoz and those others to happen to you."

"The others?"

"That's why we always stick to the brief, Dietz. I've seen them haul off other people when they come back from a drop raving about having been somewhere else. That is why we're in quarantine, after. It's not because of the physical stuff—they know right away if we're messed up there. But because of the mental stuff. They want to know if we went . . . somewhere else. Soldiers who get . . . confused get discharged. Not the good kind, latrines and labor, but discharged, disappeared. You get me?"

"Killed?"

"Nothing good. Maybe the top brass kills them, maybe they run experiments on them? Who knows? But we never hear from them again."

The tech returned, bearing a freshly serviced pair of lenses for me.

"Stick to the brief," Jones said, and we both shut up.

My display flickered. For the first time in a while, it occurred to me to check the date again. There were no clocks, no calendars. We could mark the time via our displays, and we had countdowns and timers and alarms. But the day? Was it Friday? December or March? When I tried to access that information, I got a little red flag of denial from my system.

I glanced over at Jones.

How long had we been doing this?

That's when I remembered the marks I had seen on my bunk, the first time I came back to base. Ninety-three marks.

I went back to my bunk and laid down. Stared at the smooth metal. Ran my fingers across it. There were no marks yet. Those marks I'd seen hadn't been counting kills. They had been counting *days*. Time. Days between drops? Between bad drops? I wasn't sure. But if this was my first time back to base after Mars recon, now was the real time to start counting.

I counted out the time I'd spent in quarantine, the days I'd been grounded, and recorded them each as a mark on the metal.

I was going to count all the time I spent living like normal people did.

I was going to figure it out.

And learn how to control it.

16.

The strangest thing, even after jumping around like I had, was getting introduced to a team I had already been on a mission with, and pretending like this was the first time.

It was two more drops before I got clearance to go again. I figured I only got it because I made myself a pain in the ass with the CO. Every time she came back from a mission, I requested an update. I sent messages to her superiors. I even sent messages to Jasso, telling her I was fit for duty. They made me see the shrink twice more. I stuck to my story about forgetting what I'd been through. I marked off the days on my bunk. I spent eleven days on base that time. I wanted to remember.

When the CO finally called me in, I said, "Sir, either discharge me or send me out. I can't sit here going through the same six immersives and running a treadmill. I'm going nuts. Sir."

"They cleared you. Apparently your shrink thinks you're fine. Intelligence has taken an interest, so watch your ass. I'm putting you on a squad with Jones. If you have a problem with him as squad leader, I'll just transfer you to another platoon. I heard you two had issues in training."

"Sir, not at all. I'm fine with him as squad leader."

The CO also assigned Prakash to our squad. I noted how Prakash's eyes got big when the CO announced it. The CO called her out for having hair a quarter of an inch beyond regulation—which was a quarter of an inch. Prakash ignored me for a while, but I caught her smoking one afternoon. She offered me a hit, and we stood there in companionable silence.

"My father smoked," I said.

"My mother. Every time she went out to fix our wonky knu connection. She thought none of us noticed."

"These aren't regulation."

"Pissed I have to roll them. You kill your squad?"

"No."

Hell of a way to start an acquaintance.

We got another new guy, Marino, a transfer from a platoon that had been decimated on Mars. He was more fucked up than me, maybe. Only he had watched his whole squad burst apart by pulse rifles, and came gibbering back to the drop point, still covered in the misty residue of their bodies. They didn't question him as much as they did me, and I suppose that was fair. They had all the intel on that one. When I tried to look him up, my heads-up display denied me, denied me, denied me. I wondered what kind of op it had been.

The other was Omalas, already on our platoon and also familiar to me from the banana drop. Which of course no one remembered but me, because we hadn't done it yet. She was a fresh-faced young woman built like a tank. She towered over me; twice as wide and maybe twenty-five kilos heavier. The Corporate Corps had clearly worked at getting her lean, but she wasn't meant to be that way. Her teeth flashed white in her dark face as she loomed over me. I tensed for a fight. This was going to be just like Frankie.

"You know the way to the head?" she said in a soft, even voice. Her tone was so low I barely understood her. Her eyes twinkled.

I pointed. She didn't laugh out loud then, but she did later. All I knew about them was what I saw now and what I'd seen during that weird drop, that stutter in time. Their files were closed to me.

We had some normal drops. I suppose that's important to know. I recognized they were coming, when I came back from a drop and the mission brief I had before the drop matched the mission brief I had during *and* after the drop. I looked forward to long, uninterrupted periods of linear time. It was never as good as I thought it would be, though.

The normal missions—when time was normal—those were the worst. When you got back to living linearly, it felt like soaking in a hot tub. I got comfortable. Complacent. I thought about just telling the shrink everything. Thought about sending a message to intelligence and laying out what I knew about the war so far. Thought about how lucky I was that Teni couldn't read and record thoughts yet . . . could they?

Going through normal time with a platoon, a squad, during active combat . . . it's worse. You know they're going to die. I knew Prakash was going to die. Is that why we got drunk and started fucking? Maybe. Maybe we would have anyway. I knew I was on borrowed time, marking the days off on my bunk.

Even if there was a better explanation—like me being stuck in some Martian simulation—and yeah, a lot of days, I figured that was a happier explanation—it would eventually have an end date too. Enjoy the time while you have it.

Jones got me copies of Amado's books: *Dona Flor and Her Two Husbands* and *Captains of the Sands*, and one of Machado de

Assis's books, *The Alienist*. They were real paper books sent to him from his mothers. Apparently, none of the works were allowed to get transmitted digitally. Corp policy on restricted work, even for citizens like Jones.

I figured I'd humor Jones since he went to all the trouble. I needed time away from the treadmill and the torture modules. The shrink asked a lot about the torture modules. Banned literature was easier to justify.

"Are you concerned it may be unhealthy," the shrink said, "to spend so much time in such an intense immersive experience?"

"It fucked me up," I said, "the idea that maybe I was captured on Mars. I didn't test well on the modules in training. I want to get better in case we drop on Mars again. It's only a matter of time, right?"

She ate that one pretty easily. I almost felt bad about it.

But mostly, between drops soldiers do two things: drinking and fucking. Or drinking and thinking about fucking. Or drinking and pursuing somebody to fuck. We were young. Crowded together like rats, without a lot to do. You can only run so many kilometers and lift so many weights.

"It's like this in the north," Prakash said after we had sex outside the barracks. The air was warm, but insistent. She tucked her shirt into her pants. "We smoked a lot of weed, too. We should get a weed ration."

"Evecom does. I heard."

"Shit. I'd trade cigarettes for that."

"Sounds serious."

"You and Jones fucking?"

"No."

"Landon?"

"God, no."

"We've fucked around a few times."

"What, with both? Shit, I spend too much time in the torture mods."

"Just Jones. But surely you and Muñoz were fucking."

"No. Shit, Prakash, is this orgy confession hour?"

She grinned. I saw it again. The arm splayed through her torso. I blinked furiously and turned away.

"What is that?" she said. "You look at me that way sometimes. Can't tell if you're sad or horrified. Am I scary?"

"Not you. Just thinking about the war."

"Your team. Sorry, I shouldn't have brought up Muñoz. I really liked Muñoz."

"It's fine."

"It's not. We've all lost . . . a lot of people. I've been serving three years. Can't believe I'm alive. You know the average length of service right now? Eighteen months. How wild is that? That's average, so it means lots of people are dead first day, first week. What's the point of going through all that training for fifteen minutes on the field?"

"It's them or us. You want to end up a communist?"

"Starting to think communism is better than being dead."

I raised a brow. It was easy to forget you were being recorded. I had heard of soldiers disciplined because of something they said, but never seen it. Better safe than sorry.

I probably spent more time with Prakash than I should have, knowing what I did. Or maybe I didn't spend enough. On Sunday mornings when we weren't on a drop, I'd read her *Dona Flor and Her Two Husbands*. She found the book hilarious. Jones gave us shit, but I figured he was jealous.

I knew the morning I was going to drop back out of time. Knew it because that was the day I carved a thin line into the frame of my bunk, a third line next to eighteen sets of five.

Ninety-three days.

My reprieve in real time was over.

"For those of you who haven't been to Mars," the CO said after we gathered for our brief, "this is going to be a special experience. We have been called on to secure a base that's recently gone dark. For many of you, this will be your first combat mission on Mars."

That caught my attention. Was this the combat mission Prakash and Jones had talked about? As the CO went over the warnings and precautions, I thought, *Great, this is it, Mars. Is this when I get to be some big damn hero?* Because I was really ready for that. I was tired of being a shitty soldier.

"This is a full company mission," the CO continued. "Our company is tasked with breach of the compound, with support from Tangine Company. To reach our target, we will be moving through an urban combat environment. We expect mines, booby traps, and the occasional hostile. Intel says we should not meet an organized force, but I don't need to tell you about the dangers posed by a single well-placed sniper. Heat signatures will not always be visible. Lots of their snipers use cloaking tech. The old ways of detection are still the best. Watch for the glimmer of a scope. Pay attention to where shots are coming from. I don't like being dropped into an urban combat situation, but them's the breaks."

They took us out to the drop field. I secured my pulse rifle. Jones to my left. Prakash in front of me, Marino next to her, cooing at his own rifle, and Omalas to my right, still and silent as a statue.

We began to tremble.

My teeth chattered.

I figured it wasn't likely I was going to Mars, or, if I was, that it wouldn't be now, at any rate. *Try to relax,* I thought. *Let it be a surprise.* Our forms began to judder apart. I saw Prakash's arm again, rammed straight through her body. Had to blink rapidly, confirm she was still there, still mostly whole.

I hate surprises.

We broke apart.

Interview #3
SUBJECT #187799
DATE: 26|05|309
TIME: 0100
ROOM: 99

I: We've started the recording. Third recording with . . . subject one-eight-seven-seven-nine-nine. Performed by . . . see the notes.

(SILENCE: 05 seconds)

I: Can you hear me?

(SILENCE: 07 seconds)

I: Is she awake? This seems to be a great number of scars. Did she come with all these?

(UNINTELLIGIBLE: 15 seconds)

I: We've given you a hit of adrenaline. Hold her up, please. Do you want some water? I can give it to her. Here you are. I apologize for what's happened to you. I did tell you it would be necessary. We're running out of time. I told you that. On an accelerated timetable . . . without your cooperation . . . our options narrow. Surely you understand that now?

(UNINTELLIGIBLE: 25 seconds)

I: I can't understand her. Hold her up. Is there a reaction with the adrenaline? Does she need another—

S: Go fuck yourself.

I: Ah. You're back.

S: Never left, Sergeant. Just . . . drifted awhile.

I: Where did you go?

S: The front. Always the front. You?

I: We've suffered great losses.

S: But you were never there to witness them, were you? You don't strike me as a woman who spends time on the field. You're the type to go door to door, watching as homes are busted into, gleefully bringing back subjects for interrogation. . . .

I: I saw enough. Let's not pretend there's any clean place in this war or any other.

S: You saw it streamed. You saw it on an immersive. You never lived it. You just enforced it. Round and round.

I: Does that devalue my experiences, in your eyes? Do you feel it makes me lesser than you, or is that simply because I am your enemy?

(SILENCE: 15 seconds)

I: I have lost things in this war too.

S: Things, yes . . . A sense of security. An unshakable ideal. Perhaps even faith in your cause. But people? Besides your Corporate IP Protection team, your commanding officer, some fly girl who got blown up over—

I: Are you trying to guess at my history again? You're doing poorly.

S: No. Not at all. I know more than you will ever believe. It helped me get here. You know what they started to say in the military corps in Tene-Silvia and Evecom, after the Dark? They said, "Fire when you're told. Don't disobey an order. Surrender to the first Martian you see." Know why they said that?

I: Because they were cowards.

S: Because Mars was—is—good to its prisoners. Disarmed them. Sat them down. Fed them a pack of rations. Most POWs spent the war in warm, comfortable rooms with access to entertainment options and education courses. Toward the end, you know, after the Sick, soldiers from the Big Six were hungry. Mars got a reputation for treating POWs decently. Even decadently. The Big Six . . . didn't. It's why so many of yours started to defect. Maybe you should have considered that before you invested in advanced interrogation techniques.

I: Taking prisoners has never been practical. I cannot believe you learned any better where you were raised.

S: In World War I, the what . . . Americans, they were, at the time . . . they got such a reputation for treating prisoners well that when conscripted Germans got sent off in the next war, their parents told them to surrender to the first American they could find. Sound familiar? If you think that didn't make a difference—

I: And see what happened to America, after. It became everything it accused others of being. It tore itself apart, riddled by the rot of unfettered free speech, drowned in a deluge of propaganda foisted upon an uneducated public with no formalized training in critical thinking. Liberal democracies and scheming socialist regimes were doomed from the start. You give a human being freedom and personhood as some innate right, and what do they have to fight for? Personhood is earned. Residency is earned. Citizenship is earned. If you're not earning for the company, you are costing it.

S: They won that war, is all I'm saying. They started losing when they forgot how to be decent. People will fight for the idea of decency. They will fight for someone who treats them like people. They fight for beliefs far longer and harder than out of fear.

I: The ghouls have fought well for us.

S: Right up until they could surrender to Mars and get treated with dignity. The corps think like corps—all short-term benefits. No long-term strategy. No greater vision. Just profit. Just winning. You can only win for so long before it all topples out from under you.

I: Is this your way of begging for mercy? Arguing politics? Morality? Trying to get me to see your side? A side which conveniently asks me to stop interrogating you? You think I haven't heard all this before, in some other form, from some other prisoner? I've interrogated better, smarter, and certainly prettier subjects than you. They all cracked. Every one. They cracked because they knew there was no way out of this. No going back. This isn't an immersive. It's real life. And here, I am your god.

S: Let us be honest. Words matter. You are torturing me. Stopping that would be nice, but it won't win you my loyalty, only my exhaustion in the face of continuing pain and hope for the release of death. Of course, I know we're too far into the war for that. I know you're desperate. I knew where this was going from the start.

I: You keep saying that. But if you knew where this was going, why would you allow yourself to be captured and interrogated? At the very least, you'd have already told me what you know.

S: Then I would be dead.

I: We won't kill you.

S: Of course you will kill me.

I: We may want to trade you. Prisoner exchanges are still done.

S: Trade me for whom? I'm nobody important, however much you wish I was. You could promise me anything. Promises are nothing, here.

I: Tell me about Saint Petersburg. Why did you go there?

S: It was the decent thing to do.

I: Who were you saving?

S: Everything that matters to me. Everything that can be saved. I've run through it again and again, and there's no stopping this war. There's no winning it. All I can do is save a few pieces I care for.

I: Answer one question for me, and I will have them cut you down. A single question. No bullshit.

S: Ask away.

I: What is the Russian word for doppelganger?

S: Dvoynik.

I: That was prompt. Good. You, take her down.

. . .

(SILENCE: 45 seconds)

I: There, is that better?

S: I've been worse.

I: They teach Russian on Mars?

S: I've had a lot of time to learn things up there. The Russian is so Martian soldiers can accept the surrender of NorRus conscripts. They're all conscripted ghouls, did you know that? They don't pretend military service is some glorious or noble sacrifice. It's simply about serving the whims of the corporation. It's always been the rich pushing us around, making up stories about how we're fighting for a noble cause when it's just about, what, some old guy insulting some other old guy's dick, measuring their relative genius based on how many people live stream their breakdown. You know the ratings for the war broke records? The corps made a killing on that. I heard Tene-Silvia even ran ads for NorRus and Evecom during that broadcast, it was so profitable.

I: Why did I ask about doppelgangers? You tell me. You're always giving me lectures about history and morality.

S: The word comes from the German, meaning "double-goer." To see a doppelganger of a loved one or relative was said to be a harbinger of their death or illness. If you saw one of yourself, it was an omen of your own death. The Egyptians had a related concept, a spirit double. But if you go back long enough, yes · · · the Zoroastrians, back in Babylonian times, in Persia, the idea of these doubles, these twin selves · · · they represented good and evil. You see that idea brought forward in a lot of other cultures. A doppelganger isn't just a double, but an evil double, a terrible twin to you. I always found it funny that the doppelganger is supposed to be the evil one, though, don't you? Just as likely that the original is the evil one, and the doppelganger the good. But that goes against our natural inclination to see ourselves as the heroes of our own stories, and the other as the outsider, the enemy, the one trying to take away everything we have. I · · · could go on, if you'll allow me a cup of water.

I: You answered my question, so yes. Will you get her · · · ? Thank you.

(SILENCE 35 seconds)

I: Here it is.

S: Thank you.

I: You must be hungry.

S: Less than you'd imagine. Pain lessens my appetite.

I: We believe that you may have spent the last few years impersonating one of our agents, which would explain how you acquired your intel. What do you think of that?

S: It sounds like you're grasping for straws, there, trying to throw something at me and see what sticks. Impersonating an agent sounds enormously difficult.

I: It would make it much easier to achieve what you have, thus far. Pretending to be a corp soldier. We have seen Mars brainwash some of our own, even, send them to Martian camps where they are "rehabilitated" and come out littered with new organic and nonorganic hardware. We dispatch them quickly, but they have gotten more sophisticated. Someone has been leaking communications to Mars. Someone told you Saint Petersburg was the best place to land, the city least touched by the Sick. They told you our CEO was there. The only way to get that information is to be one of our own. Yet we have destroyed all our traitors. We cut them each out at the root.

S: You sound so certain.

I: It was a very thorough purge.

S: It's a convenient theory. It's wrong, but convenient.

I: Why do you seek to destroy a free Earth?

S: Even if tossing a petrol bomb at your CEO's hotel would destroy anything, really, the fact is there is no free society on Earth. Everyone is owned by someone else. The resistance here wants to unshackle you, but that's too frightening for most people. So what does that leave us? Free people who believe they are already free? They think they have chosen their servitude, and that makes them individuals, powerful. Freedom to work? Ha! Freedom to die on the factory floor, behind a desk, pissing in place because they don't get bathroom breaks. Freedom to be fired at the whim of a boss bleeding you dry on stagnant wages you can only spend at the company store.

But the choice of the whip or the chain is a false choice. Sometimes you have to leave people behind. They're part of the old world. They aren't capable of building something new. To build something new is to admit that the lives they lead aren't what they believed. And to lose that belief . . . threatens their sense of themselves. The annihilation of beliefs is the annihilation of the self.

I: Spare me your rhetoric.

S: You asked.

I: Another question, another answer, and I'll send in a surgeon.

S: Surgeon and a vodka.

I: You will need to think carefully about your answer.

S: I'm thinking already. That's something we have in common now. I made sure of that.

I: Who ordered you to attack that building? Who told you where our CEO was?

S: You did. How do you think I knew you'd be there? How I knew it was free of plague? How I knew you'd pick me up?

I: What do you—

S: That's two questions. I want my vodka.

I: I told you to think very carefully about your answers—

S: I have. You string me back up, you'll get the same answer.

(SILENCE: 09 seconds)

I: String her back up.

S: You lose, Dvoynik. Of course, I suppose that's as good a name for me as any. You,

though . . . you are easy to anticipate.
   I: End interview.
   (END RECORDING #3)

17.

I do a lot of thinking when we break apart.

You aren't supposed to be able to think when you're just a collection of atoms transformed into light. But then, you're not supposed to be able to do a lot of things when you drop. Even my memories were muddled. What was yesterday? What was today?

We're all just animals reacting to stimuli, like runnels of water headed downhill, or blobs of mercury beading apart around an obstacle. I heard something in a biology class once about how animals can't detect things they aren't designed to. That might sound obvious, but how often do you assume that everything just sees and reacts the same way you do to the world? If we aren't designed to detect or perceive a thing, if it doesn't impact our ability to survive, then we can't comprehend it. Think about space, stuff like dark matter, black holes, the expanding universe. We spend our whole lives making up stories to explain these things because we can't figure them out; not the way we can figure out how vision works or how gravity keeps us rooted to the ground. Vision and gravity are things we have evolved to be able to sense. If we don't understand those things, we're at a disadvantage. But the universe? It doesn't matter if we understand that, does it? Maybe on a grand scale, but not day-to-day. So we never evolved the capability to understand it. We aren't made for it. It's the same with the light, with traveling the way we do now. This isn't something we're designed to do. No wonder my memory is so messed up.

No wonder I broke apart over some great golden field under a blue sky, instead of the Martian vista I'd been promised.

Oh well.

I wondered who my team would be. Wondered how long it would be until coms came online. Wondered how I was able to wonder all those things before I'd corporealized.

We came together.

I tried to breathe, but my lungs weren't ready yet. It was like sucking vacuum. The air finally came, cold, so fucking cold. Where would it be this cold? When? The bodies of the platoon were flickering in and out, still solidifying.

I scanned the horizon; just flat, rolling wheat fields as far as I could see. No buildings. No towers. I didn't say a word over the platoon channel or the squad channel. I waited for coms. I waited for the updated mission brief, just like Jones and Muñoz always told me to do.

I may be stubborn, but I can be taught.

All around me, platoons began to appear on the field. Platoons generally had four or five fire teams each, making a platoon twenty to thirty strong. It wasn't long before it became clear we were a very large deployment, probably a brigade, which was anywhere from fifteen hundred to thirty-five hundred soldiers.

Since we weren't being shot at—a nice surprise—we waited

quietly for coms.

The first voice I heard was Jones's, which was a relief. "Squad, sound off. Dietz?"

"Alive," I said. "Fine."

"Omalas?"

"Sir," she said.

"Marino?"

Marino hummed something on our squad channel. Sounded familiar, but I couldn't place it. Was that the theme to *Vila Sésamo*? I had a vague recollection of watching all those happy puppets while huddled around an LED-film projection in the labor camps with two dozen other children while a hot wind kicked up dust outside. You'd think the puppets would have been the most fantastic part of that show, but it was always the world of clean air and flat social hierarchies that felt like a cozy fantasy.

"I need an affirmative, Marino," Jones said.

"Still shooting," Marino said. "Let's carve them up."

"Deathless?"

Shit, I thought. Who was Deathless?

"Here," a woman said. She raised her rifle, so I knew she was the one next to me. She was about as tall as I was; I maybe outweighed her, but not by much.

As our trackers came online, I consulted my heads-up display, and saw her last name listed as Ratzesberger. No wonder she had a call sign. I definitely hadn't seen her in our platoon before this. I would have remembered that name.

Chatter on the line. Marino said, "Big to-do out here."

"They like to make a show up here in Canuck," Deathless said. "Get all the Martian immigrants pissing themselves."

Wait for the updated brief, I thought. The loading icon still blinked at the lower left of my vision.

"Dietz," Jones said, and my stomach sank. "You all right? All pistons firing?"

"Yeah, good." I went over the other names in our platoon, trying to figure out who else was missing. Landon was still there, Tanaka, Leichtner . . . Herrera was missing. And Markesh. The rest were the same as I remembered. Deathless must have been one of the grunts rotated in to replace one of them.

Prakash was missing again, too. I let out my breath. I didn't realize I'd been holding it. I tried to center myself in time. This was after Prakash's bad drop, probably? Before . . . was it before anything I'd experienced yet? I didn't know. Maybe not? I wondered if I'd ever see Prakash again, or if she was gone, sealed away in some memory I'd never get back, like Muñoz and the rest of my first squad.

Stick to the brief.

As if summoned, the brief popped in on my heads-up display.

We were part of a major deployment moving into Canuck to secure it after intel reported that six Martian drop ships had landed here, overrunning a CanKrushkev base in the area. Two CanKrushkev divisions had already been dispatched, but we'd lost communication with them. Our platoon was part of Dog Company, one of the four companies that made up the Ghost Battalion. The Ghost Battalion and our sister Battalion, the Midnight Marauders, together formed the Ruby Regiment. The Ruby Regiment was one of the three regiments comprising the Firewalker Brigade, which rolled up into the 91st Armored Infantry Division. Our division numbered about fifteen thousand soldiers, last I heard, but I had yet to see its full deployment.

Until now.

Let me tell you what the Martians did to Canuck. Most of the North American continent has been fought over by Evecom and CanKrushkev for decades. CanKrushkev won. Long time back, CanKrushkev and NorRus fought another big war over it. Called it the Seed Wars, and it was mostly fought over the far north after it thawed out, probably more than a hundred years ago now. The blooming Manitoba and Saskatchewan wheat fields and solar farms were way more valuable than crude oil, by then. Changing weather patterns dramatically altered the Pacific region, and that carried over far inland. Most of the southern half of North America was desert; it happened fast, maybe two decades. People were displaced. It got messy. Nobody won in that war. They blasted the whole place to hell. Turned this melting Garden of Eden into a contagious, radioactive wasteland. So much virulent shit was eating through the organics in Canuck that it became one of those dark places you threaten to send kids if they don't follow corporate rules.

When a splinter group of Martians broke their silence and offered to fix Canuck in exchange for passage back to Earth . . . shit, who was going to say no? Fix what we broke. Sounds great.

I don't think anybody figured they would fix it so well, though. I had seen the place in lots of immersives, but in real life it felt—crisper. Colder. I searched for a date on my display but got nothing. If I had to guess, it might be early autumn. There were trees in the distance, out beyond the soft undulations of the fields all around us. Clouds hung low in the sky; a black thunderhead bloomed to my left. Took me a minute to realize it wasn't clouds, but smoke.

Our objective lay over there; Martian drop ships and the missing divisions, all obscured by the billowing smog.

"Incoming!" the CO yelled over the platoon channel. Her voice sounded different. Was that Lieutenant V? That was as much warning as we got.

A massive explosion tore away the ground ten meters to my left, engulfing the entire platoon next to us.

It threw me like a freight train.

I went ten feet in the air. Crashed to the ground. Hunks of grassy earth, bits of flesh and gear, tattered slicks, rained from the sky. The smoke mixed with the reddish mist of blood. Bloody soil smeared the front of my helmet.

I tried to wipe it clear, and only distorted my vision even more. I instinctively reached for my helmet to pop it off and stopped myself. The only reason my hearing was intact was because of the helmet. I pushed up my visor—the risk of going blind preferable to getting hit because I couldn't see anything. All this tech, and they couldn't keep our field of vision clear when the shit hit.

"Jones?" I said.

"Assess and advance north!" the CO said across our platoon channel. "We are advancing! They took out our drones. You are the eyes on the ground." That definitely was not Lieutenant V's voice. It sounded a lot like . . . Who? I couldn't place it.

I hefted my rifle and kept low. My heads-up gave me direction, which was good, because the smoke was so bad I still couldn't see anything. I snapped on my oxygen line, the one we were supposed to use for Mars, figuring now was as good a time as any to use it.

The GPS marked my squad on the display. I caught up to Omalas, who was helping Deathless get free of the tumbled earth.

"Anybody injured?" I said over our squad channel.

"I'm up," Jones said. I didn't have a visual on him, but his tracker marker on the local map pivoted toward me; his and Marino's.

"I have Marino," Jones said.

"Still got my balls," Marino said.

"Dietz! Visor on," Jones said. "They're using gas. Probably sarin. Everyone, check your med kits. Secure your masks."

I wiped away the smear on my visor as much as I could and lowered it. The edges sealed around the helmet. I brought up the full oxygen mask, yanking it down from inside my helmet and securing it. The oxygen line threaded through the mask. I knew about various nerve agents, had learned about them in mandatory training, but the idea that they would actually be used still shocked me. I dug around in my med kit and found the antidote syringe labeled GAS. I had no idea if it would work against sarin, or all types of gas, or . . . shit.

"Division is moving north," Jones said The heavy *whump-whump* of artillery continued. Arcs of plasma sailed over our heads.

I kept low next to Omalas. This was heavy shit.

"Move!" Jones waved us all forward. The rifle trembled in his hands.

I slowed my breathing, trying to center myself like I did in the torture modules. The fire and fury on the field is meant to kill, but it also confuses, and confusion can kill you just as easily.

The bulk of the division moved north across my heads-up display map. They were little blue beads on the read-out, clumping and falling and reclumping. To get their names, I could focus on each individual, but I didn't want to. They fell so fast I feared getting attached even to a name. I scanned the map for the CO but broke off when another blast ruptured the ground thirty paces away.

A mass of grassy earth smashed my head. I stumbled, caught myself, and ran to catch up with my squad.

"Spread out!" Jones said. "Don't bunch up!"

We moved away from one another, trying to keep fifteen feet between every member of our squad and the larger platoon. That was the recommendation in training; it helped minimize losing your entire squad to a mine or a blast, but these bursts were big; they spewed earth and shrapnel and body parts with massive force. I wasn't convinced any of us would survive a nearby hit.

Jones went crater to crater; probably figuring the likelihood artillery would hit the same place twice was low. I was pretty sure that's not how chance worked. Smoke hugged the ground; twisting yellow and green. Sarin was clear, tasteless, and odorless.

This had to be something else.

I pushed the thought out of my mind. Heard only the sound of my own breath. The formerly flat plain was pockmarked with craters and dirt mounds and bodies. I tripped over two soldiers still writhing, soaked in blood. As we advanced, the field of bodies grew thicker. I kept my heads-up map of the area minimized, terrified to watch us all falling and dying in real time.

Minutes felt like hours. My heads-up began displaying heat signatures in the near distance.

"Three k's to the target," Jones said. "Keep moving."

"Fucknuts should have dropped us into camp," Marino huffed. "I'd come together inside some fucking red and kill him right there."

"Less chatter," Jones said. Another explosion rocked through a nearby platoon. A helmeted head careened past me and disappeared into the smoke.

Tanaka's squad kept pace with us; our platoon was strung out, and we'd taken several losses.

"This is bad intel," Tanaka said over the platoon channel. "It shouldn't be this heavy."

"Keep your heads down!" the CO barked over the platoon channel. "We advance." Whoever she was, she sounded younger than Lieutenant V.

My breath was loud inside my helmet. The forms of my platoon and those nearby came in and out of the smoke like ghosts.

Deathless stumbled; just ahead and to my left. She went down. I ran over and offered a hand. The ground trembled under another blast. Deathless lay just behind the lip of a crater. I saw nothing of her face behind the helmet, but I opened a two-way channel.

"Come on," I said.

"I can't."

"You can." I grabbed her arm, but she shrank away from me.

"That's death up there. That's death for no reason. They're running us into a grinder."

"We signed up for this. I'm not leaving you. Come on."

I hooked her under the arm and dragged her out. Forcing her to move woke something within her; the soldier, maybe, buried beneath the fear. She moved. I kept close to her, closer than we should have to avoid a double-death by bombing, but I figured seeing somebody else next to her was good peer pressure. If I was moving, so could she.

The bodies beneath our boots grew more frequent. Shredded flesh. Mangled torsos. Burst heads. Bits of helmets and broken pulse rifles, abandoned medical kits and tattered MRE wrappers. We careened past a soldier who'd gone to his knees in the middle of the dead and taken off his helmet. He wept there in the bloody dirt while the snaking tendrils of the gas enveloped him.

Deathless was right. We were all going to die here. And for what? What had the Martians done up there that deserved this show of force, this mindless run into gas and artillery? Why had they sent infantry into a deathtrap?

We caught up to Jones and Omalas. Marino weaved just out of sight, to my left. I jogged ahead to catch up with Jones, and opened up a two-way channel.

"Jones, we—"

I'm not even sure what I was going to say. We should watch Deathless? We should go back? We should tell the CO to hump us out? We should become cowards, now, when we faced a hopeless mission?

The ground exploded around me. Heat. Pattering of earth. My ears went dumb. I choked, realized it was dirt, pushed myself up. My visor had shattered. Muted groans. Screaming? My vision swam. I let myself drop back to the ground, still dazed. I turned over. My limbs, I thought. Do I have all my limbs? Are my guts hanging out?

I patted at my arms, my groin, my thighs, and lifted my head to gaze down the length of my body. I lay covered in dirt and blood; bits of flesh and shredded golden grass.

You are alive, I thought. *You are whole. You can move.*

"Jones," I said aloud, and it was like I was speaking from the bottom of a well. Ahead of me lay a smoky ruin of a crater. My heads-up blinkered; I couldn't figure out how to access it, my brain was so muddled.

I moved rocks and twisted grass away as I went toward a dark, heaping shape. My mind served up the image of Grandma's body, again: her torso torn open. "No, no," I said; the sound hummed in my ears. Like speaking underwater.

An arm. Exposed fingers. I went to grab the arm, pulling myself close enough to see that most of it was no longer attached to the body that had rolled into the crater.

I slid into the lip of the crater and hooked my arms under Jones's. Aside from the mangled arm, he seemed mostly intact, but out of it, eyes glassy, confused. His dangling arm dragged across the ground as I pulled him. The bone was sheared; jagged splinters. Tattered flesh. What was left of the arm was attached to him by two taut sinews, nothing more.

I opened the company channel; the howls of fear, of the dead, of the dying, pierced my helmet. "Medic!" I said. "Jones, the six-oh-four, needs a medic!" A dozen others called the same.

"This is the five-oh-six, medic! Medic one, this is the five-oh-six. Ferreira's down!"

"Seoane, the three-oh-nine—we need blood! Med team two! This is the three-oh-nine! Over!"

"Get off this channel! Use the evac channel!"

"Who the fuck is sending us into this shit? We all need evac! This is bullshit!"

I searched for the medic frequency. Was this new? I didn't

know it. This operation was massive; I'd had no real brief, or at least not that I remembered. I called my request again into the new channel.

Voices overwhelmed here, too.

"Med team two, med team two. This is Vásquez, the three-oh-nine. I'm hit, we're—" Gone.

"Med team, med team, I have Coelho and she needs immediate—" Gone.

"Hey, three-oh-nine, this is med team one. We are sending personnel to your position, three-oh-nine. Hold. Shit. We've lost the last of the three-oh-nine. Is the five-oh-six still—yes! We're sending three medics. Hold position. Over."

"The five-oh-six is down to one squad! I repeat, we are all down but one squad! Requesting immediate evac! Over."

"Hey, five-oh-six, this is med team one. I cannot send evac, five-oh-six. Best we can do is patch and run. Over."

I didn't dare open a higher channel. The division channel must have been a screaming mess. I'd get lost in that one.

Jones was bleeding out. I yanked open my med kit. Unraveled a tourniquet. I looped it around his upper arm, pulled it too tight, trying to stop the blood flow, knowing I was doing it wrong. Gas settled in the bottom of the craters; no harbor there.

I let go of the division channel and switched in to a one-on-one with Jones. "I've got med evac," I said.

"Leave me."

"Evac will be here soon. Hold for evac. Hear me?"

I fumbled around in the kit, looking for a hit of adrenaline. I needed to keep him conscious, keep shock from taking hold. I grabbed him under the arms and shifted him so his head pointed down into the crater, so his legs were higher than his head. Jones's breath was rapid. He kept waving his injured arm—what was left of it. The sinews strained. The stump waggled.

I fumbled for a knife to cut away the sinews, but my utility knife was missing. Where had I lost it? I leaned over and bit the sinews with my teeth, releasing his stump from his ruined arm.

"Keep it with me. Keep my arm with me."

I set his severed arm onto his chest.

"You look good," I said. "That's it. They'll fix you right up. New arm. Good as new. But you gotta stay awake for evac. You understand?"

"Go ahead. Keep moving."

"Not leaving you behind."

"Bad Luck Dietz. Bad luck."

"Think you'll do better if I'm not here?"

"I don't want to die here."

"You won't."

"My moms . . . tell them I fought—"

"I will."

"My grandmother fought. Hers before. We all fought. All citizens. I didn't have to fight. Why did I—"

"Calm down. Be calm for evac."

"I should have been a journalist. My mom . . . wanted me in intel. I couldn't. Dietz, I couldn't."

"It's okay.

"'We kill time; time buries us,'" Jones murmured; one of his Machado de Assis quotes. "My arm. Will they fix my arm, Dietz?"

"It's all right. They'll fix it."

I pulled up my local map. Tanaka and his squad were ten meters ahead of us, either dead or staying low under heavy fire. Omalas and Marino were behind me, slowly moving toward us. Deathless lay flat on her stomach in the dirt, just far enough to my left that I could barely make out her form in the shifting smoke.

"Jones!" the CO said over the platoon channel.

"Jones is injured, sir. I've called for evac."

"Tag him for the medics and leave him. Gather your squad and get moving, Dietz. Tanaka! Meet up with Dietz's squad. Tanaka, you're squad leader for the combined squad. We are still advancing on this fucking target. Keep your heads down and keep moving. You hear me, soldier? I need your head in this game, Dietz."

"Yes, sir." I stared at Jones. His visor was opaque. I could not see his expression, and I was glad for it. "Medic is coming. I have to move."

"I heard," he said.

I put the hit of adrenaline into his hand. "You start feeling like you'll black out, you hit yourself up with this. Got it? It's just the arm. The bleeding's slowed. Medic will be here any minute."

"Yeah. Okay."

I squeezed his shoulder and pulled myself up into a half crouch. *He'll be fine,* I told myself. *Medics are coming.* I hesitated.

"Lieutenant. Permission to stay with Jones until evac."

"Did I stutter, Dietz?"

"No, sir."

"And that's *First* Lieutenant," the CO said.

"Moving out, sir."

I opened the squad channel. "Deathless! Marino! Omalas! You heard the CO! Head toward Tanaka's position." I added Tanaka's squad to our channel. "Tanaka, we're headed your way."

"Haul ass! We've got some quiet. We're between rounds."

I grabbed Deathless by the arm and yanked her up. She huffed and squirmed, but kept moving. She was like a tired old engine; needed a kick in the ass to get going every time she went down.

Marino and Omalas waited for us with Tanaka's squad. As we came up, Tanaka called us all forward. The barrage had died down. I heard low rumbles in the distance. Slim chance they were out of munitions—more likely, they were loading up shells and retargeting.

Tanaka's team was short by two. Landon was with him, tall and lanky even in his suit, and moon-faced Sandoval. The third was Vela, who stood almost as tall as Omalas and twice as wide. Her name seemed vaguely familiar from one of my drops, but I could not recall her face. While we were eight strong all together, I figured the CO expected more losses, hence the larger fighting groups.

A light breeze came in from the north. The smoke around us began to rise. As we went, the only sound in my ears was my own breathing. Curtains of smoke and gas purled away from the field, revealing a sea of bodies among the broken shards of once-golden grass, now slick with fine red dew.

Ahead of us rose the shining spires of the closest city, Shabarat, home to the Martian refugees that had transformed this part of the world. A bulky line of drop ships ringed the city, just behind a massive display of artillery that took my breath away. Fighters screamed across the sky—headed away from the city, not toward it.

"Where did all this come from?" I said.

"Mars," Marino said.

"Wow," Landon said. "You've got a bright one. Where's *our* artillery? Air support? Like . . . anything?"

The ground rumbled.

"Those guns are getting ready," Tanaka said. "Let's move."

"Why . . . why are we moving into that?" Sandoval said.

"Orders." Tanaka took the lead. I made myself go after him, though my stomach turned. This was easily the stupidest thing I'd ever done. Bodies lay all the way to the first ring of artillery. About a thousand troops still moved ahead of us, picking over the bodies of the fallen. The dead far outnumbered the living.

The guns started.

"Fuck," Landon said. He stumbled and went down right

behind Tanaka.

I grabbed for him just as a projectile moved past me, about three meters away, so dense it disturbed the air; its presence even before it landed was a tangible thing.

The boom came from behind us. The patter of earth and dismembered flesh and ground-up gear. A flash of shrapnel pinged against my helmet.

"Dietz, keep distance," Tanaka said. "All of you, fan out. We're sitting ducks."

Marino's high, maniacal laughter came over the channel.

"Same," Vela said. "Same, Marino."

I kept pace with Tanaka. The sound of the guns was a physical force. Smoke swirled. The air roared. Rumbled. Groaned. Like something alive.

"Air support incoming," the CO said. "Take cover."

"Cover where?" Deathless howled.

"Drop!" I said and thumped her back. I lay on my belly, rifle pointed ahead, as if it would do any good at all.

Fighters streaked overhead as the rest of the squad lay flat. The best we could hope for was to avoid debris. The heavy guns changed their trajectory, lightning fast. Two fighters exploded in a blaze of black smoke and roiling fire.

"Pull back to the rally point," the CO said. "They want us to pull back and give air support some room."

"Could they have thought of that before?" Landon said.

"Bullshit," Vela muttered.

"That's six kilometers," Tanaka said.

"That's the closest safe point for rally, possibly evac," the CO said. "They can't pull us out; way too hot here. The reds are running interference on our trackers. They can't get an accurate bead on us."

"Copy that, sir," Tanaka said. "We will—"

That's when we lost coms.

Our heads-up displays cut out. The constant blue aurora at the bottom left of my left eye disappeared. My connection with the platoon channel, gone.

"Tanaka?" I said aloud, to no one, because their helmets were still on.

Tanaka pressed his helmet against Landon's. Came over to me, did the same. When he put his helmet to mine, I could just hear him; mostly through the vibration his voice made.

"Coms?"

"Gone for me too," I said.

He was thinking a lot faster than me; another reason he was a squad leader and I wasn't. I heard the DI's voice in my head again, yelling about how I didn't have two brain cells to rub together. Fuck him, yeah, but I heard it, still.

Tanaka waved us all south, pointing in the direction we'd been headed before losing communications. We went after him, lunging over the bodies of the fallen. Ahead of us, a few stragglers did the same. The staggered march turned into a haphazard run as terror coiled through the ranks.

Our air support circled back.

A searing rain of fire dropped between us and the soldiers in front of us, cutting us off. The fire cooked the suits from the skins of the squads nearest us, licking greedily. I fell back on my ass.

Sandoval flailed. His legs were on fire. I tackled him, rolling him across the ground like a sack of screaming meat. Our suits resisted fire, but this slick flame would not come off. Fire peeled away from him and crept up my hand. I tried to wipe it on the ground, but that only spread it; a slithering oil. Desperate, I clawed around for dirt to drown it in. Saw the open chest of a soldier nearby. I shoved my hand into the wound, dousing the flame. The soldier's guts were still warm.

When I turned back, Tanaka and Omalas were wrapping Sandoval in a Mylar blanket, snuffing out the fire. But all around us, fire still licked the sky, high and hot, feeding off the air itself. I couldn't see Vela. Squinting into the flames, I spotted her beefy form, already consumed by the heat.

Marino stood in front of the great blazing wall. He raised his rifle above his head and fired it in the air. Marino yanked off his helmet. Threw it into the flames like a great black football. "Fuck you!" he screamed. Spittle flecked his chin. "Fuck this! Fuck you!"

I pushed up my broken visor. "Marino!"

"Fuck you, too!"

The others flipped up their visors. Tanaka yelled, "We're cut off! Vela is down! Head—"

"The only fucking way we can?" Marino cackled as the flames began to encircle us on a third side.

"Move! Move!" I said. I helped Omalas with Sandoval. He seemed dazed more than anything; the fire had eaten through the first layer of his suit from his chest to his toes on his right side. I saw raw, pink flesh peeking through. I had no idea how bad the burns would be once we got his suit off.

We stuck close together as we ran through the slim opening between the flames. The heat was intense. I closed up my helmet again as much as I could, instantly parched. My heart thrummed.

More flaming pillars appeared ahead of us. The golden grass had caught fire, and burned steadily. Without coms, without our maps, we had no idea where we were. The oxygen in our suits was finite. If we didn't get out of the smoke and heat we would suffocate and burn up.

Tanaka swerved ahead, cut off by another blazing fire.

Marino screamed, his own helmet gone. He huffed away from Tanaka, yelling, "This way! This way! Born in flame!"

"Screw it," I muttered, and went after him, gesturing to Omalas to follow my lead. If there was anyone crazy enough to find a way through this or die trying, it was Marino.

I didn't stop to see if anyone else followed us. Without coms, I didn't technically have any orders from Tanaka or the CO that contradicted where I was headed. I guess you could argue I should have followed Tanaka, and maybe I could argue about that technicality at my court martial. Hope springs eternal.

Marino darted over heaps of stone jutting through the grassy, burning fields. The ground sloped upward here. I was out of breath. Sandoval sagged in our arms. His right foot dragged.

I pushed my visor up again, and Sandoval's too. "Hey, hey," I said, smacking his check. His eyelids fluttered.

"Yeah! Yeah!" Marino stood atop the ridge, another fifteen meters up. Then he disappeared.

"Marino?" I said. "Hold on! Omalas—"

"I have him," she said.

I left Sandoval with her and scrambled to the top of the ridge. The ridge fell off into a rocky, shallow canyon. Marino lay at the bottom of it, rifle in his lap. A lazy stream wended its way past him. Further ahead—thick copses of trees. I pivoted, gazing back the way we had come. Fire still raged below. The fighters no longer ranged across the blue, blue sky. The tremulous Martian city, rising like Oz from the golden prairie, spouted great gouts of flame. Fire ringed the towers, feathery things putting off plumes of sooty smog. Her smoke rose up forever.

The rest of our squad struggled up the rise. Omalas and Sandoval, Tanaka, Landon, and Deathless. Behind us . . . nothing. After that bombing . . . there was no moaning or sobbing on the field. There were no whole people, no one capable of sound.

Everything smelled of blood and smoke.

I went down and helped Omalas drag Sandoval the last few meters to the top of the ridge.

Tanaka joined us. "Let's get down in the gully. We're exposed up here."

We climbed down after Marino. Deathless slumped next

to him. She yanked her helmet off, revealing nearly two fingers of dark brown hair. I wondered when the CO had stopped complaining about regulation haircuts.

Omalas and I set Sandoval down along the waterline, figuring cold water might be soothing, if not exactly sterile. I searched my med pack and shot him full of antibiotics and painkillers.

"We have to call for evac," Sandoval said.

"Our trackers should still work," Deathless said. "Even with coms down, they can track us."

"Maybe." Tanaka scanned the trees on the other side of the stream, rifle up. "Dietz, when you were on Mars, they disabled your tracker. For your squad, too. Then yours got removed."

"That's what they told me," I said.

"Could have done it here, too," he said.

"They took mine out. I got ID'd by a civilian."

"They could still work?" Landon said. "If we sit tight here—"

"That fire's out of control," Tanaka said.

"The ridge might act as a firebreak," I continued. "The stream, too. The city's on fire now. It'll create its own weather." I raised my hand. "Wind is moving over us, toward the city. That means the fire will head away from us too."

"Anybody remember the evac point?" Deathless rubbed distractedly at her arms.

"I do." Omalas pointed across the stream. "Past the woods, across a bridge over a river. It was an open field on the map."

"They'll tap into our trackers," Deathless mewled.

"If they work," Tanaka said. "If everyone's coms and trackers went out, they'll expect us to rally there. They'll send standard air pickup."

"Like they sent air support?" Landon's sarcasm was thick.

"War is messy. Logistics fucks up sometimes." Tanaka, with the corporate line.

"Easy for them," Landon said. "They aren't on the ground."

"Hydrate," Tanaka ordered. "We'll rest here a quarter hour and keep moving. Dietz, watch that wind?"

"Sure." I pulled off my helmet and strapped it to a carabiner hooked to my belt. I washed my gloved hands in the stream; my gloves were still covered in rotten innards and char. When they were clean, I pulled the gloves off and splashed water on my face. The cold hit me like a slap; I remembered what the woman had said to my father . . . who was she? Some Corporate Intellectual Property tough. *The Nazis were high as balls,* she'd said. I understood why. I wished I could take whatever they had taken—the future be damned.

Omalas folded her legs and sat beside me. She pulled out a protein bar and offered me a hit from her water slug.

"Thanks. You want to refill it here?"

"Yes. I have tablets."

She meant iodine tabs. I'd half hoped for methamphetamines. Oh well.

We all sat in silence, listening to the sound of the burning prairie. The exhaustion hit me. I wanted to keel over into the stream and never get up.

"You all right?" I asked Omalas, which was a dumb question. None of us were all right, but the silence frightened me. The silence invited me to think.

"They say you grow up in war, but only parts of you do. Other parts . . . they get suppressed, eroded."

"How old are you?"

"Who can say? I have been fighting this war a long time. Once you begin to drop, time becomes a luxury, an outdated thing, like the idea of voting or equality or freedom that meant anything but freedom for the rich from the burdens they force the poor to carry for them." It was the most I'd ever heard her speak.

"Is that a quote from something?"

She smiled without showing her teeth; a sad smile that never reached her flat black eyes. "No. Only a statement of truth."

Tanaka got us going again. Maybe he had some drugs we didn't. He bent next to Sandoval. "You think you can march?"

"I'm good. Good painkillers."

"Great. Need help?"

"No, no. I'm good now."

Tanaka helped him up, and Sandoval limped forward. I hoped those painkillers would last until the evac point.

"This is bullshit," Deathless muttered, and I couldn't disagree.

All I had was, "You want to stay here?"

She grumbled at me.

"Marino?" Tanaka said. "I want you up here with me. Dietz? Watch our ass."

"And the wind." I pointed at the fire.

"And the wind."

It still blew toward the city. Small blessings.

The seven of us hiked across the stream and into the trees, following worn paths. We came across a few abandoned structures; or, I hoped they were abandoned. Doors and windows were fixed tight. Parts of the fields had been burned. We found a paved road that wound toward our objective. From here I could just see the ripple of a wide river.

"Split up," Tanaka said. "Stick to either side. Sandoval, Marino, Omalas, with me. Dietz, Landon, get over there with Deathless."

Staying to the side of the road would make it easier to break for cover. Just like avoiding sticking close together on the field reduced our chances of getting blown up all at once, staying on opposite sides of the road ensured at least half of us might survive a mine blast.

The world had gone silent. Nothing above us. We passed a few more residences, all boarded up. No smoke here. No barking dogs. Not even bird song.

"More smoke." Marino pointed over the trees. Great gouts of black made heavy plumes above the tree line.

"Another city?" I said.

"Ridge up here," Tanaka said. "Deathless, run up and scout."

She forged ahead, lighter and nimbler than the rest of us. Outside the kill zone, she moved a lot faster.

She headed back down to the road, said, "Couple of trains, looks like. Fighters must have hit them."

"Hope that wasn't our evac." Landon headed up the ridge too. I followed.

We stood on the rise overlooking the flaming trains. A large vehicle on the track had halted the first train; a second train had backed up behind the first. The bodies inside writhed like shadows.

"Why didn't the second train turn around?" Marino scoffed. "Dumb shits."

"Probably lost coms like we did," I said. "I bet they were fleeing the city. They couldn't turn around and go back. Maybe they thought they could bump the other train out."

"Dumb shits." That explanation probably made Marino feel better. We all wanted civs to die because they were stupid, because they deserved it, not because we were the bad guys.

Tanaka came up beside me. Marino spit and headed back down with the others. For a long moment, Tanaka and I watched the burning trains. There must have been a thousand people on those two trains, all charred, twisted wrecks now, like the vehicles they had tried to ride to safety.

"Think they were . . . maybe soldiers?" I said.

"No. Probably civs."

"This isn't what I signed up for." Paladin. Hero of the light. This wasn't heroic at all, throwing ourselves at Martian artillery, blowing up regular people fleeing for their lives.

"You ever see *War of the Worlds*?"

"Sounds familiar."

"It's about Martians invading Earth. But the original . . . my sister loved old media. Radio dramas. You know what that is?"

I shook my head.

"Like a movie, but just the words. The sounds. Like closing your eyes on the battlefield. People used to sit around these big wooden boxes, listening to this stuff. All you got was the voices. *War of the Worlds* got broadcast like it was a news report. Lot of people believed it. Went crazy. Thought giant Martians with tentacles were invading. Called the law. Totally freaked out."

"Like the Ebola riots in Europe, before Evecom."

"And the ShinHana Panic, back in '75. Exactly."

I watched the burning train, not following his line of thought. "It's easy to get confused when you're scared," I said. "Maybe they didn't mean to blow up these trains. Thought they were something else."

"Dietz, what if we're not at war with Mars?"

I turned. Wanted to see his expression. "That would be . . ." And I thought of the Ebola riots, and his story about *War of the Worlds*, and stopped.

"The corps are all united in this war. That's what they all tell us. What if they're lying? What if this is another corporate war like the one that took out Elosha, made the Big Seven the Big Six? Only this time, we're fighting to the death?"

"One corp to rule them all?"

"Yeah."

"Why lie about it?"

"Maybe there's nobody up there on Mars, but us. Just our own colonists. No free Martians at all. Maybe the refugees are the last of the real Martians."

"And we're . . . killing them to cover that up? Doesn't make sense." Not that a lot of this war made sense. "Mars goes dark and—"

"Killing them as insurance. Maybe Mars went dark because everyone is dead up there."

"But we're fighting on Mars."

"Yeah, but who, Dietz? *Who* are we fighting on Mars? There are corp settlements on Mars. We've seen them."

I had no memory of going to Mars, though everyone else assumed I'd been there at least twice. I dredged my memory, hoping for some revelation, but as ever—nothing but what I already knew. I couldn't square anything he was saying with my own experience. People go crazy during war. I knew that as well as anyone.

He said, "I wouldn't say this if coms were online."

"Yeah, obviously."

"What if the Martians didn't blow up the moon? What if it was some corp accident?"

"You sound like a conspiracy theorist."

"So does war with Mars. We can move people around with light. Nobody on Mars can do that. Who can just disappear two million people like in the Blink?"

"You're saying *we* moved them?"

"I've had a long time to think about it."

"How long?"

"Dietz, I've been at war . . . forever. I feel like we just keep going round and round."

"You know what year it is?"

His piercing blue eyes searched my face. "Do you?"

"No."

"Me neither."

We gazed as one back to the trains, to the burning soldiers, to the black smoke rising against the bloody red sunset.

18.

The river lay on the other side of the trains. We gave the wreckage a wide berth. Sandoval sweated heavily, though the air was cool. The bridge over the river was a rocky ruin, but enough of it was left that we could pick our way across. On the other side was a public park, a grassy expanse ringed in a mix of evergreen trees—the evac point.

The park was deserted.

No soldiers. No vehicles.

"We'll set up here," Tanaka said. "Clear skies, which is good. It's going to get cold. Not sure if I want to risk a fire, though."

"Pretty sure there's enough smoke to mask it," Landon muttered.

I knew what he was thinking. I wanted a wash, some food, and a lot of warmth. The slicks were good at absorbing our bodily fluids, recycling them into clean water and excreting the rest, but there was nothing like real warmth, real water, real food, for morale.

"Omalas," Tanaka said. "You take first watch."

She nodded.

We chose a site at the edge of the clearing. Landon and Marino dragged over two picnic tables.

Marino sauntered over to a grill. Pulled off his gloves. "Still coals in here!" he called, and the grin on his face was the most honest, least mad I'd seen on him yet.

We heated up our MREs—a luxury—as the sun set. I sat at one of the tables, rifle in my lap, watching the bruised red sky blaze. All the smoke made for a hell of a sunset. With my gloves and helmet off, I felt the wind change.

"Tanaka," I said. "Wind's turned toward us."

"Got it. River might slow it down, maybe stop it."

"Maybe." The smoke roiled toward us, blooming like a forest of mushrooms.

"If evac comes, it comes here. We'll stay as long as we can."

"These suits aren't fucking fireproof," Sandoval said.

"I hear you." Tanaka did not look at him.

They drill discipline into you during mandatory training. As the seven of us sat here, cut off and abandoned, probably presumed dead as fire threatened to consume us, I understood why. In the heat of battle, yeah, you need it. But adrenaline and protecting the guy beside you are usually good enough motivation. Here, though, here—the waiting, the time to think—that's when you had to lean hard on the discipline. I watched Tanaka. He chewed on a long blade of golden grass, gaze fixed on the trees on the other side of the park. Omalas had eyes on the south, where the city burned. Sandoval gingerly tended to his inflamed skin, slipping second-skin adhesives onto the raw patches.

I thought I might feel better in the dark—less exposed. But as dusk enveloped us and there was still no sign of air or light evac, I found the blackness cloying and claustrophobic. The blaze of the city continued to make the north glow. Embers and ash drifted over us, borne by the soft wind. If the blaze jumped the rocky gorge and the river, it would light up all the trees around us and move fast, far faster than we could run. Fires were common in the trash heaps where I grew up, fueled by toxic waste and unnamed flammable fluids, often sparked by the heat generated by the mounds of composting garbage. When the fire came, you checked the wind and gathered your shit and ran. The community made a series of fire breaks around the landfill, but the corp kept filling them in.

Sitting at the picnic table here, entranced by the glow, I found myself back there, my hand in my mother's slick palm. The stench of smoke. She roused me from dreams of catching geckos, of geckos pouring out of our cupboards, roaring from beneath the bucket we used to drain water from the sink.

"Mama," I said, and I was very young here, my brother wasn't even born. "What about Papa?"

She said nothing. Firmed her mouth. She was an imposing figure to me, then: all hard angles, sharp elbows, skinned knees, sinewy forearms. I didn't see my father much in those days. He was a mythical figure to me.

We climbed into the deep, damp ditch with dozens of others. She pressed her body over mine. The heat and smoke rolled over us. I screamed and clung to her, suddenly desperate to get out, to run. I feared the walls of the ditch would close on us, sealing us in like a tomb.

"Dietz?"

I started, still lost in the smell of earthy loam and burning diesel. "Yeah?"

Tanaka stood over me, partially outlined by the glow of the sky. "I want to walk the perimeter of the park. See if we missed anyone. You up for it?"

"Sure." I hefted my rifle and started after him.

"You have the squad, Omalas."

Tanaka followed a path out behind the tables, well-worn and

scattered with pine needles. We walked in silence, keeping to opposite sides of the path. I kept the quiet, wondering what he was thinking. I was so used to keeping my mouth shut because of the heads-up recording that I found it difficult to think of something to say. Cut off, alone, fire on all sides.

"You have someone back home?" Tanaka asked.

I started. It wasn't a question I expected. "Girlfriend. Broke with her before this, though. Got tired of losing things. You?"

"I was married. Already military when this all got rolling when the moon . . . She was up there, when it happened, or . . . that's what I heard. It's where I was stationed. I was doing some training exercise. Saw the whole thing break apart. They can't confirm it. No body. They could have taken her prisoner, the Martians. . . . When this war ends . . . I'll look for her. The kids are all right, though. Were back on Earth, visiting my parents."

I couldn't help but gaze through the twining branches overhead, the big black sky, and the whirling shards of the moon, just visible as the ghostly smoke breezed by. A remnant of the moon streaked across the void like a big bright firefly, and was blotted out by another plume of smoke.

"You believe it was the Martians?" I said.

"I don't know anymore."

"You saw something."

"Maybe."

"What did you see out there?"

"The future."

A chill rode up my spine. I cast a look at him, trying to read something from his profile. I remembered Muñoz pointing him out, how our tastes differed except in this. A man with a strong jaw and a kind face. Still, looking at him, I could not help but miss Vi. Miss how she fluttered around like an anxious bird, parroting stories about hostage negotiations and how to power-prime yourself before a test. She had a life ahead of her that I could never be a part of, though I seemed to be the only one of us who knew it. Vi would get into corporate IP, corporate affairs. She would excel. There was no place for me in that life, nursing at the tit of the corp. I had known it then. Knew it now. Even when she decided to take a year off and do the work she did . . . I never figured it would last. She'd get into one of those shining towers soon enough. I wouldn't.

But here I was, not just sucking off a corp but dying for it. It's funny, how sometimes you run so hard away from something that you find yourself exactly where you started.

"What kind of future?" I said.

"The war. This war. It didn't matter who it was—another corp, free Martians. They were going to start a war over it. Most of the corps had left the moon. Low losses on all sides. Mostly research. Convenient most of the soldiers stationed there were out on an exercise that day."

"Had you been to Mars?" I remembered my mother and father doing their cargo runs to the asteroid belt.

"Yeah. Before."

"Before?"

"Before they went dark. Before the war. One day we just . . . didn't go to Mars anymore. No explanation."

"You had contacts there?"

"Naw. You didn't talk to anyone there. Just dropped off supplies, took on cargo."

We kept on the path as it circled the green parkland. From here I saw the warm coals of Marino's grill still glimmering. The MREs had not been made much more palatable heated, but it was a nice change, I guess.

Continuing on, as the world burned. We kept along the path, making half the circle back to where we had come, perhaps two kilometers.

"Tanaka, how long have we served together?"

He paused. Turned his face to me, and I lost myself. Lost all sense of time, of who and what we were. Instead, it was just the two of us, two grunts on a long walk, hoping this wasn't the end.

I still have the Mars combat mission, I thought. *I still have a chance to be a hero.* But beyond this? Maybe this was the end? Maybe this was how we died—cut off from the others, swallowed up by fire.

"You tell me," he said.

"Not a fair ask. I haven't experienced things like . . . normal people."

"None of this is normal."

The trees thinned. We broke into a clearing, still shielded from the park proper. A stream—little more than spring runoff—gurgled at the other edge of it. I envied the Martians who had made a home of this place. They had transformed this blasted heath into a vibrant, secret garden. Why had we come back to destroy it all again? What was the point?

On the other side of the break, Tanaka slowed, then stopped. I came up short. He walked over to me, rifle pointed down, eyes intense.

"I wanted to ask you about Mars," he said softly. He stood close, only a forearm of distance between us. He softened his grip on his rifle.

"I don't remember anything."

"You're sure?"

"I lost my squad, Tanaka. I would love to remember how. I can't."

"There's nobody recording. You can be honest."

"I am."

"I don't know anyone else who came back from Mars after getting captured. Thought you could speak to my theory."

"Sorry. If it's a corporate mindfuck, it's a good one."

He nodded and started walking again. His manner bothered

me. I wasn't sure what this was all about. I didn't follow him. When he noticed, he turned back.

"What's this about?" I said. "You should have had Omalas and Landon do this walk. You didn't need to. Is this just about Mars?"

"No." He came back over to me. My pulse quickened. "You going to punch me if I kiss you?"

"You outrank me. You going to pull rank if I don't?"

He laughed. "I haven't outranked you since before we dropped, Dietz."

That hit me like a gut punch. "What?"

Tanaka grunted. "Check out your display on the heads-up," he said.

I accessed the local map and opened my vitals profile. There it was: Corporal Dietz. "Huh," I said, because anything else invited more thought. More questions. I deflected. "Thought you and Jones were a thing."

Tanaka raised his brows. "You go giving one guy a hand job and everybody around here thinks it's a marriage proposal."

"Truly, romance isn't dead."

"What do you think, Corporal Dietz?"

I figured, hey, you only live once. I shrugged my rifle over my shoulder and took his face in both hands and kissed him. He was taller than me by a head; he leaned into me. The last time I touched anyone like that was Prakash, and it was for the same reasons. When death is all around you, you want to prove you're alive.

We fumbled toward a patch of grass, peeling off armor, yanking away our slicks. Fucking after you've almost died is a heady thing. Intense. You've never fucked anybody until you've done it frantically, joyfully, after surviving a slaughterhouse.

After, we lay in the grass, trying to catch our breath. The smoke had moved over the stars.

Tanaka traced my bare collarbone. "No scar," he said.

"From what?"

"Mars."

I closed my eyes, barely suppressing a groan. "Right. Which time on Mars? I get them all confused."

"When you were captured. I saw it happen."

I hitched myself up on one shoulder. "Intel told me no one saw it. Or . . ." What had they said? A Martian ambush. Smoke, an EMP, and . . . something else that made us impossible to track. "Anyway. This is the first I've heard of it."

"Nobody talks about what we saw up there, with our heads-up recording all the time. You were hit here." His fingers just beneath my collarbone again, rough and calloused. "I thought that was it for you, for our whole platoon. But they only took you and your squad."

"They shoot anyone else? How did it go down?"

"You seriously don't remember? That's not just a show for intel?"

"You wanted to fuck me to prove it?"

"No, that's . . . sorry, it wasn't that."

"I'm not slow, Tanaka."

"There were rumors about you."

"Bad luck?"

"That you were part of the Light Brigade. I just figured you were the strong, silent type."

"The Light Brigade?"

"It's a joke. Some people go through the war . . . I don't know. It does something to them. They experience things, remember things differently. It's freaky shit, honestly."

"Try living it."

"No thanks." He sat up and reached for his undershirt. "That blast took you right in the shoulder. After the smoke. You all took some fire. It was a good hit, though, Dietz."

"Maybe Martians have great health care."

"Maybe."

I rolled over and pulled on my clothes, grabbed my slick. My rifle sat within reach, safety on. I considered what would have happened if either gun went off while we fucked around, blowing us up instantly. Death might be a relief from all this madness.

"You ever beat the torture modules?" I asked, pulling on my boots.

"Take control of them, you mean?"

"Yeah, force a restart."

"No. I hated those things. Never touched them after training."

I strapped on my armor and shouldered my rifle as Tanaka got into his boots.

I said, "What if we could . . . if we could control where we dropped?"

"Us? Grunts? I don't know how the tech works. Sounds . . . doubtful."

"So does breaking apart into light."

"Fair. But if that could be done, wouldn't someone have done it already?"

I thought of all my weird drops, hopping around in time and place. "Maybe they already have."

A low rumble.

"Shit," Tanaka said.

Spotlights appeared over the open field of the park. "Evac?" I suggested. I stepped toward the clearing.

"Wait. Let's go back on the path."

We ran back the way we had come. I kept gazing into the clearing. A single ship hovered there, shining big searchlights below. In the brilliant white light near the tables, I saw Marino step out, rifle up.

"Hey, you fuck faces! The fuck you been?" Marino yelled.

A beam of energy surged from the ship, destroying the table right next to Marino, pelting him in splintered wood. He screamed and fired on the ship, backing up toward the woods as he did.

"Cover! Cover!" Tanaka shouted. "That's not one of our fighters!" He raced ahead of me.

We met the squad on the path, coming toward us. Marino limped along behind Sandoval, the right half of his face seared and peppered in splinters. A wedge of wood as big around as my thumb stuck out from his hip; another handful had made his ass into a pincushion.

"Warm fucking welcome!" Marino barked. "Who the fuck are those people?"

Omalas brought up a fist. "Listen. You feel it?"

My body trembled. I'd thought it was fear, but Landon's teeth were chattering too.

"Logistics must have found us at the same time," I said.

"Still no coms," Landon pointed out. "Can logistics get us out before this rogue ship fucks us up?"

"This is a bad place for logistics to evacuate us," Tanaka said. "We need to be in the clearing."

"Ship's moving!" Omalas called.

The ship rotated. A light exploded through the woods just behind us, leaving a precise hole burned right through the forest; the sheared branches and perfectly carved trunks still glowed red. Whoever was in that ship, they didn't want us getting beamed out of the park alive.

"Up here!" I said. The clearing Tanaka and I had found on the other side of the trees would give us a little more breathing room for a light evac. Even as I moved, my legs spasmed. Sandoval hissed and fell over. Omalas grabbed him.

The ship shot at us again; a burst of light that cracked through the woods between me and Marino. He howled and shot back at them. "You fucks!" he yelled. "You fucking red illegals! We are going to fuck you!"

We made the clearing. I fell to my knees, helmet thumping against my ass from where it hung on my belt. My whole body shook. We were easy targets here.

The rumble of the ship increased. It was coming over the tree cover to our clearing. We spread out around the clearing, over the crushed grass.

"Where's Landon?" Tanaka asked.

I turned back to the path. Landon limped along, going tree to tree. Had he fallen and hurt himself?

"Landon! Get out of the trees!" I shouted. I thought of all the bad drops, the bad retrievals. The less physical interference in our drop zones, the more likely we were to come back with all our digits, instead of half a tree rammed up our ass.

The ship droned. My teeth chattered. It was a race between the rogue ship and logistics.

"Dietz! Dietz!" Landon yelled, breaking from cover. His rifle was gone. Dirt smeared one cheek. He held out his hands.

"I've got you!" I said. I reached for him.

My body spasmed. My jaw locked. Logistics had us. They'd pull us out.

The ship appeared above us. Its searchlight hit me full in the face. I froze like an animal caught on a midnight road.

Landon flailed toward me, blotting out the light. I could feel my body begin to come apart.

We were going to make it. We were—

My fingers snatched Landon's wrist.

Landon exploded in my arms.

Blood sprayed across my body. Wrecked bits of flesh stuck to my face, my chest. A clump from his scalp dropped from my face onto my shoulder.

The ship's light pierced my vision again through the red mist of what remained of Landon's body. I shielded my eyes, and saw the ship's logo. I knew that logo pretty well. The blue sickle and thirteen stars. I'd hauled enough scrap with that logo on it to recognize it immediately as NorRus. Not a Martian ship. One of the corps. Firing on *us*.

I was next.

I broke apart.

19.

The light between things.

Why do people keep going when they know they should stop? Why do we fight for something, even when it starts to come apart?

I'm not stupid. I don't believe everything they pump us full of. I don't believe all the networks. When I came apart, covered in Landon's blood, my mind was not a blank tapestry, a blackness. Time passed there, in the space between things.

I considered the São Paulo Blink. Why did they pick São Paulo? And, why did these aliens come down from Mars but the others didn't? And, the question Tanaka had posed, which was how Mars had done something like São Paulo with tech they had never used again. Tech that looked a lot like how we traveled. But most of all—that NorRus logo on the ship that fired at us. Who were we really fighting?

They don't like us to ask questions. They try to train it out of you, not just if you're a corporate soldier, but for citizens and residents, too. The corp knows best, right?

When I was dating Vi, we talked a lot about sociology. Or, rather, she talked and I listened, because it was pretty interesting, and I'm bad at small talk. She said there's this thing called escalation of commitment. That once people have invested a certain amount of time in a project, they won't quit, even if it's no longer a good deal. Even if they're losing. War is like that. No one wants to admit they're losing. To end a war, you have to give them some way to save face, to pretend the sacrifice was worth it.

You know what you are. What you're becoming. And you can't stop it. You're committed. It doesn't matter how much people scream or how many you kill whose faces look like yours. This is your job. This is what you're trained for. It's who you are. You can't separate them.

I came back together still shaking. My rifle hung beside me. A soft wind blew, making the rifle clack against my helmet. All around me, the other soldiers looked the same, though the way they were spaced out, it didn't appear to be many of us had made it back from whatever our last drop was. Their suits were well-worn, their armor threadbare and patchy.

I pulled off my gloves and used them to wipe the blood and viscera from my face. It was sticky, still fresh.

The blue coms indicator blinked at the lower left of my eye. I brought up our platoon map, wondering where the fuck in space and time I was. Was I changing anything, jumping around like this? Or was it all decided already, like running through an immersive?

"Dietz?"

I minimized the map. Swung my head.

Jones had taken off his helmet. He stared at me. "What . . . where's—? Shit, Dietz."

I flung my arms around him. "You're alive. You goddamn bastard."

"What the hell are you covered in? What's this?" He pulled

away. His hand knocked the piece of Landon's scalp off my shoulder. "Shit, Dietz."

"Who else is alive?"

"Our squad made it." But of course that didn't mean anything. Everyone who'd been on whatever mission they were on had made it, but it clearly hadn't been the shitty Canuck mission I'd just survived.

"So evac came for you," I said. "You survived? But Landon—"

"Dietz, I think you need to see intel again."

"Fuck intel."

"Hey, First Lieutenant," Jones said over our squad channel. "We got . . . a Dietz thing again."

"Hold there," the CO said. It definitely wasn't Lieutenant V here either. What had happened to her?

A lean woman walked over to us. Two medical personnel moved ahead of her to run everyone through the post-drop check.

The woman pulled off her helmet, revealing thick, curly black hair. She had shorn her head up from the nape to the middle of her ears, making the nest of curls look like a jaunty cap. For a minute, I didn't recognize her. She peered at me.

"You told me you were Light Brigade," Andria said. "I didn't believe it."

"Andria? When . . . ?" I stopped.

She raised her brows. "Wow, Jones."

"Yeah," he said. "To be fair, that wasn't a fucking good drop for anybody. But at least it's over."

"I'd send you to intel," Andria said, "but they're pretty busy after that last run. We lost a lot of people. Come on in. Time for quarantine. I'm sure your shrink misses you."

20.

"Have we met?" the shrink said, holding out her hand.

"Yes. You probably see a lot of people like me."

"A few." She perched in the big easy chair. "Let's continue where we left off last time then. How long has it been?"

"Don't you have a record of that?"

"I'm interested in your personal recollection."

"Have you had problems with other soldiers and recall?"

She smiled thinly. "You know I can't breach the confidentiality of other soldiers. It's just a question we ask."

"Except to our superiors."

"What's that?"

"You can breach confidentiality, to our superiors."

"Does that surprise you? You understand that your contract is owned by Tene-Silvia. Do you understand the terms of that agreement?"

"I read it." That was only partly the truth. Nobody reads the full terms.

"Last time we spoke, you had some thoughts about death and mortality."

"So you do have records?"

"I understand this can be confusing."

"I don't remember talking about death."

"I see."

"I keep feeling like I've done all this before."

"Déjà vu? When you think you've seen something you've seen before. It happens a lot, though we aren't certain why it happens to some more than others. Soldiers seem to experience it even more than those with epileptic seizures. We believe it has something to do with electrical discharges in the brain that cause faults in the way you store memories. It's not that you've really seen what you believe you have. It's that your brain already wrote the memory, but your consciousness doesn't realize it yet. You *feel* like it was a long time ago, but it wasn't. Time is highly subjective. Its interpretation relies on the brain's ability to interpret and imprint memories correctly. There's a tremendous amount that can go wrong."

I told her that made sense. It's just a faulty memory. It's just being a soldier.

You see things other people aren't supposed to see.

"Can you tell me about your last drop?" she asked.

"I . . . don't remember."

"We have a record of what happened to Specialist Landon."

They would have tested whose blood and flesh I had smeared all over me.

I shivered. "When did it happen?"

"Some time ago."

I began to shake in earnest.

"Perhaps that's enough for today," she said, rising. She had known, I realized. Maybe she had always known what was happening to me. Intel knew it, too. The Light Brigade. A whispered name, one Tanaka had told me in that field. But here, now, whenever this was, it wasn't a secret.

Quarantine lasted forty-eight hours. Once again, I spent quarantine alone. I lay in the shower for over an hour, just letting the hot water beat down on me. I slept a lot. I considered tapping into an immersive, or practicing with the torture modules, but I wasn't up for it. The shrink had given me something to sleep; every time I closed my eyes, I saw Landon coming apart.

The second night, I tapped into the knu and searched for a piece of media. "You have *War of the Worlds*?" I asked the knu. It returned twenty different films, sixteen editions of a text, but no radio play. Radio *drama*. That's the word Tanaka had used.

One text said it was a history, and included a transcript. "Read it to me," I said, and the knu picked up the soothing default voice I had programmed into my heads-up, and told me a story about how little towns went crazy thinking the Martians were invading, back during the days of peak capitalism. *What makes people believe this shit?* I thought as I lay there listening. But it was easy, wasn't it, when people were isolated. When information was scarce or siloed. People would believe whatever you put in front of them, if it fit their understanding of the world. Bad Martians. Logical, well-meaning corporations.

I opened my eyes, alone in quarantine, with only these softly spoken words for company, and I understood.

When they let me out of quarantine, the shower water in our barracks was much worse, barely tepid. The food in the cafeteria was mashed tubers on toast, and that made me think of Muñoz and her shit on a shingle. Everyone I came in contact with had the dead-eyed stare of exhaustion. I was still feeling too sick to see who was alive and who was new on the platoon map, but just walking around, I saw a mix of old and new faces.

"At least it's over," Sandoval said at a nearby table. I sat by myself, nursing a very poor cup of coffee. All the food seemed watered down, strung out. The tubers tasted of sawdust, a common filler. The coffee could have been filtered through underwear.

I glanced over at Sandoval, grateful to see he was still alive. Like the others, he'd grown out his hair. Was this an Andria thing? Was she just lax about regs?

"Lot of dead Martians," his table companion said. I didn't know her. "But yeah, I guess this is probably it. At least for Martians on Earth. They'll be pissed though, won't they? Retaliate?"

"They'll see what we did," Sandoval said. "They'll know we could do it up on Mars too, if we wanted."

I trudged back to the barracks, ready for my own rack. I crawled into the bottom bunk and lay peering up at the slats of the bed above me.

My stomach twisted.

There were more marks there. Hundreds of them. I felt my dinner coming back up. I rose and put my head between my legs. When I was ready, I counted up all the lines scratched into the slats.

Nine hundred and sixty-seven marks.

I had spent nine hundred and sixty-seven days between missions here since my first drop.

What had happened during all that time? What was *going* to happen?

21.

They called it the Sick.

I woke the next morning to see my platoon crowding the screen in the rec room. Going in there, I didn't even pay attention to what the corporate spokesperson was saying, at first. I was noting who was alive.

No Prakash. I had expected that, but it still hurt. No Landon. They had confirmed that. Jones sat on the edge of a chair, legs on the back of a couch. Omalas stood with arms folded, closest to the screen. I recognized Deathless, though she was thinner than I remembered, her face little more than skin stretched over bone. She leaned in a doorway, sucking at a flameless cigarette. I had already seen Sandoval, and there was Leichtner, chewing on her thumbnail at the back.

No Marino.

I wondered when the war had gotten him. Maybe he had gone AWOL. I hoped.

Tanaka? I scanned the group, but didn't see him. The rest were new faces, about twenty of them. Way too many new faces.

I tuned in to the corporate spokesperson then. She stood in front of an imbedded press pool, all hand-selected people with approved questions.

"Can you tell us where the virus originated?" one of the reporters asked.

"We cannot confirm it's a virus," the spokesperson said, "but we believe it is Martian in origin. It originated in Canuck, after our great victory there."

"The war was supposed to be over. Is this a new front?"

"The war is over," the spokesperson said. "Our final solution initiative was successful. Mars has gone dark again. This new development is one we expect to eradicate quickly. A virus is not a war. We have contained and quarantined those affected. We expect a quick resolution."

"How can citizens and residents protect themselves?"

"We urge anyone with flu-like symptoms to report to the nearest corporate wellness center. We are working diligently on a vaccine and expect it to be in trials very soon. But again—if you do not present yourself to the wellness center, we cannot treat you. Please speak to your friends, your neighbors, your coworkers, and urge them to come in. If they are reluctant, contact your local corporate security liaison."

I kept to the back of the room, in the doorway. The war was supposed to be over? I thought of those nine hundred and sixty-seven marks. That was a lot of living that I couldn't remember.

"Dietz?"

I turned into the hall.

It was Tanaka.

I let out my breath. Didn't realize I'd been holding it.

"I listened to *War of the Worlds*," I blurted, like an idiot. It had been, what, years since we had that conversation. But for me . . . three days ago.

"It's you," he said.

"Isn't it always me?"

"No. You want to get out of here? Go for a walk?"

"What's happened?" I asked as I followed him down the hallway. "Since . . . Landon."

"You just came back from the grinder. The fire. They said you had his blood all over you."

"Yeah."

He stared at me; I wanted warmth, but there was something fearful in him, remote. I remembered he had a missing wife, children. He would want to go back to his children, and keep looking for his wife. The war was over. At least now I knew how it ended.

"You have to tell them next time you drop," he said. "Tell them what's going on here."

"The war's over. There's no next drop . . . right?"

His gaze moved over me, to the screen. "You still have gaps in your memory?"

"Yeah."

"Then you still have drops."

"Shit."

"Shit is right. I always check with you, see what's coming next. You told me how bad this gets."

"How bad what gets?"

He nodded at the screen. "The Sick."

"How bad does it get?"

"Bad. You're on the right track with the torture modules. That's what you wanted me to say to you. To keep going. That maybe you could . . . change this."

"What else?"

"That's . . . it." It wasn't it; I could see it in his face, but I let it lie. Who really wants to know their future? I didn't like the one I was seeing.

I wondered why we weren't being hauled away by intelligence, the both of us.

"We still being recorded?"

"Yeah," he said. "Just . . . not monitored as much. After the Dark, we started running out of people. Lots of intelligence got reassigned from babysitting us to restoring everyone lost. Still, better to talk to you now, when they're monitoring all of us, seeing our reaction to this."

"Do I want to know what the Dark is? Was?"

"We lost coms."

"Like in the last . . . like in Canuck?"

"Something like that. All over, though."

"Mars?"

"That's what they say." He no longer looked at me, but at the screen. "I didn't believe you. About all this."

"I wouldn't have believed me either. Figured everyone thought I was nuts."

"Hey, Dietz!" It was Andria, our new CO, coming down the hall.

"Sir," I said.

I broke away from Tanaka, putting some distance between us. I wanted to hug her. Wondered how long she'd been CO. What had happened to Lieutenant V?

"My office," Andria said.

I followed after her. We didn't say anything as we walked down the hall. She turned into the old CO's office. It looked about the same. Maybe there were more scratches on the table. Worn armrests. The only new addition was a large wooden globe in the far corner, about chest height.

She shut the door. Gestured to the chair. "At ease. Just us. Want a drink?"

"Yes." I sat.

She opened the top of the globe with her left hand, the one that had been rebuilt, revealing a selection of hard liquor. Her curls were twisted back with a hair band, making a little tail at the end. I scrutinized her face. We had joined up at eighteen. We weren't much older than that, were we? Twenty-one, twenty-two at most? Unless those marks on my bunk were wrong. Shit, could we have been deployed for long periods that I'd lost track of?

"This is going to sound stupid," I said.

"War is shit. Vodka?"

Vodka? When had Andria started drinking?

"I know we've talked before."

"It's all right." She pulled something from her pocket and set it on the middle of the table. A pocket watch. The little flicker of my heads-up display went out. "That's a scrambler," she said. "We've got privacy as long as that's on."

"When did you get these?"

"I heard about it from you. Corp owns everything, but we pass stuff around. I asked about it. I know you'll ask some of the same questions again. It's all right."

I'd assumed it was Mars that cut off coms back in Canuck. But this was our tech. Corp tech. What one corp had, most corps had: corporate espionage, buying out contracts on individual assets—it could have been any one of the corps that blinded us. It could have been Teni.

"I didn't get kicked out, when you all figured I was . . . doing this?"

"The shrink has known from the start. It's why they're here. Intel . . . well, they believed what most of the Light Brigade folks like you said, at first. Some remembered stuff, some didn't."

"The ones who remembered went missing. They hauled them away."

"Yeah, early in the war."

"Not anymore?"

"Not since you told us about the Dark."

"Did it help?"

"Not really. But . . . some shit went down. You weren't the only one telling them about it. It helped us figure out that mission we just came back from, which was a shit show. But . . . maybe it's over? I don't know. Maybe it just keeps going."

"How many more are like me?"

"I've met three. You, a kid called Rache, and Rubem. You remember Rube?"

"He still alive?"

"No." She handed me a vodka. She'd filled the glass with it. I hadn't eaten since breakfast and it was already past lunchtime. I tried to gauge how she was feeling about Rubem being dead, but her face was a blank.

"I know what it's like to lose somebody close." I drank half the glass in one go and set the rest on the table. The burning in my stomach felt good.

"It's war," Andria said. She drained two thirds of hers. Kept the glass in her hand.

The warmth of the vodka began to ease the tightness and anxiety in my body. I opened myself to it, let it take me down, down, away. Liquor made the edges of life bearable.

"I think Muñoz had weird jumps too," I said. "Jones told me about it later."

"Muñoz . . . from your first squad."

"Yeah."

"Weird that these are all people you knew."

"You and I just know people in common. I'm sure there are other people. Other teams."

"I've talked to other COs. Most people who have bad drops die. Go mad, coming back. Or come together in the ground, or inside some wall, raving about where they've been. And you're the only one who's jumping around that's not only lucid on coming back, but who's still alive here at what should be the end of the war."

"You don't think it's the end?"

"I haven't gotten this far by blindly believing the corporate line. Maybe at first . . . you know, we signed up for one another. You, me, Rubem . . . Shit, did you know Garcia and Orville dropped out? Marseille died on her first drop. Timon and I kept in touch until the Dark. He was in Beijing. Poor bastard."

"We're it."

"Yeah. You sign up to fight a war. You keep fighting the war for the people next to you. Not the corp."

"You said I couldn't change anything. If that's true, what's the point of all this? Breaking apart? Seeing a future you can't change?"

She shrugged. "I'm not in logistics. Just glad they haven't disappeared you. Me, Jones, Tanaka . . . took a lot of work to get you this far."

"Maybe it'd be better if I disappeared."

She sipped her drink. "You helped wake me up, Dietz. Helped me see what the fuck is going on. And you're a good soldier."

I snorted. My hand shook as I drained my glass. "Why did you ask me in here?"

"Because I want to help you beat the torture modules."

"You've done it?"

"Yes. You're going to hate it."

"I feel like I've been living one."

"I get that. This thing that's been unleashed, this . . . virus. You told me that when it hits, the war isn't over. It's just the endgame. If that's true, we'll have some time. Nobody's getting sent home."

"Does anyone ever get sent home?" I asked, thinking of Tanaka. "Anybody get to really leave the war?"

She shook her head. "You wouldn't tell me."

22.

Reality is a constructed thing.

Imagine us all standing in a circle, trying to describe an object to one another, and as we agree on its characteristics, the thing at the center of our circle begins to take form. That's how we create reality. We agree on its rules. Its shape. Different cultures have created different realities just by all agreeing about the thing they described.

The first time I understood that my reality wasn't the same as someone else's was when my brother brought home a beige coat. We were residents already. My father had been taken away again, leaving the two of us there with our dying mother. She spent most of her time by then gazing at the world through a morphine haze.

"Where'd you get that coat?" I asked. The fabric was nice, clean.

"Bought it," Tomás said. He was twelve, shooting up like a broad tree already. He must have been well over eighty kilos, and a hand taller than me. No one guessed he was so young.

"With what? What do you need some ugly brown coat for?"

"It's green."

"It's not." I picked it up. Shook it at him. "It's tan."

"It has a green tint."

"Are you high on something?"

He snatched the coat away from me. "Fuck you."

I slapped him.

He was big, but he didn't slap me back. Just gazed at the floor. My cheeks burned. I felt bad. But it was just the two of us; I was older, I was in charge of him. He needed to respect me.

His eyes filled.

"Sorry," I said. "You just . . . you shouldn't talk to people that way."

He picked up his coat and went to his room and quietly shut the door. I felt like an asshole. What kind of person was I, to treat a kid like that?

I knocked on his door. "Tomás? I'm sorry. I'm a shit." I opened the door.

He sat on the edge of the bed, the coat in his lap, crying.

"Hey, I'm sorry," I said.

"I stole it. The coat. I'm sorry."

"Shit. Did anyone see you?" But that was a dumb question. If anyone had seen him, there'd be corporate security busting down our door. Our ghoul was showing. Teni would punish us severely for it. "They expect us to steal and lie and cheat. We can't be like that."

He shook his head. "I just wanted it. It was so nice. I've never seen anything so nice."

"Papa will come back." I sat next to him. Put my arm around him. He leaned in to me and sobbed. His hair needed a wash. His shirt had a big tear along the hem that needed to be mended. Residents had some rights, mostly the right to work, but we had little safety net.

Our mother died three days later. They released our father for the funeral. My brother wore his stolen coat, and I stood next to him, holding his hand.

We embraced our father. He had lost more weight. He took the cuff of Tomás's coat in his fingers and smiled and said, "That's a lovely green coat."

I blinked at him. Peered at the coat. Still beige, to me. I slowly pivoted, gazing at the walls of the little mourning room we had been assigned at the crematorium. White roses. Fake gilt on the picture frames. The ubiquitous eyes of the cameras. What else did I see differently from everyone else?

"Papa," Tomás said, "when are you coming home?"

It was only the three of us in the room. Two corporate security techs waited for my father outside, to escort him back to . . . wherever he was being held.

"Soon," my father said. "Soon."

It was one of his many lies.

We never saw him again.

What I learned, as I looked back on those times, was that the lies are what sustained us. The lies kept us going. Gave us hope. Without lies we have to face the truth long before we are ready for it.

Long before we are prepared to fight it.

23.

I hung at the center of the interrogation room. The chains bit into my wrists. Left red welts. My toes just touched the ground. The stone walls were bare; the room looked like something out of a medieval dungeon.

Andria's avatar stood at the big wooden table in front of me, surveying the surroundings. "You and your grimy medieval settings!" she said. "Why do you always choose these?"

Always? I thought. *How would she know?*

"I was thinking of, like, *The Count of Monte Cristo*."

"Shit, you have been spending a lot of time catching up on media, haven't you?"

"I ran through a game based on it," I said. I didn't tell her I'd played paladin. She knew that already.

"Ah shit. Yeah, I remember that."

"You ready?"

"No. I fucking hate these."

"Well, I'm here. You concentrate on me. You listen to me. You can't kill your way out of the modules."

"How did you beat them?"

"I took control of the narrative."

Four interrogators in black armor moved through her and into the room. They bore shock sticks, like the last time.

"I turned up the real factor," she said. "You had it on easy mode."

"Andria!"

The first hit burned my right leg. Another hit my chest. They went at me fast and furious then. I felt every blow.

"Stop!" I yelled.

"I'm not doing it. It's your construct."

I had let her program the safe word that would turn off the program. I already regretted it.

"You're tougher than a construct," Andria said. "Listen to my voice. Just my voice. I'm going to move you through this."

The hits kept coming. I gritted my teeth and stared at their identical faces. Steely, impersonal; they sweated, and their hair was slick. The stink of sweat and damp mildew.

"Andria—"

"None of this is real," Andria said. She began to move around me. "This reality, more than even the one we see, is a complete fabrication. It exists in your mind. Like pain. Like pleasure. We are all of us just beasts, you know. Reacting to stimuli. That's all we're doing here. Pinging those parts of your mind that respond to inputs. You're complicit in your own torture, here."

"It comes from outside. It's made by the software!"

"It's a trick. It doesn't work unless you accept it."

"I don't accept it! So why are you all still here?"

I thought of my father. Had they done this to him? Put him in a torture module? Or had they done it for real?

"What are you afraid of, Dietz?"

"Nothing."

"Dietz."

"Dying. Maybe. I don't . . . make them stop!"

"You make them stop, paladin. What did I always play?"

"Tank. You always took the hits."

One of the men hit me across the face. I reeled. The chains bit into my wrists. I drooled. Too much real for me. Too much. I saw Landon blowing apart again. Prakash's arm. Tanaka tracing my collarbone, asking about a missing scar. My mother eating that bird in three quick bites.

"It's all real," I said. "That's the—"

"You're made of light," Andria said. "We're all made of light, did you know that? We are mostly empty space. They shake those atoms apart when they deploy us. Makes it easier for us to move through the world. We disintegrate and come together again."

A shock to my kidneys. I screamed. A stick across my face. One of the men yanked at the chain, heaving me completely off the floor. I dangled.

"Where do you want to be?" Andria said.

"São Paulo."

The construct shifted. Stuttered, like interference. I caught a glimpse of a smoggy yellow sky.

"Home?" Andria said.

Life was simpler in the labor camps, or maybe it just felt that way because I was so young. The whole world seems simple when you're a kid. Food, shelter, family. Try not to die of some infection, or overheat during the hot, dry summers. Hard, yeah, and short. But you live, you live—you live for that day. No other day. There's no future.

No future.

I gazed at the ceiling, past my chafed, bleeding wrists. Above me, a jagged tear in the fabric of the construct. Some blip. Programming error. We are all made of atoms. Pieces of us flung around the universe at the will of the corporations.

The hits still rained down. I closed my eyes. Concentrated

on Andria's voice.

"We are all of us just meat," she said. "You can control what you react to and what you don't. You can change how you react to pain. Pain is simply a message, a ping on your heads-up. Acknowledge it and move on to the problem. What a lot of people don't get about these modules is that half the experience relies on you believing in it. The more you believe, the more intense it is. The more real it becomes. People do get lost here. I've seen that. But because half of this reality is a reality you construct, you can break it. Break your chains, Dietz."

I kicked out at my captors, but my feet went right through them. Why? Why did their blows land and mine didn't?

I am the construct.

I am creating half of this.

I took a deep breath. Focused again on Andria. A single, real thing: her voice.

I lashed out. My foot connected with one of the interrogators. He fell back, nose bloodied.

Not a real nose, I reminded myself. This is my world. My construct.

An alarm sounded.

"What's that?" I said.

Andria gazed at the ceiling. "Shit. Proximity alarm. End construct. Safe word: Rubem."

The environment fell away. I gasped. I came to on the reclining seat in the game lounge. An alarm blared.

Andria lay on the seat next to me. She opened her eyes and peeled off her restraints.

Boots sounded in the hall outside. Two other soldiers from my platoon were in the room; Sandoval and a woman I didn't know yet. They both ran out into the hallway.

Andria's left eye lit up with something from her display.

"What is it?" I said.

"Report to the parade ground. We've got some company from corporate."

24.

The drop ships arrived just as I got into formation next to Jones. The air was hot and muggy, unbearable if not for our slicks. The whole of Dog Company came out to greet the ships, all three platoons. Our company captain came out front and inspected our platoons. I knew her immediately: Lieutenant V.

She wasn't dead. Just promoted. Andria couldn't have just told me that? But of course, I hadn't asked. I'd feared the worst when I saw that Andria had taken Lieutenant V's place.

The drop ships vomited their contents: two dozen black-clad Corporate Intellectual Property enforcers. They scouted the area, eyes flickering as they scanned us. Seemingly satisfied, they got in formation near the lead ship. The front opened and two more suited techs walked out. Behind them . . .

I saw the red boots first. Then the white trousers. The hem of the white coat.

The tall, lean woman wearing them came into full view. I knew her face instantly, though she was older, thinner, just like the rest of us. I had not noticed her eyes, back then. I'd spent a lot of our meeting on the floor while she interrogated my father and then dragged him away. Her eyes were black. Her hair now boasted silvery streaks of gray, as if someone had combed through it with tinsel. She held her hands behind her back. Her gaze scanned the crowd. I turned slightly away; like the BLM agents, she would have facial recognition integrated with her display.

Lieutenant V went to meet her. Held out a hand. The woman didn't take it. Said something long and windy instead. I could imagine it had something to do with some dusty bit of history that made her feel like she was smarter than the rest of us. Fuck her.

They spoke for a few minutes more, then headed inside. When they were well gone, the platoon COs got word that we were dismissed, and back inside we all went.

What was that display for? Why was this woman coming in to see the troops?

A message pinged in my heads-up display.

Andria, saying, "Company captain wants you and me present in the conference room. Bring your party shoes."

I started a message back, telling her that was a bad idea. But what did I know? I didn't even know what had been going on the last nine hundred plus days. Shit.

I left the parade ground and got waved into the CO wing. I raised my hand to knock on the conference door, but Andria was already there. She steered me to the observation room adjacent. Put her fingers to lips. Raised her pocket watch.

"We've got an update," she said, bringing me into the dark little room. We stood behind a transparent LED film, giving us a view inside while displaying a generic projection to those in the room. On the other side: the woman in white and her IP techs, Lieutenant V, and the captains from the other two companies. I recognized the major general of the brigade,

Major Stakeley; and Colonel Jemison of the Regiment; as well as Lieutenant Colonel Bowman of the battalion.

Andria put her pocket watch on the desk in front of the mirror.

"What's going on?" I whispered. No idea why I whispered. They all just felt too close, I guess.

"We're getting briefed. Corporate said it was too sensitive to do over coms."

"Real information? How are we—"

"Captain V. Whatever you said to her after you came back from that burning Canuck mission, you convinced her we're fucked. She wants you to take this back with you, whatever they give us, when you drop back. Light Brigade shit."

I sure hoped I could come up with something witty by then to convince them all this was real. The yawning promise of those nine hundred and some days overwhelmed me again. I didn't want to keep going. I wanted to end the war here with the rest of them.

"You've been briefed on the . . . incident?" asked one of the men dressed in black.

I had a moment of dissonance as the woman in white leaned back in her chair. Was he in charge? Had they hustled him in under cover? Who was he? The face was vaguely familiar.

"We have six divisions in quarantine," he said. "Colonel Jemison, what's your status here?"

"Isla Riesco is well isolated." Jemison was a tall, lanky woman, another one of the ageless COs. I noticed the top brass here still had some meat on their bones. More than we did, anyway. "Or, we were, until you announced yourselves."

"We're clean," he said. "The executive suite and the board are also isolated. I assume the other corps have done the same. Our intel is spotty."

"This is a bigger deal than your mother let on," said Jemison.

His mother. The CEO? Not the CEO of Teni. She had no family. The CEO of some other corp. Was this a takeover?

"Yes," he said. "Captain Norberg?"

The woman in white said, "We suspect that our . . . final solution may have let loose a violent pathogen."

"Christ," Jemison muttered.

Another man, the head of the regiment, spoke up. "How violent are we talking about?"

Norberg shrugged. "We've seen a hundred percent casualty rate. It's a lovely little thing, tailored perfectly to act quickly, but not too quickly. While your troops may be quarantined now, they were there on the mission. It's quite possible you're already infected."

"Why are you here then?" Jemison demanded. "You have a death wish?"

Norberg laughed.

"Tell them," the man said.

"We've come from Saint Petersburg," Norberg said. "They've synthesized a vaccine. We'd like to inoculate your people."

"You synthesized a vaccine in less than a week?" Jemison asked.

The man said, "The only safe place in Evecom right now is Saint Petersburg. They've barricaded and quarantined the entire city. We had an idea of what was coming."

"And how did you know that?" Jemison snapped.

"That's not important," he said, dismissively. "What's key is having soldiers who can move through this thing before it mutates."

"How fast is it mutating?" Jemison said.

"It's killing at an unprecedented rate," the man admitted. "It may have already mutated beyond what we can cure with this vaccine. But it may stave off the worst of the symptoms. In tests, it's improved the survival rate by fifty percent."

"Fuck me," said the head of the regiment.

"How many of us are still in play?" Jemison said. "I want the real intel. Not the bullshit."

"You're answering to Evecom right now," the man said. "The merger with Tene-Silvia just went through. We'll be announcing our rebranding plans shortly."

"And with Masukisan and NorRus down," said Jemison, "that leaves us with three corps. And a defeated Mars. If we can survive."

"Consolidation was always the endgame," Norberg explained. "Losses were expected."

"Whose virus is it?" Jemison asked. "Evecom's? I don't recognize the son of Evecom's CEO giving us orders. Not until I hear it from Tene-Silvia's chief executive of war."

"War is hell," Norberg said.

"What do I tell my soldiers?" the head of the regiment asked. "We say you've got some wonder drug?"

"You tell them we are protecting them," the man said. "Just like always. They will line up and get their shots and head back out there. This isn't over."

"Mars is defeated," Jemison reminded him.

"Nobody gives a shit about Mars," the man said. "Mars is the past. The moon is the past. We're looking outward. The belt. Jupiter. Pluto. The goddamn Andromeda Galaxy. Our future is bigger than this system and the cold rocks we call neighbors. But we aren't going to get there unless we're united."

"How you expect to get there with a planet full of dead people?" Captain V asked.

All gazes turned to her. Jemison guffawed.

"You can take it up with the chief executive of war," the man said. "She reports directly to the CEO."

"Be glad we're offering a vaccine," Norberg quipped. "The Eighty-Second and Seventy-Ninth divisions got sent in to quiet down the riots in Buenos Aires and Bogotá without it. They should all be dead in another seventeen hours."

"Why aren't we showing symptoms yet?" Jemison asked.

The man shrugged. "I said we suspected you were exposed. It's entirely possible you weren't, or that you were infected with the original strain, which takes longer to present itself. I'm offering you the vaccine."

I watched the spectacle play out through the film, chewing on my fingernail. I wondered how much of the world was really left out there. In that moment I wanted nothing more than to drop . . . someplace else.

The man stood. "Your choice,"

"Our choice?" Jemison said. "This isn't a choice."

"I'm not endorsed by the board yet, I understand," he said. "I came here to try to help ahead of the merger. So much can get lost in all the red tape. But I saw no need to hold the vaccine until all the paperwork was filed. I have good intentions."

"You think he's consolidating power?" Andria asked me. "Getting on our good side so he can use us to overthrow his mom during the mess of the merger?"

"I'm worried she's already dead," I admitted. "I'm worried everything's dead." I wanted to ask about the CEO of Teni and what happened to her.

"We fucking murdered ourselves," Andria muttered. "They threw us up north and obliterated all those Martian refugees, for what? Some family game these shitheads are playing."

"We take our orders from the chief executive of war," Jemison said. "You have her call us up with an order, and we'll carry it out. You desk jockeys in your pretty little suits think this is all some power grab. These are my soldiers' lives. I will obey the chain of command. Who the fuck do you think you are, coming in here and feeding us some story, trotting along that little silver knife Norberg with you? You think we don't know who she is?"

"I counted on you knowing who she is," he said.

Jemison said, "We still talk about you at the academy, Norberg."

"My record still stands, then."

"You beat the torture mods in thirteen seconds," Jemison said.

"I trained in the real thing." Norberg waved her hand as if dispelling a particularly annoying fly. "The mods aren't nearly as effective as the real thing."

"And you're here telling me to shoot up my soldiers at this kid's word?" Major Stakeley said. "I don't believe either one of you. I've seen too many like you both. Greedy and power hungry, letting others do your dirty work. Thinking you're too smart for the rest of us. I'm done with this meeting. I'll await orders from the appropriate channels."

As he stood, Norberg said, "Have you ever experienced a coup, Major Stakeley?"

"Not in my lifetime," he said. "I want to keep it that way."

"But you had to learn about them, of course," Norberg said. "In officer training. You had to learn about those grand old battles. Tactics and logistics. That part of warcraft always appealed to me. Such things happen slowly . . . and then all at once. The ground must be carefully prepared, often for generations. Corporations had been chipping away at the authority of governments for a century before the Seed Wars. They experimented with company towns, and then outrageous benefits for employees. As health care became more expensive, one didn't even have to offer private transport and free meals. Simply helping pay the cost to cure grandma's cancer was enough to ensure blind obedience. That's how you keep them loyal. Foster distrust in the democratic governments that are actually accountable to them. Show them that only the corporations can save them from themselves. You still see this war as one of bullets and bombs, but the rise and fall of Mars was engineered by intelligence forces like mine. Why did your grunts sign up to fight this war? Because of the moon? Because of the Blink? If you think I can't engineer a story to make them turn on you the way I fostered a story to get them to throw themselves into war, you're more delusional than even I assumed."

"I will wait on word from the CEO," Major Stakeley repeated.

"You'll be waiting a long time," the man said. "She's dead. So is Evecom's CEO. The virus took out most of the executive suite."

"Who the fuck is in charge, then?" Jemison asked.

The man leaned forward. "That is an interesting question, isn't it?"

"Goddammit," Stakeley said.

I glanced at Andria. "Can they confirm anything that guy's saying?"

"No. Media is his, probably, if what he says about the CEO is true. Everything's dark. There are some back channels. . . . I've been hearing rumors from people on the ground, but I don't know anybody high enough up."

"They don't have the staff to monitor us," I said. "That's why everyone's so lax."

"Been that way awhile."

"So he could be right, about leadership? That there's a power upset because of the merger?"

"That's the shit thing about systems. They get so ingrained . . . they can putter on awhile longer, even when you chop the head off. You don't know you're dead until six more steps down the road."

Norberg stood. I gazed back at her. Remembered how she had stood over my father. "My advice is to take the vaccine," she said. "You don't know what's going to happen to you otherwise."

"I need to go," the man said, pushing back his chair. "I have some things to put together in Saint Petersburg. I anticipate your response to my offer. We'll be at the Taleon Imperial. Norberg?"

She inclined her head. His bodyguards went ahead of him, all dressed like him; same haircuts, his same age. It was a pretty smart ploy, I thought, traveling like that. I wondered how many people wanted him dead.

The whole corp was falling apart. Andria looked at me expectantly.

"What?" I said.

"You think you can fix it?"

"Fix what?"

"I don't know . . . when you drop again, maybe? If you know this is going to happen, you could prevent us from going, right? The final solution? Then maybe this virus—"

"I'm one person. And how do we know anything that guy said is true?" I still had no idea what his name was. I didn't keep track of politics; the son of the CEO? I had no idea.

"The captain said—"

"What does the captain know? Our friends are dead. Landon blew apart in my goddamn arms. Blew apart! Prakash . . . shit. I still haven't lived through the aftermath of that, but I see her every fucking time I close my eyes. And—"

"You think you are the only one with ghosts, Dietz?"

The door opened. I started.

Captain V stood in the threshold, regarding us. "Well?"

"Fuck!" I said. "What did I tell you? Why did you have me listen in on this? I'm nobody. I'm a grunt, and I'm fucking nuts. Just like you said I would be."

She regarded me quietly. Waited until I was done. Still seething, I stood and saluted her. "Sorry, sir."

"You have one more drop left in you, Dietz?" she asked.

"No."

"Me neither. Go line up for your shot."

"We're doing it, then? Getting vaccinated? Working for this

guy?"

"We're soldiers without a corp, Dietz," Captain V said. "Our options are limited."

They had us line up outside the medical bay. Follow orders. Take your medicine. I got my injection and went back out into the hall outside the medical bay. From the windows there I watched the drop ships take off. I hoped that was the last I'd ever see of Norberg. But knowing my luck, well . . .

As the ships moved over the jungle, I heard a commotion from down the corridor. The cafeteria. Loud voices. Gunshots. Not our pulse rifle blasts. Those sounded altogether different: a wet punch, not a bang.

I tensed. We didn't go around the base armed. Our weapons were stowed in lockers between shooting drills and drops.

"What is that?" asked the kid just ahead of me. My heads-up said her name was Tau.

"Not sure." I shifted my weight so I stood between her and the door into our corridor. Shouts. Boots on linoleum.

The line of soldiers waiting outside the med center for the inoculations started to get antsy.

Tau tried to push past me, to the door.

"Wait," I said.

"The fuck should I—"

The door burst open. A soldier slammed onto the floor, her head busted in.

I saw Andria coming in behind her, running full tilt.

"What's going on?" I said.

"Get out!" Andria yelled. "Get out! Go drop!" She threw something at me.

Her pocket watch slithered across the floor. I snatched it up. Raised my head.

Figures behind her. A huffing sigh. A wet punch.

She blew apart.

Blood spattered the hallway. I turned, pushing Tau ahead of me, slipping in Andria's blood, smearing my handprints all over the walls as I wheeled around the bend in the corridor.

A few soldiers stayed on, dumbstruck.

I stuffed the pocket watch into my trousers and came into the cafeteria just as someone on the other side opened fire.

Sandoval ran past me. "What's—," I began.

"Major Stakeley is staging a goddamn coup," Sandoval said, and kept running. He was headed to the rifle lockers.

Shit.

I ran to the barracks, taking a longer route that I hoped would avoid most people. I ducked into a bathroom as a squad of bloody armed soldiers went past. Were they my platoon? No faces I recognized, but that didn't mean anything. When we had lined up to greet the drop ships, I barely knew anyone.

I crouched and pressed open the door to the barracks just enough to get a look at it. A bunch of soldiers were funneling out through the back door. I recognized Jones, holding it open for them.

"Jones!" I said.

He waved at me. "Get over here!"

I took a quick look around, verifying I couldn't see anyone with a gun.

"Where are you going?" I asked.

"Come with me." Hand out. Blood on his fingers.

"What's—"

"I'll take out your tracker. We took out ours. Stakeley's been planning this since the Dark. We knew it'd give us cover. Take out your heads-up and come with us. My moms will—"

"Your moms work in intelligence!"

"There's no Teni anymore. We'll make something new."

Screams behind me. His gaze over my shoulder. I stared beyond him, through the open door, across the parade ground, to the woods. I remembered how we had trekked through the forest together with nothing but a map and a compass and live rounds. I wondered if it was him who shot Grandma that day. Wondered if Muñoz's team shot first. Wondered if any of it mattered at all, after everything we'd been through.

"I can't, Jones."

"Why, we—"

"I have to drop again."

"You're fucking insane."

"Yeah." I hugged him, fast and close. "Go."

He ran. I watched until he met the rest of the little group; I recognized Leichtner. They had torn down the broken tangle of the perimeter fence. Jones scrambled over and joined them. Sounds of gunfire, inside and out. But he kept moving. Kept moving. Disappeared into the jungle.

It itched between my shoulder blades, the place where I'd gotten my own tracker. They had pulled out one another's trackers, thrown off their displays, like slaves throwing off their shackles. Is that what we were? No, we had choices. We had pay. No one owned us, not really. Right? Our choices were limited here, though, just as they always were. They hadn't been inoculated. There had been no time. They were running off into the jungle, but they'd be killed by that virus, the corporate nightmare we'd unleashed. Our fate. Their fate. The fate of this whole stupid world.

When did it start?

It started with the Blink.

"Hands up!"

I lifted my hands. Did not otherwise move.

"Turn."

I turned.

It was Tanaka. He pointed a pulse rifle at me.

"You with us?" he said.

I wanted to punch him. Scream at him. Because in that moment I had no idea who "us" was.

"I'm here to fight the bad guys," I said.

"Then you're with us," he said, and marched me to the cafeteria with the others.

25.

anaka was promoted to platoon leader, which came with another bump in rank.

"You want my old squad, Dietz?" he said. "You're a corporal. You should be a leader by now."

"Leader of what?" I said, because there weren't many of us left.

But the corp—whatever corp we were now—still had a use for us.

We got to round up the bodies. Shoot people who left quarantine. Hunt down deserters. I spent six weeks driving truckloads of the dead out of Fortaleza to a mass grave site. The smell was overpowering. The work, numbing. The flesh comes right off the bones when a body has gotten ripe enough. The scalp slides away from the skull.

I remember baby shoes and tattered men's ties. I remember how there weren't enough medical staff to help civilians with gangrene. We took off their limbs: arms and legs. You ever carried a limb? It's like carrying a baby. Hunk of dead weight, still warm.

I was standing with Omalas at an all-night takeout diner, picking through the canned goods in the back to feed our squad when the news came on a flickering LED film in the main dining area. A lot of the power still worked in the places the military went. Our engineering corps made it a priority.

"Thank you for your patience, TenisanaCom," the company spokesperson said. It was just her up there, a young kid, maybe twenty—shit, I thought, what am *I*, twenty-two?—and I felt sorry for her. Thin hands folded on the table in front of her. Dark hair swept back from a severe face. She wore makeup, but I saw the telltale raw pink patches on her throat and wrists: one of the early signs of the illness we called the Martian pox, though by then most of us doubted there was anything Martian about it.

"The fortitude you have all shown is truly extraordinary," the spokesperson said.

Outside, a tank rolled past. The spotters up top wore night vision goggles and gas masks. A few of the locals blamed the military for the sickness—they were probably right—and had been attacking us with Molotov cocktails and homemade pepper spray.

The bubbly spokesperson continued, "Our CEO, Papa Martin, assures you that our liberation is nearly at hand. A violent Martian traitor has been arrested in Saint Petersburg. We will have answers soon."

"Bet that Martian is glad to hear that," Omalas said. She picked at her teeth.

"You like spiced cabbage?" I held up a can of it from the cupboard.

"Only with vodka."

I nodded and added the can to my pack. Anything in a can was bound to taste better than MREs. I was so goddamn sick of MREs.

"When did this go wrong?" Omalas asked, gazing at the

screen.

The spokesperson gave a weather report, like anyone cared. "And now," the woman chirped, "we have more soothing programming from our cultural affairs committee."

Our new corporate logo filled the screen.

"It was always bad," I said. "That's what I'm just getting, you know? Feels like something changed but it didn't. It was always rotten. Just took a long time to see."

"Could it have gone another way?" She scratched at something on her arm.

"Don't know."

I grabbed two more cans of beets and a jar of cocktail olives. I hefted the pack and came over to her. "Anybody out there?" I asked. The tank rumbled in the distance.

"No."

I saw the raised pale patch on her dark skin, then; the flaking wound. We had all been inoculated by then, but the virus was mutating rapidly. Like the flu, different strains of it were moving through population centers, sometimes taking out every last person, sometimes leaving half, sometimes only taking the old and the young. Then it would mutate again, and the cycle continued.

She met my look. Shrugged. "Irony, yes?"

"None of this was our fault. Why are we suffering for it?"

"We pay for the sins of those that came before."

"That's bullshit."

We made our way to the truck. I'd parked in the back. There were no bodies in the truck bed, but the smell still permeated everything. I drove us to the rec hall we were using as a base of operations. I needed a shower, even knowing the smell wasn't going to come off.

Tanaka met us as we got waved in through the makeshift gates.

"What's going on?" I asked. He had his rifle out.

"Captain V needs volunteers for a drop," he said.

"Nobody's dropped since—"

"We got clearance for a drop." He met my look. We hadn't spoken since the coup, not really. I didn't trust him any more than I trusted myself at this point.

"Where?"

"Captain Norberg needs backup for a project," Tanaka said. I gazed at him, trying to keep my expression neutral. "There's been some chatter. She thinks there may be a Masukisan squad trying to infiltrate one of her interrogation sites. You up for it?"

"You're sending *me*?"

"Who else would I send, Dietz?"

I noticed, then, that he had the marks on his throat too. He wiped his nose on his sleeve. Made a little bloody smear.

The end of all things, I thought. When was there going to be a mutation that took me out, too?

"I'm sending you down with a squad Norberg picked. Most of ours are in quarantine."

"Whole world's in quarantine," I muttered.

"Sandoval won't last the night," Tanaka said.

I had no idea what to say to that, so I said, "Can I eat first?"

"Think you'll come back?"

"Here? I don't know."

What would Andria tell me to do? Take control of the construct. Might as well tell me to just take control of the world. The world didn't work that way.

"Then eat first."

I slid out of the truck and went to the makeshift kitchen with my canned goods. Laid them out for the kid in charge of rations. He awarded me a can of beets for my troubles. Even opened it for me.

"You're a doll," I said, and sat up next to the barred window with a plastic fork jammed into my can of winnings. I saw things when we broke apart. Heard things. I remembered breaking up over the Cape, the long serpentine tail of the mountains there. I closed my eyes. Sipped at the beet juice.

"You all right?" Tanaka asked.

I didn't turn. Watched his reflection in the window. "No," I said. "None of us is all right." I stabbed a beet.

"I'm not the bad guy."

"No. We all are."

"I don't think that's true."

"Whatever helps you sleep."

We hadn't been stationed in our barracks for a long time. I'd lost count of the days. No way to tally them up on the bed frame. I could have cut my arm or something, but I was worried about infection. Medicine had become harder to come by, including antibiotics. I had visions of surviving this whole war only to get murdered by flesh-eating strep.

"I told you some things a long time ago," he said. "They were all true."

"You afraid Norberg's listening in? You think she's got time to flip through our boring lives now?"

"If anyone would, it'd be her."

"All right, Tanaka. Why do you give a shit what I think?"

"You still don't have that scar, do you?"

I turned to look at him. While he watched, I rucked down the tab at my collar, pushing my armored padding away to reveal the smooth skin just above my heart.

"Maybe you remember wrong," I said. I folded the tab back; the slick came together easily, like a second skin.

"Come out to the deployment room at oh-nine-hundred," he said, and left.

I didn't sleep well that night. I didn't sleep well any night. I dreamed of Norberg, her pale hands around my throat, her eyelashes covered in shards of glass that ground into the seams of my face.

I woke at oh-four-hundred, sweating on the makeshift bunk in a room I shared with Omalas and a young kid named Ross who jerked off twice every night without fail. Who had the time or the energy? I wanted to yell at Tanaka, have him tell the kid to run laps for an hour every night before bed. Why did I feel so old?

I took a shower. The water smelled faintly of sulfur. It ran cold for ten minutes before I decided to just go for it. The weather felt like spring. I had seen a few calendars around on people's desks, depressing things that told me that I'd been at war for more than three years. A lot of time had passed after the coup. Are you as old as your physical body, or as old as your memories?

I'd have to ask Ross.

I got dressed and went down to the cafeteria, but the cook wasn't up yet. I wanted some coffee. Someone had left the filter in one of the industrial coffee makers overnight. I poured more water in the thing and drank it cold. Tasted like old socks.

I climbed up the back staircase. A track ran along the second floor, all ringed in windows. I watched the sun come up, sipping the terrible coffee.

As the sun rose pink against the far horizon, I realized how much this felt like my childhood. Secondhand coffee, scavenging for food, watching sunrise from some building we were squatting in. It was like I'd come full circle.

What had my father said . . . ? Something about how I swallowed all the corporate bullshit, and how it would keep me safe, but I shouldn't believe it once I got older.

The corporations fucked us over. He was right. All their scheming and manipulating, all the propaganda and fearmongering led by people like Norberg. And yeah, me. I was part of this too. I was the fist attached to the arm of the corp.

When Tanaka sent us all out, where were we going to go this time? Or, rather, where was I going to go? And what would happen to my squad?

I felt stuck here, endlessly repeating mistakes, a loop on repeat.

I reached into my trousers and pulled out the pocket watch Andria had thrown to me. It didn't keep the time. I'd even tried winding it, but the winding mechanism was the part that turned on the scrambler.

I stuffed it back into my pocket. Made up my mind. I trudged down to Tanaka's room. Knocked.

He was already awake and dressed. Hair combed back. Eyes still bloodshot. Unshaved.

I held up the pocket watch. "You know what this is?"

"Yeah," he said.

I turned on the scrambler. Lost coms.

"Andria gave that to you?" he said. "I was looking for it."

"She did. Before one of you shot her."

"It wasn't me."

I motioned him back into the room. These had once been offices for the rec center staff.

"Send me alone," I said. "Just send me on the drop."

"Norberg's expecting a crew."

"Maybe she'll get one. Listen, people who travel with me . . . If I fuck something up, I don't want to murder them too."

"Like Muñoz?"

I prickled at that. I still didn't want to believe Muñoz or the rest of my first squad was dead. "Yeah."

"You think you can control it?"

"Yes? No." I sighed. "Maybe. There's just me, right?"

"Far as we know."

"And we're probably all going to die here, eventually."

Barely perceptible nod.

"Then fuck it," I said. "It will get Norberg, too, eventually. Send me."

"I have to send you with a team. Sorry. You still don't know what will happen when you go. What if you really go there? You don't always jump out of order. Someone needs to have your back. You could go . . . shit, anywhere. Forward, back. Shit, I hope there's a forward."

"Then I'll tell her I went rogue or some shit."

"You think you can stand up to a Norberg interrogation?"

I thought of my father. "I'm sure she'll be pleased to meet me."

"Norberg handpicked a team to go. I'm telling them you were a last-minute request. That's all I can do. I do that, and we're even."

"Were we not, before?"

He shook his head but didn't elaborate. A few hours later, just before oh-nine-hundred, he came back to our nearly empty barracks and waved me over. He led me down to the rifle lockers. Signed out my weapon. We walked down to the deployment area behind the rec center—a giant overgrown football field scattered with plastic wrappers, old chip bags, solar cells, and tattered clothing.

A team already waited there. As I approached them, Tanaka said, "You don't know Akesson and her team. They're from a different division."

The sound of that name hit me like a sledgehammer. The tattered group of four turned to watch me approach, and it was déjà vu all over again.

"No," I said softly, "I know them."

Dirty blond Akesson, pale and soft-jowled. Tall, dark Chikere chomping on bubble gum, giving me the once-over with her piercing eyes. Sharpe, standing awkwardly on one foot while she dug something out of the bottom of her tattered boot. And of course, Toranzos, who stood there wolfing down what remained of a greasy sandwich that I knew he was going to be vomiting up on a beach in Southern Africa in just a few minutes.

A roaring filled my ears. My pace slowed, and I stopped ten meters away.

"Tanaka, I've done this before."

"What do you mean?"

"I know what happens."

"What?"

"I already did this jump, with this team. Norberg. Shit, it was Norberg we were looking for. It went bad, Tanaka."

"How bad? Did you die?"

"I . . . don't know. Fuck." What if this was my last jump? What if I'd already been to the end? "What if I don't go?"

"Then nothing changes."

"What if nothing changes anyway?"

He put his hand on my shoulder. Met my look. "Then you make sure it does."

"Tanaka. I want to know—"

"You already know too much. If you see me, tell me not to be an asshole."

"You think that will work?"

"No."

"If you don't remember me saying it, I must not have."

"I have no fucking idea how any of this works. Maybe you jump around and make other futures. Better ones? Maybe in that one I won't be an asshole."

He strode forward. I followed, though my stomach hurt and my hands shook.

"Akesson," Tanaka said.

"Sir," she said.

"This is Corporal Dietz. A last-minute addition from Norberg. Has bad drops sometimes. Be extra vigilant on this run."

Akesson raised her brows. "You're Bad Luck Dietz?"

"Sorry," I said, because I knew how this turned out.

"No big deal. You listen to me, and this will be just fine."

I got into position just behind her.

"Logistics? This is Corporal Tanaka. I have a team in place for deployment. Stand by for coordinates."

I began to tremble.

Tanaka moved away from me, like I was some giant bomb about to go off. Maybe I was. Maybe *we* were.

My vision stuttered. I went taut as a wire.

The last thing I remembered was Tanaka looking past me, behind me, with a look of terrible fear and awe. But there had been nothing behind me but the trash-filled field.

Nothing at all.

His chest burst open, spilling viscera. His body blew back. The world rumbled. A shock wave.

Everything burst apart.

26.

How do you keep living through the present when you already know the future?

Can you change the future if you've already experienced it, or only ensure that you live the future you were promised?

It's a goddamn mindfuck, is what it is.

You're not supposed to see things, when you become the light. I know that. I say it every time, but it doesn't help, because I keep seeing things.

I heard Andria's voice this time: "Take control of the construct."

Reality is made up. Reality is what we agree on. Had I agreed to this?

Darkness, this time; a constant buzzing.

I want to tell you there's a humming sound, when you start to break apart, but they all say that's impossible. Light doesn't hear things. They tell us that we can't see or feel anything either, but that's a lie. I was starting to think that anyone who's been through it and tells you they don't see or hear anything is lying because they don't want to get grounded. We all see things in transit. It doesn't mean you're bad or crazy. It doesn't mean you're a bad soldier.

I don't want to be a bad soldier.

I don't want to be part of the Light Brigade, either.

But here we are.

Knowing the future, heading forward? Or back?

I would know soon.

No, no—I needed to make it so. I needed to control it. What had I missed? Mars. I wanted Mars.

I wanted to be a goddamn hero.

I dropped, I dropped . . .

Cold. Ice cold, like huffing dry ice.

Wheezing. Grabbing for the oxygen mask hooked to my shoulder. My body heaved. I vomited. The mask didn't come off in time. I sank to the dusty red dirt and kept gagging, forgetting about the soiled mask, but nothing else came out. My body: light, springy, alive! As if I were a child again. I felt infinitely younger. Gravity. Something about the gravity.

Where's . . . ?

Mars.

On Mars I'd be half the . . . wait, no, just 38 percent of what I was on Earth. I was about seventy-seventy kilos on Earth; which meant I weighed twenty-nine kilos now, plus my gear, if this red soil . . . I flipped up my visor. Stupid. The grit blew into my face. Even with my lenses in, the dust collected at the corners of my eyes and made them water madly. I snapped my visor shut.

I hadn't weighed twenty-nine kilos since long before we got residency. Shit, I'd been starving so long it was a wonder I got up to an adult weight.

"This is nice," Omalas said over the squad channel.

Before the end. Must be. Right?

Or did we go back to Mars after the Sick?

The heavy *whomp-whomp* of artillery roared from just ahead of us. I hit the dirt behind Omalas.

"The fuck!" I yelled.

"Sound off!" Jones said.

Jones. My eyes filled. Dumb reaction, but an honest one. Jones still here, still squad leader. I had gone back, after all. Not forward.

"Dietz here." My voice broke.

"Prakash."

I tried to find her on my heads-up map. But coms weren't online yet. I wanted to wrap my arms around her. Squeeze her hard. I'd kiss her if I didn't smell like vomit.

"Omalas, aye."

"Still alive," Marino barked. "Got my dick and both my balls."

"I don't give a shit about your dick unless you sprout two of them," Prakash said. "Then we'll worry. Otherwise you keep your goddamn dick to yourself."

"What if my dick falls off?"

"Hardly a life-threatening injury," Prakash said. "You men and your delicate fucking dicks."

I laughed. Why did I laugh at this stupid joke? Because it meant we were alive.

The CO, over the platoon channel. Captain . . . no . . . Lieutenant V? Shit. I needed the coms map up. "Heavy fire! Stay down! Wait for coms!"

Red Martian dust puffed all around us. Coms with base were offline; our heads-up displays were dead in the water. I felt naked, alone, like I was missing half a world, and yeah, maybe I was.

They said Mars was mostly habitable, made that way by atmo plants and terraforming projects funded by the corps in the early days, before the Martians betrayed us and went dark. But hearing it's habitable and sucking oxygen through a mask while your elbows churn up dust that won't settle is slim comfort. Marino had dropped to Mars before; he'd only talk about the dust if you got him going. No useful intel there.

The *whump-whump* of artillery fire. The ground shook. I had my rifle up, but the dust was so bad I couldn't find a target.

"Are we taking fire?" I said over our squad channel.

"Can't see shit," Prakash said.

"Hold," Jones ordered. "Don't hit a friendly. Wait for a shot."

"Sitting fucking ducks," Marino muttered. "Same every goddamn time."

My heads-up was giving me heat signatures on what looked like another force on a ridge just to the north of us, but I couldn't determine if it was friendly or not. All the corps used slightly different tech; even when they teamed up to fight Mars they knew enough to guard their IP. Flagging a force as Evecom or ShinHana would have helped us on the ground, but also would have opened up their secure systems to ours. In truth, it would have been fairly easy to hack, pretending to be one force and not another. Martians could be passing themselves off as corps easily if all they had to do was emit a specific digital tag.

The ground rumbled.

Something hit my head. I yowled, thinking it was shrapnel. The object rolled into the dust next to me. It was a large white bird about as long as my hand, body limp. Another bird tumbled to the ground ahead of me.

"Poor babies," Omalas cooed in her soft, deep voice.

I gazed up; a cool wind blew away the dust. A large flock of white birds moved across the butterscotch sky—right through the artillery fire. They dropped in pairs, in groups; feathers exploded above us, drifting lazily on the wind. Gravity here was low. They seemed to barely beat their wings, and when they fell, they fluttered to the ground like leaves.

The artillery ceased. Chatter on our platoon channel.

"Strike on their position was successful," the CO said. "Wait until the dust clears, then secure your area."

We had come down just behind a great stone ridge. Jones led our team up the left side of it, scanning for hostiles. Our boots crunched over gravel and harder layers of rock beneath. A fine yellow-green lichen grew over the rock. Here and there I spotted leathery-looking succulents, like cacti, that sprouted giant white flowers.

"I thought Mars was mostly dead," I said.

"Not at all," Prakash said. "That's how they could come back and engineer Canuck. They learned here."

"Sad to be at war," Omalas murmured, "with a people who can create all this beauty."

"Earth is nice too," I said. It just came out. Like there was much of an Earth left at all, from where I'd just been.

"Save your air," Jones huffed. He was panting, even with the mask on.

After we'd secured the position, the CO brought together the platoon and said, "For those who weren't paying attention! We've lost contact with a frontline outpost on Tempe Terra. They were tasked with bringing down the defenses for the bombardment of the Utopia Basin. Our orders are to determine what happened to the formation, and—if necessary—resecure the position. Those defenses over the Basin need to stay down.

"Jones, Estes—I want your squads guarding our ass. Garcia, Khaw, Tanaka, your squads are with me. Swihart, take that ridge up there and give us tactical support with Leichtner and her sniper shot. Marked it on your display. Are we understood?"

"Understood, sir!"

I stumbled after Jones as he waved our squad forward. We waited for the bulk of the platoon to go ahead of us and took up the rear. That gave me some time to get my bearings.

"You all right, Dietz?" Jones asked. He put his hand on my

shoulder. I jerked away from him.

"Fine."

Mars. I'd decided to go to Mars. Was it a coincidence that I'd dropped to Mars, or had I helped make this my next drop by . . . *willing* myself here?

I patted at my trousers. Felt the round heft of Andria's pocket watch. It was real. All that had been real. A wave of vertigo overcame me.

"Didn't expect this," I muttered.

Prakash said, "I'm sure the chief executive of war will do better at keeping you personally informed."

"Bad drop. Sometimes I don't know who we're fighting."

"The bad guys," Prakash said, and snorted.

"They already told us what we need to know," Jones said. "You ask way too many questions, Dietz. Stick to the—"

"The brief. Sorry. Asking questions must be the ghoul in me. Citizens are better at following orders." It just came out. Like old times.

"So are soldiers," he snapped. "What's wrong with you? Your helmet is scuffed. Your gun looks terrible. Why are you wearing that old slick instead of Mars grade? Shit, this isn't . . . you didn't leave the barracks this way."

"It's a long story, Jones," I said. "Let's just . . . complete this mission." I was still waiting for coms and the comforting blink of the heads-up display. It wasn't going to tell me much more than the CO had, but I'd have the chance to figure out who was alive and who wasn't. I almost told him, "I'll tell you everything back at base," but I don't think I had, last time. I wasn't sure if I got do-overs or not. So far, not, but if I could control it?

I didn't know.

Last night I was eating out of a can of beets I scavenged from an abandoned diner in Fortaleza, I thought. Bet my shit was going to be red with those beets. But here I was on some Martian jaunt.

How many times had they told me I'd been to Mars? That awful Mars recon mission I had no memory of, and . . . there was only that other one, when Lieutenant V said I was some hero. This had to be that one, right? My brain needed the logic of that. My mind wanted to untangle the pattern and make sense of it.

Control the construct.

Jones headed after the rear of the platoon.

"Heads-up, Dietz! Eyes on my six!"

"I've got you." I raised my rifle. He was right. My gun was dirty. We'd gotten lazy in those last days of the war. My hair was damp and scratchy inside my helmet. I hadn't cut it in weeks.

The vertigo came again, stronger this time. I paused. Squinted. *Keep it together,* I thought. *You know this drill. Let your body lead. It knows what to do.*

We trudged through the shifting Martian sands. The lower gravity was a blessing; I had trekked over sandy beaches along the Atlantic before, and it was always a slog. Here, we could step more lightly. The air was cold, thin, but not deadly. Red, yellow, and gray lichens carpeted the stones. Little white flowers and tiny fungi littered the ground. I stepped over them carelessly, wondering how many people had sweated and died to make anything at all grow in what had once been a hostile wasteland.

The ground rumbled. I sweated hard in my suit, my body suddenly reminded of the artillery in Canuck, the blazing prairie and choking smoke. I felt the warm, many-tentacled fingers of anxiety unspooling in my chest. *Deep breaths. Keep it together.*

Omalas opened a two-way channel to me. "How are you, lovely?" she asked.

"Not good."

"One foot in front of the other."

"Trying. Yeah." Saliva poured into my mouth. My stomach heaved.

I flipped up my visor and tore away my mask. I heaved again

all over the pristine Martian soil. I sank to my knees, coughing and choking. Mars smelled of salt, rotten eggs, and my own vomit. "Pleased to meet you, too," I said to the dry red soil.

Omalas came over and whacked me on the back.

"I'm fine," I said, coughing. Fine.

"You're vomiting blood," Omalas said gravely.

"It's just beets."

Jones came over. Stared at the vomit. "Where did you get beets?"

Those fucking beets. "It's nothing. I'm just nauseous. Bad drop."

Jones flipped up his visor and stared at me, eyes wide, brow furrowed.

It occurred to me I probably looked like shit.

"Dietz—"

"Stick to the brief," I croaked.

I saw the bob of his Adam's apple as he swallowed. A nod. He flipped his visor back down, replaced his mask. "We're going."

I spit a couple more times, then put my mask on and secured my visor.

We came over a low, sandy rise. The mangled ruin of siege artillery met us first. Their bulbous forms lay shattered and overturned like sad, menacing giants. Sand built up at their bases, carried there by the persistent wind.

"Watch for mines and booby traps," the CO said over the platoon channel.

Our squad waited for the ones ahead to scout out a path. We kept our attention to the rear, scanning the low hills behind us for insurgents. When the last squad was clear, we went after them, winding our way through the towering masses of artillery. I wondered if these were the same type of artillery that had shot at us in Canuck . . . that *would* shoot at us. Through the maze we went; we kept chatter to a minimum. The squads at the lead would take the worst. I knew Tanaka, Sandoval, and Landon were up there. Deathless? I hadn't checked for her. Tau wouldn't be here yet. At least I had my own squad near me. Unless something happened that I didn't understand, it was possible we'd live through this one. Unless that wasn't how it worked. This time-shifting shit was a pain in the ass.

Omalas and I were the last two to come around the final corpse of the artillery. Below us was a Martian settlement lay across a two-kilometer-wide stretch of the basin. Willowy trees lined circular footpaths. The remains of a suspended tram or train system that connected the settlement across the basin gave off threads of smoke. The modular panels of the geodesic domes of the housing would have all been printed here on Mars. What I didn't expect was the yellowish vegetation twining up over the seams of the domes. Pops of blue and lavender peeked out from the wreckage of shattered domes and apartment buildings stacked four and five stories above the basin floor.

On the other side of the settlement, nestled into a rocky outcropping, was the base we'd lost contact with. From here I could already see the communications equipment was damaged. Char and peeling organic skins gave the exterior a patina like something sucked up from the bottom of a flooded basement. Beyond the base—fields and fields of those willowy trees with needles that grew straight up, like Cyprus trees. The forest went on as far as I could see. I wondered if the trees were a food or building source. They must have gone on far enough that logistics figured chancing us through a kilometer of the settlement was a better option than going through the trees. I imagined the city would give us better cover if it turned out the base had indeed been overrun by insurgents.

We descended into the settlement, keeping to a route that local drones told us was clear of obvious traditional mines and human-generated heat signatures. That no one had shot down the drones yet was, I figured, a good sign. I didn't want another Canuck.

The streets of the settlement lay dormant. Bits of trash skittered across the porous roads. I had never seen such narrow byways; not much larger than pedestrian and bike paths back home. A few abandoned vehicles lay in the streets, rickshaws powered by compact solar cells.

A flurry of movement ahead of us. One of the squads at the front let off a shot. The pulse burst disintegrated the entire side of a cracked dome. The structure above it rocked dangerously in the Martian wind.

"Hold fire!" Tanaka, over the platoon channel.

"What was that?" the CO said.

"That was me," Sandoval answered. "Sorry. Some kind of animal—"

"Just a . . . cat, or something," Tanaka said. "Martian cat?

"There's cats on Mars?" Landon quipped.

"Or something," Sandoval said. "Sorry."

"I see it." Prakash padded a few steps down a side street.

"Stay with the squad." Jones raised his rifle.

"It has six legs," Prakash squealed. "This shit is fantastic."

I cast a look ahead where the CO and the front-facing squads were moving again. The bulk of the base loomed over the settlement; its physical presence became more ominous the closer we got. I caught the glint of something up on the walls of the base. A scope? Reflection from a helmet?

Prakash jogged toward us.

I was feeling all right about this drop, maybe because other people had told me how great it'd gone.

Getting cocky is always a mistake.

Getting cocky gets people killed.

Guarding the rear of the platoon, we had good reason to figure the worst of what we were headed into had already been poked with a stick and not come up hissing.

I was suffering from severe jet lag . . . time lag, maybe. I had no business being here.

I heard the shot.

The force of it blew Prakash back on her ass. Her head whipped against the ground.

I went to my stomach. Jones took cover behind the nearest dome. Omalas sank next to me. Marino screamed and fired his rifle in the air. A second shot exploded the dome next to him. Marino staggered forward. The dome took the hit cleanly. What the sniper was using clearly wasn't a pulse rifle, or Prakash and the dome would have been in pieces.

"Prakash?" I said. It killed me that I yearned to gather her up into my arms, even knowing how this ended for her. *Keep it together, Dietz.*

"Hurts like hell," she said.

"Is your suit punctured?" the CO said.

"No. Didn't get through the armor."

"Stay down," the CO ordered. "You move, you make noise, they'll shoot again."

Prakash stayed down.

I scanned the surrounding buildings. The base had no line of sight on her. The shot had to have come from somewhere in the settlement. The many-faceted eyes of the geodesic domes glimmered back at me. I'd get these fuckers.

"Can we get a heat signature sweep?" I asked. "Is there a drone?"

"Already en route," the CO said. "Jones, eliminate the sniper. Tanaka, your team has rear guard. We are going to continue advancing."

Shit, I thought. She was leaving us alone in the settlement? I knew a single sniper could do a lot of damage, but the mission objective reigned supreme. You want to believe your CO loves you, and maybe some do, but whatever her orders were, breaking us away from the platoon was considered a worthy risk.

"Watch for more ahead," Jones said.

"We're clearing," Khaw said.

Fuck you, Khaw, I thought. *You didn't clear this one.* Anybody who tried to go in after Prakash was going to get hit.

Fuck it, I thought. I'd already lived through enough of this war.

I ran.

The shot came past just as Jones yelled, "Dietz!"

I saw the flash. The telltale fire of a midlevel sniper rifle. That was some precise, old-grade shit. One street up. It had come out of a bit of the broken topmost dome on a three-level.

I dropped and rolled.

Two shots hit the dirt next to me, sending up puffs of Martian soil.

I found cover in the shadow of an abandoned rickshaw.

The sniper had hit my helmet. I didn't dare take it off to inspect it, but I sucked in the sulfur-smelling air.

I hesitated. If I shot and hit nothing, I'd give away that I knew the sniper's position, and they'd have a chance to run.

Jones must have sensed my hesitation. "Wait for the drone," he said.

My heads-up had the drone en route, about thirty meters up and to our left. Ten seconds. The drone swooped low. I caught the gleam of it.

The drone operator must have thought the drone was well out of range.

Three quick shots shattered that notion. The drone dropped like a stone; a wounded mechanical bird the size of a basketball.

"Fuck this," Marino said. "I got a sight on it." He let off his pulse rifle, firing six bursts at the busted wall of the dome.

"Omalas," I shouted. "You come with me?"

"Hold on," Jones said.

"You and Prakash go in the back," I said. "Marino and me will take the side entrance. Marino? You listening?"

"Anything that involves killing shit," Marino muttered. "Tired of being a fucking target."

"What if that—," Prakash began.

"Marino!" I said. "Covering fire while Prakash evacs."

"Goddamn right."

We both fired at the dome. My shots went high. I corrected. I'd forgotten about the gravity. Hunks of organic sealant shattered; rained across the street at three-quarters speed, like feathers back on Earth.

Jones swooped in next to Prakash and laid down more covering fire as she darted for the relative safety of the next building.

I scrambled to keep up with Marino as he made for the rear entrance. I sure *hoped* there was a rear entrance. . . .

What we found was another side entrance. Marino kicked in the door with some help from his pulse rifle. I reached for his shoulder to indicate I was ready to breach, but he didn't bother waiting.

It was a wonder he hadn't been killed yet. Why did idiots die last?

We went up a winding ramp, the Martian stairwell, I guess. It was certainly easier to huff up it than stairs. The rooms all lay open. This may have been a school, before. The furniture was all undersized. Martians were supposed to be tall and mostly thin because of the gravity. We cleared the big school room and went upstairs. This was a play area of some kind. Big bouncy balls. Massive blocks. Craft stations. Funny how much of that stuff was the same. A powdery red dust covered everything; the cracked domes had let it filter in.

Not a body in sight, though. Whatever had happened here,

they had enough time to get out. So what idiot had stayed behind? Probably someone dangerous. Dumb like Marino.

As we came up the third ramp, Marino slipped and bashed me in the helmet with the butt of his gun. My head snapped back. My visor finally shattered completely. My head slammed against the wall. I swore, flipped up what remained of my visor, yanked my mask. "Watch it, Marino!"

His visor was already up. He swung back to look at me, mask hanging against his throat. "Smell that sweet Martian air, Dietz."

I pushed his shoulder. "Stay on point. I don't want to die today."

"Dying's the only way out, Dietz." He grinned, showing a chipped front tooth. His brown eyes had a glimmer of gold at the edges. He had that strong jaw that all the streams liked. I wanted to bash it off his face. Little fuck.

Marino swiveled back to the half-open door ahead of us. On the upside, he was the sort of guy who would lead a clearing team and take the first hit and say it was fun. I appreciated that.

Marino kicked the door clear and swung his weapon to the right.

We entered an open space, the hub of the topmost dome. Trash littered the ground; plastic floor? Concrete? I couldn't tell through my boots. A massive pile of junk took up the far corner, half covering the other entrance. If they had tried to barricade themselves in, they had done a poor job of it. I scanned the left while Marino scanned the right, so I was last to see the massive object positioned along the shattered wall facing the street. The gun was mounted on a tripod; it stood at least as tall as me.

Marino approached it, his own gun still level.

On the blunt metal side of the gun closest to me, I recognized the NorRus logo. I made one last sweep of the room and then lowered my gun.

"This automatic?" I said and shut my mouth. Like Marino would know.

Marino mashed the gun with the butt of his, succeeding only in knocking the whole contraption over. The clatter made me start.

"Shit," I said. "Don't touch anything. It'll go off."

"I'll go off on it."

I heard something: a sigh, maybe, an exclamation. Sounded like it came from the heap of junk by the second door. I raised my rifle and scanned for heat signatures.

The wavy orange wisp of warmth curled from beneath the corner nearest the door. The bowl of the heat signature made no sense to me. Too small, maybe another cat? A heated dinner stuffed into the pile?

"Come out," I said.

Marino swung his head toward me. "What you see?"

"Heat sig."

"There's nobody here."

A knock came at the opposite door. Then, over the squad channel. "Dietz?" Jones.

"Yeah," I said. "It's . . . mostly clear. I have a weird heat signature. You'll need to push the door good. Got some shit here next to it."

With three of them on the other side, it didn't take long to bust in the other entrance. Jones, Omalas, and Prakash rolled in, rifles up.

"Automatic gun," I said. "We think. Only." And I gestured to the aura of the heat sig. "Anybody know Martian?" I knew Portuguese, but only because I'd grown up speaking it in São Paulo; it wasn't an official Teni-Silvia language. I couldn't imagine they spoke Portuguese on Mars. But fuck, weirder things had happened.

"Publichno zayavit," Omalas said. "Uill ne prichinit vam vreda."

It sounded Russian. The heat sig wavered. The trash trembled. Marino raised his rifle.

I pressed my hand over the top of his barrel, forcing it down. "Give them a minute." I tried a few phrases in halting English. That got me a withering look from Omalas.

"Got any other ideas?" Prakash asked. "The heads-up can translate some stuff, but not very good."

"I'm unsure my Mandarin is better than the display," Omalas said, and then picked her way through. "Bù huì shānghài ni ˇ. . ?"

I wished I'd spent more time on languages. What was left? "Anybody know French?" I asked.

"Badly," Jones said.

Omalas grunted. "You think mine made sense?"

"Uh . . . ," Jones began. "Je . . . ne te ferai pas de mal? Uh . . . s'il vous plaît sortir?"

"Shit," Prakash said. "You drunk during that class, Jones?"

"Just light it up." Marino yanked his gun back up. I batted it down again.

"Why you have to fuck everything up, Marino?" I asked.

"The fuck you think we're here for, Dietz?"

I grabbed the butt of his rifle. He puffed up his chest. Faced me. I straightened. He towered over me. I met his cold stare. Got ready to bash him as best I could, just like with Frankie. I was done with bullies.

A scrabbling in the trash heap.

We both turned.

A small head popped up from the refuse. Skinny, big-eyed, deep circles under the tawny skin of the black eyes. How old was he? Seven? Eight?

The child scrambled away from the trash, fixing us with that luminous gaze.

Jones tried to talk to him, but the kid babbled in something else. Mandarin? The kid held up grubby hands. He wore a too-big gray smock and tatty trousers tied with a rope around his skinny waist. His belly puffed out, as if he were malnourished or parasite-ridden.

Omalas took over, muddling through with more gut-churningly bad Mandarin.

"Did he operate this gun?" Jones said. "Ask him?"

Omalas flipped up her visor and peered at Jones. "And then what?"

"Then we clear him," Marino said.

"We were told to clear the sniper," Jones said. "If he was the one who operated this gun—"

Omalas growled, "I didn't sign up to murder children."

"Masukisan," the boy said.

We all rounded on him.

"Tu est avec Masukisan?" Jones asked.

"Tout à fait," the kid said. He pointed at us. "Evecom?"

"No," I said. "Tene-Silvia."

"He trying to say he's a corporate kid?" Marino said. "That's bullshit. If he's Masukisan, where are all the fucking Martians? We came here for Martians."

"He's definitely Masukisan," Omalas said. "This isn't one of those free Martian cities. It's one of the old corp settlements. I bet he's speaking a dialect. The rest is just stuff he's picked up."

The conversation I'd had with Tanaka in Canuck came back to me. The idea that we weren't just fighting free Martians, but using it as a cover to fight the other corps under some pretense. I examined the kid a little closer. His tattered tunic bore the Masukisan logo on the collar, frayed and dirty as the rest of him. NorRus equipment, a kid wearing Masukisan gear. Was it staged? A setup? Were we all just fighting one another here on the bones of these poor stupid colonists?

"We should stop asking questions," I said, very aware that our heads-up displays were recording.

"Our mission was to eliminate the sniper," Jones reminded us, as if we'd forgotten.

We all looked at the kid again.

"I'll do it," Marino offered.

"He's a prisoner," I pointed out. "We can take him with us."

"We can't do that," Jones said.

"Then tie him up here and leave him," I said. "We'll come back."

"I'll kill him." Marino, more loudly.

"We heard you the first hundred times," Omalas said.

"No," Jones said. "Tie the kid up, Dietz. Bring him with us for now. That's fine. Maybe we can get some information from him."

I wasn't sure how much an eight-year-old had to say to us, but if it kept us from committing another goddamn horror, I'd go along. I had nothing to bind the kid with, though. Corps regs of war required us to carry restraints, but I sure hadn't used them until now. It felt good to do something different, even if it might not matter to anybody but this one kid.

As Omalas bent to bind the boy, a blast rocked the room. The *whump* of the hit roared. The child screamed. A hunk of metal crashed into my helmet. Omalas shielded the child.

I peered at the ruin Marino had made of the big gun on the mangled tripod.

"You feel better?" I asked.

"Yes," he said. Half the big gun now lay outside the clear, broken pane of the dome, like a tooth still attached by one tremulous root.

"Eliminated." Marino huffed off down the stairwell.

"Let's move out," Jones said, like leaving now was his idea.

I wanted to yell at Jones for not taking on Marino. Jones was squad leader, but shit, I didn't blame him. When the bucket of rage that was Marino finally boiled over, it was set to burn everything around him.

We followed. I took the rear guard with Omalas; the kid walked in front of her, behind Prakash and Marino, with Jones catching up to the lead position. The kid slowed us down, of course. We were all more quiet than usual. No one wanted to say it out loud. Except Marino, probably, but as I watched him sashay ahead, I figured he'd already moved on to seeking out the next thing to be outraged about.

"Jones! You there, over?" The CO, on the platoon channel.

"Affirmative. We're a few hundred meters from your position."

"We've hit a stretch of mines. Khaw and Tanaka are down. We need your squad immediately. Double time."

"Affirmative, sir. We . . . uh, we have a prisoner."

"You have a what?"

"Prisoner, sir. Uh, over."

"No, you do not, Jones. You were to eliminate all threats."

"The threat is eliminated, sir."

A long silence. My heart clenched.

"Get your ass over here, Jones. Move."

Omalas hefted the kid over her shoulder. He screeched. She said something to him in Mandarin, and he quieted. Maybe she mentioned Marino and his gun.

We darted down the ruined streets. I covered the rear, gazing back, always back, at what had come before.

The positions of our platoon lay over the street grid on my heads-up. But I heard them before I saw them. Howling.

Tanaka lay on the ground; I barely recognized him. His helmet had been blown right off. His left foot was a tangled mess of flesh; Sandoval knelt next to him, holding the tourniquet that kept him from bleeding out. Khaw was further up the street, her legs completely gone. Two of her squad still tended to her, their voices too loud, panicked. Shit.

The CO strode toward us. Visor up, oxygen mask dangling. I had not seen her face so angry before. "Are you fucking kidding me, Jones? We don't have time for this."

Omalas put the kid down. The kid tried to hide behind her, but she pushed him before her.

"It was my idea," I said. "It's just a kid. We don't even know if he was operating the gun. He may not even be a combatant. I thought—"

The CO pulled her sidearm and shot the kid in the head.

It happened so fast my mind struggled to accept it.

The boy's blood seeped across the dusty road, mingling with the blood of our own soldiers. The kid didn't even shudder. Just a twitch. The glassy eyes.

In that moment, I thought of my brother. When had I last seen him? Six weeks after our mother died, months after our father was disappeared by the corp, Tomás announced he was going back to São Paulo.

"Why?" I asked. "We have residency. Things are better now."

"Are they?" he said. We were packing up the house. As two unaccompanied minors, we were required to move to the unaccompanied minors' barracks. By then, Vi and I were serious enough that we wanted to apply for a place. But I didn't want to leave Tomás alone.

"We have access to good jobs," I said.

"You do. What will happen to me?"

"I'll take care of you."

"And what if you die?"

"I won't." I took his hands. "We have each other. They won't take that away."

"Why not? They took everything else." He gazed out the

window to a blooming cherry tree. "Papa said they would give us some new life. But we didn't get anything new. It all came with rules. New rules. And we weren't supposed to learn them. Because they only apply to certain people. We're still no one. We're no one with a better name."

"Don't say that. We're somebody."

Tomás was quiet, then. I should have known what would happen. But I was thinking of Vi, of our own life, of what I would do after school. Thinking of myself. Always myself.

"Everything we really are is in São Paulo," he said.

"That's a bullshit life."

"At least we were free."

When I came back from school the next day, Tomás was gone. He left a note saying he was going back to São Paulo. To the friends we had made in the squatter camp. To eating wounded birds and going to bed hungry and worrying about gangrene and broken bones and wounds that wouldn't heal.

At least I will be free, he wrote, and it was as if he had wrapped his fist around my heart and squeezed. *Free to die terribly,* I thought. But being a resident hadn't saved my mother. Hadn't saved my father. Why did I think it would save us?

I told myself, when he left, that he was crazy. How could anyone trade the security we had for the unknown bullshit we had put up with in the labor camps? Was it my fault? Should I have made it clear that me and Vi would always care for him, that he could stay with us? Or did he just see more clearly then what had taken me an entire war to realize?

Staring now at this dying boy, I understood. When you are under the thumb of a corp, they own you. They say you have freedoms, choices. When your choice is to work or to die, that is not a choice. But São Paulo was no choice, either. It was a bad death, when this world was more than rich enough to ensure we could all eat, that no one needed to die of the flu or gangrene or cancer. The corps were rich enough to provide for everyone. They chose not to, because the existence of places like the labor camps outside São Paulo ensured there was a life worse than the one they offered. If you gave people mashed protein cakes when their only other option was to eat horseshit, they would call you a hero and happily eat your tasteless mash. They would throw down their lives for you. Give up their souls.

Like we were doing. The Corporate Corps.

They made sure we had no good choices.

"Fuck you," I said to the CO, low and cold. "Fuck this war. He's Masukisan, not Martian. What the fuck is going on?"

"They're all Martian, Dietz," the CO said.

"Fuck you!" Louder. I felt it. Deep in my gut.

She hit me; not an open slap, but a punch right in my exposed face. I staggered back. Fell on my ass.

"You stand down and you follow orders, Dietz," the CO said. "Stick to the motherfucking brief. You disobey a direct order again, and the next bullet out of this gun is for you."

It had been a long time since I felt like crying. The spike of pain in my sinuses, the rush of tears; it was like some awful foreign sensation. Something that happened to other people.

Omalas held out her hand. I stared at it. She, too, had her visor up. I liked that, because I could see her eyes. Cool and black, like staring into some clear, cold pool. It comforted me. I knew she didn't want this any more than I did. This boy had trusted us, hadn't he? We may have been the only living people he saw today.

I took Omalas's hand. She pulled me up.

Prakash came up next to me. Put her hand on my arm, opened a two-way channel. "You all right?"

"None of this is all right." I closed the channel.

The boy's body lay in front of us. The CO had already moved away. She gazed at the incoming medical evac drones as they swooped in to pick up Khaw and Tanaka.

I found myself oddly detached about Tanaka. I knew he would live, didn't I? For a while. Unlike Prakash. Her time was more limited. But Khaw? How long did Khaw have? When was the last time I saw Khaw in the platoon ranks? Was this it for her? Should I mourn or be happy that she escaped this fucking circus?

"Jones," the CO said. "I need your squad to take the breach of the front. Sandoval will be doing breach of the back."

"Yes, sir."

The drones arrived. Two evac units painted with the crescent moon and cross of the medical corps. I watched Sandoval and Leichtner load Tanaka and Khaw up and then I was moving again, right after Jones, heading to that fucking base on the hill.

Fuck.

Our squad, one of the two still intact, approached the base directly. I won't lie, I was trembling. We were completely exposed. I came up the front with Jones, leaving Prakash and Omalas at the back, and Marino yanking his dick in the middle, looking for something to fuck up.

Jones and I approached the main entrance. He motioned me forward. Yeah, of course, I had to breach this fucker. I hated the idea of trying to shoot in the door. There could be people on the other side.

"I have the code," Jones said, just as I reached for the door.

The door sagged inward like a wilted flower. I exchanged a look with Jones.

He motioned me forward.

I pressed the massive door open further. Metal. Heavy, even in Martian gravity. The darkness inside swallowed the pale burst of sunlight that preceded us. The place relied on solar power; I'd seen the compact solar cell towers from a distance. Even if they had been damaged, there should have still been some juice in the solar-charged batteries. If the lights were off, it was either because of a catastrophic system failure, or—someone had turned them off on purpose.

I rolled into the doorway, rifle up. I had a light attached to my rifle. It illuminated the narrow corridor. Gave me a clear view of the second doorway, set opposite of the entrance. I went to the inner door. This one was locked.

Jones punched in several codes; the system kept booting him off. I heard him conversing with the CO over a two-way channel, no doubt getting more options third- or fourth-hand from some nerd back on Earth in a stuffy intelligence office.

Marino muttered under his breath. No doubt he had an itchy trigger finger.

The sixth code worked. Jones pushed inside.

We padded into the corridor. In here, the lights were on. I wanted to say over the squad channel that . . . you know, clearly, there were no signs of a prior breach, but didn't. However this place had gotten cut off, it wasn't by anybody outside of the base.

We continued through the corridor, heading toward the beating heart of the station itself.

Here: the dead. Crumpled bodies lay in a heap at the center of the compound. Civilian bodies. All dressed in bright Martian colors, faces smeared with red dust. What had come through here? It was difficult to say. I swept my rifle across the corpses of about a dozen people, all lying around the core of the base's operations. Bubbling blood. Red dust. Charred smears along the wall. The smell of vodka and sulfur and death.

The CO, over the platoon channel: "What is the status of the base? Under our control, or the Martians?"

Jones said, "To be determined. There are casualties. Stand by."

This is why I liked not being squad leader. I couldn't be this composed. I'd tell Lieutenant V that we were fucked. That nothing was what it seemed. I wouldn't stick to the brief. I was turning into Marino.

A rattling sound came from the floor beneath us. I trained my rifle along it.

"Whoa," Prakash said.

"Hello?" Jones said. "We are—"

On the other side of the room: a rattling shiver. One of the fallen cabinets moved across the floor, propelled by two dirty hands clawing up from beneath it. I recognized the work of a pulse rifle; someone had used one to melt a hole in the floor and hide there. A shaggy-haired man in the dirty suit of a Teni officer crawled out.

I trained my rifle on him. "Identify yourself!"

The man shifted his mealy gaze to me. Stared like a dog that needed to take a piss in the yard.

"The fuck is this?" Prakash said.

"Sir!" Jones said, saluting.

I saw the ranking on the man's cuff right after Jones. Lifted my hand . . . and froze. The name was on his shirt. Kowalski. I stared hard at the bearded face, covering the strong jaw. The wild brown eyes, the runnels the sweat made across his dusty, familiar face.

No way.

"Frankie?" I said. "Uh . . . sir?"

Franklin Kowalski stared at me. My god . . . how the hell had he gotten here?

I lowered my rifle.

"Dietz," Frankie said. "Dietz, have you seen it?"

"Seen what?"

"The end of the war. You haven't, have you? No, you haven't. Because there's no end, Dietz. It just goes round and round, one big circle. We're trapped. All trapped. No way out."

"Frankie, uh, sir, what happened here?"

"I tried to save them." He ran his fingers through his greasy hair. Came forward. I lifted my rifle, instinctively.

Jones stepped between us. "Sir? Is there anyone still alive? Anyone who needs medical evac?"

Frankie seemed to become aware of the bodies all around us for the first time. His mouth trembled. "Oh my God, oh my God. I tried to save them."

"From who?" I asked. "These are civilians. Why bring the civilians here? Where are your soldiers?"

"We were bombing the city," Frankie said.

"This is a war, Frankie."

"Don't call me that."

"Okay . . . sir."

"I know you see it," he said. "There are people they shouldn't break apart, people who make all this unstable. You're one of them. So was . . . it's not important. But you haven't been there, have you, the end of the war? You haven't seen it yet."

"No."

"I knew it."

"Doesn't mean it's not there," I said carefully. His face was so red I feared he might burst something.

"It's not there. Once you break it, it can't be fixed. They broke something, Dietz. Broke our minds, maybe. Our bodies. Broke the world. We can't fight our way out. I knew you hadn't seen it."

"Did you kill all these people, Frankie?"

"Me? No, no. It was *you*. You, Dietz. You did all this."

Marino said, "Fucking nutter."

"Frankie, I've never been here."

"No, no," he said, and he lunged at me. Jones caught him. I reared back, startled. "You did this, Dietz. You started all this!"

"Fuck you, Frankie," I said.

"No," he said. "Not me, not me!"

"Enough!" Jones said. "Corporal Kowalski? What has happened here? We don't —"

"We murdered them!" Frankie snarled, and pulled himself from Jones's grip. "This is a Masukisan settlement! They aren't Martians. That's Masukisan artillery out there. Our bombers came out here to back us up. I told them there was a mistake. They had to go back. But they kept coming. Wave after wave . . . I did my part. Completed the mission. I secured this base. Me and my people . . . all gone now."

He seemed to lose something, some vital energy that was keeping him upright. He sagged to the floor.

"Mistakes happen sometimes," Jones said. "It's not your fault."

Frankie swept his hand at the dead. "Does that look like a mistake to you?"

"You still haven't answered—," I said.

"I brought them here to save them from the bombing," Frankie said. "There were no soldiers here but the ones in my company. No free Martians. It was a civilian Masukisan settlement. But the Teni brass must have figured out what I was doing, and they dropped something . . . some disease that made us all go mad. What are any of us, but test subjects? Corporate dogs. They started . . . we started killing one another."

"Lieutenant," Jones said, and I figured he had opened up a two-way channel to the CO. I couldn't hear him over the platoon channel, only out loud. "We have a situation in here."

Whatever Lieutenant V was saying . . . well, I could imagine.

"Frankie," I said, because though all I wanted to do was kick his face in, I had to know what happened. I had to take it forward . . . or backward, to wherever I jumped next. I wasn't a passenger. I couldn't be. I thought of Andria tossing me the pocket watch. Of the look of terror and awe on Tanaka's face as it blew apart. Prakash . . . and Vi, fuck . . . Vi, the only one who could have gotten through this, I knew, because I had let her go, but look how that had turned out?

"Give it straight, Frankie," I said, "for once in your life. Did you fuck them the way you fucked everything?"

"How are you so low, Dietz?" he said. "Why haven't you advanced?"

"I like being a grunt."

"Dietz, this is your fault. I could not save them. Because we were all locked in to this from the start. Do you understand?"

"No, I don't."

"We're just killing corporate civilians. Why? Why all this death?"

I didn't rise to the bait this time. Let him hang.

He peered at me. "You know what happens, don't you, Dietz?"

"Yes, sir," Jones said, over his two-way with Lieutenant V. He raised his head. "Corporal Kowalski, the rest of our company is incoming. I suggest you have a seat and wait for them. We will have a medical team for you."

"No," Frankie said. "No, no, no." He turned and ran out of the room, bolting through a corridor we hadn't cleared yet.

I went after him, with Jones and the others just behind me. More dead littered the hallway. Here and there, I saw the armored bodies of Tene-Silvia soldiers. Had Frankie told the truth? Did he and his company try to save these people, and Teni had them killed for it? Or was he just mad, broken, incompetent? Maybe he'd done all this himself. I wouldn't put it past him.

The hallway led to a large common area open to the sky. Frankie stood at the center of it, struggling to get himself over more bodies, many of them blown apart, half-submerged in fine Martian soil. The ground here was pockmarked with craters.

"They bombed us!" Frankie shouted, raising up his hands. "Teni bombed us. They sent a sickness. Made us mad. Made us kill each other. They fucked us, Dietz. It wasn't me. Not me."

I heard movement behind us; the CO approached with the

rest of the platoon. On the other side of the parade ground, the rest of the company moved in as well. We surrounded the sea of dead.

"You are all being played!" Frankie yelled. "This is one big fuck fest! It's all a fucking joke!"

The CO came up behind Jones and said, "He's gone mad. We have orders, Jones."

"I know," Jones said.

Jones walked across the parade ground. Held out a hand to Frankie. "Sir, we need to go."

I felt for Frankie in that moment. I realized it could just as easily be me up there. I'd been able to keep myself buttoned up, so far. But if this had been me, the only one left alive out here?

"I need you to come with me," Jones said.

Frankie pushed him.

Jones pulled his sidearm. Frankie wrestled it away from him. He shot Jones in the chest. Jones went down. Frankie came at me, waving that gun.

I shot him in the head—one smooth, instinctual movement. It's how they train you.

No thought.

No questions.

Action.

Killing.

Frankie burst apart.

27.

I stood over Frankie's body like some dumb puppet, staring.

"Dietz?" Jones said.

For a minute, I didn't know who either of them were.

"You're okay," Jones said. "It's all right."

Omalas whacked me on the back. I coughed. "Okay," she said in her calm, soothing voice, and that did it. I came back.

I lowered my rifle. I gazed across the courtyard. A flicker of movement caught my eye. A figure peeked into the room, so briefly I thought it might be a trick of my eyes. But I knew that figure instantly.

"Muñoz?" It was her. There was no doubt in my mind. The soldier raised her head, caught my look—and bolted.

"No!" I ran after her, over the piles of corpses, across the courtyard. I peeled into the corridor I had seen her dart down.

"Dietz!" Jones, over the squad channel. "The hell you going?" Frankie's shot hadn't been lethal. Our suits could easily endure standard fire.

"It's Muñoz!"

I came to the end of the corridor just as the soldier jumped into a refuse chute. I went after her, sliding through the slimy chute and hurtling out the other end. I came up in a mass of composting bio-matter. Lifted my head just in time to see the soldier jump into a vehicle emblazoned with the Martian flag.

She met my gaze again, eyes wide, like she had done something wrong. And I read recognition there. She knew who I was. It was absolutely Muñoz.

"Go, go!" she yelled at the driver. The beefy woman at the front had tattooed X's on her knuckles, and a sheared mohawk of yellow hair. It was Squib. Who else? But how? Had they been captured on that Mars recon mission? Were they working for the Martians?

The vehicle peeled out, spitting Martian dust. I lay in the compost heap, dazed, staring at the whirls of red particles they had kicked up.

"Muñoz!" I screamed it again and again, until I was hoarse.

"Dietz?" Jones, over the squad channel.

Then, "Dietz?" and he was next to me, knees in the compost heap. Took my face in his hands. "Dietz, I need to know you're still here."

My eyes filled. "I'm here," I said. "Fuck, I'm here."

"Me too." He pulled me into his arms, and I clung to him, but my gaze still followed the wispy remnants of the dusty path kicked up by Muñoz and Squib's vehicle.

They were still alive.

They were on Mars.

How the fuck had they gotten to Mars?

"Did you see it?" I asked.

"What?"

"It was . . ." And then I stopped, realizing how it was going to sound.

"Wait, look at this, Dietz."

All around me, in the refuse heap, were dozens and dozens of cast-off NorRus uniforms. I waded through the pile and came down the other side. There was a printer recycling station nearby; all this refuse was meant to be pulped and reused in onsite printers to make new clothes and materials. I'd seen this tech in the refuse heaps outside São Paulo. It was always a scramble for us to get out what we could before it got shoveled into the recyclers. It's why we spent a lot more time along the beach than at dump sites.

"Why were they tossing NorRus uniforms?"

"Looks like NorRus infiltrated the station," Jones said. "I bet he was trying to cover for them."

"What, they took off all their uniforms and put on Teni ones? And he was okay with that? I don't get it."

"What makes more sense? That he was a traitor collaborating with NorRus or Teni killed this guy's whole platoon?"

I wasn't going to give my opinion out loud. I wouldn't put it past Teni to dump a bunch of uniforms here for the drones and snaps to see and then beam a story back home about how Frankie was a traitor. I realized I might never know what really happened here. War was all about the annihilation of truth. Every good dictator and CEO knows that.

"Good find, Dietz," Jones said.

It didn't feel like a good find. It felt like I'd made everything more complicated.

When we brought Lieutenant V out, she accessed the base's coms and recordings to verify what had really happened. I waited outside the coms door, but she closed it behind her. Whatever she saw, she didn't share it with any of us. She just patted me on the back, said, "You did pretty good this time, Dietz. Just keep following orders."

"You aren't going to tell us what happened?" I said. I wanted to know if she'd seen Muñoz or Squib on the recordings. Probably not; Frankie had cut the power to the security systems around the perimeter.

"Stick to the brief, Dietz. Secret to every successful grunt."

Goddammit.

The cleanup at the base took a while. Jones's suit had protected him from the worst of the shot; it was a standard sidearm, not a pulse rifle, but he had a good bruise to show off underneath when the medics got to him.

I wanted to stay on Mars longer. Wanted it to last awhile. Maybe because I didn't want to see what happened next, because I already knew what was coming. Maybe because I hoped to see Muñoz again.

"What's the line from Teni?" I asked Omalas after the two of us finished carrying bodies from the corridor and into the evac ship. I had that déjà vu again, remembering Omalas and I during the Sick, hauling around the dead.

"Some Martian bug," she said. "Killed the civs. Made the soldiers go crazy."

"You believe that?" I asked.

She tapped my forehead. "That was the brief. It's what we have to believe in."

"You aren't even curious? What really happened?"

"What would the truth change? We follow orders."

Omalas offered me half her protein bar. I took it and we stood a moment in silence, gazing at the abandoned Martian settlement, both of us reluctant to go back into that stinking deathtrap of a base.

"Want to buy some illusions?" she said. "Slightly used."

I laughed. I don't know why. Maybe I just needed to laugh. "Better platoon name," I said. "The Disillusioned."

"You think we'll see the end of the war?"

I gazed up at her; thought of beets and truckloads of the dead. "Yeah. We will."

When the dead were sorted thirty or so hours later, the CO

marched us back through the settlement to our drop point. We got in formation. The Martian wind was high; dust coated everything. I tasted sulfur.

Prakash knocked me on the shoulder. "Good job out there."

My big damn hero moment: Shooting Frankie in the face. Trying to save a civ that got shot anyway. Not letting Prakash die yet. Sticking to the brief.

The air began to tremble.

I gazed at the butterscotch sky.

Where to next?

I closed my eyes. I needed to go back.

Time to go back again.

Interview #4
SUBJECT #187799
DATE: 27|05|309
TIME: 0300
ROOM: 100

I: Interview beginning at · · · see notes. Subject is one-eight-seven-seven-nine-nine. Let's commence. You're looking better.

S: You know how to sweet talk, Sergeant, but you have poor taste in vodka. Is this really all that's left?

I: That's better than our officers get.

S: The sweet talk, or the vodka?

I: Both.

S: I see you're warming up. Feeling good about yourself, are you? Got some answers to make your superiors feel better? I'm doing my best to keep you upright, Sergeant. Can't do to start over with some new guy, after all we've been through together. We've developed such a fine relationship, after all.

I: I've struck your comments from our last meeting. As a show of good faith.

S: For me, or you? I wasn't bullshitting you.

I: It's impossible I sent you to Saint Petersburg. Don't insult me. My superiors want you strung back up.

S: I didn't say you sent me, you just put the idea into my head. You don't remember where we met for the second time, do you? Then, as now, you had no idea who I was. That's not uncommon, especially when there are power differentials. The higher-status person forgets the lower-status person. I was a grunt, a cockroach. Before that, you saw me as a ghoul, the child of an insurgent. You shared intelligence with my CO. I just tagged along. But I remembered you. I remembered what you said about Saint Petersburg.

I: You seem to have very good intelligence. You're telling me I gave it to you?

S: You gave it to the brass. I just took a peek.

I: I am an intelligence officer. As you have seen, I do not engage in advanced interrogation techniques. But your continued evasiveness is tempting me.

S: You asked about doppelgangers. But that's a bit of a tired old idea, isn't it? Hardly easy to do with today's advancements in organics. What do you know about time distortions caused by corporate deployment technology?

I: Why don't you tell me?

S: I want my shoes back.

I: Answer and I'll consider it.

(SILENCE 45 seconds)

I: I have all the time in the world, Sergeant. Do you?

(SILENCE 110 seconds)

I: Go get the shoes.

(SILENCE: 140 seconds)

I: Is that better?

S: Yeah, I'll need these later.

I: For all the jogging you're going to do?

S: Oh, look at you, feeling feisty. I knew

you had a sense of humor. And a keen interest in the past. Did you know Martian POW camps give you access to unrestricted media? I'm sure I mentioned that. The first thing I listened to was <u>War of the Worlds</u>. You know what that is?

(SILENCE: 7 seconds)

S: I'm uncertain if that look means yes or no. After a few months of media access, I understood why the corps restricted so much of it. It shows you different ways people have lived. It offers options. Gets you to thinking . . . well, is this really the only way that a society can organize itself? Was the past really a socialist cesspool of want and disease? Were people happy? What sort of problems did they have? You'd be surprised how little what drives us has changed.

I: If you aren't a Martian infiltrator, how do you know what you do? Are you a defector? I admit we have seen some of those fools, but they didn't live long. If that's the case, why would you defect to Mars?

S: Why does anyone defect? Some defect for financial or personal freedom, certainly. For enough wealth, people will do anything. Others defect, simply, because they discover the world they believed they lived in proved to be false. There is a province in Shin-Hana that was once split into the north and the south. The north was geographically isolated, and supported by the old . . . oh, what was it? One of those long-winded acronyms. For seventy, eighty years, this regime controlled everything that people saw and read and heard. It was a small enough country that it was easy to restrict everything, to a far greater extent than any of the corps do now, even with our advanced surveillance and tracking systems. They were raised to believe their tiny spit of land ruled over by some doddering dictator was the center of the world. And you know what? It worked, mostly. For a long time. The war there was entirely a war of propaganda. The rest of the world worked to let the north know that there was another life beyond the one they knew. But there are always people who are more comfortable with what is certain and known than what is just . . . a promise. A what-if. The tipping point comes when you have nothing to lose. When you can't stand it anymore. If your life is in danger, or your future is grim, then shit, why not defect? There's nothing to lose. That's the trouble with regimes that get too cruel. People need to feel like they have free will. They want to believe that nobody else is as free or happy as they are. If they aren't citizens yet, well, shit, that's their fault. They aren't working hard enough. People disappear in the night, and you think, of course they must have done something wrong. Good people are rewarded. Bad people are punished. Many fought hard to get messages into the north, to share their own propaganda, and people defected, certainly. But only the very daring or the very desperate. The rest did not want to believe. This is something we don't talk about · · · what happens when you are presented with a truth that contradicts everything you believe in? The widespread proliferation of information in the early days of the open knu, back when it was the wild net, should have made truth easier to find. But it turns out most of us don't want truth. We want stories that back up our existing beliefs. Flood the world enough with information, and I will pick out only those bits that uphold the virtue and rightness of whatever corp I've been taught to love.

I: But you stopped doing that, clearly. What turned you?

S: Sometimes, to save the world, you have to let it break. You let it break because even as it breaks, there will still be those who believe its demise impossible, even as they watch it disintegrate. Monsters do not die quietly, not the corporations, not the corrupt democracies and kleptocracies before them, and certainly not the monarchies, the feudal lords, the god-emperors, and the oligarchies. Most of those old leaders had to get their heads chopped off to step aside. That's what moved them, finally.

I: You advocate violence, then? A terrorist radical.

S: Don't tell me every revolution is peaceful. Revolutions rely on the tireless work of faceless masses whose lives mean so little individually that their names weren't known to their movements even when alive. There is no bloodless revolution, only necessary revolution, when a system becomes so deeply broken you can't affect change from the inside. When the system itself has become calcified so permanently that change is not possible . . . that is when the knives come out. I used to believe, as others did, that we could work within the existing system, that moderate change was possible. But when you take away the ability of the people to effect change within the rules of the system, those people become desperate. And it is desperate people who overthrow their governments. The corps tell us each individual should reap the profits of "their" hard work. But the reality is the corps made their fortunes on the backs of laborers and soldiers paid just enough to keep them alive. The corps did not labor. Do not labor. The shareholders and upper management sit in their glass towers and drink liquor spiked with our blood. Instead of sharing that wealth with those who broke their backs to attain it, they hoard it like great dragons. Any human power can be changed by human beings. That is a truth, a constant. Humans can't build power structures that cannot be destroyed. We are the power structure. There was a time when human beings believed they were their governments. They understood they had power over them, because they created them. They did not simply wait around for their governments to give them rights and freedoms. They demanded them. People should not be afraid of the corporations. Corporations should be afraid of the people.

I: You're a communist then.

S: Let's say I'm old enough not to be dazzled by Ayn Rand.

I: Truth is a point of view.

S: So says every great tyrant. You mistake the interpretation of a truth with the truth itself. There is still objective truth. The truth that the sun comes up in the east. The truth of gravity, which keeps us tethered to this spinning ball of space stuff. Those are truths. The rest is made up.

I: Was it the pursuit of truth that made you defect?

S: The more I lived, the more I understood that I was ill-informed about the world. I had grown up with a story of how things were. And . . . the world was not that way. As a POW, I gobbled up all sorts of other stories. I learned about piecing together evidence. About paradoxes and loops. About mathematical equations and what each society considered an acceptable amount of force. They enjoyed giving me genre shows. They considered those least powerful, least political. But those taught me other things. My favorite detectives, Sam Spade and Columbo . . . the rogue detective in Despiadado. That endless series about the Barnaby family, and Saga Noren. Ah, Saga! Gallium Martinez. Sasha Oriphant, from the early show Evecom made. Ortega, from Detective Muerto. That was an early Teni one, back when we were called Teniente Azul, after the arms dealer. The world was a much more complicated place before the corporate consolidation. So many different countries. Different rules. Difficult to keep track. But many did believe in rightness. Objective truth. The rule of law. They were all fantasies, the same way our media is fantastic; full of hopes and wishes and stories about the world we strive for, not the world we live in.

I: So you defected because you wanted to watch a lot of bad media? Is that what you're saying?

S: What do you believe in, Sergeant? Do you believe in TenisanaCom?

I: TenisanaCom has always been fair to those who are worthy.

S: But you did not always side with TenisanaCom, or Evecom before it. You worked for Teni, before the consolidation. I was there, Sergeant. Were you always with Evecom, a secret agent rolled up into its citizen schools until you could engineer the merger with Tene-Silvia, or was there a moment you turned and sided with another corp? I wonder, often, if you were in this from the beginning. If you knew the end as I did.

I: We are free to barter citizenship.

S: You were bartered?

I: My contract was up for renegotiation.

S: A euphemism if I ever heard one.

I: Not at all. I'm a skilled citizen.

S: Then you made a choice. To give up what

was known and head into the unknown. Why did you do that, Sergeant? Was it because the known had become so terrifying?

I: Money and opportunity. Isn't it always thus? Is that what Mars offered you? Money and opportunity?

S: No. Mars offered me rest, Sergeant. Rest from a very long war. An infinite loop of despair. Defecting also offered me a chance to know the truth.

I: The truth?

S: About the war. About myself. You get a lot of time to think about things when you're in a cell.

I: And what truth did you learn there?

S: That the war with Mars is a lie. That the only idiots on that rock are a few thousand free Martians staying low until you destroy one another. The rest are just corporate civilians caught in a war that started between the corporations on Mars, and then came here.

I: You're here to spread misinformation?

S: That's your job. I just answer questions.

I: Why Saint Petersburg?

S: You are so obsessed with that stupid question. I already told you. I went there because you were there, and I needed you to get me here.

I: And where is here? You have no idea where we're holding you. That's by design.

S: On the contrary. I know exactly where you're holding me, because I've been here before.

I: Riddles and nonsense.

S: Not at all. Time displacement, remember?

I: That's a theory only. It's not been proven.

S: I'm disappointed. You're in intelligence. You should understand what's happening.

I: Enlighten me.

S: We're in a basement on Robben Island. And I'm about to liberate myself.

I: You're a mad little grunt, aren't you?

S: I've never been saner in my life.

I: End interview.

(END RECORDING #4)

28.

Some of us came back together.

Some of us didn't.

Prakash lay in front of me, flopping like a fish. Blood bubbled from her mouth, frothing.

I threw off my helmet and crawled over to her. The others were still coming together; not everyone saw her. Maybe I was looking for her, because I knew, always knew, this moment was coming.

Her hand jutted out of her chest, the arm mangled to shoot through her. I knew it was possible to get put back together wrong. They went through it in training. I'd seen it happen to other people. But knowing it would happen and then finally seeing it happen to someone on my squad was something else.

I pulled Prakash into my arms. Her eyes were already distant, the far-off look of someone retreating into death.

"Don't, hey," I said, like it made a difference. I took off her helmet and put my hand to her face. I wanted to touch her one last time, before this all went full circle.

But the medics took her away from me. Another medic grabbed me by the shoulder and started walking me through the protocol.

"Show me your digits!" she said.

I held up my hands.

"Name and rank," she said, and I choked on my words because I had no idea what my rank was at this moment in time.

"Sorry. I'm a little confused."

She shone a light into my eyes. I blinked rapidly, trying to figure out where I was in the order of things.

If Prakash was . . . we had just come from the banana fields. Where I had shot the Martian girl. Early in the war. My heart fluttered frantically, like it was trying to come out of my chest.

I wanted to throw up. I buckled over, but nothing came up. I couldn't breathe. My body sagged, suddenly weak, and I broke out in a cold sweat.

"What's happening?" I said. "What's—"

The medic called for a stretcher. I started hyperventilating. I clawed at the collar of my slick, tore it loose.

Two more medics hustled over. Gave me oxygen. Threw me on a stretcher. I shook so badly I thought I'd shake right out of my body. I pressed my hand over my heart, willing it to stay still. I kept trying to work out what was happening; it was like I had left my body, like I was looking down at some unreasonable thing happening to someone else.

I saw Jones staring at me; Jones, who was going to defect, in the end, and I didn't blame him, not at all, though the look on his face now . . . he still had something, this early in the war. Some feeling of rightness and duty to the corp that had yet to be broken. Omalas watched me go too; Marino was presumably already halfway back to the drop that would take us to quarantine, no doubt thinking about a beer and a fuck. Blackness ate at the corners of my vision, and I closed my eyes then, fearful that I would pass out.

In medical quarantine, they hooked me to a line and ran some tests. They gave me something that cooled the edges of reality. After half an hour or so, I felt like I was ready to float away.

The doctor came in, a tall woman with a beak of a nose and bushy orange eyebrows that were at odds with her stark white hair. I hadn't met her before, not that I remembered anyway.

"Private Dietz. Are you feeling better?"

"Yeah." My voice sounded far away.

"It looks like you had a panic attack. It's very common, after a drop."

"Prakash," I said. "Did she die?"

"I'm afraid I can't comment on that."

"Who can? Is she dead or not?"

"She's being treated. That's all I can tell you. I'm sorry. As for you, we'll keep you for observation for another two hours, then release you to quarantine. I'm going to have your company medic administer a powerful sleeping aid for you the next few nights. You were badly dehydrated, and you're underweight. I expect your CO will also have something to say about your hair."

I touched my scalp. My hair had grown out at the end of the war with nobody to keep track of it. How long had I been there, after the Sick? A long time. Months, at least. Maybe a year?

"Intelligence is coming, too, aren't they?" I said.

"That's not my department," she said, "but based on your condition, that's likely."

She left. I zoned out, my tumbling train of thought castrated by the drugs.

When was the last time I slept?

I fought it as long as I could. Some part of me was afraid I'd wake up in another time, that everything would be different again, that this was the drop they found out I really was Mad Dietz, just like my father, and I'd be the next one they disappeared.

29.

The soft blue walls of the intelligence debriefing room comforted me. After seeing how chaotic things were at the end, all I wanted to do was eat and sleep. Talk seemed counterproductive. Lieutenant Ortega was back, which I also found soothing and familiar.

She sat across from me, alone this time, though I knew there were other people guarding the door, and probably some watching us on camera. I would expect no less.

They hadn't even let me have a shower yet. My hair was greasy and long. My stomach rumbled so loudly I thought Ortega could hear it.

She swiped open a display on the table and turned two snaps around so I could see them side by side.

The first snap showed me in formation, no doubt right before the last drop. The banana run. I had a fleshy, sunburned face; a shaved head. The second snap was me in the hospital bed. I didn't remember anyone taking it, but there are cameras everywhere. In this one, I'm much thinner, my hair's a messy tangle, and I have that faraway, blank look I've seen on so many other soldiers who have seen too much shit.

"Can you explain this?" She tapped the photo of me in formation. "We took this right before you dropped. We prefer to have these on file for occurrences like this, when people come back . . . different." She tapped the second snap. "This is you now."

I peered at the faces. They could be two different people.

"Private Dietz? Tell us what happened during your last drop."

I rubbed my finger on the projection of my new, thinner face. "Sometimes we come back wrong. Like Prakash."

"These differences can't be explained by the deployment technology."

"What happened to Prakash?"

"We all know the risks of deployment," Ortega said. "She had to be lethally quarantined—put into stasis to halt any further damage."

"You going to lethally quarantine me, too? Put me on ice until you figure out what to do with me?" Prakash wasn't dead, though, not yet. That was something.

"Do we need to?" Ortega leaned toward me.

"I don't know what happened." Something caught in my throat. All the lying catching up to me, maybe. I couldn't even look at her.

"That's the story you'll stick to?"

"Ask your logistics people what happened. Then maybe you can start giving *me* answers, instead of the other way around. I'm the one bleeding and shitting for the fucking corp. You owe me."

"The corp owes you nothing."

"Then I don't owe them anything, either."

"That's not what your contract says."

I folded my arms. "I want a shower and a hot meal. I haven't had either in a while. You still consider us human at all? Or are we just ghouls to you? My parents died to get me residency and it means shit, doesn't it? We're all just a means to an end."

"What was your mission brief, Private?"

"Round up some insurgents. I shot a Martian on accident. Prakash complained about her arm. That's all I have for you."

"So you do remember," Ortega said, triumphant.

"I know the brief."

"You're in a dangerous place. If you can't give us answers—"

"You still need soldiers. I can be a soldier. Just because I came back wrong . . . that shit isn't my fault, any more than it was Prakash's. Don't fuck around with me, Ortega."

"Lieutenant Ortega."

"Whatever."

I got a day in the brig after that, for talking back to an intelligence officer. It was worth it. I needed some time to myself anyway. I got my shower. Blood and grime collected at my feet, swirled down the drain. I found myself pressing my fingers to the space just below my collarbone, where Tanaka thought I should have a scar. Who was I? Who was I *supposed* to be?

When I got out of the brig, quarantine was over. Got my hair cut at the barracks barber. I watched him shave off my curly black hair, revealing the skinny, narrow head beneath. The face looking back at me could have been a stranger's.

I got a new set of clothes, and an appointment with my shrink. Dr. Chen looked just the same.

When she came in and got sight of me, she did a double-take. Her left eye lit up as she accessed my file, no doubt confirming who the hell I was.

"It was a bad drop," I said, and my mouth turned up at one corner.

"I see."

"We've met before," I said, before she could ask.

Something passed between us, maybe for the first time.

What number was this meeting, for her? Our third? Fourth? It all blended together.

"You lost a colleague," she said. "How has that made you feel?"

"Lost a lot of things."

"Tell me how you're holding up."

I wanted to tell her I wasn't holding up at all. I was busting down. Busting apart. What if I told her everything? Got myself locked up for the rest of the war? Maybe I needed to be lethally quarantined. What if there was no way out of this loop but to just remove myself from it? I moved my hand to the pocket watch.

"Private Dietz?" Dr. Chen said softly.

When I opened my eyes, she was leaning slightly forward, her retinal display still flickering.

"I'm not feeling well. Physically."

"According to your file, you were in medical quarantine after the drop. Do you want to tell me about that?"

"I'm tired. I just need time."

"Did they discuss your body's cellular degeneration?"

"No."

"It's taking place at an advanced rate."

"Oh, that. Yeah, I have heard that before."

"It's accelerated since our last discussion."

"So what does that mean?"

"It means there's no shame in anything you are feeling. The panic attacks are a normal response to extreme stress."

"They going to put me on a medical leave?"

"Would you like that?"

"You're the experts."

"Reviewing your physical and mental health, I would recommend to your commanding officer that you remain confined to the barracks for six weeks, just as a precaution. We can meet once a week and discuss your mental health. Can you tell me more about how you're feeling about the loss of your colleague?"

"No."

She asked a few more questions, but I was done. After twenty minutes of one-word answers, she let me go. I went to my bunk in the barracks for the first time since I'd come back. My steps slowed as I approached. I was afraid to count the marks on the bed frame.

Jones was already in his bunk. He had out one of his Amado books, but it lay flat on his chest, unread. Omalas was asleep in hers two rows down. No one else was in the rack. We had an hour before lights-out; I figured most were playing games or engaged in immersives.

"You look like shit," Jones said.

"Yeah."

"Everything come back all right?"

"Giving me some downtime."

He nodded, once. "Sorry about Prakash."

"Sorry for all of us."

He wouldn't look at me. His hands were shaking. I sat at the end of his bunk. Scrutinized his face. I patted his knee; anything more felt intrusive.

But he sat up and hugged me. A brief embrace, like he was my brother. And he was. They all were. My brothers and sisters. The family closest to me. Another family I'd lose.

Jones pulled away. Wiped at his eyes. "This fucking war," he said.

"Yeah. It's confusing as hell."

"Muñoz got confused too. After her first drop. Kept thinking things had happened that . . . didn't."

"How often?"

"I don't know, you know how it is. We all want to stick to the brief."

"She ever . . . say she could change anything?"

"I don't follow."

"When she saw things . . . I feel like we're all on this big speeding train. Out of control. It's heading over a cliff, and there's no way to stop it. We're just passengers."

"If I was on a speeding train I couldn't control, hey . . . I'd jump off."

"You would."

"I would."

That was all the talking I had left in me. I stripped and went to bed early. Lights-out came and went.

Losing Prakash made me think of Vi. I couldn't help it. I pressed my hands to my face, willing away the memories. I had met Vi at the beach. I remember the day because even in my memory, it's like a dream. A blazing blue sky. Warm, milky water. Something from an immersive, the type you want to dip into over and over.

She came out of the water laughing; I didn't know at what. She was talking to someone on her heads-up; I saw it flickering with an image.

I was learning to surf with some other residents I'd met in class. I was seventeen, and I'd learn later that Vi was almost five years older than me. It wasn't so much a legal taboo—sixteen was the age of consent—but a social one. She was a citizen. I could tell immediately. Clear skin, easy confidence, a walk like she owned the world.

She saw me looking and flicked her gaze away, pretending she didn't notice. Maybe she didn't.

I watched her the whole time we were on the water. When we came back in and started a game of soccer on the beach, I tried to think of all sorts of ways to engineer an excuse to talk to her. Ultimately, I couldn't figure one out. How do you just, like, go up to a citizen like it's no big deal?

It was sheer luck that I saw she was giving a talk at the local university. The university was government, but residents and citizens were allowed to attend talks. It was my mom who pointed it out to me on the events screen. My mother lay in bed, one of her bad days, and she pointed at the programming. "Look at that," she said. "It's a free talk about corporate negotiations. You should go, little cabbage. Know your enemy."

"They're not the enemy, Mama," I said, rolling my eyes, but it was Vi's face on the program.

I went.

I was the youngest one there, one of just a few residents. I sat near the front, and felt like an idiot the entire time. Nothing was really free, and we had to get scanned in to attend, so the corp could sell us more stuff later, track our interests.

But when Vi got up there, I was rapt.

"How many of you think that you view the world objectively?"

A lot of hands went up. Mine too.

"I'm going to tell you about a man who was under a tremendous amount of stress," she said. "Turn on a screen and you see talk of corporate wars. Bad business deals. Residents losing their rights. Citizens who are bartered away to other corporations against their will. We have disease. Food riots. Scarcity. Poverty. He saw all these things, and the worse it got, the more he felt like it was all connected. He began to write elaborate theories and spread them around the knu. He could connect all these events into one grand, elaborate structure. There was only one problem."

She paused for effect, and I saw a little hint of triumph in her eyes. "None of it was true. Under stress, the human mind is more likely to see patterns in everyday noise. Show them a picture of random black-and-white dots while primed to remember a moment when they were out of control, and they are more likely to see an image in it. The more stressed we are, the more we believe we can alter outcomes. Understanding this tendency is crucial to intuiting how both you and your business adversary see the world around you."

Vi went on for about half an hour, and then opened it up for questions. I had come with a bunch of questions, including dumb things like asking her out for a caffeine hit right there, but I figured that was creepy.

I raised my hand. She called on me and I said, "What happens when they're right?"

Everyone laughed.

I shook my head. "I mean, I agree that this is clearly a thing that happens. But if we were smart enough to be able to truly perceive all the complex ways the world interacts, could we connect them? See the future? Isn't it a matter of the human mind not being smart enough to put it all together yet?"

I sat down.

Vi said, "If that was true, we could train an algorithm to find that pattern. So far there's no algorithm that can accurately predict the future. This is in part due to quantum theory, which I understand isn't the topic here, but it's related. There is no way to predict the future because the future is always changing, always uncertain, at the quantum level. Quantum particles behave unpredictably. Unpredictability rules us at the most basic level. We yearn for certainty, but the fact is that certainty and absolutes are a fiction. Another question?"

I stuck around after, trying to figure out a way to ask her but not ask her out. To my relief, Vi invited those of us left at the venue to head over to the bar across the street for a drink. The six of us went.

By the end of the night, only the two of us remained.

I'm still not sure how that happened. I found her fascinating. When she asked me what I planned to do with my life, I said, "Be a hero," and that got a laugh.

But it was true then.

It was still true now.

I woke in the barracks sometime after midnight, straining to hear what had woken me. The grunts and sighs and shifting sheets, just a couple of people fucking around, somewhere on the far side of our sleeping quarters. I closed my eyes again. They were being pretty quiet, all things considered, but I was wired. My heartbeat started banging hard in my chest again. I took a few deep breaths. *There's nothing to panic about,* I told myself, but my body didn't want to listen. Frankie's headless torso. Prakash flailing in my arms. Landon. Fuck, Landon, spraying blood and viscera all over me. His fat baby. Round little wife. Where were they, now? What was going to happen to them, during the Sick? Dead, probably. All of us dead, and for what? So the corps could consolidate power. One corp to rule them all.

I closed my eyes and focused my breathing. In and out. *Focus on something you can control, Dietz.*

Control.

My mother yearned for control. Over her body. Over us. Over our circumstances. She yearned for control over the weather. I remember her shaking a fist at the sky when it hadn't rained in two months, cursing it out in French. The only French I ever learned from her were the curse words. Her family had come to São Paulo as refugees after the end of Masukisan's war with a small regional corp called Sarko-Molina. Sarko-Molina was swallowed up and merged with Masukisan, its citizens and residents busted down to ghouls and forced to reapply for status. When I asked what city she came from, she said it was Abidjan, and she pointed it out on my father's old world map, a city on the African continent that hung off the back of the elephant's ear there, dangling like an earring.

"Most of the city flooded in my grandparents' time," she told me. "We were far inland, behind great towers in the sky, before

Masukisan came. Much of eastern Africa is desert, of course, but the Sahara bloomed, as the world got warmer. My great-grandmother remembers when they thought the world wouldn't warm as quickly as it did. But there was beauty in it, also. Some deserts turned to forests. The tundra became wheat fields. We were never hungry. The solar farms, the hanging gardens . . ."

"Were you a citizen?" I asked.

"A resident. But the war . . . well, there are some things you cannot control. But we could determine how we reacted to the war. Masukisan would wreak retribution on us, I knew that. We would not sit there waiting for it."

"How did you know when to leave? Why did so many people stay?"

"There isn't a precise time when you know you must leave. It's like putting a lobster in a pot of cold water and turning up the heat. It warms slowly. Then there is a moment, though not a moment past, when there is no going back. You must move before that moment."

"But you can never know that. You can never know when it's too late until . . . until it is."

"That's right."

I would learn later that she had no living family back in Abidjan. Only my grandparents and her sisters—those who had fled to São Paulo with her—were still known to her. Whether they were dead or lost, scattered to some other place, she never knew.

"We were someone once," she told me. "We'll be someone again."

"We've always been people, though, Mama," I said. I was young.

"You have to make yourself, little cabbage."

I didn't like the idea that all I could control was how I reacted to what was done to me. I wanted to prevent the corporate wars, the displacement of people like my mother and her family. But who could do that, who but a leader, a CEO, a prophet, some big man in a tank. I wasn't good at any of those things. Even during this war, I'd never made squad leader, and the highest rank I seemed to have attained was corporal at the very end. Probably because a bunch of other people died and I simply outlasted them. I wasn't good with people. Not technically proficient. Not charismatic. All I had was what was done to me—this weird way of jumping. What was I going to do with it?

I gazed up at the marks on the bunk above me. I'd been so tired I hadn't counted them. I did so now.

Ninety-three.

The same number as when I left on that mission to CanKrushkev territory, that banana drop, but really ended up clearing out Robben Island. I added three more marks to cover my time in quarantine and today.

I knew that when I jumped to the Sick, there were more than nine hundred marks here. Which depressed the fuck out of me. That was a lot of experience to get through, from here until then. I listened to the culmination of the fucking in the barracks. I won't lie; my hand strayed to my crotch. Shit, after all this, you just want to *feel* something. I turned my head, looking for who? For Prakash? For Tanaka?

I closed my eyes. Vi.

If I'd listened to Vi, if I'd gone after her, I wouldn't be in this shit. I wouldn't be in *any* shit. It would all be over. Like a sinking fucking ship.

Above me, Jones continued to snore softly along with the rest of the platoon.

Knowing how this all ended, it occurred to me this ship was sinking too. It's just that not everybody realized it yet.

30.

We have a little announcement to make," the CO said.

She stood on the parade ground with us, flanked by some of the top brass. One of them, Major Stakeley, waved over another officer, who broke formation and saluted him. I was ten rows back and couldn't make out much of the new officer's face.

Major Stakeley said, "First Lieutenant Valenzuela has been promoted to captain and will become your new company commander. This is First Lieutenant Andria Patel. She will head up your platoon going forward."

I strained to get a look at Andria, but in her suit and hat, she looked so much like the rest of us I couldn't make out any distinguishing features. I clutched at the pocket watch again. Would I find her, or would she find me? She must have looked at our dossiers and known I was here, but I could not catch her look.

"I've heard you're a good bunch of grunts," Andria bellowed. "Some of you I know, some I'll get to know. I expect good manners. Exceptional fitness. Divine obedience. In return I'll do my damnedest to make sure you don't die without a good reason. Understood?"

"Understood, sir!" we shouted.

After we were dismissed, I made my way over to Andria. She nodded. I saluted.

"Sir," I said.

"At ease, Dietz."

"Permission to speak with you privately, sir?"

She narrowed her eyes at that, but nodded. "Come into my office."

I thought she would take me to the CO's old office, the same one I would later see during the Sick. But Lieutenant V must not have been out of there yet. Instead, we headed upstairs to the rec room, where only the brass was allowed to go. I hesitated at the steps, but she urged me up.

"They're all in some meeting," she said.

She pressed her hand to the security plate and got us entry. The LED film covering the walls lit up, giving us a view of a deep, wet jungle, like something you only saw anymore in Patagonia or Western Australia. Mats lined the floor. A rack of free weights took up the back wall. Just beyond that were two immersion chairs and a cabinet I figured held the booze, because that's where Andria headed first.

"Shut the door," she said, popping open the cabinet. I had never seen so many bottles of liquor all in one place, and that was saying something.

"How did you become a first lieutenant so fast?" I asked.

"Be in a platoon with a high casualty rate," Andria said, "and don't fuck up too much when they run you through abbreviated officer training."

"Well, I'm right out, then."

She pulled a bottle of scotch from the cabinet and poured me a brandy glass full of it.

"I haven't eaten, Andria; not sure I want to chug this."

"You won't." She snickered.

She poured herself a mere two fingers of pale amber scotch.

"Have a seat." She gestured to the immersive chairs. I pushed up an armrest and sat sideways in the chair. I wanted to stay upright. If I laid back, I feared I'd fall asleep. I took a gulp of the drink, barely hesitating as I got a whiff of the peaty stink of it right before it burned my throat. I winced.

"Like that?" Andria laughed. "Rubem got me into it. Satisfying. Like drinking the war."

I took another swig and closed my eyes. I rolled the swallow around on my tongue. It reminded me of burning Canuck; the smell of Marino's smoking grill. The loam and salt of Tanaka and I fucking in that field. Taste of our heated MREs covered in ash from the coals. It must have been Andria who was our CO on that mission; that's why I didn't recognize Captain V's voice. How could you long for a time and a place that had been hell on earth? I swallowed the scotch and opened my eyes to find Andria scrutinizing me.

"You know why I'm here?" I asked.

"I know coms don't work so well in the rec room. I figured you'd appreciate that. It's been a while, Dietz. For you. For me."

I turned on the pocket watch and set it on the floor between us. The blue aura of my coms went out. Intelligence was muted.

Andria stared at the watch like it was a malevolent insect.

"Where the hell did you get that?" Andria breathed.

"From you."

Andria dug into her pants and set a nearly identical watch next to the one I'd put there. My version was shabbier, a little scuffed, and still had a bit of Andria's blood on it.

"This was my grandmother's," she said. "Passed on from her grandmother. How the fuck do you have it?"

"Does yours take coms out like this one? Have you done that yet?"

Andria took her original pocket watch and slowly stuffed it back into her pocket. "You did that? How do you have . . ."

"I need your help. Not just now, but later. Have you heard of the Light Brigade?"

"What, like . . . the charge of the light brigade?"

"No." I didn't know what that was. "Soldiers who have bad drops. Deployments that happen . . . out of order. When they break apart."

"I've read your file. Rube told me to, when he heard I got this promotion. He had a feeling."

My chest tightened. Could I trust her this early in the war?

"I don't want to get grounded. I have to learn how to control these drops. You helped me, ahead of now. That's how I have that pocket watch. There's going to come a time, you'll know it, after a mission they call the final solution, when we all get sick. That's when I need your help most."

Her fingers tapped her glass.

"You talked to Rube?"

"No." I almost added, "He's dead, how could I?" but didn't. I could see it in her face, her tone. She was talking and thinking about him like he was still alive. And he was, for now. My head hurt.

"What do you want from me?"

"I need you to help me finish what we started in the future."

I expected her to call in a medic right then.

"Tell me?"

I told her—about the drops, about burning Canuck. The Sick. The torture modules.

"I have to figure out how to beat the torture modules. Can you help? You know how."

"Sure, I learned back in mandatory training."

"But you didn't go into intelligence?"

Andria grimaced. "I don't torture people."

"Aren't torture modules torture?"

"Yes, but not with real people. You're beating an algorithm designed to act like a person. It has rules. Like any program. There are rules."

"Like . . . physics." I searched my memory for my basic physics class. "Basic rules. Conservation of mass? Right?"

"Mass can't get created or destroyed, only rearranged. That's why we don't generally lose people. They come back wrong. Also, theory of relativity . . . shit gets heavier the faster it moves."

"What was the thing about heavy stuff?"

"I see where you're going. Heavy objects distort space-time. And if you're moving at the speed of light—"

"We'd get heavier."

"Sure, but massive star heavy? And wouldn't all that heavy gravity fuck up stuff like—"

"The moon?"

Andria leaned back in her chair. "Huh." She poured herself another two fingers of whisky. "I'm listening."

"I'm just spitballing. I have no idea what I'm talking about."

"Yeah, but whatever it is you have no idea about kinda intrigues me. Rubem was saying science shit like this."

"So you're listening because of *Rubem*? Well, remind me to thank him." Before he ended up dead.

"Let's say I believe you're living this war out of order," Andria said. "We'll say that logistics fucked up, like they did with Rube. Happens all the time. It's new tech."

"And I'm not the only one it's happened to. That's how you know I'm not crazy."

"You're the only one to talk about it in detail. Rube clams up about it."

I pointed at the pocket watch. "I'm only talking because coms are down. If they were recording this, I'd be grounded. Nobody wants to be grounded. And Jones said people who had bad drops weren't always just grounded. They disappeared. I wasn't going to talk about that with anybody."

"But you are with me? We haven't seen each other in . . . a long time."

"For you, maybe. It wasn't that long ago that I last saw you. When I meet you again, in the future, you said I'd talked to you. That I'd somehow convinced you to help me. I have no idea what I said. I'm hoping this is it."

"Better turn coms back on, or someone's going to ask questions. I can only blame the bad reception in this room for so long."

I reluctantly took the watch into my hand. "You going to report me?" I said.

"I remember what they called your father."

"I do too."

"You signed up to fight this war, even with what they did to him."

"I believed it was the right thing to do."

"I never told you how my aunt died, did I?"

"One of the two you lived with?"

"Yeah. They looked after us, after my parents died. And one of my aunts fought in the corporate wars. Fought for Teni, too. Good soldier. Good woman. She's the reason I wanted to go into the service at all. I was already a citizen. I could have done anything. But something happened to her in the service. I didn't know what until earlier this year. All I heard was she died. They gave us all these great benefits. Sent her ashes home wrapped in a flag. Neat and tidy. I got drunk with a sergeant major on leave, and she remembers my aunt. She tells me she spoke up for my aunt when my aunt was court-martialed. It's the reason my aunt wasn't dishonorably discharged. The sergeant major was the reason we got some happy story about her and got to keep our benefits and citizenship."

"What did she do?"

"She saw something she shouldn't have. That's all the sergeant major would say. I wonder, though, about all the shit going down in the Corporate Corps, especially the last few years. I wonder just how far they'll go to beat the other corps, to consolidate us. It's been moving that way for a long time."

I let out my breath. I didn't realize I'd been holding it. I raised the watch. "Ready?"

She nodded.

I pressed the switch, and the blinking light flickered at the corner of my left eye again. I put the watch away.

"I'm happy to help you work the torture modules," Andria said. "But you look like shit. Take another couple days. Work on your meditation. Then we'll head down to the immersive cave and talk about volition. I heard you're grounded for six weeks. That should give us some time unless the platoon is called out on an extended mission."

"Thank you, sir." I stood.

"And Dietz?"

"Yeah?"

"Wait to be dismissed next time."

"Yes, sir," I said, and saluted. I backed out of the room. When I got into the hall, I realized my hands were shaking. When was the last time I tried to change anything in my life instead of just reacting to it?

I hadn't even tried to change for Vi.

More the fool, me.

31.

I rolled into my first immersive with Andria a few days later during free time. I wasn't looking forward to it. All I had to go on was Andria's future insistence that this would work. The Andria I sat next to on the reclining immersive seat parallel with mine didn't seem as confident in what the fuck we were doing as Future Andria, but I suppose I should have expected that. The thing is, when you're doing something you know is a little bit nuts, you really want to have somebody on your side reassuring you that it's not really nuts, and this is fine, really fine. And she wasn't quite there yet.

As I slipped into the immersive experience, I tried to blot out my memories of the future. I wanted to believe Andria was doing this for me, but she was doing it for Rubem. Rubem, who would be dead by the next time we talked. And I never even asked her about it then, never said, "How did he die?" The dead were all blurring together, muddled as the events I was experiencing. Follow orders. Follow the brief. Jump, jump. Do as you're told. No time for anything else.

Vi used to tell me about this experiment, the Milgram Experiment, where some college professor got ordinary people to administer electric shocks to students until they believed the students were dead. He did it by telling them that he would take all responsibility for what happened, and that if they didn't administer the death-dealing shocks, the experiment was ruined.

That's the easy way to live, and the way the Corporate Corps wanted it.

It wasn't until I opened my eyes and stepped into the immersive experience with Andria that I remembered that study. Ordinary people would do anything for authority figures, as long as they could be insulated from the blame. But they would do anything for the people they loved, too. Even if it meant disobeying orders. Why didn't anyone do an experiment on *that*?

The immersive bloomed around us. A dingy, brick-lined torture chamber. This was the first time, chronologically, that Andria had seen it.

"How very medieval," she laughed.

I hung at the center of the room, bound in chains attached to the ceiling. At the edges of the darkness, I sensed the hulking forms of the guards, the torturers, the interrogators, waiting to seethe inside and end this.

Andria picked up a whip lying on the big wooden table in front of me. It was, by far, the most innocuous of the weapons laid out on the counter.

"Something you want to tell me, Dietz?" she said, waggling the whip.

"It's the default setting."

She shrugged. Threw the whip back. "Oh well. So tell me about what you're experiencing."

"Everything fucking hurts." I hadn't put on the settings. Andria had, again. That scared the fuck out of me. The torturers could do anything they wanted, until I used the safe word that triggered the program to shut down. It occurred to me that this time I might know the word, though, if she reused them.

"Why does it hurt?"

"I don't get that question."

"You understand you're in a simulation. You know it's fake. You're in control. So, why does everything hurt?"

"Because my brain says so. It says that—"

"What's the purpose of your brain?"

"To interpret . . . stimuli."

"So what is this?"

"Stimuli . . . but listen, what's the difference, then, between this and the real world, if they're both just processing stimuli?"

"Exactly." The torturers came in dressed all in black, a mix of faces and skin tones and hair textures and crisp uniforms. I didn't want them to look like Martians, whatever it was we had been told Martians looked like—tall and thin, tending toward the pale, clear skin, squinty eyes, snub noses. I knew the enemy was not a tone or a texture, but a system.

Andria picked up a jagged black knife on the table. She cut each of their throats cleanly. The torturers dropped like flies; far more quickly and quietly than any human person did in real life unless they had a blood clot or an aneurysm. An uncle of mine—a man I called my uncle—had once died of an aneurysm. He had been running along a popular pedestrian pathway, and then simply dropped dead, like a marionette whose strings were cut. It was an astonishing thing, to watch someone who was there one moment, and gone the next.

The bodies of the torturers bled out and faded from the module.

"There you go," Andria said.

"You aren't coded like me."

"On the contrary. I'm dialed in to this simulation with the same constraints you are."

I closed my eyes and focused my attention, the way I had the last time she and I had done this, in the future. I heard the second wave of torturers head in.

As their boots approached, I felt Andria move. I opened my eyes to find her face peering into mine. The cold blade she held kissed my neck.

"What will you do?" Andria said.

Behind her, the torturers came in, garbed in their black.

I met Andria's gaze. I reached.

The chain around my right wrist warped and melted away. I yanked the blade from Andria's hand and lashed out at the nearest assailant. Plunged the knife into his neck. Then the next. The next.

They threw themselves at me, one after another, wielding their buzzing batons. Their hits landed. Pain. But pain was just a message, a firing in my neurons. This pain did not exist outside my head. It was confined.

As the last woman fell, I found my breathing was still even. I had not broken a sweat. Of course not.

This isn't real, I thought. That's the understanding one had to have. The realization that made it possible.

"Very good," Andria said. She pointed to my left wrist, still bound by a chain. "Fatal flaw there, though."

I jerked at the chain. It remained fast.

"Goddammit," I said.

You win some, you lose some.

32.

Three weeks into my grounding, the platoon got called on a mission to eastern Africa, Masukisan territory. That left me in the barracks with the support staff and a few other soldiers from the wider company who were out on medical leave like me, either for physical or mental.

It was not an especially memorable time. I marked the days on my bunk. I saw the shrink. We discussed my bullshit feelings about nothing. I talked about my own boredom, my weariness of the war. She wanted to talk endlessly about the Martian I had shot on my last mission, but that Martian was the least of the horrors in my brain, now. When I woke during these stretches, it was from nightmares of vomiting blood onto my boots on Mars, and running, always running, after Muñoz across the rusty Martian dust; she always stayed just ahead of me, laughing, looking back.

I didn't tell the shrink about those nightmares.

When my six weeks were officially up, my platoon still wasn't back from their last deployment. Those of us left in the barracks weren't given any updates. Information was, as ever, at a premium. I got put on guard duty around the barracks, and started attending classes to work on my specialist promotion. Most of this was the shrink's idea. She didn't like me spending so much time in torture immersives. I suppose it doesn't look good, being on some mental health leave and volunteering to get virtually tortured. But I had heard about aversion therapy for PTSD; some of the other soldiers talked about it, and I surfaced that idea in one of our discussions. Maybe it was good for me to face the things that I had experienced in a controlled environment. Let my body burn off the anxiety.

By the time my platoon got back, I'd been awarded my specialist promotion, proving that I did, in fact, have more than two brain cells to rub together. I wanted to message the DI and tell him, then wondered if he was dead. That would be fitting, wouldn't it?

When my platoon got out of quarantine, I counted fifty-six additional marks on my bunk. It continued to be the only way to keep track of days, as I had no access to a calendar. Duty lists and company-wide events were communicated through a countdown clock, and never more than seven days in advance, as if knowing too far out about a holiday or a parade march would result in a mass revolt.

Jones was the first one I saw come back from quarantine. He walked with a limp. He did not look at me as he slid into his bunk.

"Alive," I said.

"Did you know that even blood can burn?"

"I didn't," I said, and left it at that.

We had lost Herrera on that drop. I learned later that he had corporealized inside of a big dirt pit and died before they could get logistics to route him out again. That left us down not one, but two people, counting Prakash.

The brass rotated in the new girl the next day, and when I

saw her name pop in on my heads-up, I wasn't surprised. I knew exactly whose squad she would be assigned to.

Ratzesberger.

On this, our first chronological meeting, I was struck with how young she looked. I had no idea how old I was by this point, but she seemed years younger, sixteen if a day.

"They recruiting kids now?" I grumbled.

She straightened her spine and said, "I'm seventeen! Advanced classes can sign up at—"

"Fresh meat." Marino sat on the trunk at the end of his bunk, cleaning his gun. "They just keep getting younger and younger."

"How long was your mandatory training?" I asked.

"Three weeks," she said, defiant.

"Holy Mother," Omalas muttered, and crossed herself.

"They sure are squeezing you through," I said. "It was six weeks when I did it."

"Well," Ratzesberger said, proudly, "it's a different war now. Very serious."

Marino belched and grunted, "I give you one drop."

"Don't be a dick, Marino," I said.

"I can't die yet," Ratzesberger insisted, "I just got to the front! You can't die the minute you get here!"

Marino snorted. "You know how many kids die their first drop? Dumb grunt."

"Don't mind him, Deathless," I said. "I'll give you the tour."

"Deathless," Jones repeated. "I like it."

"That pretty much guarantees she dies first," Marino said.

"Maybe it'll fake death out." I motioned for Deathless to follow me, and realized I was the one who had given her this goddamn stupid nickname.

Of course. This time line had a grim fucking sense of humor.

33.

How many days did I have to go?

A lot, it turned out.

I guess the bunk could have told me that, again and again, but I still didn't trust my own reckoning. As I'd found out after the Sick, I knew I wasn't always going to be here in the barracks to count everything.

Turns out that was a good guess.

Logistics started encountering issues. That was how they put it. Our experience was different. A whole platoon from Tangine Company came back wrong. They dropped into the deployment field as a mass of contorted bodies, arms and legs attached to the wrong torsos, heads facing backward, spines made impossibly sinuous, feet twisted like claws, when they were recognizable as limbs at all.

I didn't see them come in, but somebody put out a bootleg recording, and I downloaded and watched a copy before the corp had them all purged—including the soldier who shared it. What shook me wasn't even the images as much as the sound.

The grunting, sobbing mass of them, like listening to a squealing bunch of pigs in a pen destined for the slaughter.

They weren't the only platoon lost that day; we heard rumors of others, though information was hard to come by. They grounded all of us after that.

When Dog Company got called up again, I feared where they would send us. Captain V was company commander, and gave us the pre-drop briefing inside the big barracks cafeteria. Outside, the rain came down so hard it sounded like liquid thunder.

"Logistics is undergoing some issues," Captain V said, "as you no doubt heard."

There were some guffaws at that.

"Our full company has been assigned to do some babysitting out in São Paulo," she said.

My stomach dropped. A few of us exchanged glances.

"No doubt you don't believe there's much left in São Paulo to babysit," Captain V said, "but our CEO is having a big to-do out there, nice show of military might, and we're to be part of it. Your duties aren't just to look pretty, but also to guard the asses of the contractors tasked with building the new Freedom Monument. You probably haven't heard, but there are some liberals and anarchists out there intent on keeping São Paulo a bare patch of ground, monument to Martian terrorism. Luckily, we're good with saboteurs, huh?"

A loud, collective, "Yes, sir!"

I brooded over what she'd said the whole shuttle ride out to São Paulo, or, where São Paulo had been. We were packed into the back of a troop carrier shuttle, no windows, so at least I didn't have to see from the air what Mars had left of everything I ever loved.

When we stepped off the shuttle, I tried to keep my head down, but you couldn't help but see it. There were still buildings left near the crater; a good chunk of the city remained. Whatever weapon the Martians had used had been incredibly tactical. It was as if a giant ice cream scoop had dipped into the eastern part of the city and carved away a massive hunk of it. Most of that area had contained labor camps.

São Paulo had been an extraordinary powerhouse of a city once. That's what we grew up hearing. It lay only about seventy kilometers from the Atlantic Ocean, but was well above sea level. Lack of water, unrest, and the early Corporate Wars left much of the city abandoned and in ruins. The upheaval transformed the face of the city into the one that I knew: the shining new citadels built by corporate interests after the war, the massive solar towers, and the endless sprawl of the reclaimed city ruins where ghouls like me and my family had eked out a living after getting barred from the cities inhabited by citizens and residents.

I felt a chill, though the day was warm. The camps around the corporatized bulwark of the central city had been razed some time ago. No smoke lingered. All that remained were the charred skeletons of structures.

"What happened?" I gazed at the ring of ruin around the shining city.

Jones saw me looking and said, "Yeah, they were planning to bulldoze out everyone in the labor camps right before the Blink. The Blink took out everyone from the camps, carved it right out, but left some of the city."

I stared at him. To his credit, he looked abashed, as if just remembering where I was from.

"There's still half a million people living here. The Blink only ate a million and a half maybe, but there were more living in the core of the city. Teni burned out and bulldozed whatever was left of the camps, though. Mostly ghouls."

"It didn't bother you? That they lied?"

"Lied? They didn't lie about Mars. I mean, you can see the crater. They did Blink most of the city."

"But . . . not what they talked about in the media. The media acted like there was nothing left here."

"I guess it was . . . well, useful to the war effort. I guess . . . they didn't think as many people would sign up if they knew Mars mostly just killed ghouls here."

"Fuck this place," I said. "Fuck Teni."

"Sorry," Jones said. "I didn't think . . . Sorry."

Why would anybody ask what had happened to the ghouls here? Why would anybody care? Why would they question the line from the corp? The real fate of São Paulo wouldn't have made it onto any corporate-run media stream. As a kid policed by BLM agents continually, it wasn't like I was going to get the real story. How stupid was I, to believe everything the corp had told me? I'd eaten it up. Maybe I'd wanted to believe it. I wanted to believe the Martians destroyed the whole city, from here to the sea, because it made it easier to sign up. Made it easier to follow orders. Believing lies just makes everything . . . easier, when those lies prop up your worldview. Would I have believed it if someone told me Teni-Silvia burned out and murdered a million and a half São Paulo ghouls to make way for the resurgence of some shining corporate city?

No, I would have called it poor propaganda from Evecom, or liberal anarchists, or socialist insurgents.

Even now, I wondered if Jones was wrong. If his mother in intelligence could have made it up. There's a tremendous moment of dissonance, like leaving your body, when you discover that one of the core defining moments of your life is mostly a lie.

"Dietz! Let's roll." Andria's voice, over a two-way channel. At least she wasn't calling me slow in front of the whole platoon.

I huffed after her and the rest of the company, off to make a show of protecting the interests of a CEO who had no qualms about murdering people like me with impunity.

34.

The protests in São Paulo were massive.

I had never seen anything like it.

The new Freedom Monument spanned the breadth of the crater in the east side of the city. The crater itself had gathered water, transforming it into a perfectly spherical lake. The seething mass of protestors surrounded the lake. They had pitched brightly colored tents and parked their beat-up old vans and desert vehicles and solar ATV's. The protestors were young. Shit, *I* was still young, but to me they looked like kids, all bright eyes and joyous faces they thought were fierce. The young have nothing to lose.

Soldiers guarded either end of the Freedom Monument, letting contractors past. I had a vague recollection of what the shining monstrosity was going to look like, in the end, but for now it was a hulking mass of a bridge shot through with half-completed columns and spires, all crisscrossed with cables and marred by the swinging arms of great cranes balanced precariously on barges in the lake.

The protestors had set up their own crane, from which dangled a flag. I had to zoom in with my heads-up to make out the words: TENI MURDERED SÃO PAULO.

Andria met with us that night in the temporary tent that was our platoon's barracks. "We have a mission to secure the area around the monument before tomorrow's speech from the CEO."

"What does that mean?" Deathless, ever the astute one.

"What the fuck you think it means?" Marino laughed.

Omalas stared into her hands.

"It means we clear the area around the crater," Andria said, "by any means necessary."

I had my rifle over my knees. I had just finished cleaning it and putting it back together. "Sir, does that mean lethal force? On our own people?"

"They aren't our people," Andria said, but her heart wasn't in it. "Most are paid protestors. We're doing a job, just like they are. They were told to disperse or face force. They know what's coming."

"They aren't even armed," Omalas murmured.

"Some may be," Andria pointed out. "That's why we have to clear them. We may not even need to use force." When none of us looked at her she said, more loudly, "This is an order from the chief executive of war, which comes direcly from the CEO. Most importantly, this is an order that comes from me."

Whatever happened out here tonight, Andria wanted me to put it on her. She'd put it on Captain V. Captain V would blame the lieutenant colonel of the battalion, who would blame the colonel of the regiment, who would blame the major general of the brigade, and up and up, until what happened tonight rested on the peacefully sleeping head of some CEO who would never get her hands dirty. Never see the blood pumping from a mortally wounded friend. Never watch the life leave the face of some poor dumb kid who believed the world could be a better place.

We moved out.

Our company struck the protestors' camps a little after two in the morning. It was never going to be a fair fight. It wasn't meant to be. I put the safety on my rifle before we hit the camps. A lot of soldiers didn't.

The protestors fought us with fists and rocks and sticks. As they came awake, they used crude petrol bombs, but those weren't enough to get through our suits, which had been made to endure the sort of violent incendiary that we'd encountered in Canuck. Even the bullets from the few standard guns they had stashed in their vehicles or under their sleeping bags didn't faze us much.

We advanced, we advanced . . . and I found it easier if I saw this as a collective action. A "we" and not an "I."

Deathless, so fearful on a real battlefield, found this poorly matched slaughter far easier to bear. She was the second in our company to fire her pulse rifle into the screaming, rock-throwing crowds, obliterating one protestor and parts of two more. I didn't see the expression on her face when she did it, because her visor was down, but I could imagine it. The rush of awe. The surge of power.

She raised her rifle again.

I plowed past her, after Andria, who was doing her best to goad the protestors with riot spray and an electric truncheon. But the protestors had decent defensive tactics. They were not complete fools. They came equipped with homemade power-nullifying vests, pepper-spray triage kits, and they had painted their faces to evade the face recognition software in our heads-up displays. Drones surged through the sky, ours and theirs. I admired the janky little craft they employed against us. It made me think of Mars, and the little boy Lieutenant V had killed. How fearful did the CEO have to be, to encourage us to murder children with homemade explosives and milky pepper-spray remedies? We were killing the symptoms, but not the disease.

I wondered what I would tell my shrink after this. How would she tell me to soothe my conscience over this one? Just a war, just orders, just following protocol for the good of Tene-Silvia?

I raised the butt of my rifle and prodded at a kid ahead of me, telling her to move, in Spanish. She responded in Portuguese. Hearing that language made me stumble back, nearly lose my footing.

"What are you doing?" she demanded. "We're your own people! You're murdering your own people! Put down your gun and join us!"

My grip on the rifle tightened.

My people.

I stood there amid the throng of screaming humanity. Pulse shots sailed past. Human flesh, viscera, blood collected around my feet. The buzz and clatter of the fighting drones mingled with the screams and protests of those around me. The protesters had begun a chant, in Portuguese:

"Join us, brothers and sisters. Power belongs to the people."

I fell to my knees. Blood mixed with the heavy dust, turning it to mud. I flipped up my visor and pulled away my mask and took a huff of the filthy, choking air. I dug my hands into the earth and took a whiff of its familiar scent; death, diesel, the tang of char that still lingered from the Corporate Wars when most of the sprawling city had been demolished.

As I raised my head to the young woman who peered over me, her eyes hopeful, triumphant, she blew apart. Her torso simply disintegrated, spraying me in a fine red mist, and the rest of her collapsed like a discarded pig carcass.

Behind me, Deathless came over, hefting her rifle. She offered her hand to me.

"Let's go, Dietz."

I took her hand.

35.

Morning dawned warm and drizzly. Our platoon stood in formation with the rest of the company on the east end of the half-completed monument, right behind where the CEO was speaking. She stood on a massive silver podium that shone the light right back into my eyes.

All signs of the protestors' camp had been cleared out by noon, just in time for her scheduled appearance. We disintegrated most of it using our pulse rifles, which was faster than burning it. The bodies went into trucks and were carted off to the crematorium. Those who survived were taken away by local BLM agents. I wondered how long they would survive in custody.

Since we were behind the raised stage, someone had put up screens so that we could watch the speech like everyone else. It was surreal to stare back at your own company, lined up as a living backdrop behind some CEO talking about how her troops were accomplishing the mission they had undertaken right after the Blink.

"Our enemies understand that Tene-Silvia is stronger than

ever," the CEO said. I found it telling that she didn't explicitly mention Mars. She wasn't talking to Mars. She was talking to the other corps. She was talking to her own people. She was talking to us. "Today we dedicate the Freedom Monument to those who perished here. Let it stand for a thousand years, a tribute to our will to carry on, to restore Tene-Silvia to the greatness of our forebears of Teniente Azul!"

Beside her, on the screen, I saw a conspicuous figure dressed all in white. Her pale hair was pulled back tightly into a bun. She did not applaud along with the prompted crowd. She did not smile. She simply stood behind and to the right of the CEO, planning and plotting, as she always had. Norberg had already begun her ascent into the inner sanctum of Tene-Silvia, no doubt well on her way to convincing our CEO to broker a deal with the son of Evecom's CEO.

The worst part about knowing the future was feeling that I had no way to stop it. It all seemed so inevitable. Frankie had certainly seen something during his jumps. Muñoz, too, and Andria had said Rubem talked of it. What did we all see? A loop. A world at perpetual war.

"I am proud of the fine soldiers here with me." The CEO smiled warmly. "They represent the very best of Tene-Silvia. I am pleased, then, to announce that anyone who joins the Corporate Corps is now eligible for citizenship after ten years of service." The CEO waited for applause. The ripple began on the outer edges of the gathered crowd, prompted by her PR team.

Marino nudged me. "Hey, Dietz."

I couldn't bear to look at him. "What, Marino?"

He opened up his tactical jacket, revealing one of the home-made petrol bombs the protestors had lobbed at us the night before.

"Shit, Marino, put that away before the BLM's snipe your ass."

He giggled. The sound of him giggling creeped me out. "Going to call him Hal," Marino said. "My little baby Hal."

"Just . . . keep that shit away from me, Marino."

He giggled again.

"We serve those who serve Teni," the CEO continued, and another wave of applause filled the air at her use of the affectionate name so many of us used for the corp.

Ten years, I thought. We weren't going to survive that long. Maybe she knew that.

When the parade of bullshit was over, we got assigned to do more cleanup duties, and finally retreated to our temporary barracks.

I couldn't sleep. I got up sometime after two in the morning and sat outside. The lights of what remained of São Paulo were dimmed, part of the energy conservation initiative. I gazed skyward, searching for the constellations I'd never been able to see in my youth.

Jones came out a few minutes later and offered me a joint. I didn't ask where he'd gotten it. The best part about being deployed with a lot of other troops is all the bartering you could do. I took it.

Neither of us spoke for a long time.

A shooting star streaked across the sky, so fast I thought I'd imagined it. But there was another, and another. Some celestial event. A rain of pretty but ultimately harmless meteorites, or maybe pieces from the busted moon, a new wave of debris finally hitting reentry.

Jones tilted his head with me, gazing at the free show.

"They were ghost messages, weren't they?" he asked.

I released the smoke from my lungs. "In training?"

"Yeah, those messages you deleted. From that ex-girlfriend.

They were ghost messages?"

"Yes."

He nodded. I passed him the joint. "I'm sorry," he said.

"Not your fault. Vi wanted to go to São Paulo to help people. She was full of big ideas. I got those messages from my brother, too, my cousins, after. But hers kept coming for a long time."

As if what they had done to São Paulo wasn't bad enough. Whatever tech they had used to obliterate the place caused the local servers to go haywire. The knus were all controlled locally by centralized nodes, and the one for São Paulo went nuts. They kept coughing up old video, voice, and text messages, usually from dead people, for at least a year. I hadn't seen any messages from Vi since mandatory training, though. Maybe it was over. Maybe the dead would be quiet, so we could move on.

"She was a citizen?" Jones asked.

"Yeah. Older than me. Fancy degree in Corporate Negotiations. She wanted to spend a year in São Paulo advocating on behalf of ghouls. Bleeding heart bullshit."

"Sounds like a nice thing to do, to me."

"Doing shit like that makes people feel good. Vi had always been a citizen. It's like, all these rich people swooping in, handing you a bottle of water and a candy bar, and yeah, you make it another day, sure, and they go off and feel good about themselves. But where does that leave people here? Sitting around waiting for another goddamn candy bar. Real change takes time. It's not something you can do on your gap year. I wasn't going to endorse that bullshit. I had things to do at home."

"Like what?"

"Like finish school. Join the corps."

"But you didn't join the corps until after São Paulo, right?"

"It tipped me over, yeah. I wanted to do some good."

"Like she did?"

"This is different."

"Is it?" Jones took another hit from the joint. The world was starting to get fuzzy at the edges. "I sure don't feel like I've done anything good for a long time."

"But we joined to do good."

"I don't know if intent matters at this point." He passed me the joint.

"Jones, when this all goes to shit, you're going to get the fuck out of here. I want you to know, now, that I totally support that."

He laughed. "You're a fucking trip, Dietz."

36.

Days turned to weeks turned to months in São Paulo. There was a lot of cleanup to do, and our company got the short straw for guarding the monument from further incursions led by protestors and saboteurs. I tried keeping track of the days in a little notebook I bought off a kid hawking shit to us from a basket. I figured we had been in São Paulo thirty days or so by then, and put that down, then put a slash down that night before lights-out.

That's how I managed to figure we spent eight months—give or take—guarding the gargantuanly ugly Freedom Monument. By the time we were rotated out, only about half of it was done; the progress seemed slow, to me, for something that Teni wanted to put up as the backdrop on every newscast. They ended up using the composite image, the one drawn up by the architects, to announce to everyone that it was finished when it wasn't even close.

I remember watching that newscast with the others in our temporary barracks while playing Go with Omalas. Neither of us said a word, just bowed our heads back to the game, but Marino laughed maniacally.

"You're a great bullshit artist, Teni," Marino cackled. "It's why I love you."

They shuttled us back to our base on Isla Riesco, though by all accounts, logistics had more or less figured out its deployment problem. I had learned not to rely on the newscasts for information like that, only my fellow soldiers. Even if we were being recorded, you found little ways to beat the system. Like Jones had told us in training, you avoided using certain phrases. We had gestures that meant, "I'm being sarcastic," or "No shit this is the truth," that we could append to all our statements.

Logistics, then, was mostly back online.

Not that that did me much good.

Andria thumped me on the back when we arrive at our base. "You ready to tackle the torture mods again?"

"Sure."

"Hey, by the way. You're promoted."

"Huh? Yeah, I earned my specialist promotion before the drop."

"You're a corporal now. You've put in enough drops. Performed well on a number of occasions. Captain V approved it."

"Why?"

"I figured you needed the pay grade."

"I don't . . ."

She made one of those signs at me, the one that meant, "Shut the fuck up I'm not giving it to you straight because the shitty corp is watching." I shut my mouth.

"All sorts of benefits to corporal," she said. "You can access more types of media and information from the knu. Great, huh?"

"Great."

She was unlocking more doors. Maybe she believed in my

bullshit after all.

But we didn't get the chance to go back to training in the immersives.

The morning after we got back, Captain V called the whole company together.

"We've got a good one this time, children," Captain V said. "A full operation. Six divisions are being deployed, including ours. You'll get a debrief from Major Stakeley shortly. What I can tell you right now is it's going to be the biggest deployment most of you have ever seen. That means it's going to be easy to get confused. I need you all to respect the com lines. We will have a medic channel for medical evac. Do not call for a medic over the platoon or company channels. We need to keep those clear."

I glanced over at Tanaka and his squad, standing just to the left of me and mine. Time for the Canuck jump, wasn't it?

I didn't want to do that jump again. I didn't want to go back either. I wanted to go forward. To see if there was anything after the Sick. Forward. Ever forward.

We geared up and they dropped us onto the deployment field. A fine rain fell. I found myself shaking.

Andria glanced back at me and opened a two-way channel. "Can you tell me how this goes?" I figured she was relying on logistics and intelligence being too busy to actively monitor our conversation.

"We lose Vela, and Jones gets his arm blown off. Fire gets my squad and Tanaka's cut off. It's . . . a fucking bloodbath. I told you about this one"

"The rogue NorRus ship?"

"I'd love to be wrong."

"How can I change it?"

"I don't fucking know," I said. "That's the fucking problem. But if you could point logistics at that park to pick us up before we get roasted, that would sure be good."

Our bodies began to shake. My teeth chattered. The contractions bent me back, tried to split me in two. My whole body bursting apart. Bursting apart . . .

No, I thought. *I am going to stay together. Stay focused. I need to go forward.*

I came apart into trillions of pieces, transformed into light. I soared. This time, I felt it; I kept a thin grasp on my consciousness as the fabric of reality warped around me.

We rose and shot off through nothing, through blackness, in the spaces between things. We careened, floated, danced, swam.

North America. Canuck, again? No, I didn't want to do that run again, I didn't want—

A burst of white light. Searing pain. Had I ever felt pain while deploying, before?

I spiraled down over the great wheat fields of Canuck, heading toward a shining city untouched by the war.

A new, vibrant city to be razed.

37.

A virgin target.

Totally untouched by drones or bursts or rapidly deployed soldiers made of light.

I had heard of the city below me, seen it in immersives about the regrowth of the north.

Nasakan.

Déjà vu.

We were a blazing ball of death.

I saw a glowing green field full of bodies heaped up like hay bales. They weren't alien bodies. They were *us*. Our suits. Our faces. And they spread out all around me, as far as I could see. Something had gone badly here. We had done something very wrong, and we had paid for it. I stretched the moment out, tried to hold it. I didn't just get a few seconds this time, but a couple minutes. And I could sense myself there, like I was visiting Nasakan during two different futures.

I had this moment of dissonance as I was coming together over the drop zone, both versions of Nasakan lying one atop the other, seeing another way this ended. Another possibility.

Blink.

And then, I dropped.

We started corporealizing over the Martian refugees' biggest port city, the shining pearl they had carved out in Northern Canuck. It unfurled from the flat black desert they had turned into a golden prairie, the way I imagined old explorers dreamed of the Lost City of Z. This time of year, the sun didn't set. The waterways up here didn't freeze in winter anymore. The Martian refugees had grown fat in the far north, complacent.

It was beautiful. The pinnacle of some great civilization. Not a Teni civilization, but something much more earnest. Much more alien. So clean and light and new. New like nothing on the rest of Earth was new, all of us building on top of the dead cities that had come before us, the ruined landscapes. Seeing their untouched city, even our most prized cities made us look like what we actually were—vagrants living on the bones of something greater.

We landed and scattered inside the spiraling towers. I arrived a good two minutes after everyone else, and I heard the screams of those who had corporealized inside buildings or walls or those who'd gotten stuck in the pavers. The whole division was here; coms came online almost immediately, and I saw the full extent of the company all around the city. But we had paid for the speed, and the coms, and the brief, yes, shit, I could already access the brief! We were online, had come online before we'd even come together, and paid dearly. Paid with our bodies.

What had they done to us?

One soldier waved her arms at me; she was stuck halfway into the ground. Others I passed were already dead, their fleshy shells put back together in a steaming mess of broken meat.

Overhead, waves of our drones came in behind us to draw fire from the shining city. They swept across the neatly tilled fields and buzzed over us. I expected to hear the enemy's defensive guns or the wailing of their artillery in response to the onslaught. But the air was silent save for the soft whirring of the drones and the chuffing of our boots on the paving stones.

I saw movement in one of the buildings and shot off a burst from my pulse rifle, reflexively. The facade cracked and wept brown sap, like something alive. But I didn't see any Martian refugees, or anyone else, just us in our boots.

I reviewed the brief, and my blood went cold. We had come here to end this city, and possibly more than that—*you have been hand-selected*, the brief said, *to deliver the final solution to the Martian problem on Earth. Here are your instructions. . . .*

What they proposed was self-destruction.

What had the Martian refugees ever done to us that we hadn't done to ourselves? But that didn't matter at all. What mattered was destroying everything that they had built on Earth. Destroying the very evidence of their existence here. Because if anything at all about Mars was good, what was there to stop our people from taking their side?

I was starting to wonder myself.

We crawled over the entire city looking for insurgents. But the city was deserted. Maybe they'd abandoned it, or they'd found out we were coming and hid in bunkers or left earth intentionally. I didn't know.

"What's going on?" Deathless said over the squad channel.

I'd been so sick and fearful, coming together inside a city, that I hadn't stopped to do a squad check. We hadn't done the usual sanity and digits check, either.

I swept over the names of my squad: Deathless, Jones, Omalas, Marino. Where did that put me in the time line? I had no fucking idea.

Marino screamed his head off and ran ahead of us. He fired his rifle into the air, blasting holes into the pristine architecture.

He yanked off his helmet. "You fucks!" he yelled. "Where the fuck are you?"

"Marino," Andria barked, "put your helmet back on."

Marino began to hum that little tune from *Vila Sésamo*. He walked into a breezy park and did a little dance on the soft green grass, shaking his ass. "Surrender to the first real Martian you see!" He laughed. "Just kidding! There are no more fucking Martians!"

He reached into his tactical jacket and pulled out what looked like a bottle of booze. I recognized it a moment later. It was the petrol bomb he had smuggled out of São Paulo. How long had he kept that with him?

"What do you think, Hal?" he yelled at his bottle.

"Marino!" Andria said. "Get back in formation. Stay on mission. That's an order."

"I love you too, Hal," Marino crooned. "We are the best of friends, you and me. We are going places. Going places no Martian can!"

"Marino!" I shouted. "Stop being a little shit!"

He rounded on me. He was still a good forty meters away, but I saw his face contort. "You saw what happens."

I remembered his inaccessible file, his missing squad, his madness and hysteria. Whose future had I seen before we came together here? Had he seen that future too? Was that the end he had seen from the beginning?

Marino pulled a lighter from his pocket. He yanked the plastic wrap from the top of a petrol-soaked rag that served as a fuse. Flipped the lighter.

The rag caught. Marino smashed the bottle open with his gun, pouring petrol all over his arms, splashing his face, his suit.

"Goddammit!" I ran toward him.

He raised his gun at me and fired just above my head, burning all the while.

I felt the wave of the blast and staggered.

Then Marino turned the gun on himself, and blew off his own head.

His flaming corpse crumpled to the pillowy green ground.

All around him, the members of our company were eerily quiet.

I pulled off my helmet and listened to the pop and crackle and hiss of his burning body.

"Dietz?" Jones opened a two-way channel. "You all right?"

"Why? You think that's how I'm going out?"

Silence.

Mad Dietz.

Major Stakeley came in over the division channel. "We are nearly in position. Dog Company, we need you to catch up."

We couldn't just come all this way for nothing. We had to do what we came for. We had to be weapons. No matter the price. We were the price. Nasakan was the price.

I read the brief over again and felt a moment of dizzying vertigo. What would this solve? How many of us would die in this stupid exercise?

I opened a two-way channel with Andria. "We have to stop this," I said.

"I need you to hold your breath, Dietz," Andria said softly.

I saw Tanaka ahead of me, and grabbed his shoulder. "Tanaka!" I said, swinging him around. He had his visor down. I could not see his face. "We can't do this. None of us should do this."

He shrugged me away. "You talking to me now?"

"What?"

"Finish the mission," he said.

"Who the fuck are you?"

He flipped up his visor, revealing his pale eyes. "No, who the fuck are you?" he said. "It's like you're a different person every time we deploy. You want to stop this? Don't fire."

"I won't," I said, "but we need—"

"How do you know? You haven't lived this one before, have you? You don't know. That's the fucking problem. All this jumping the fuck around means nothing. It's a dead end. Just like the war."

He put his visor back down and moved out.

Jones said, over our platoon channel, "Dietz, we need you here. Move."

My heart sank. Tanaka was right. And Andria? What was going on? What had happened right before this?

We assembled around the heart of the city's square. Just as the brief told us to do, we raised our pulse rifles and flipped them on the new setting, the one engineered specifically for this mission. We pointed our weapons across the broad square at one another, sticking to the brief. Set the rifles at a high charge. Waited for the signal.

But, scouring the brief, I realized no one had actually tried to use the light like this before, no living person. It was something they'd done with simulators and robots. Now they wanted us to shoot at one another just as we were coming apart. Shoot the people you'd take a hit for.

I'd fire into my own face first.

I opened a two-way channel to Andria. "We can't do this."

"I know. We're out of options."

"Fuck you, Andria. Fuck all this."

She cut the connection.

I swore.

I started to vibrate.

We had to wait for the signal. Be patient.

The brief said to wait . . . and then we should fire on one another.

Madness.

Mad fucking Dietz, they all said, and I was the only person here who seemed to have any sanity left.

I yanked off my helmet and kicked it into the circle. Raised my hands. The cold Canuck wind made my eyes water. "Stop this shit! Don't do this!"

I kept the safety on my rifle, and ran out into the center of the circle.

I was part of the Light Brigade, and I no longer believed in doing what they told us to do.

The vibrating got worse. Then the cramping. My body seized up. I gasped. Somebody shot their weapon; too soon. A scream. A body down. Another shot. Too soon.

Goddammit, hold it together.

"Listen!" I shouted. "There's got to be another way. Don't let them—"

The contraction stopped.

The world snapped.

I didn't look at the mirrored helmet of the soldier across from me. I looked at the light on my map, the little tag that told me it was Sandoval there, across from me, Sandoval, who was going to shoot me.

Everything burst apart.

Our company fired on one another.

I was aware of the blooming fire of the explosion we made, busting down our component parts.

I whirled up and up and up with the rushing plume of fire. The city crumpled like a child's fairy garden. Trees flattened and stripped away.

The searing explosion kept moving, on and on.

I watched it from above, still conscious, somehow, in limbo between the darkness and the light.

The reaction was so massive it obliterated half the northern hemisphere.

Everything the Martians had made grow again in Canuck we turned back into dust.

We were the weapon.

We were full of light.

I would like to tell you I knew what I was going to do, before that. But I had not seen the true measure of the destruction that the corporations were willing to wreak to consolidate their power.

I wanted to be brave. To be a hero. To carry out orders like a paladin would. I did those things even knowing what the outcome was going to be. I wanted so badly to be the good guy.

But it truly was not until that moment, after I had destroyed everything still good in this world, that I realized I wasn't a hero . . . I was just another villain for the empire.

38.

There weren't many of us left to see what we did, and maybe it was better that way. I stayed broken up there in the ether between things for a long time. I didn't want to go back. Didn't want to come together.

Take control of the construct.

And I did.

A part of me, a conscious part of me, cruised the coms and tipped a toe across the world, trying to understand what had happened. We were all just bits of data.

It was all over the networks, the destruction of half a continent. They didn't say we shot one another up to do it or say how many of our people died in the explosion, their essential elements obliterated. And right beside these pictures of this barren, smoking wasteland were pictures of our own people cheering in our dingy little cities built on the bones of our ancestors. We had scorched the fucking earth, but everyone cheered because we'd gotten back at those aliens, those liars, those immigrants.

I saw the streams and I knew what I had to do. I still wanted to be a hero. I had a chance. But it meant giving up everything I believed in. Betraying everyone I cared about. Being everything I'm supposed to hate.

I knew what I needed to do because I'd seen it. We'd been moving here the whole time.

A loop.

I knew what was next.

They had lied to us on the networks. The Martians weren't bumbling refugees that we had benevolently allowed to stay here. They had come to help us, come to share what they had learned when they transformed Mars. They had made a beautiful world from the over-heated toxic desert we'd created, and we hated them for it, because they were free to create a better world. No one owned them.

Betrayers, they said, on the networks. *Liars. Martians.*

They had made the land grow things again, but that was *all* they were supposed to do. They weren't supposed to be free because no one is free, and they weren't supposed to be able to defend themselves because no one can, not from the corps. The corps won't allow it. The corps take care of you, as long as you give them everything.

Now that I'd been light, I started thinking that maybe all those ghouls in São Paulo didn't die after all. Maybe they just went somewhere else. Maybe the Martians found out what we were too, and tried to save us from ourselves.

The São Paulo Blink showed the corporations what was possible.

It was the Martians who had given us the light.

Nearly two million people, gone in a blink.

And our response: half a continent scorched of all life. A ruined Martian landscape. Murdering our own children.

Maybe the light was our downfall. Or maybe we'd been falling the whole time.

39.

I fell back to Earth like a busted drone, shattered and exhausted, split into a million pieces.

We need to go back, back . . . I thought as I came together, fearful of losing myself, of breaking so far apart I could not be retrieved.

I came together, experiencing the rush of inhabiting a body on the cusp of the corporeal. Is this how ghosts felt? I held up my fingers, marveling at them. I reached for my helmet before I'd fully come together, something you aren't supposed to do, but it felt natural. I lifted it from my still fuzzy head and tossed it to the ground. It sank into the soil and came together within it, half submerged.

I fell over, and my hands hit solid ground. Ten fingers. I huffed in a long breath, feeding my newly formed lungs.

As I raised my head, I saw a wide expanse of grass all around me. The sky was dark save for the flickering image of the cloud-streaked moon and her satellites. I leaned back on my heels. I was alone on the deployment field.

From a little guard tower up on the hill, a flashing light approached. Sound of a motorbike or ATV. Two technicians rode down. One leaped from her vehicle and came straight to me.

"Name and rank?" she demanded.

"Dietz, corporal."

"My God. We thought we'd lost you. Your platoon came back six days ago, before we lost power. You were listed MIA."

"Well, now I'm found."

She shone a light into my eyes. I always wondered what they were checking, with that. Could you see if someone was an alien agent, by looking in their eyes? Maybe test for sanity?

Whatever she was looking for, she seemed satisfied. She turned to her colleague and said, "Call in medical. This one needs to go straight to quarantine."

Once again, I was in quarantine alone, my own platoon having gone in and out four days ahead of me. I wiped my hands over my skull. Hair still short. My stomach wasn't shrunken. It was hard to get a line on anything else, though, in quarantine. I expected to hear from intelligence first, as usual, but instead it was my shrink..

The doctor came into the medical room, wiping her hands on her blue skirt, the same color as the blue walls. She looked harried.

"No intel?" I said.

"I'm sorry?"

"We've met," I offered, before she could ask. "I was missing for a week, they said. What happened? Nobody will tell me anything."

"I'm sure you will be debriefed. I apologize. There have been some events that took intel away."

"They said the power went out, but the lights are on?"

"Generators. We have been on emergency power. There was an attack on power grids."

"Which ones?"

She sat across from me, tucking her skirt under her legs. "All of them, I believe."

"That's . . . a lot."

"They thought it was an EMP. And in many areas, it was. We had some protection here from that, most bases did, but not civilian areas, unfortunately. What most concerns us now, however, is your mental state after your ordeal. Do you have any memory of where you've been?"

"I was hoping you'd tell me."

"Your squad came back from a very stressful mission in the far north of the North American continent. Do you remember that mission?"

"Which one?"

"Your squad leader, Jones, was injured. He lost an arm. How did that make you feel?"

"The fuck do you think?"

"I'm trying to assess where you are in—"

"In time?" I suggested, and she started. "Yeah, me too."

She leaned forward and whispered. "The records server is offline due to the attack. What you tell me here is in confidence."

"What I tell you here belongs to Teni."

"Trust me."

"No. You trust me. You tell me what the fuck has been happening to me."

"We know some of you are experiencing this war . . . differently. But the results are highly individualized. Some only cross once, some twice, and most have no observations to share that amount to anything except a profound sense of confusion. They are overwhelmed, just following orders."

"You mean, cross . . . to other parts in time."

"You remember, don't you?"

"Yeah."

Her tone became energetic, almost frenetic. "That's wonderful! You're the only one who has retained full awareness and memory throughout your experiences, or so you say. You must understand—for years we assumed you were all experiencing psychosis. There was no way to prove the crosses were real, especially because so many would simply tell us about events we had already seen. The people like you, you are giving us insights into events that could be days, months, or years into the future. We had no idea how to prepare for that future without having more details. When we pulled you back, our locators told us you were physically in one time, and of course, the issue was not your physical location. The issue was how your brain recalled those experiences. Our best guess is that breaking you apart changed the structure of your mind in some way."

I blinked at her. What more had I expected, really? "We're just some test to you. Some experiment. That's the best you can do?"

"The human mind has always been among the deepest mysteries of our bodies. We want to pretend science has all the answers. But it simply gives us the tools to uncover those answers. It doesn't mean we have them. It's why so many still cling to religion. We need answers to the unknown."

"You threw us all out there without knowing what you were doing. You—"

"Every soldier is a sacrifice. You are owned by the corporation, or the state, before it, or the king or landlord before that. It's the first thing they drive into you in training, isn't it? Your body is not yours. Most soldiers died of disease and infections before the rise of antibiotics and the seemingly basic knowledge that one should wash one's hands before sticking them into a man's guts and wash again before hacking off another's leg. Soldiers were the sacrifice. We needed an advantage over Mars. This technology did that. The losses, the side effects, were calculated to be worth the advantage they gave us. We are all of us scrambling around in the dark."

"Like now," I said bitterly. "In the dark. You knew this whole time."

She nodded eagerly. "How many times have we met?"

"I have no idea. This has been a long war for me."

"It ends with the sickness?"

"How did you hear about that?"

"Other soldiers—"

"Like who?"

"That . . . I cannot tell you."

"How about Frankie Kowalski? How cracked was he by the time I shot him on Mars?"

"Corporal Kowalski . . . did have some unfortunate drops."

"And what did he see?"

"That's what's so stimulating," she gushed. "*You all saw different events.* Different futures."

I lost my breath. Had to sit back in the bed. "But there's only—"

"One would think. And yet."

I considered that, the idea that Rubem, and Frankie, and Muñoz and me—maybe Marino, too—all saw some other end to the war, and then looped around and experienced it again and again.

"Do you think a lot about mortality?" she said.

I had no idea where that had come from. "Now? Sure."

"What are your thoughts on it?"

"I never thought much about dying when I first signed up," I said carefully. It was a relief, I realized, to sit here with someone who believed me, even if I was just some test subject to her. But I wasn't a thing. I was alive.

"Nobody really does," I continued, "even when you see your friends stuck inside walls, or watch their torsos bust open, or hold their guts in your hands. It takes a while to really get that it could happen to you. You're the hero of your own story. The hero doesn't die, can't die, because then the story ends. But I've had a long time to sit with death, now. I have stared death in the face. I don't like it much. I want to choose how this all ends. I don't just want it taken from me. When I'm old and dying, wheezing my guts out, my organs failing, I want to walk out the front door of some old farmhouse on my own land, maybe forty, fifty hectares of it. I want to find a cool place in the woods under some old oak tree and settle down there and die as the sun comes up. I want a death rattle, a final breath, a body intact that can then be torn apart by scavengers, riddled with worms, my limbs dragged off to feed some family of little foxes, my guts teeming with maggots, until I am nothing but a gooey collection of juices that feeds the fungi and the oak seedlings and the wild grasses. I want my bleached bones scatted across my own land, broken and sucked clean of marrow, half buried in snow and finally, finally, covered over in loam and ground to dust by the passage of time, until I am broken into fragments, the pieces of my body returned to where they came. I could give back something to this world instead of taking, taking, taking. That's the death I want. The death that means the most to me. That is the good death, the best death, and that is the death I wish not only for myself, but for you, too. Our lives are finite. Our bodies imperfect. We shouldn't spend it feeding somebody else's cause."

Dr. Chen was quiet for a bit. I waited her out. I didn't want to say anymore. I'd said enough. I was always saying too much.

"Are you working toward that end?" she asked. "What do you think about life after the war?"

"That's it. That's about all I think about it."

"Death?"

"Sure."

"Your brother was killed in the Blink."

That didn't sound like a question.

Silence, again.

"A lot of people ask how you can be a paladin and be a soldier," I said. "Even if you take an oath of vengeance. But you're committing to fight the greater evil. It doesn't mean you won't sometimes do some evil yourself. It doesn't mean that you aren't sometimes fighting for the empire. It just means that in the end, you do the right thing."

She leaned forward. "But that's the vital question. What *is* the right thing?"

40.

Fuck if I knew.

But I was determined to find out.

Dr. Chen had fucked with all of us this whole time. Knew everything. All of them knew pieces of it. And here I had been, fearful of talking to anyone and getting disappeared, when they were doing this to us on purpose, rolling us like dice to see which of us came up with a way to win the war.

But none of us did, did we?

Because they were going to lose the war. Everyone loses in war.

I came out of quarantine, and it was Tanaka who got up and ran over to me. He wrapped his arms around me like I'd been dead, and I suppose they had figured I was.

I pulled away from him, remembering his words in that Martian city. Little fucker hadn't listened to me, and here we were. But as far as he knew, we had just fucked in the woods a few days ago.

"Dietz?" he said. "You all right?"

"No."

Omalas and Jones, Deathless and Sandoval, and a few others crowded around. I saw Marino up in his bunk, paging through a comic book someone had smuggled in.

"Where were you?" Jones said. "You did another one of those weird . . . Dietz things you do."

"How's your arm?" I asked.

He grinned. Rolled up his sleeve to the scar around the area where it had been severed. "Good work, huh? These medics are fucking magic. I'm glad I made you keep my arm."

"Me too."

"But where *were* you?" Tanaka echoed.

"I just got . . . caught somewhere, I guess. Where we all go when we jump."

Tanaka narrowed his eyes. I gave him the "bullshit" sign so he knew I was giving them a show. Deathless was the only one who didn't catch it. She was still too new.

"I've never gone anywhere but the drop," Deathless said. "They all say you drop funny, you come back somebody else. Like, you get remade."

"I wish," I said. "Sorry. Same bullshit."

"Dietz!" Andria, from her office.

I went.

She ushered me inside. Shut the door. Produced her own pocket watch. "Got mine fixed up," she said, and peeled open the inside to reveal a scrambler chip.

"You figured it out?"

"I sent Captain V a recording of what you told me, before that drop in Canuck. Fuck, we lost Vela, and Jones and his arm . . . I made him a priority evac. Probably only reason he kept that goddamn arm."

"And you sent our evac?"

"Yeah. Barely got ahead of that NorRus ship. Thought we

could get Landon . . . I'm sorry." Andria set the watch on the table and pulled out two liquor glasses. "That's when Captain V confided in me about what the fuck they figure is going on with you and the others. The Light Brigade."

"Motherfucker," I said.

"Yes."

"Had a chat with my therapist, too. She knew. The brass all knows. What the fuck are they playing at? It's working, though, the torture modules. Have you said that to me yet?"

She shook her head. "Not sure when that comes along."

"Fuck." I sat down.

She poured again. Sat.

"How are we going to fix this, Dietz?"

"I tried," I said, "during the final . . . shit, you told me to shut the fuck up. I don't know what that was about. You—" *You died before I could ask,* I thought, but shut my mouth.

"What else happened?"

"Listen, the shrink thinks we all saw different wars. Different futures. All the ones who jumped out of order. You think that's possible?"

"I don't know," Andria said. "I know you can see shit and then it happens. I just don't know how to change it."

"Me neither. Sorry."

"For what? It's not your fault. The war's not your fault. Not my fault either." But she said the last part differently, like she didn't quite believe it, and downed her drink.

I wondered if she was right to have that tone, though, because it *was* our fault, wasn't it? We fought this war willingly. We gave our bodies to it, even if we're only here because of the lies Tene-Silvia told us. What if there was a war and nobody came? What if the corp voted for a war and nobody fought it? You can only let so many people starve. You can only throw so many people in jail. You can only have so many executions for insubordination to the latest

CEO or board of directors.

Why did we make all this possible? Why didn't we just go home and take care of our fucking dogs and tell the corps to fuck themselves?

"Andria," I said slowly, reaching for the second drink. "I don't like what I'm thinking."

"You going to share?"

"No. Just remember to tell me the torture mods are the key, when I come home with Landon's guts all over me."

Andria raised her glass. "To Landon," she said.

"To Landon."

41.

The brass was full of ideas. Aren't they always?

It took another nine months to get the power back up and running. We spent a lot of time guarding power plants and knu nodes and being bored out of our minds.

I managed to get some time with Tanaka during that long dull period while we both got guard duty. Coms were still spotty, but I used the pocket watch anyway.

"Shit gets bad, Tanaka," I said.

"It's war."

"No, listen. People get sick. They die. This whole war takes us out."

He glanced over at me. With so much of the power out all around us, the stars were visible. We kept pace with each other around the parade ground. I found his presence soothing, still, despite him not listening to me in Canuck about the final solution. The world was moist and loamy; a fine drizzle fell.

"How do we stop it?" he asked.

"I don't know. I've been trying."

"Maybe you're not trying hard enough."

"Fuck you." I tried to read his expression, but he was gazing ahead again.

"Why can't the Light Brigade end this fucking war? What's the point of all this if nothing changes?"

"I've been trying to change it. I told you. They call it the Sick. Everybody gets some Martian virus. Or maybe a corp virus. We think the war is over, but it isn't."

"How do we make sure it's over?"

"I don't know. Not fight Mars."

He laughed at that. "Good luck."

"Well, you tell me the torture modules will help. When the Sick happens and I bounce back, all right?" *And don't be such a fucking asshole,* I wanted to add, but didn't. He didn't exactly look and sound like somebody who wanted to hear that right now.

"What about my family?" he asked.

"What?"

"Did you find out what happened to them?"

"When the fuck would I have time for that?" It probably didn't come out the best way, but it was a shitty, myopic thing to ask. "Have you been thinking about yourself this whole fucking time?"

"You haven't? You haven't been whining about losing your family?"

I wanted to smash his face in. Instead, I picked up my pace and left him behind.

Why did I feel so alone in this bullshit? Why wasn't there anyone else still alive who could do what I did? Had it driven them all mad because they knew that there wasn't any way to stop what was coming?

I got myself another notebook, and tried to capture all the days, but they ran through my fingers like vodka. I knew the marks on the bed frame weren't accurate, not like I thought they would be in the beginning. Time was slipping away. Instead, I used the notebook to come up with a shorthand code to record my thoughts on how to engineer my next drop. Even though the count of days on my bunk was useless now, I knew it would be useful to me later, so I added marks when I could. It was a rough span of days, but I would need to get a sense of the stretch of time involved in all this in order to plan for this moment. What a mindfuck..

Tanaka kept trying to sit down with me at mealtimes; I'm sure he wanted to make up, but I couldn't stand the idea that all this time he was trying to use me to figure out his own shit. I didn't blame him, I couldn't, because he was right that I was focused on my own past.. He reminded me too much of myself and my own failings. How was I any better, always going back, instead of looking ahead? I turned inward, more than I had at any other time. I ran through the torture modules and kicked Andria's ass.

It was during one of those extended sessions that I broke my chains and wrapped her in them.

"The fuck!" she said.

"All the claims you make follow a logical path," I said. "It's 'I won't, I can't,' but you have to make it to '*I will*. I will. I do.' It's powerful. That's the power of volition. That's the power we can tap into when we jump. When we become the light. What directs us, always, is volition."

"I think we need to stop now, Dietz."

She was right.

When we came to in our immersion chairs and pulled off our rigs she gazed over at me.

"Life is a grind," she said. "Your best bet is to find people who will endure it with you."

I fist-bumped her. "Here's to endurance."

She was going to die. I was going to die. Tanaka was going

to die.

But until then—we'd live.

Nine months is a long time to live linearly, that late in the war.

Nine months is a long time to hold on to the people closest to you.

We deployed several times. At first, Andria was upbeat and supportive, looking forward to the next drop. But when we did drop—to clear an abandoned hospital in the dusty streets of Odessa in southern North America, I dropped without incident. That threw her off. I guess I hadn't told her about the times I was able to go through drops linearly. I hadn't done it since the beginning of the war. It bothered her. We got drunk over it. We argued over it.

Her and Captain V and the brass started hanging out more. I don't know what was said. I was never sure how the war was going. All we got were the government-approved news channels and the old, weary media.

"Hey," I asked Andria one Sunday afternoon, after we got out of quarantine from another linear drop in Turku. "You want to get a drink?"

"Got plans, Dietz," she said, and she was distant. I recognized the inward-facing look, the same one Tanaka had gotten the last time we talked.

What is it with people's memories? It has to be in their face constantly before they get it. Before they realize they can't just look away and expect it to all be fine.

"You still have my back, Andria?"

"Sure, but they have some really great ideas right now. I think they have some tech that could end the war."

"Like blowing one another up?"

"Nah, not like that. I have to go. Just . . . they . . . maybe we trust Teni, just this one time?"

"You dumb fuck."

Her face crumpled. "Watch your mouth."

"Yes, sir."

People are emotional creatures.

Nobody ever won a war on logic.

It's why I wasn't surprised when Captain V called the whole company together, and Andria and the other platoon leaders were there with her, happily lapping up at the latest corporate story.

"We need some volunteers," Captain V said, and I had a good idea of what they needed volunteers for, because I'd already done it. "The brass has discovered a way to end the Martian threat on Earth."

We needed to destroy them all.

It was the only way to go forward, now that our infrastructure was back up.

The only way to protect our way of life.

The only way to be free.

Mars would never let us be free.

"This is an experimental procedure," Captain V said, as if anything we'd ever done during deployment wasn't experimental. "None of you are under orders or obligation to go on this mission. But I can tell you that you will be heroes. You will be part of the hand of light that smites the Martian threat from Earth and casts them back to that red rock. If you don't want to go on this mission, you step aside."

I stood in formation with Jones and Marino. Tanaka was two spots up, with Sandoval. Omalas and Deathless stood just in front of me. And the rest of the platoon—all that was left after this bloody parody of a war, this grinding endgame, they stood at attention with me. Next to me. My brothers and sisters. The heroes of the light. The shock troops for the empire.

We weren't in mandatory training anymore. We were made

of tougher, stupider stuff. We had survived this war for one another, and we would end it together.

No one stepped out of line.

I wasn't going to let them go alone. Because I knew that if this was when I was about to drop to that shining city, I was about to drop out of order for the first time in over nine months. I realized I hadn't agreed to go on the final solution mission because I thought I could stop anyone. I'd gone because it was my chance to break the loop.

When they took us out to the drop field, I decided this was going to be my last drop, my last real drop. It was time to take control.

I knew what I had to do, now. We had all experienced a different future, the shrink said. It was up to me to make one that broke this cycle.

Sometimes, though, to break the loop . . . you have to go back to the beginning.

All the way back.

I inhaled deeply. Closed my eyes.

We began to vibrate.

I could already smell the coppery sulfur stink of Mars.

First drop.

Let's do it right this time.

42.

Unstuck in time.

Broken apart.

The smell. That fucking smell.

Go back. Do it again.

It's the only way forward.

I heaved in a great mouthful of Martian air and squinted at the butterscotch sky. Coughed uncontrollably.

"Dietz? Dietz?"

My eyes filled at the sound of the voice. Her hand touched my shoulder, and I sobbed.

"Fuck, Dietz," Muñoz said. "You all here? Show me your digits."

I choked on another sob and brought up my hands. Coms weren't online, but she had pushed up her visor, and I could see her face. Her real face. I put my hand up, tried to touch her, but she batted my hand away.

"Shit, you're a wreck," she said. "Don't be hysterical."

Squib stood a little ways distant, patting the pockets of her tactical jacket. "I need a joint."

Abascal stood over Jawbone as he heaved his guts out. The rest of the platoon was here, the first platoon—Tanaka and Herrera, Vela and Khaw, and there, up on the ridge, the familiar squat form of Captain, no, Lieutenant V. I wanted to bundle them all up into my arms and kiss them.

Instead, I collected myself as best I could and grabbed the front of Muñoz's helmet and brought her face to mine.

"Jesus, Dietz!"

"What was the future you saw?" I said. "When you jumped wrong? What was the future, Muñoz? Tell me now before coms come online. In mine, there's a sickness. It gets let loose. Everyone on Earth dies. What was yours? I have to know."

Her eyes got big. She took my helmeted head in both her hands and said, "You die on a Mars combat mission. You kill a kid on Mars, and Marino kills you. In the end . . . just light, explosions. We bust everything apart. The whole fucking world. Desert. Darkness."

The flicker of our coms pinged at the corner of my vision. She yanked herself away, stumbling back on her ass.

We stared at each other a long moment, then she was moving.

"Report in, show me your digits!" Muñoz said over the squad channel.

"Jawbone . . . intact."

"Squib, still not high and really fucking upset about that."

"Abascal, admiring Dietz's ass."

"Dietz," I said. "All here."

I felt the first wave of a panic attack. Breathed in and out through my nose. I bet all those futures were dead ends. If they weren't, we wouldn't be stuck. So how could we unstick ourselves?

Fuck.

I followed after Muñoz, trying to get my bearings.

"Muñoz, I need your squad up on that ridge," Lieutenant V

said over our squad channel.

"Copy that."

I went after Muñoz, scanning the ridge ahead. What had Tanaka said? An ambush. We were going to be ambushed. All right, what could we do to avoid . . . No.

Don't go back.

I knew what I had to do, and it clawed at my heart. Muñoz would never forgive me. My squad would never understand.

Muñoz humped up the ridge, and we went after her. I saw the flash of a scope almost immediately. The Martians had scouted out this area ahead of us and planned an ambush for the entire platoon there, between those two ridges.

I took one last look at Muñoz, and then threw myself down the ridge.

I rolled, kicking up incredible amounts of red dust. It got into everything, seeped into my mask.

The squad channel got busy. "Dietz? Dietz?" Muñoz yelling. Lieutenant V shouting.

I came to a stop in the little valley between the ridges. When I looked up, Muñoz and the rest of my squad were coming after me, punting great waves of dust. Muñoz again, on the squad channel, calling for backup. "Dietz is down! I've got movement on my heads-up. We need—"

I grabbed the pocket watch and turned on the scrambler, obliterating our coms before she could tell them any more.

I turned, saw the flash of a scope, and stood up, hands in the air. My rifle hit the dirt.

The shot took me in the shoulder.

I went down hard.

The breath left my body.

"Dietz!" Muñoz, next to me. Abascal, shooting.

Martians, shooting back.

"Don't shoot!" I yanked off my helmet. "Don't shoot!" I

raised my hands; my left shoulder burned. "Abascal, put that down!"

"The fuck?" Abascal hesitated though, and that was enough.

"We surrender!" I yelled, and tried it again in English, and hell, Portuguese, too.

"We do not!" Muñoz said, yanking at my arms. I was bleeding out. I could feel it.

"Muñoz," I said. "This is the only way we break the loop. Listen. Right now. You tell them you're intelligence. You're smart. You give them anything they want. I need you to break me out and send me back to Saint Petersburg at the end of the war."

"Are you insane?"

"Yes," I said. "Saint Petersburg is the only place I know isn't going to get hit by the sickness. And the CEO and fucking Norberg will be there. Believe me, Muñoz. I've been over this a million times, in what feels like a million lives."

"How the fuck—"

"You'll figure it out. You all have information I don't. Make something up. But get me out. Stay here, after. You'll be pretty safe on Mars, as long as you stay with the resistance. Don't come after me."

"I—"

"Keep those hands up!" A small squad of soldiers dressed in scrappy red armor huffed into the valley. They spoke Spanish, which was a relief. They lobbed smoke grenades between us and our platoon, and a couple of flash-bangs for good measure.

I yanked Muñoz's hand up next to mine.

"We surrender!" I said again.

The squad moved toward us.

Jawbone threw down his gun. Abascal raised hers, defiant. They shot it out of her hand, taking most of her hand with it. She howled and went down.

"Don't shoot!" I said again. "We all surrender. Really."

"Your friend doesn't seem to think so," the woman at the front said. She had sand-coated black hair and spoke with a Masukisan accent.

"What day is it?" I asked, because it had been so long since I knew the fucking date that I was thirsty for it.

"Tuesday."

"No. What day? The date, the *year?*"

"Are you serious?"

"All these fascist zombies are mad as exo-colonists," said one of her companions.

"It's July seventeenth, of oh-five."

"That's the Martian year?"

"No, the fascist one. You're a fascist asking for it. Why would I give you a Martian year? It would fuck up your head even more."

"That's . . . okay," I said. I could center myself in time. This was absolutely the Mars recon mission, my first drop. I'd done it. I felt suddenly lightheaded. I was still bleeding. I pressed my hand to my chest.

"I take it back," the woman's companion said, "you're too addled to get any more mad."

"Whole squad's cracked," the woman said. "What year do you think this is, private?"

"I've seen the spring of oh-nine."

"Well, well, well. Interesting. How's the war gone, then?"

"Badly."

"For you? Good."

"Yes," I said. "Very good."

I jabbed a thumb at Muñoz. "She's in intelligence," I said. "She'll tell you anything you want to know to keep your little Mars resistance away from insurgents. So will I. I know exactly when they will hit your colonies on Earth and here, and when. I can save your people on Nasakan."

"That remains to be seen," the woman said, and hit me on

the face with the butt of her gun.

I couldn't blame her.

I had it coming.

Interview #5

SUBJECT #187799

DATE: 25|05|309

TIME: 2100

ROOM: 101

I: This is the fifth session with subject one-eight-seven-seven-nine-nine. Audio only. See intelligence notes for prior briefs. I'm afraid this may be our last meeting, friend.

S: Don't get all emotional on me.

I: I admit I didn't expect you to be so mad. Now that you've had time to settle down, do you want to tell me why you thought you could liberate yourself?

S: You must have taken me seriously, since you took my shoes again.

I: Not my decision. My superiors are cautious. I'm less impressed by your optimism. But it does make me curious. Why are you so relentlessly foolish?

S: I figured out your game. Took a long time. What was left of free Mars was never going to be free if I didn't play this out. And Mars is the only hope for a free future in this solar system. We gave our lives to the corporations in exchange for clean air, clean food, infrastructure, shit we could have collectively done for ourselves. We forget that people are power. It's why they work so hard to control us.

I: You talk like a Martian.

S: I spent a lot of this war on Mars. And here. It was a two-fer.

I: I have a theory.

S: Do share.

I: I think you are the agent who committed the Blink.

S: I suppose that's a good guess. You no longer think I'm a doppelganger?

I: I think you are something much more special. The irony is that if there were no Blink, there would not have been a war.

S: That's a lie, just like it's a lie that the people in Sao Paulo would have lived if the Blink never happened. The Big Six were going to war. You can't let socialist ideas spread. If Mars was successful here, and up there, it would have undone all your careful propaganda. The showdown was coming.

I: How do you hide for years without us finding you via your tracker?

S: I didn't have it. We'll get to that.

I: I have questions about time travel. How did—

S: I'm not here to talk about time travel, though I'm glad you finally figured that shit out. Who'd you talk to? You had a singular line of questioning you pushed here during the last days. None of it related to that.

I: Your socialist democracy can't survive on Mars. They never do. People succumb to fear, no matter the government. The everyday person doesn't want war, but it's remarkably easy to convince them. It's the government that determines political priorities, and it's easy to drag people along with you by tapping into that fear. I don't care if you have a communist mecca, a fascist regime, or a representative democracy, even some monarchy with a gutless parliament. People can always be convinced to turn on one another. All you have to do is convince them that their way of life is being attacked. Denounce all the pacifist liberal bleeding hearts and feel-good heretics, the social outcasts, the educated. Call them elites and snobs. Say they're out of touch with real patriots. Call these rabble-rousers terrorists. Say their very existence weakens the state. In the end, the government need not do anything to silence dissent. Their neighbors will do it for them.

S: Maybe so. Everything comes around again, doesn't it? But this time, your time . . . is over. It's mine now. Ours. I suppose it's an old story, isn't it? The oldest story. It's the dark against the light. The dark is always the easier path. Power. Domination. Blind obedience. Fear always works to build order, in the short term. But it can't last. Fear doesn't inspire anything like love does.

I: You aren't going to win this by telling a pretty story and holding hands.

S: There was never anything to win. All we had to do was survive. The Big Six killed themselves. It's a rotten choice soldiers are given. Kill your enemy to save yourself, save your friends, and commit murder. But don't pull that trigger and you might die, your friends might die . . . you may even lose the war, because of that choice. But it's a soldier's choice. It's the same argument for those who can get pregnant, you know. Now, of course, most of the corps have to give you a license to have kids. But there was an argument, a long time ago, that to continue a pregnancy or not, while a terrible decision, was a decision only the pregnant person could make. It's that way with soldiers. You have the choice. None of it's good, but it's yours.

I: Why was it you who could move through time when deployed?

S: How should I know? I'm not in logistics. The Mars Reconnaissance was the last mission I engaged in, but the first time I was actually deployed. Took me a long time to figure that out. You look at time as a circle, say, all these events spinning around and around. It's like we're all tied to a wheel. What you did when you broke us into pieces was break us from that wheel. We bounced around inside of it, popping in and out of time, experiencing it all out of order. I spent this whole war in two places.

I: That isn't possible.

S: Sure as shit is possible. The Big Six knew it, too. Tene-Silvia sure did. They didn't realize how bad it was, though, thought they could keep us going with enough therapy, and trying to guide the person who traveled to the right future, the future that favored them. My shrink sure as shit was complicit. They knew I wasn't crazy. They just didn't know how deep it all went. We were all a bunch of guinea pigs.

I: Why come to Saint Petersburg at all, then? Why not just watch out the end of your little game safe on Mars?

S: Because I needed you, Norberg. I needed you to bring me here to this cold little cell in Southern Africa so we could come full circle.

I: The Blink-

S: It's all a big circle, sweetheart. Time is a mindfuck, isn't it?

I: How do you know who I am?

S: You still don't know? That doesn't surprise me. I was no one, to you. That's what it is, with bullies. The things they do to you shape your life profoundly. But they often don't even recall your face, let alone your name. You don't know? I'm Dietz, Norberg. I'm the kid of some guy you disappeared back when you were a sergeant, a guy you probably don't even remember. I signed up with Teni right after the Blink.

I: That's . . . not possible.

S: Anything's possible when you're unstuck from time, Norberg.

(LAUGHTER)

I: You need to tell me how that's possible. You arrived in Saint Petersburg on a Martian shuttle, already vaccinated against the Martian pox. How? Did the Martians give it to you?

S: All right, Norberg. I see from the look on your face that I'm about out of time. I can feel it, too, did you know that? I can feel the jumps coming. But to tell you everything you want to know, I need to start at the beginning. And . . . ah yes, here we are. You've got a little Masukisan squad out there fucking up your perimeter, which is about to take out your security. And my squad is just arriving.

(RECORDING ENDS)

"I have you," Norberg said. "Why do you continue to be so good-spirited? You have nowhere to go. We're scooping you up like rats from a burning cane field. There is no more Mars!"

"I'm good-spirited because I know something you don't," she said.

"And what is that?"

"There was never a Mars to fight. You were obliterating corporate holds on Mars. The Mars resistance? The real Mars? I told them everything. Who you would hit, what cities, and when. We got out ninety percent of civilians before your soldiers, before I—ha, yeah, me!—even hit the dirt there. This was all a big corporate circle-jerk. But it produced a Martian resistance that's going to outlast you. My team up there is going to outlast you. And me, here? I'm going to checkmate this whole motherfucking time line."

43.

Flash-bangs.

Always a good sign.

I leaped across the table and took Norberg by the throat. It felt good. Probably too good.

She hacked and coughed. Alarms went off. Shots fired. I heard more flash-bangs. I smashed Norberg's head against the floor.

Two guards came in, but I was ready for them. Turns out, you spend a few years in a Martian POW camp, you have a lot of time to think about the future you've already seen. The future that's finally here, this moment.

I took down the first guard. Palm strike. Throat. Smashed the kneecap of the other one. It was over in four seconds.

I gazed down at their smashed faces and thought of Frankie, from all those years ago. How I would have handled myself then, if I knew what I knew now.

But I wasn't going that far back.

I slung the guards' guns over my shoulder. Grabbed

their flash-bangs and the most important thing—the EMP overloader—and ran into the hallway. I knew the turrets would be there because I had seen them before, of course, from the other side. I shot out the turrets. They exploded.

I ran down the hall, bare feet slapping against the metal. I rounded the corner and came upon the basement. The smell, shit, the smell was the same. The reddish dirt. The salty air from the sea.

The burst from the turret had stunned them. I shot twice. These rifles were standard ammo. All I needed to do was stun them; shoot something that wasn't their heads. I tossed the EMP overloader into the room. That took them out.

The bodies of the squad—my squad, myself—fell in a heap. They joined the other bodies there, some squad of Masukisan misfits trying to breach the compound. The ones who conveniently set off all those lovely alarms and triggered the room's defenses.

I came upon them and stopped, dizzy and exuberant. *Oh fuck,* I thought. *Oh fuck, I did it. This is it.*

I gazed at the knocked-out bodies before me. Akesson, Chikere, Toranzos, Sharpe . . . and there, in front of them all, guarding them bodily like some big damn idiot—was me.

I seemed so small. So young. I had a long moment of dissonance, brought back to myself only because of the blaring alarms.

I suspected Norberg didn't have many more guards in there. But I shut the big doors to the interrogation hall nonetheless, and barred them with one of the pulse rifles. Mine, as it turned out. Shit, this doubling thing was fucked up.

I pulled the utility knife from the belt of my other self, my younger self. I could not help but pull back the cuff on the collar and note the clear skin over the chest. I rubbed at my own scar reflexively, the scar Tanaka insisted I should have. The scar I would have, I did have, now.

I cut out the tracker from between the shoulder blades of my younger self, and swallowed it. I wouldn't need it very long. I pulled out the heads-up lenses and inserted them into my eyes. I gathered my own body up into my arms, and let out my breath.

Focus. I needed the tracker, because it connected me to logistics. To the web of light. To the breakdown of time. I paged into the platoon channel and said, "This is Dietz. Team is down. We need immediate evac. Immediate!"

"Copy that, Private Dietz, hold for evac."

Oh, to be part of a small squad again.

We broke apart.

I saw nothing. A wall of blackness.

I heaved myself backward in time, so heavy, so desperately heavy that I broke the fabric of time and space itself.

I corporealized at the edge of Cape Town, a bustling Cape Town with a busy beach and curious children who gazed at me as if I were some mythological monster come to life. And maybe I was.

I set my old self down here gently, so gently, pushing the helmet back, murmuring, "We can do this. We can break the loop. I believe in you."

I burst apart again, still only partially corporealized.

Volition.

Control the construct.

I needed another time.

Another city.

Go back, Dietz. Go back.

Back to the beginning.

Another city. A sprawl.

I knew when and where I needed to be. I knew where this started, and it was where it would end.

I knew this city because I had grown up here. It was as if I were four years old again, staring into the lights of São Paulo. I could smell the sea on the wind.

I knew this place, and this day, because it was before the end of everything, before the beginning of the end.

I came together on a dirt street running between two rows of squatter houses, all lovingly put together with whatever the owners could find. The colors are what impress you; the people out sweeping their front stoops as if they are residents of some grand city. And it was. It is. The São Paulo I knew, the labor camps, we were grand. The people were grand.

I lifted my head, and saw him there in the doorway of the nearest shelter.

My brother, Tomás.

He gaped at me. I held open my arms.

Tomás ran, and I embraced him.

I wanted him to be safe forever. I wanted us all to be safe.

"I knew you would come," Tomás said.

"Is Vi here? Did she find you?"

He nodded and took my hand. "She's helping, up here. Free legal advice!"

I didn't correct him. Vi wasn't a lawyer. It didn't matter. My stomach churned; a flutter in my heart. What would she say?

Tomás led me to a temporary tent at the end of the lane. And there she was, standing behind a makeshift table, her pinched face so serious, her once-soft hands dirty and calloused. She pushed a curl of her hair up over her forehead, and squinted at a piece of old paper one of the men in front of her presented.

For a moment I could do nothing but stare at her.

"Come on," Tomás said. He tugged my hand.

We came within a few meters of her, and then I had to stop, and I could not move, because the sight of her rooted me to the spot. In that one moment, that terrible and wonderful moment, I saw what this was all about. I had taken an oath of vengeance to get back at Mars for what they had done to her and Tomás and my cousins here. I started this whole thing for these people they had taken.

And I had found them again.

She saw me.

Our eyes met across the table. My palms began to sweat. What if she rejected me? She had every right. What would I do then? Just burst apart into nothing?

Vi came around the table, mouth half open. "Gina?" she said.

"Hello," I said, and I let out my breath, because it had been years since I heard someone use my first name.

"How did you—no, Tomás, of course, I just didn't expect—"

"I didn't know how to tell you what I meant, when you said you were going here. I got offended. It was like you couldn't even see me. See . . . us, this. You're . . . but it doesn't matter. Vi, something bad is going to happen here, and if we don't leave now, it's all going to come apart."

The days of trying to change the system from within were long over. Sometimes you had to let the whole world burn behind you.

"I need you to trust me, Vi. Just one last time."

"What about them? We can't leave your family. Your brother, your cousins, and all these people—"

"I'll take them too. As many as I can manage."

"But where will we go?"

"I don't know. Do you want to find out with me?"

"Gina? I didn't think you would come."

"Is that . . . good, or bad?"

Her eyes filled. "Good." She opened her arms, and I pulled her to my chest and felt her heart beat against mine.

We broke apart over São Paulo.

I was a massive wave of energy, disrupting the bodies around me, transforming everything my altered atoms touched.

We became millions of points of light.

We Blinked.

You can't save them all. But I could save some. I could take us all . . . someplace else, to some other time or place where there's no war, and the corporations answer to us, and freedom isn't just a sound bite on a corp-controlled news station.

I was high above the city now. So many people lost.

What if there was a war and nobody came?

Was I deluding myself? Millions of people of every class and position, ghouls, residents, citizens . . . people like Vi and Tomás. My cousins and citizen stakeholders. They will want to rebuild a world like the one we came from, won't they? A world where the same people were in charge. Because it was known. It was comforting.

All I could hope was that some other place would give us a chance. There was no future here, only the past. Leaving them here condemned them to die with the rest. If I couldn't save the world, at least I could save the people I loved.

This is not the end. There are other worlds. Other stars. Other futures. Maybe we'll do better out there. Maybe when they have a war again, no one will come.

Maybe they will be full of light.

AFTER

"Whatever's busted in your life—
you can use its pieces to make the life you want."
—Warren Ellis

I still believe in the military. I believe there's sometimes a greater evil that must be vanquished. But more often than we'd like to admit, there is no greater evil, just an exchange of one set of oppressive horrors with another. Wars are for old people. For rich people. For people protected by the perpetuation of horrors on others.

I don't regret what I've told people about my motives in this conflict. I don't regret what got me here. Maybe you wanted a different story. One with more answers, less ambiguity. But that wasn't how I experienced this war. It's like Machado de Assis said: *"I know your excellency preferred a delicate lie; but I do not know anything more delicate than the truth."*

This is the closest I could get to the truth.

I have two sets of memories now. I have my own memory of being on Mars, spending all those years in a POW camp, listening to books on history, geography, intelligence. And I have my memories of the war as it happened, all experienced through the vision of my other self, a younger self, out there being a big damn hero.

They were different wars. The same war. The war I never want anyone else to experience ever again.

I will forever remember the protestor in São Paulo telling me to drop my weapon and join her. I know now I was never the hero.

It was her. It was *us*.

The heroes were always the ordinary people who pursued extraordinary change.

The power of the corrupt governments and entrenched corporations feels inevitable. No doubt so did the rule of the kings and landowners before them.

But I know better now. I know there is a greater power, and it is ours. The greater power is *us*.

And that is the world we will build out here, somewhere, when we bring all our pieces back together.

A future made of light.

Acknowledgments

Tremendous thanks to my agent, Hannah Bowman, who suggested extending my short story "The Light Brigade" into a novel. This was a hell of a book to figure out, structurally, and she helped me dig and navigate the trenches on this one.

Special thanks also to Joshua Bowman, for figuring out the mathematical graph Hannah and I needed to run characters through to see if the events in this book all lined up correctly. I'm told it was "a directed Hamiltonian path through a bipartite graph." This resulted in a structured time-travel path that overcame all the corners I'd painted myself into. I owe much of the theory behind the time-traveling events here to Carlo Rovelli, who wrote *The Order of Time,* which provides the closest thing to science in this science-fiction novel.

Kudos to my editor, Joe Monti, for enduring the lateness and resulting abbreviated editing time line for this novel. He was the good cop to Hannah's bad cop: a great two-punch editing duo who enabled a half-formed idea to become a novel.

Also: god bless copy editors.

My assistant, Denise Beucler, put in a lot of hours on this project as well (in addition to all the many other ways she has assisted me). Many thanks to her for the particularly brutal crunch that got this book to its first sales-ready presentation.

As ever, special thanks to Jayson Utz for enduring my drunken rants, self-immolating deadlines, and particularly grim wit. I'm a pretty funny gal.

There are many cribbed references in this particular work. I'll let you all enjoy ferreting them out, but know that yes, they are—in nearly every case—willful homages. This ain't my first rodeo. Don't @ me.

Finally, all my love to you, the truest fans of Team Hurley, for the support, cheerleading, book buying, reviewing, and general goodness you bring to the world.

Don't just fight the darkness, friends. Let's be the light.

The Big Red House
Summer 2018

UNDER THE PENDULUM SUN BY JEANETTE NG
PAPERBACK & EBOOK
from all good stationers and book emporia

Two Victorian missionaries travel into darkest fairyland, to deliver their uplifting message to the godless magical beings who dwell there… at the risk of losing their own mortal souls.

Winner of the Sydney J Bounds Award, the British Fantasy Award for Best Newcomer

Shortlisted for the John W Campbell Award

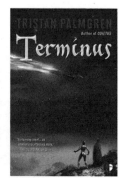
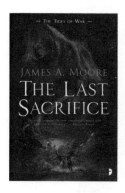
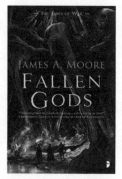

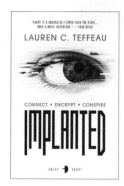

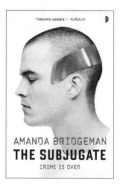

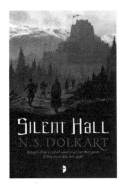

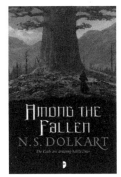

Science Fiction, Fantasy and WTF?!

@angryrobotbooks

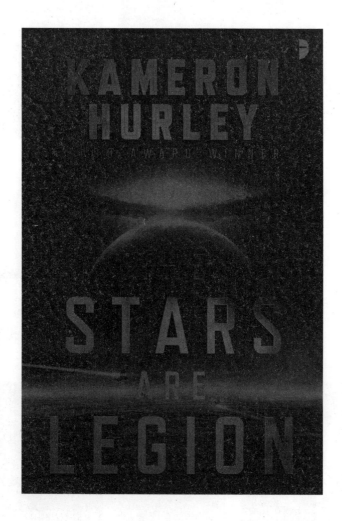